# HOME STREET HOME

*Further Titles by Elizabeth Webster*

A BOY CALLED BRACKEN
CHILD OF FIRE
JOHNNIE ALONE
TO FLY A KITE

# HOME STREET HOME

## Elizabeth Webster

This first world edition published in Great Britain 1993 by
SEVERN HOUSE PUBLISHERS LTD of
9–15 High Street, Sutton, Surrey SM1 1DF.
First published in the USA 1993 by
SEVERN HOUSE PUBLISHERS INC., of
475 Fifth Avenue, New York, NY 10017.

British Library Cataloguing in Publication Data
Webster, Elizabeth
  Home Street Home
  I. Title
  823.914 [F]

  ISBN 0-7278-4562-4

Typeset by Hewer Text Composition Services, Edinburgh.
Printed and bound in Great Britain by
Redwood Books, Trowbridge, Wiltshire.

For Ben and Hilo
and all their friends


Elizabeth Webster will be donating a percentage of the proceeds from the sale of this book to The Depaul Trust, a charity providing for the needs of the young, street homeless.

For further information please write to:

The Depaul Trust
247 Willesden Lane
London
NW2 5RY

# I

# THE SWING

The swing lay on the ground. Hilo stood with the sheared rope in her hand, too white and cold with shock to speak. She stared down at the scuffed grass in silent outrage. There, on the worn brown turf, lay all her private world – her hidden citadel – in ruins. The bright bubble broken. Childhood gone.

She looked at the spite on her mother's face with disbelief. The cobra-striking eyes, the thin, pale mouth, seemed to reflect a kind of triumphant satisfaction. It appalled her. How could she bear to go on living with that wantonly cruel smile?

She searched her mind for reasons and could find none. There had always been war between them, a bitter, unending conflict that never got resolved. Sometimes it was violent, sometimes buried under deep resentments which she did not understand, and sometimes softened by sudden moments of contrition and extravagant affection which puzzled her even more. She had learnt to endure the swift unexpected blows, the sudden rages and sullen silences, with a kind of stoical patience. It did no good to hit back – to answer back. And the sudden bursts of affection were even harder to respond to. It was better to keep silent and not let her father know how far the war had gone.

But this? The swing had always been her refuge – the place of dreams and visions, safe from intrusion in its hidden green shade.

You went up into green. It was all round you. Rich and thick – and deeply private. The world turned, and there was blue air under your feet. Sky under your feet. You were flying, swifter than any bird. Flying through blue air, with the green all round

1

you, all thick and strong below you, holding the world at bay. You were flying free. You were free.

And the world turned. You went through blue air into green. There was green over your head. There was blue beneath you. There was sky in your eyes. And leaves – fat cushions of leaves – to lean on as you fell.

You fell. Like Icarus from the sky, the blue air racing past you. Breathless, you fell back into green – those welcoming arms of green came rushing up to meet you. The green received you, enfolded you in softness. You were drowning in green.

But it did not hurt you. It left you free. You leant on the air and it supported you. It lifted you up and flung you to the sky. Oh, you were swifter than a bird, swifter than a dragonfly, swifter than a falling star. The sky was all about you, in your eyes and in your mouth and in your streaming hair. You were flying free. Free of the heavy pull of the earth, of the stain – of the pain. You were free.

The blue air was cool upon your face. Cool and soft. The gold and silver nets of the sun caught you and held you in their blazing arms. You burned with their fire, pierced by their sharp and brilliant lances, pierced till you cried out with their fierce and loving pain.

And then, like Icarus, you fell.

"Down to earth, my girl!"

"What?" She was still too dazed, too bound up in shattered dreams, to understand.

"Life is for real now. No more nonsense. I'll see you *inside.*"

Her mother turned, the shears still in her hands, and went into the house, back stiff, head still tilted in anger like a striking snake's. Hilo watched her go and said nothing. What was left to say?

This garden – this small green refuge – this quiet sanctuary – was gone from her for ever. No-one had understood its value – its desperate importance to her in her threatened world. No-one except her father.

Her father. Those quiet eyes that saw everything and gave away nothing – grey, like the rest of him. Neutral. Kind. Hair that was grey too young, the long, scholar's face already grey with despair, beset by that scolding tongue, that unpredictable, lightning-flash of destruction.

But he hadn't been grey the day he made the swing. She remembered that day. He had been young and laughing then. She remembered the recklessly laughing face, brown with the summer sun, hair tangled by the apple boughs as he stood and pushed her to and fro on the new swing. She had been laughing too, hair flying, head tilted back so that petals fell into her open mouth from the blossom-laden branches. She had rushed forward into sunlight and back towards her father so that she saw him upside down and laughing, laughing, his white shirt open and boyish, and his eyes as bright as the daisies in the grass.

She had been five when he made her the swing – on her fifth birthday – and the world was all green and gold and full of laughter.

No, not all laughter. There was her mother. Her mother who quenched laughter like a dowsed flame – who cut things down to size (not only swings) and who endlessly scolded her for dreaming. Scolded her father too. Distrusted that gentle, librarian's patience and detachment, his love of books, his love of words themselves, which he passed on to his small daughter with devoted attention.

"Soaring . . ." he sang to her over the dappled grass of summer. "Soaring high, soaring low . . ."

"High . . . low, High . . . low," she sang back at him, tilting her world towards the sunlight, swinging through green and gold.

"That's it, little Hilo. Fly free as a bird."

From then on it was always Hilo with her father. Her mother said it was silly, and Rebecca was a perfectly good name which went with Fielding. Sensible and respectable. Hilo was ridiculous. What would the neighbours think?

Hilo didn't care what the neighbours thought. And her father's nickname stuck. "Hilo, Hilo . . ." she sang to herself, skimming over the daisy sea.

*"Get down off there!"* shouted her mother. *"Stop dreaming and do something."*

Do something? When the world was all green and gold and scented with summer flowers.

3

*"How d'you expect to look nice for your party? You look like a scarecrow."*

She hadn't expected to look nice. She never did. Too plain, too thin and gawky, too small, too dark, all arms and legs, her mother said. She knew she was a disappointment to her mother, – not being pretty and blonde and blue-eyed (like her friend, Rosalie) but dark-haired like her father, and grey of eye like him, too. Not fit for frilly party frocks and knickers with lace on, and pink bows in her hair.

*"Hold still, can't you, while I fix your hair! Though why I bother, I can't think."*

She couldn't think why, either. It never did any good. She still didn't look like Rosalie. Still disappointed her mother at every turn.

Five isn't very old, she thought. How can I remember it all now? It's all so long ago. So many dreams wasted, so much hidden darkness. I feel old. But then the world was all new. The colours were so bright, the shapes so clear, and the sounds . . . Oh, my father's laughter and the singing of all the birds in the morning! Perhaps that was just childhood, all that brilliance, all that joy. Joy? Brilliance? Where have they gone, I wonder? Now that I'm not a child any more.

Her mother had no time to waste on things like joy or brilliance. They frightened her. She shouted at dreams, hit out with a sudden vicious hand at silences, and sneered at the pale, uncomprehending face of her bewildered daughter.

*"Look at you! How I ever had a daughter like you, I can't imagine."*

Nor could Hilo. Her mother never saw the sky, or how a bird sailed downward on tilted wings. Or the shape of a leaf cut sharp and black against a moonlit night . . . Or clouds riding high . . .

"Clouds," she murmured, aloud. "Sky?" and thought of her father.

He understood about dreams – and sky. He knew Hilo's mind. He knew how she felt. But, like Hilo, he had learnt to say nothing, to hide things deeper and deeper, to go greyer and greyer with the effort of concealment, until the day that was greyest of all.

4

She remembered that day. The heat in the little suburban house, and her mother's endlessly scolding voice. (Surely, she must have been ordinarily kind and pleasant *sometimes?*) And her father patiently trying to read, to shut out the storm.

*"You never do a thing but sit around all day with your head in a book – just like your useless daughter."*

(It was always *"his* daughter" when Hilo was to blame for something.)

*"Yes, dear."*

*"Well, get up then. Do something. At least you could mow the lawn."*

*"Yes, dear."*

Hilo had retreated to the swing again – like so many other times when the scolding got bad or the blows got too fierce. She had sat there, furiously swinging to and fro, aching with anger, watching her father drag out the heavy mower, watching him try to start it over and over again, watching him fall. *Watching him fall.*

She had run to him then. The sky reeled as she leapt off the swing and ran across the sunlit grass. But it was too late.

He lay there, clutching his chest, his breath coming in strange, uneven spasms, and that awful, nulling greyness spreading over his face. He only managed two words: *"Hilo . . . sky . . ."*

He might have meant God. But she knew he did not. His quiet mind was somehow beyond such obvious acceptance. There was a note almost of surprise in his voice. She had looked up at the sky, and it was blue and passionless. But beautiful. And colossally empty. When she looked down, he was gone.

Passed away, her mother and the neighbours said, between sniffs into neat white handkerchiefs. But Hilo knew better. He had simply gone. There was a tired shell on the summer grass – a shell that looked up at the sky in mute surprise. But her father had gone.

"Sky" she repeated to herself, and now there was a hint of tears in her voice. Only a hint, though. Hilo never cried.

She had not cried then, she recollected. This seemed to annoy her mother even more. She remembered the cold, pretty face, the curled-up puffs of yellow hair, and the thin, downward curve of that mouth that could spit such venom, the hard, accusing stare that offered no respite.

*"No heart at all. Always sitting on that flipping swing. I've a good mind to cut it down."*

Fear had caught her then. Her only refuge taken from her? Where could she hide then?

*I have got a heart. The swing is where I think of him. And who are you to talk of hearts when you killed him?*

She hadn't known she had spoken aloud, but the stinging backhander had nearly knocked her off the sun-baked wooden seat. For the first time since her father's death, she had tears in her eyes.

*"Get inside. Just because your father's dead is no excuse for mooning about."* The harsh, high voice was pitiless. It followed her inside, out of the sunfilled garden, up the sharp stairs to her room at the back of the house. It was hot and airless, and looked out on to the road towards the busy high street where her mother worked as a hairdresser. No glimpse of the quiet garden.

*"And do your homework. Exams matter more than ever now. I won't keep you for ever!"* The screech rose higher.

Hilo knew exams mattered. She always had known. After all, she and her father had nursed a secret dream about college – about reading English like her father, and perhaps following him into the library service. She had even hoped – vainly, it seemed – that her mother might "come round" to the idea and be proud of her. Some hope.

The more she tried, the more her mother carped. She wondered sometimes what the trouble really was, and if she could do anything about it. What was it all about? Apart from not being pretty or fluffy, not taking to frilly clothes and girlish shopping jaunts, and being a general disappointment all round, what else had she done wrong? She knew her quiet (almost secret, by necessity) discussions with her father about words and books and the hidden realms of magical exploration that he had always opened up before her only seemed to fuel her mother's wrath. To fill her with exasperation and suspicion.

*"Always nattering on. What do you talk about in there?"*

Or: "Head in a book again? About time you saw the real world, my girl."

6

But what *was* the real world? Was it fear that beset her mother – that turned her into a cold-eyed shrew? Fear of the unknown? Fear of being shut out? Fear of anyone cleverer than she was? Fear or jealousy? Two people ganging up on her, exploring worlds she could not reach and could not understand? Hilo did not know.

Once she had heard them arguing about her – her father's voice gentle and reproachful: *"She's quite a clever child, you know. They think highly of her at school . . ."*

*"Clever? That sullen lump? She hardly ever speaks. I've no idea what she thinks about."*

*"No,"* agreed her father quietly. *"I know."*

Yes, he knew. But he could not tell her about Hilo's dreams, and Hilo could not tell her either.

After her father died, Hilo had wondered whether she might get through to her mother somehow. Maybe now she had no-one to gang up with, her mother would not feel so threatened. Maybe, Hilo thought hopefully, she will relent and we could start to be friends instead of enemies. I'd like that . . .

But her mother did not relent. If anything, she got tougher and more abrasive and Hilo's attempts at reconciliation shrivelled and died.

She had thought, for her father's sake as much as her own, that she ought to go on with the college idea. He would not be there to see it, of course, and she had no ally now to back her up, but she could work hard to get there on her own, given half a chance.

But she wasn't given half a chance. All that was gone now, she knew. Her mother would not see her through college. She would insist on a junior's job in the hair salon as soon as Hilo was old enough to leave school. Money mattered now. More than words. It always had, of course, to her mother.

*"And no scribbling in that blasted notebook, either!"*

Scribbling. Even to her father she had not confessed about the secret folder, kept hidden, added to in lonely moments of childish grief or despair. (Or ecstasy? But she would never admit to that – not to anyone.) Only one had she shown her father, a translation of a Spanish song, asked for by her other ally, Robert Butler, the music master at school. Since it was going

7

to be shown to him anyway, Hilo also allowed her father to see it. She remembered those words – words that now seemed to belong to a life that was gone. A world that was innocent and unspoilt.

"In rose and pearl
Fades the sky,
Wide distance grows
As colours die.
Pure silence deepens
In blue air,
And faint and far
The pale stars stare.
Time swings and circles
Through the night,
There is no end
To darkening sight.
The inmost heart,
The core of light
Pulses beyond
The farthest height.

And O, how small, how frail are we,
Groping for worlds we cannot see."

*"Why, Hilo,"* her father had said, his voice soft with wonder, *"that's beautiful."*

Yes, beautiful, she thought sadly. I was young then. I believed in an unspoilt world. Beauty could hold me. But now I feel old. And beauty is dead.

Robert Butler had approved of it too. He understood about words – almost as clearly as her father. Being a teacher, he was mostly tired and disillusioned, but his face lit up with extraordinary warmth when he was pleased about something. He had held the paper in his hand, looking from the scribbled lines to her face in astonishment. *"Well, well –* " he had begun, and then failed to say any more.

But he had done his best for her, dear old Robert Butler, until her mother spoilt that too. He had fostered her love of words –

8

put work in her way – given her space to think in the haven of his quiet music room.

*"The shape, Hilo – the rise and fall, the curve of a phrase, like music. A pattern on the air."* He had smiled at her then, and said obscurely: *"I think you'd better learn the flute."*

She had learnt the flute and understood the arching shapes, the lift and fall, the marvellous contours that music drew – that words drew – on her listening mind.

But even this fragile respite her mother had destroyed. *"Music? Are you sure that's what he keeps you late for?"*

Hilo had frozen. She could not explain – could not admit to her mother the sense of relief, the wealth of freedom given her, the extraordinary reassurance of Robert Butler's understanding mind. It was impossible to put into words. And now it would not be the same. The innocent delight of music and words was suddenly stained with undeserved guilt. Other words with sinister undertones hummed about in her mind. She shrank from them, and grew silent and cold once more.

Butler noticed the change in her, she knew, but he said nothing until she announced abruptly: *"I can't come after school any more."*

Then he protested: *"Why, Hilo?"*

She could think of no way to answer him and the silence went on much too long. But at last she had handed him her latest furious scribble. It was not specific. But she thought he might understand it without being told.

> "Your eyes were knives,
> Sharper than words,
> Or swords.
> They cut
> And I was killed.
> Each day a death.
> Each bitter glance
> A dying.
> I never knew why
> They struck.
> Lightning has no rules.
> Each time

I shrivelled
And died,
Each time
The fire flashed out.

Always, always I got burnt.
I never learnt."

(I was fourteen when I wrote that, she thought. No, thirteen, I think. I wonder what he made of it?)

Robert Butler had read it silently, nodded, and then handed it back, saying simply: *"I see."* But then he had added quietly: *"It's all right, Hilo."*

She had stammered then, shamed and defeated by her mother's suspicious mind. *"D-dayspring . . .?"*

*"Dayspring mishandled cometh not again?"* He had sighed and shaken his head. *"Not true, Hilo. It comes again and again. But –"* his quirky smile had challenged her, *"you have to fight for it."*

She had almost allowed herself to believe him then, a kind of stoic acceptance settling inside her that was harder than courage. *"Yes. But it's such a long, long war."*

Yes, it was a long, long war. And it got worse. Horrendously worse. For her mother took a lodger into her home, and into her bed. That should have made things easier, but the trouble was, one bed wasn't enough for him. He seemed to be under the impression that every bed and every person in it was his by right.

Steve was large and blond, with big red hands, a little boy grin, and something wrong about his eyes. They were rather small and set close together, and they shone with a pale blue light that should have been cold but was somehow hot. They burned with a strange fire, especially when they looked at Hilo, and she felt herself shrivel in their peculiar heat.

One night she woke to find him standing by her bed. He stood there slowly taking off his clothes, and his shadow was huge on the wall as he stooped over her.

She did not tell her mother. She knew she would not be believed. Steve would simply deny it, call it the ravings of a mixed-up adolescent, and she would be labelled a slut and a

10

liar. (She could almost hear her mother saying it.) And Steve had threatened worse violence (but could there be worse?) and even direr consequences if she didn't keep her mouth shut.

So the persecution went on; and though she shrank and froze at his touch, it didn't deter him. But though she did not dare refuse him (could not, physically, repel him unless she took to violence herself and got hold of a knife), still something inside her fought desperately for freedom, still waited for the moment of escape to come.

She grew even more silent and withdrawn, and there were more and more unexplained absences from school. She concealed these by setting out as usual, waiting till her mother had gone to work at the hair salon and Steve to his building site, and then creeping back to have a bath and lie shaking with reaction on her bed. But though she scrubbed and scrubbed until she was sore, she never felt clean any more.

She had tried to make some sort of decision about her life, lying there on her bed in the empty house. All day, shut in her room, she argued with herself about what she should do. She saw the remorseless pattern of her future in this cramped, unhappy house. Without her father's gentle presence there was no longer any ally to protect her from her mother's malice or from Steve's incessant demands. There was no-one at home to stand between her and violence, no-one calm and quiet and neutral to rely on. She had only herself to turn to – herself and the leafy solace of the swing in the empty garden. In despair she had fled there once more, like a child (but no longer a child), aching for comfort.

And then – shock.

Her mother returning, beside herself with fury at her truant daughter. *"You lazy slut. You mindless lay-about. Why aren't you at school? I'll teach you!"*

The garden shears – her father's garden shears, last ironic betrayal – and the swing lay on the ground.

Something within her died in that moment. More than when her father left her, for she could remember him with thankfulness all her life. More than when Steve laid his hot hands on her, – though that was a kind of death, too.

But here, on this scuffed patch of grass, lay all her dreams, her childhood innocence. All broken, and all gone. She would never

11

be young again. And while she stood there, looking back at the bitter pattern that had led her to this point, she realized at last that she had the power to escape. She did not have to submit to Steve and his hot eyes and groping hands, or to her mother's ceaseless accusations. She could just go.

She did not tell anyone of her decision. But she did try to leave a clear explanation behind. She had written it down in despairing anger and grief, – and she left it carefully placed on the pillow of her tumbled bed. Let her mother make of it what she would – it said enough. It was called "To Steve."

> "Did you ever stop to think
> What you did to me,
> To a child's faith,
> To a child's belief
> In good?
> Violation, they call it.
> Did you know?
> Not only bruised limbs
> And a room that will never feel safe,
> A child that will never feel clean
> Again.
> But a bruised mind.
> I had a heart once,
> I had a soul.
> Bright innocence still lay
> Across my sky.
> All gone now.
> All done.
> All gone.
> All I can do is die."

She left it lying there, collected all the rest of her scribbles into their folder, packed a small rucksack, and left.

No-one heard her go.

At the gate, she looked back once to the garden, once to the place where her father had lain and looked at the sky, and once to the fallen swing on its patch of faded brown. Then, without any sense of regret or fear, she walked away from the little suburban

12

house, from her childhood and all her dreams, towards the main road to London.

She was not yet sixteen. She had no money except the loose change in her purse and a post-office savings book with less than fifty pounds in it. And she had no assets except a sheaf of unsaleable poems and her own young strength.

But the world was wide. And at least she was free. Free to begin again. Squaring her shoulders, she set out for a brave new world.

## II

# COMPUTERS AND FOSSILS

Ben went home warily these days. He was never sure what kind of a mood his father would be in. Usually the carping was merely exhausting, but sometimes it got beyond endurance and he wanted to hit back. But he never did. You couldn't hit your own father, could you? Especially when your mother stood there, white-faced and anxious, trying to keep the peace between you somehow and tearing herself to pieces in the process.

So far he had managed to keep going to his classes at Tech, and keep his part-time job in the local computer software shop. He only got that job because he was good at demonstrating the new models and understood a bit about graphics. But his father went on and on about "a proper job" (like his own on the factory floor) and "wasting time poncing about" on useless occupations that got you nowhere, and Ben couldn't seem to get through to him.

Jobs were difficult enough to get these days. He was lucky to have this one. Particularly in something to do with graphics which he wanted to do anyway. But you couldn't explain that sort of thing to his father. To him, a job was turning screws on the factory shop-floor, on the same day-shift, in the same grey echoing concrete building at the shabby end of town, for more than twenty monotonous years. Ben wanted more than that out of life. He was good at graphics. They were the up and coming thing even in his small town, and if he got really skilled at design and presentation he might go far. Far is where he would like to go – travel to distant places, and explore strange lost wildernesses . . . He wasn't going to stay in Stanbridge all his life, like his

14

Dad. Oh no. He would have liked to go to art school and study graphics and design properly. But of course his Dad would not hear of it. All those long-haired layabouts who smoked pot and never did a day's real work in their poncy lives. (Poncy was his Dad's word for everything he didn't like or understand). No son of his was going to go down that road. No, sir. Better find out now that real life was tough and a bit of a grind, and stop having stupid dreams.

Stupid or not, Ben still had dreams. He was a merry boy on the whole, a curly sort of boy, what with his upspringing hair and uptilting, quirky mouth. Even his eyes had a slight upward tilt to them, and glinted with laughter more often than not. But behind the laughter, he still dreamed of those far-distant places, still half-believed in heroes and high endeavour. Why not? There was plenty of scope in life for adventure if you took your chance.

Today he had felt adventurous and shut in by the grey north midlands townscape, so he had done his morning shift in the computer showroom and then seized his bicycle and ridden out to the nearby hills. He had parked his bike by a stone wall and climbed the steep meandering sheep-track path to the top of Brown Jack, which was the highest of the little range of bracken-covered hills called the Long Withians rising brave and clean above the industrial murk below.

Along the top of the ridge he suddenly began to run, kicking his legs up like a child in absurd delight at the emptiness and space, at the spicy scent of curling bracken and the racing cloud-shadows on the hills. He felt tall and brave and strong, like his childhood heroes, like a Viking, like a Roman centurion, like a marauding Scot running on these high hills – or fighting in Arthur's army to rescue the oppressed countryside he loved from tyranny, pillage and murder. Yes, one of Arthur's knights, riding along the secret hill-paths to round up the last of the defeated enemy . . . Riding? But where was his horse?

He laughed, and kicked up his heels again in a derisive leap of irrepressible amusement. Horse indeed! Knights and white chargers! He was a dull, ordinary boy with a bike, doing a dullish job in a dullish north midlands town in twentieth-century recession-grey England. How Arthur would have laughed. But up here it didn't matter. The hills had stood here, sturdy and

15

silent, long before Arthur was even thought of, long before the Vikings came riding in over the sea in their long ships, long before anything Ben could even imagine, – and they would still be here long after Ben and all his daft dreams had gone.

"Daft," said Ben, and picked up a stone to throw down into the darkest dip in the hills. "Daft, that's me." But something about the shape of the stone in his hand made him look down, and he found it was a perfect shell fossil that he was holding. "Beautiful," he murmured, turning it over to look at the delicate symmetry of the fluting. Thousands of years old, he thought. Formed when these hills were under the sea. And here am I, holding it in my hand.

Sobered suddenly by the enormity of time, he stopped his wild dash for freedom, and paused to look at the shape of the hills and the sprawling mass of the smoky town below. They'll still be here, he thought, no matter what I do. Even when the town has gone, they'll be here. But I'm going to do *something* with my life. I *am*!

He walked on until it was nearly dark, and then he thought he'd better turn for home. If he was late for tea it always led to trouble, no matter how innocent the cause. On the way home, he met his red-haired friend, Mick. At least, Mick *had* been his friend at school, but lately he had been running with a curious gang, and Ben didn't trust them much.

"Hi, Ben," shouted Mick. He sauntered up to Ben's bike and laid a detaining hand on the handlebars. "You're into computers, aren't you? Got one of your own, have you?"

"Some chance!" sighed Ben. "Where would I get that sort of money?"

"I know where I can lay my hands on one." Mick looked at him sideways, squinting into the sun. "Get it for you cheap."

"Why?" Ben's voice was flat. "Hot or something, is it?"

"Legit," smiled Mick, spreading out his hands. "Bankrupt stock. You know – Yardlers. They went down last month."

"Tycoon are you, these days? Bought up the lot, did you?" Ben didn't trust that smile an inch.

"I got friends," said Mick, still smiling. He laid a finger against his nose in the time-honoured gesture of the unquenchable wide-boy. "Less than half price – screen and keyboard and all."

Ben did not speak, so he went on, even more persuasively. "Proper job, Ben. Amstrad, with a mouse. You know the gen." He waited, the question in his voice lingering on the air.

Ben was tempted. "You *sure* it's not hot?"

"Sure," agreed Mick. "Straight up. Proper receipt if you want."

There was a pause. But it was too good a chance to miss. Think of all the practice he could get on his own computer – the patterns and colours he could play with . . . Colour?

"Colour?"

"Sure. Glorious sickli-colour all over. Plays those computer games, all bright and breezy – you know."

"OK." Ben made up his mind. "How much?"

"Fifty, all in."

Ben whistled. "What's the catch?"

"They're not complete. Bits missing. Plenty of spares, though. Guess you could fix it . . .?"

"If I had a specification."

"You got it."

Ben could hardly believe his luck. "I get paid Friday. And I can draw out the rest from the post office. That do?"

"Deal." Mick held out a cheerful hand.

Ben took it, but he still felt a curious reluctance about the whole transaction. *Was* it legit? The price was too low, of course. But he did know that incomplete models went for a song these days. There were always new ones to follow on. Still, there was something about Mick nowadays that bothered him, though he couldn't put a finger on it. But he needed that computer. Shrugging off his doubts, he made his way home through the half-dark of the tea-time streets.

"You're late," said his father, looking up from a plate of sausage and chips.

"Oh Stan, not very," protested his mother, already in a flutter of anxiety about impending trouble.

"Sorry." Ben fetched his plate from the cooker and sat down at the table. "I went up on Brown Jack. It was smashing up there." He glanced at his mother and smiled, his curly mouth lifting, his whole face lighting with laughter.

"Skiving off again?"

"No, Dad. I'm doing mornings at Foster's this week. I had the afternoon free." He reached for the bottle of brown sauce. "And my Tech class isn't till seven."

"Huh," grumbled his father. "It's all right for some."

Ben didn't mention the computer. Better smuggle it in when Dad was at work. Let it become a permanent fixture up in his room before his father discovered it.

"You'll be seventeen next month," announced Stan Roberts suddenly. "Time to stop poncing about with that footling job."

Ben went cold. "What d'you mean?"

"I've had a word with the foreman. They'll take you on – as a favour to me."

"But, Dad – "

"As a *favour*, mind. I've been there twenty-three years come Michaelmas. Counts for something. But you'll have to work – or I'll look all sorts of a fool."

"But, Dad – "

"Do me proud, son. Time you got down to the nitty gritty."

Ben got up and pushed his chair back. "Dad! I don't *want* to go into the factory. I'm happy where I am."

"I'm sure you are – doing nothing but sit on your arse playing computer games." He snorted in derision. "There's no future in that poncy job."

"Dad, computer graphics *are* the future." He didn't say there was no future in working on the assembly line in a run-down factory at the wrong end of town. But the inference was clear.

His father's neck went red above his collar. "You don't know what you're talking about!"

"Yes, I do. Ask the class-tutor at Tech. He'll tell you."

"I'm not letting any f – poncy teacher tell me what to do!"

Ben sighed. It was hopeless. The row would go on and on if he defended his chosen subject. Better say nothing now. Let it ride. "I'll be late for class," he said, and headed for the door.

On the way out, he turned his head and winked at his mother. Anything to take that anxious look off her face. He watched her smile back as he turned to go.

It was always like that. Day after day. His father shouted and laid down the law. Benny protested. His mother tried to keep

18

them apart. The explosion never quite came. But one day, Ben feared, it would. And then what?

On Friday he paid Mick for the computer and smuggled it upstairs without anyone noticing. He was a bit surprised when Mick actually came into the computer showroom where Ben was demonstrating graphics on a super-sophisticated new set-up, and stood looking around, waiting for him to stop work. But Mick was perfectly civil and kept his voice down and didn't try to show off, and outside when they clinched the deal he helped Ben load it on to his bicycle to carry home.

Ben discovered when he examined it that there were only a couple of small parts missing. It didn't take him long to put it all together and get it working. It was wonderful to have all that screen space to himself (though, of course, it was a bit primitive compared to the new ones he had been demonstrating at Fosters), and he spent more time than ever upstairs in his room, shut away from his father's disapproving glare and his mother's worried frown.

He liked his mother. She was still pretty, with brown hair that curled (like his) and had reddish lights in it, and big eyes that were more violet than blue and inclined to have sparks of laughter in them (like his) when they weren't so worried. She worked part-time in a baker's shop in the town, but his father permitted that because women couldn't be expected to work as hard as men, and anyway he wanted her home in time to cook his tea, didn't he? Ben remembered the time when Edie Roberts had been quite young and skittish. She used to drag his father off to the Saturday night discos at the works canteen. One year she had been crowned Disco-Queen and had worn a glittering paste tiara on her head and a shiny blue dress that flared out when she twirled.

"Look, Ben – it's like wings. I can fly!" she had cried, and lifted him up and twirled round and round, waltzing with him in her arms.

That kind of nonsense was all over now, of course. Life had tamed her – or his Dad had tamed her. She was no longer the impulsive, absurdly joyful girl she had been then. Now, Stan's uncertain temper put worry lines on her forehead, and the clash between him and Ben made her permanently afraid. Ben knew she was scared, but he didn't know how to reassure her. He couldn't cave in to his father's old-fashioned ways altogether, could he? She wouldn't want him to be stifled, would she? But there didn't seem to be any way out that would please everyone.

And Ben wanted to please. He wasn't naturally a trouble-maker. He liked life to be cheerful and full of laughter for his curly mouth to lift to. A scowl did not suit it.

"Dad," he tried once, "there's more to life than being behind the factory gates – isn't there?"

"Not that I've noticed," growled Stan.

"But – you used to go out and enjoy yourselves, you and Mum, didn't you?"

"That was a long time ago." He was still growling.

"But you're not *old*," said Ben, who thought his Dad was, but wasn't going to allow it. "You could still have a whale of a time – the two of you."

"Costs money," Stan grumbled, and rustled his paper to indicate that the subject was closed.

"But – you've *got* money," persisted Ben. "With you and Mum both earning – and I give her a bit too . . . Couldn't you –?"

"No, I couldn't," snapped Stan. "Savings matter. Never know these days." He glared even more fiercely at his son. "Do you good to think on that, too!"

But Ben didn't want to think of his savings – especially as he had blown most of them on his computer – so he said nothing.

The next day, though, out of some obscure sense of guilt about his mother's drab existence, he went out and bought her a bright silky scarf and a bunch of chrysanths for her birthday. "Cheer you up," he said, and tried to infuse as many sparks into her smile as his own. "Do you remember twirling? See if you can do it again!"

Edie put the scarf round her shoulders and seized Ben round the waist. They were dancing madly round the room, alight with laughter, when Stan came stumping in. "What's this, then?" he said. "Who won the war this time?"

The magic was broken, of course, and Edie at once looked frightened – but some of the sparks still lingered in her eyes.

Ben thought: Maybe I can keep her happy and keep Dad at bay
– if I try.

But then the trouble started. There was a ram-raid on Ben's
computer showroom, and a lot of valuable gear was stolen.
Before long, it became clear that his friend (his erstwhile
friend?) Mick was involved, and all his clever unscrupulous
gang with him. Ben could have kicked himself, for it was also
clear to him that the wily Mick had been "casing the joint" when
he was being so pleasant and obliging about the computer deal.
The computer deal? Ben went cold at the thought.

The police also questioned Ben about his association with
Mick. He told them truthfully that he knew nothing about the
raid, but he didn't think they believed him, and the upshot of
it was, his employers didn't believe him either, and he was
sacked.

"Told you so," said his father. "No-good poncy friends and a
no-good poncy job. Now perhaps you'll see sense."

Ben saw, all too clearly. The factory gates were closing round
him. And then his father found the computer.

*"Where did you get this?* Stolen property, is it? I won't have
stolen goods in my house."

In vain Ben protested that he had paid good money for it,
honestly he had, legitimately, and got a receipt. Here, look at
it. But Mick had been the seller – and Mick was involved in a
series of ram-raids round the town, wasn't he? So this *must* be
stolen. Stands to reason. Stan wasn't born yesterday.

That was the trouble really, thought Ben sadly. Stan wasn't
born yesterday. He was old-fashioned and unyielding, suspicious
of anything new, and he believed a father should lay down the
law to his wife and son and be obeyed without question.

"Start on Monday," he ordered. "No arguments. Get rid of
that bloody machine. And give up that stupid poncy course."

Despair settled on Ben. Even the curls at the edge of his mouth
went straight. But he knew that to keep the peace he would have
to obey.

However, his mother, Edie, behind her frightened gaze, had
plans for outwitting Stan in her still-curly head. She went quietly
off to see the foreman's wife, Betty, whom she knew quite well,
and a long and interesting conversation took place.

When Ben reported for work on Monday morning, head held high but heart sunk low, the foreman looked up and smiled. "Report to the drawing office, Ben."

"What?"

"Been doing a bit of graphics, I hear. Useful, that. They could use you, they tell me. Try it?"

"You bet!" crowed Ben, and set off to find the drawing office, walking on air.

His father was furious. But there was nothing he could do about it. He could not even insist on Ben getting rid of that suspect computer machine at home now, because apparently there were things Ben had to work out on it for the drawing office in his spare time. Ben tried to explain that a go-ahead company had to have new products, new ideas, new designs, even new packaging and new publicity. His father did not understand a word of it. He simply rumbled on about poncy rubbish and no good would come of it, you'll see. There's no room in a man's world for all this fancy stuff.

What happened was the reverse. The fancy stuff prevailed, the man's world crumbled. It was even worse than Ben could have imagined. His father and a third of the older-generation work force were made redundant. But the design office staff were kept on.

Something dreadful happened to Stan when he was made redundant. He became a different man. Having been the bread-winner, the head of the family, the undoubted ruler of his little roost, he was suddenly no-one. He had no role, he contributed nothing and no-one paid him any attention. He was a failure.

He took to going down to the factory gates and hanging about outside, jeering at the younger newcomers and telling anyone who would listen that it was a scandal to lay off a man after twenty-three years of loyal service. The men were sympathetic but they didn't want any trouble. They had their own jobs to consider. Mostly they avoided him, and once or twice when he got really stroppy they sent the union man out to talk to him.

As for Ben, – of course it was all his fault that his father got the push. It was a conspiracy against him. Taking on an inexperienced boy like Ben into that poncy office, and giving his father the sack. It was outrageous. Ben ought to protest. He ought to go and demand Stan's re-instatement or he would leave. He ought to leave anyway. He had no right to take that job when his own father was being thrown out. And so on. And so on.

Ben also tried to avoid him. He took to going the long way round to the main road goods entrance instead of the normal gates. That way he did at least get to work without a scene. But coming home was harder. The goods gates were closed, and he had to go the short way, the way that led past his angry, bewildered father. He took to staying on late in the drawing office, working on new designs, until he thought Stan would have gone down to the Crown and Thistle in search of comfort. Then Ben heaved a sigh of relief and slipped home through the shadows, alone. But then there was tea to get through, and the rest of the evening to be spent somehow avoiding a confrontation. His mother grew steadily paler and more worried as Stan got wilder and more unreasonable, and Ben was at his wits' end to know what to do. He was sorry for his father. He understood his rage and grief and wished there was a way to cure it. But he minded more about what it was doing to his mother. He could not bear to see her getting more and more fraught, especially knowing he was somehow responsible for all this family tension.

Edie had persuaded the bakery to take her on full time now, so she was out of the house all day, and there was still money coming into the house. Ben himself was on a Government Training Scheme, so his wage was low, and he still had to go to his graphics evening classes (to his relief, they were a compulsory part of the job). So he could get away in the evenings at least twice a week. His mother could not.

He said once, after a more violent spate of invective from his father than usual: "Mum, would it help if I moved out?"

"Out where?" asked Edie, already on the verge of tears.

"Anywhere. A room or something?"

"You couldn't afford it. Not on that wage. And I can't help, the way things are."

Ben looked at her. "We've got to do *something*. Or there'll be murder done."

Edie shivered. "Don't say such things."

He could see that the mere idea of him leaving had upset her.

23

Maybe she needed his support more than he realized. But it only made things worse with Stan and Ben did not like to see her so divided.

"I – I'll think of something," he said, and left it at that for the moment. Maybe something would happen that told him what to do.

It did. One day the design office closed early because of a computer failure and Ben was sent home an hour before the usual time. He came into the hall of the little terrace house to the sound of strange smashing noises upstairs. They seemed to be coming from his room, and he went up the stairs two at a time, wondering about burglars and break-ins. He flung open his door and paused in astonishment. His father stood there, a lump hammer in his hand and a ruin of computer parts all over the desk and the floor.

"Dad!" Ben started forward. "What on earth are you doing?"

"Can't you see?" snarled his father, looking strange and wild, and somehow curiously out of focus. "Getting rid of the junk."

"It's not junk!" Ben protested. "There's a couple of hundred pounds' worth of equipment there."

"Rubbish!" shouted his father. "Rubbish! All of it. And your poncy job, too!" And he swung the hammer up and smashed it down again on the splintered wreckage all round him. "And rubbish you are, too!" he yelled. "A son that takes his father's job and ruins him." And this time he lifted his hammer and swung it dangerously near Ben's head.

"Don't be daft," said Ben, suddenly enormously sorry for this pathetic wreck that was his father, and he went calmly forward and took the hammer out of Stan's flailing hand.

For a moment Stan resisted fiercely, and it looked as if a real struggle might develop, but then all at once the fight went out of him and he seemed to collapse in a heap on to the nearest chair.

Ben, without hesitation, laid an arm round his father's shoulders and spoke softly above his head, soothingly, as if to a frightened child. "I'm sorry, Dad. I'm sorry it's happened like this. But I never took your job away. It wasn't my fault."

Stan nodded dumbly, not able to speak for a moment. Then he said in a gruff, gravelly voice: "I know that, son . . . It's just

24

that – '' He looked up suddenly, and his eyes were bleak and bewildered in his ravaged face. "I don't know who I am any more."

Ben knew what he meant and his heart ached for him. But somehow he could not say: "You're my Dad, of course, and Mum's husband – same as always," because it wasn't the same as always. Something had changed between them for ever. So he gave the sagging shoulders a little helpless pat and said lamely: "You'll get another job soon."

Stan shook his head. "I'm too old. No-one wants you when you're old. It's the day of the young – kids like you – and all that new technical stuff. I can't keep up with it."

Ben knew this was true. But how could he say it to that obstinate, grizzled head? "Things'll work out," he murmured, rather uncertainly. He found himself obscurely embarrassed by his father's collapse. "Shall I make a cup of tea?"

"Tea?" echoed Stan, still dazed by his own rage and his own collapse. He was a strong man, and he was not used to weakness. He didn't understand what was happening to him, and he was frightened. The blue, defeated gaze had a sheen of tears about it as he looked up at his son. "I might've killed you."

"Well, you didn't," grinned Ben, and turned to go down the stairs and make a cup of tea.

But his mother stood in the doorway, horror on her face as she took in the scene of carnage. "Stan!" she whispered. "What's got into you?"

"It's all right," Ben told her cheerfully. "No harm done."

No harm? His father was an even more shattered ruin than his computer, and between the two of them lay a broken relationship that could never be the same again.

"No *harm*?" repeated his mother. "Are you hurt?"

"No, of course not."

"Edie – " Stan stammered. "I – I wanted to kill him – " and he gave a kind of despairing groan and covered his face with his hands and began to cry. Edie gave Ben one swift appealing glance and then went forward and folded Stan in her arms, rocking him to and fro like an errant child who has had a tantrum. "There," she crooned softly. "There then, Stan. All over now. There, then."

All over now, thought Ben. I can't stay here any longer. He won't want to face me after this – won't be able to look at me. And if he gets in a rage again, anything might happen. No, it won't do.

He realized as he slipped out of the room that the two of them scarcely saw him now. They were wholly concerned with each other and Ben was somehow irrelevant. Maybe, without him there, they would be able to pick up the pieces and make a go of it. But with him there, a constant reminder of his success and Stan's failure, it would never work.

He went down into the kitchen, but he did not make a cup of tea. Instead, he got his old rucksack out of the back of the broom cupboard and looked round to see what clothes he could salvage. He could not collect any from his room while his parents were still weeping together in the midst of the wreckage, so he simply took a couple of shirts off the clothes line by the stove, and a spare jersey from the mending pile, grabbed a hunk of bread and cheese, and walked out of the house.

As he left, he felt in his pockets for any loose change, and his fingers encountered the rounded shape of the shell fossil. For some reason this comforted him. It was very old. It had seen enormous, cataclysmic changes. His little problems were really very small.

He did not leave a note. There was nothing he could say that would put things back where they were before. His mother would know anyway why he had gone. It was better this way.

Sorry, folks, he said to himself with a flick of slightly off-balance humour. You're on your own now – and so am I. Good luck to us all, I say.

Maybe it was the row, or the struggle, or the shock or something, but he felt curiously light-headed – no, light-*hearted*, he told himself, almost facetious – and he gave a little skip of absurd, childish mischief on the edge of the pavement under the streetlight. Footloose and fancy-free, he said, and couldn't tell if the ache inside him was laughter or tears. On an adventure at last! Oh well, Benny-boy, you always said you wanted to see the world.

He walked down the road, and hitched a lift on the first lorry he saw. It was up to him now.

# III

# THE PIANO

It was the greyness that shocked Hilo most. She hadn't realized, fresh from the comparative cleanness of her small suburb and its leafy gardens, how huge and grey and dirty a big city could be. The streets were grey and covered in a greasy wet scum of rain and oil and trampled mud. The buildings were grey, and much too tall, so that you could hardly see the sky. And what sky you could see was grey as well. So were the people – grey and sparkless, and always hurrying by without looking at anyone, as if they were ashamed to be alive.

The first few days, she stayed in a Y.W.C.A. Hostel, whose address was given to her by the friendly lorry driver who set her down in central London. He also pointed to a card pinned up in his cab which said: "Message Home?" and explained how she could phone in and leave a message on the answering machine to tell her folks she was safe. "Mothers do worry, you know," he said casually, cocking an eyebrow in her direction.

"Not mine," stated Hilo flatly, – and at the look on her face he said no more.

From the first she had to fend off men. She was by no means pretty, but something about the thin, straight young body, the rough cap of mouse-brown hair and the grey-green eyes with distance in them was curiously attractive. She looked defenceless and vulnerable, – almost unbearably young to some of them. But when they put out a hand to touch her, the slight figure strung taut as steel. "No!" she said, and something about that unyielding tension made them pause.

27

Even before she ever got to the hostel someone tried to pick her up. "You look a bit lost. Nowhere to go?"

"I'm all right, thanks."

"Would you like me to help you find a room? I've got some friends . . ." The eager, over-bright eyes looked her over with speculative calculation.

"No."

"You can't just wander about on the loose."

"I'm not on the loose. I know perfectly well where I'm going. Did she? In all that huge and frightening city she had not one friend, not one address except the hostel to go to . . . No-one she could trust.

"I could – "

"Go away."

"I was only trying to help – " The voice was injured now.

"I don't need any help." But she did. Only to this predatory, foxy face she could not say so.

"Listen, if you – "

"If you don't go away, I'll call a policeman." Where would she find a policeman anyway?

But he saw the gleam in her eye, the hard, straight line of her mouth, and he went – still grumbling that he was only trying to help.

She knew that kind of help. In a way, she reflected, she ought to be grateful to the awful Steve. At least he had taught her to distrust all men. And she had already sworn to herself that she would never let any of them come near her, not ever again.

The hostel was gloomy and full of careful restrictions – but safe. She stayed there three days, which was all they would allow, and then found a small shabby room in a tall shabby house, where she and two other girls shared a tiny boxroom and took it in turns to sleep on the single, springless bed.

The other girls were older and a great deal more experienced than Hilo, but one of them got her a badly paid job as a washer-up in a sleazy café in a back street behind Notting Hill Gate. The girls tried to be helpful, but they found Hilo difficult to deal with – positively prickly, in fact.

First of all, they told her, she ought to do something about her appearance. She resisted fiercely.

"Don't you want to make the best of yourself?" Sue, the oldest and toughest, sounded just like her mother.

"Not particularly."

"You'll never get a boyfriend looking like that."

"I don't want a boyfriend."

There was a moment's astonished silence. Then both girls laughed. "You must be joking."

"No, I'm not." Her mouth went straight. "I don't want to let any of 'em within a mile of me – not ever again."

"*Again?*" queried Sue, with a knowing smile.

But Josie, who was kinder and more observant, shook her head and murmured: "Have it your own way," and left her alone.

Sue, however, was more persistent. She tried to lend Hilo a trendy mini-shift because she looked like a squared-off drainpipe. But Hilo refused.

"I told you – I don't *want* to attract men, thank you." She spelt it out again with fierce emphasis.

"You don't?"

"Not that kind."

"What kind? They're all alike," shrugged Sue. "Only after one thing."

"Well, they aren't getting it from me," snapped Hilo.

They were standing in front of the spotted mirror on the wall, while Sue held up the meagre scrap of black mini-shift. Hilo's straight grey-green glance met Sue's disbelieving brown one defiantly.

"They aren't all like that," said Josie softly, from across the room.

But Hilo did not answer.

After a few weeks of washing up and steam by day, and badgering by Sue in the evenings, Hilo got raw hands, a racking cough, and a permanent headache (which she rightly interpreted as a sort of claustrophobic longing for space and peace and quiet). The cafe manager (with a gleam in his eye that was not exactly kindness) took her aside and told her she could be a waitress if she dressed a bit better and took care of her hands. He offered to buy her a dress, but she refused abruptly, saying she would buy it out of next week's wages, thank you. She did, however, permit him to buy her a pair of rubber gloves for washing up, which he should have provided in the first place.

So then it was working as a waitress, which was tougher and more exhausting, but better paid. It was all she could do at fifteen, with no training. But the noise and constant demands of the job defeated her. She had no time to think, no time to breathe, and as she got steadily more exhausted she made more and more mistakes. At last, one day when the manager got extra fresh and pinched her bottom too hard, she dropped a trayful of dirty crocks on his feet, and left.

The girls were furious. "You can't afford to throw a job away!" they told her. "Now what are you going to do? You won't be able to afford the rent."

"I'll manage." Her mouth was one hard line.

But they had to take on another girl to help pay the rent, even of that one cramped room, and there simply wasn't the space for Hilo as well. She moved out and found herself a corner in a near-derelict house occupied by a group of squatters in a run-down street off Shepherd's Bush. Most of them smoked pot or other curious things and couldn't be bothered to clear up much. The house was rapidly becoming a rubbish dump but Hilo kept her corner with its single, threadbare blanket as clean as she could and even scrubbed the floor.

The others teased her a bit about being "squeaky" but let her go her own way. They offered her pot, and she tried it once or twice, but found it clouded her mind rather than causing any elation, so she stopped. "Crack?" they offered. "Ecstasy?"

"Not that kind," she said, and wondered why they looked so uncomprehending. But from then on she refused all the other curious pills they offered her from time to time "to take off the edge".

"I don't want to take off the edge," she said, mystifying them still further but she could not tell them about her secret folder and the occasional extra sheet of scribbles she stowed away inside it. The writing was different now, tougher and more fierce – and sadder. The days of lyric sunlight and her father's garden – the memory of his gentle presence – seemed far away. But the mere fact of putting words on paper seemed to keep him alive inside her, in spite of the uncomprehending grey world of the big city.

She did write one protest about the greyness – a silent cry which she showed to no-one. But she felt fiercer and less frightened when she had written her grief down on the page and put it carefully away with the others. She called it "*Gone*."

"The colours are all gone.
The bright days,
Each outline crystal clear,
Blue space, and spiced snow-scented air,
Splintered sunlight, and moonwashed seas,
Dayspring and starshine,
Cloudless ecstasy.
Gone – all gone.

Now it is all grey,
Grey half-light and blunted shapes.
A world of shades and echoing silences.
Each leaden moment hangs
Like unshed tears,
Dull drops of water on a sodden leaf
Waiting to fall.
Nothing but shadows
Waiting to fall.
Where has it gone,
The spark that shot the world with fire,
The comet tail,
The shimmer,
The promise of light still there?
Gone – all gone.
Only greyness here."

She did not tell the others of her despair. Or the loneliness that clouded the long, slow days. But one evening she weakened when they told her there was a party somewhere that night, and went with a crowd of unknown young people in a car to some secret destination. She did not know why it was secret, or that the word *Party* meant much more than it said these days, but there seemed to be convoys of cars, all converging from different places on to one dark road that led to a disused warehouse on the edge of a trading estate.

The strong, inescapable beat of rave music blared out from the doors in a wave of unbearable loudness, and strobe lights flashed and dazzled through a haze of smoke over the packed arena of gyrating bodies inside. Hair flying, arms flailing, bodies twisting, feet stamping, shuffling and lurching to the hypnotic insistent beat, blanched faces, blank eyes half-closed in the flickering gloom, – the frenetic crowd of young ravers abandoned themselves to the fierce, engulfing oblivions of the night.

Pills were passed from hand to hand, drinks were laced and spiced with unknown hazards, eyes grew glassier, smiles got dreamier, thoughts flew off into realms of dark ecstasy or brilliant unreality, – and still the relentless beat went on, the bodies jigged and wriggled in frenzied persistence, and the crowded space got hotter and more nightmarish with every frantic second.

Hilo thought it looked like a scene from hell. She stood it for a little while, and found herself dancing feebly, half-crushed in the crowd of twitching bodies, unable to escape. One hand was clutching a bright blue capsule that someone had thrust at her, but she had not attempted to swallow it, being much too afraid of what it might do to her mind to dare take the risk. And now, suddenly, the awful pressures of the evening, the packed bodies, the zigzagging lights, the incessant, ear-splitting, shattering drumbeat, seemed to bear down on her with frightening intensity. She had to get out. *Had to!* She could not think or even breathe in this horrendous atmosphere, – and a wave of panic swept over her as she fought and struggled to escape from the crowded space and get out into the clean air under the night sky.

At last, gasping and shaking, she managed to fight her way to the door and push against the incoming tide of still-arriving party-seekers to the comparative peace and freedom of the cindery floor of the car park.

"Freaked out?" asked a voice from the gloom. "Phased?"

"No," said Hilo. "Tired," and sank down wearily on to the gritty ground.

32

The owner of the voice was a gangling boy with a tangle of longish hair and a longish face to match. He was sitting with his back against a concrete bollard, smoking what looked like an ordinary cigarette, and looking at Hilo with what looked like ordinary friendly concern.

"Not your scene?"

"No." Hilo shut her eyes, and breathed in some cool night air.

"Not mine, either," the boy admitted, drawing lazily on his cigarette. He glanced at Hilo sideways, seeing her face lit by the pale glow from the open door. "How you getting home?"

"No idea," said Hilo, eyes still closed. But then she opened them swiftly and added: "Not with that lot," and waved a hand at the madly jerking mob inside.

Her companion was just about to agree with her when the wail of police sirens began in the distance, and two panda cars with flashing lights came into view.

"Oh-oh," said the boy. "Here they come. Better melt, I think," and he took Hilo's hand and dragged her away into the shadows. "If you got anything on you, throw it away," he urged. *"Now!"* He was making her move quite fast towards the quiet empty road behind the trading estate, away from where the police cars were already converging on the overcrowded warehouse. "We still might get picked up," he muttered, and went on walking away from trouble, with Hilo still held in a hard, determined grip. "Main road not far," he said. "Safer to hitch in twos. Where you heading?"

"Hammersmith."

"That'll do. The flyover. Come on."

Hilo came on, thankful for once to be ordered about and told what to do. The nightmare quality of the evening still oppressed her. She knew she was a fool to have gone there at all – the noise and chaos still seemed to be echoing in her brain, leaving her helpless and shaken.

Before long her decisive companion had thumbed down a lorry and they were travelling back towards Hammersmith in a noisy, bone-shaking cab that made conversation impossible.

Hilo wasn't sorry. There was nothing much to say, and she was still ashamed of having allowed herself to get mixed up in such a frightening orgy of noise and self-indulgence. The faces of the young ravers kept coming back into her mind – blind and desperate in the white glare of the lights, dancing themselves to death in the Halls of Hades . . . And somehow the despair behind their frenetic enjoyment was all too visible in their glassy smiles.

Hilo shivered, and her companion turned and gave her an encouraging grin, sensing her distress.

"It's a tough old world," he said, above the roar of the engine. Hilo only just heard him, but she nodded grimly and did not try to answer.

At last the lorry-driver put them down by the Hammersmith flyover, and thundered on towards the city, leaving them staring at each other in the cold gloom of a London dawn.

"You OK?" asked the boy.

Hilo nodded. "Thanks."

"A coffee would help," he said, looking round and spotting an all-night stand on the corner.

They stood warming their hands on the plastic cups, and staring out over the still-sleeping city.

"Steer clear of that lot," said the boy suddenly. "Bad news."

"I know," Hilo agreed. "Stupid."

He grinned. "Me, too." Then he put down his cup and prepared to move off. "See you around," he said as he turned away.

"Sure," answered Hilo, and watched him go, knowing he would not. Then she went back to the squatters' house and her loneliness, and tried vainly to put her life together.

She went down to the job centre every day, but there never seemed to be enough work to go round. They told her she was too young for the jobs offered, too young for the dole, and anyway she hadn't got a fixed address so she couldn't apply for a job, or for social security benefit. She looked on notice boards and peered in papershop windows, and at last found another exhausting job filling supermarket shelves. But at this point, the police raided the squatters' house and took away various bottles of pills and two of the squatters.

Hilo had been warned in time by the youngest and kindest of them – a shock-headed young giant called Rod, who said succinctly: "Split, kid."

"What?" Hilo didn't understand the score.

"You're not into this scene. Go on. Get!" And, as an after-thought, he thrust a five pound note at her.

Gravely Hilo returned it, saying: "Thanks, Rod, but I don't need it," and left him staring after her with doubt in his eyes.

So she went off by herself and wandered about for two days and nights before she found another corner in a seedy house the wrong side of everywhere behind the railway sidings. She had slept in the park for the two chilly nights, wrapped in her one and only blanket and some newspapers. But she was lucky. The police did not move her on, and the coffee-stall owner on the corner gave her a bowl of soup and a hunk of left-over bread for 5p at two o'clock in the morning because he was "packing up and going home, kid, and so should you, too."

The new house was full of West Indians who were mostly friendly and kind, full of absurd pranks, and who made a terrible noise on Saturday nights.

One evening the party got so wild that she was driven to sleep out in the park again, but this time a young policeman did pick her up. After one look at her he gave her his sandwiches and took her back to the house behind the railway sidings which was spilling over with singing West Indians and loud pop music.

He surveyed the scene for a moment in appalled silence, and then said: "You live *here*?"

"Afraid so," admitted Hilo.

"I can see why you wanted to sleep out."

"Yeah." Her smile was bleak. "But they're not breaking the law, are they?" She sounded quite anxious on their behalf. After all, they had been kind to her.

"No," said the policeman doubtfully. "Will you be all right?"

"Sure," she said, fending off one wildly singing boy with a bottle in one hand and a tin tray in the other which he was using as a drum.

The policeman shrugged helplessly, but he did get hold of one of the revellers who looked slightly less high and slightly more responsible and muttered several words in his ear. So the music was turned down a shade, and the shouting and singing subsided a little, as well as the tin-can orchestra. Hilo slept.

The supermarket job did not last long, as they were making

staff cuts, and the next one was as a junior in a hairdresser's. (Shades of her mother). But that folded soon, too – and the one after that was in a bar. But then the bar-keeper found out she was under-age, and she was out of work again.

It was at this time that she discovered the river – and a whole new world of meaning in the word "grey".

It wasn't grey at all. Not *just* grey. It was blue-grey and shimmering with light one minute, brown-grey and murky near the water's edge where the Thames mud got stirred up by the marauding ducks and wandering grey-lag geese, and almost black the next minute when the shadow of a river barge went by. It was pure silver some evenings, pure gold some mornings, greeny-grey and dove-grey, and even rose-grey when the sun was setting in a haze of city vapour towards the west. It was all the colours you could imagine, and some you couldn't, though they were most often muted and softened by the filtered London light – and they were always different. Every time you came it was different. At dawn when you were cold and hungry – at mid-day when the sun was high (behind the haze) and you had managed to afford a hot pasty from the corner stall – at quiet evening, when the traffic had almost stopped except on the roaring main road and there was scarcely a ripple on the old river's silken surface – and at night, with the sodium lights reflected in the water and snatches of music and laughter coming from the riverside pubs, and the smell of food, oh the smell of heavenly food, drifting over from the busy restaurants along the river walk. Even if you were still hungry there was always the water to look at, blue-black, inky and dark, sparkling with golden gleams of light . . .

So far, life had not been insupportable for Hilo. She had been in work enough to be able to eat, and only once or twice totally homeless. And, up to now, the weather had been more or less kind. Bearable, if you didn't have to sleep out more than one night at a time. It was cold, but not freezing, and if it rained, it didn't happen to do so on the nights she was sleeping rough.

But she knew it would. And that the time would come when she could not find anywhere to stay, could not find any work, and could not pay for anything – either food or shelter. What would she do then, she wondered? And shuddered a little. But then a sudden shaft of light from a watery sun lit up the river,

36

and Hilo forgot her fears and stood in rapt enchantment as dusk came down with swift violet wings to cancel out the gold.

There was one boy among the singing West Indians who had taken rather a shine to Hilo. He was a tall, willowy, golden-skinned youth with soft doe eyes and wild hair, and his friends called him Rufty. He was always kind to Hilo, always smiling and cheerful, but one evening he decided that she needed a bit of extra comfort (including a lot of extra rum) and got altogether too kind.

Hilo resisted fiercely, outraged at this invasion, and finally hurled the rum in his face.

He was bewildered when she threw him out, along with the rum, and swore at him with a fury that was as white-hot as it was unexpected.

"What have I done?" he asked, clutching at his wild hair in amazement.

"Get out!" she screamed. "This may only be one small corner of one small room – but it's *my* corner and I want you out!"

"But – "

*"Get out of here!"*

She could not tell him that for a moment he had almost breached the high wall of loneliness and pride that kept her going – the wall that kept her own private world safe. It would have been so easy to give in, to accept the warmth and comfort of those friendly young arms . . . to let someone else take charge, even for a little while, and to feel herself loved and wanted and protected . . . But she couldn't. Oh no, she couldn't. Not after the mindless tyranny of Steve. Never again. Never again would she let anyone come that near.

Rufty, still not understanding, went ruefully away.

Of course she was wrong in some ways. People came near whatever you did. You couldn't shut out the world. Not for ever. You thought you'd grown armour. You thought you were safe. But you weren't.

The next time it was a musician called Max, who had fizzy black hair, black eyes snapping with mischief, a burning fiery furnace sort of face, and a violin tucked under his chin. He was busking at the entrance to the underground station, and Hilo stopped to listen, because he was really good.

One minute she was alone, listening to a stranger playing Brahms to a heedless crowd, and the next minute he had winked at her over the heads of the passers-by, and a slender, perilous bridge had been built in the listening air. A bridge she was afraid to cross. She stood there, breathless and scared, while he went on playing until the rush-hour ended. Then he scooped up the money from his open violin case, put his violin away, and said: "Come on. I'll play you some real music."

He did, too.

His room made Hilo gasp. She was so used to cramped and squalid quarters by now. But this room was different. It was a split-level affair at the top of an old warehouse down near the river. It was huge and airy, and painted white. On the top level there was an upright piano, some electronic equipment and a couple of speakers, and not much else. Down below was a futon mattress on the floor, a table and one hard chair, and several large white cushions. And nothing else.

"So much space!" breathed Hilo.

He glanced round carelessly. "Not mine. Sam's."

"Who's Sam?"

"My boss. Runs a club. He lets me use it." He turned to his electronic switchboard and said: "Violin Concerto, with orchestra – or piano without?"

Hilo looked at him. "Which is you?"

"Oh, piano."

"Well then, piano, of course," said Hilo, and sat down on the floor to listen.

For over an hour he played to her, or rather to himself, for once his hands reached the keyboard he forgot everyone and everything.

She did not understand his music, of course. But that didn't seem to matter. New worlds swam into being, huge horizons opened, starry heights and wide, empty wildernesses grew in the pulsing air. Clouds bloomed and sailed, seas and cataracts poured, wild, swift eagles soared, flames leapt and burned, and dark, cool caves echoed with dripping space. Strange, fierce ecstasies and griefs assailed her, sudden rages and equally sudden calms and innocences, great striding nobilities, and small quiet oases of tenderness. They fell on her unguarded heart in a ceaseless stream of sound.

She was utterly lost. Such marvels and miracles, and – above all – such total freedom of spirit, were utterly new to her.

When Max finally stopped playing and looked round, he was almost afraid of the tearless white enchantment on the small face before him. Had he done that to her? (He admitted, wryly, that he had been showing off a little.) But such surrender? For the first time in his self-absorbed existence he had a faint desire to protect someone. He wanted to put his arms round her and say: "Don't look like that. The world's a terrible place, and you'll die if you stay that open to hurt."

Instead, he got off the piano stool and said: "I'll make us some coffee."

After a little while when the dreams and visions had receded a little, Hilo said shakily: "What do you do?"

He raised an enquiring eyebrow. "For a living? Busk – as you saw. And play in a club."

"No. I meant – how do you survive, with all *that* inside?"

His grin was wise, and older than his years. "I'm a natural survivor."

She was looking at him almost in disbelief, as if he wasn't quite real. "But – how?"

"How do I come down?" He lit a cigarette. It was handrolled and rather shaggy at the edges, and he gave it a sardonic glance. "Mostly, with this . . ."

"Pot?"

"Or something." He handed it to her, but she shook her head and handed it back.

"Doesn't that – cloud things?"

"Yes." His mouth grew grim. Then he relaxed and laughed. "So I never smoke till I've finished working."

She still looked unconvinced.

He made a wide, sweeping gesture with his hand, half in defence, half in humorous resignation. "Listen. Everyone has to come down somehow. You sit there, sky-high and lit, with 'All this and heaven too' written all over your face in flaming letters ten feet tall – and someone's needled by the blaze and switches off the neons. Click."

Hilo blinked.

He laughed again. "You see? I've knocked you down. Now you have to pick the pieces up and try to put all that bright bubble together again. And you can't." He leant forward, looking at her intently out of those startlingly brilliant black eyes, his fingers curled tensely round his coffee mug, the smoke from his cigarette spiralling blue in the air. "You *can't*. Can you?"

Hilo sighed. There were tears in her eyes now. She knew about those starry heights. That coming down. "That's what I meant. How can you bear it?"

His face changed. It astonished him that even after this rough treatment she was aware of his own hurt. And concerned about it.

"You a musician?"

"No." It was on the tip of her tongue to confess to that folder of scribbles. But what could she say? No, I'm a poet. How ridiculous it would sound. Besides, what *was* a poet? She didn't believe she had the right to such a claim. No, better keep quiet. Keep it hidden, as usual. Safer that way. No-one could knock her down if she didn't give them a chance. So she said nothing.

They stared at one another, and the silence was long and strange. At last he said, with a hint of anger behind the teasing voice: "You know too much."

"Sorry," she said, and got hesitantly to her feet. "Shall I go?"

"Yes. Go on. Go." He drew hard on his cigarette. "Leave me to wallow in self-pity. What else have I got?"

She stood still, and her face blazed with sudden passion as she turned on him. "Your music," she said. And turned to go.

Max saw the thin young body strung taut with resolution. The set of her shoulders was absurdly brave and proud, and he could not bear it. He came across to her in one swift movement and laid an arm round those stiff, unyielding shoulders. For a moment he thought she was going to hit him. But instead she looked up into his face searchingly and said in a humble voice: "I won't invade."

He stood looking down at her in surprise and shock. He saw how aware of pain that vulnerable young mouth was, and how clear and far the visionary grey-green eyes seemed to see – and he was troubled. It seemed to him that the face before him was

40

both too old and too young – too inexperienced and yet too wise for its time. Like his own tired grin, had he known it.

He sighed. "OK. No invasions." His smile grew a little when he saw the flash of relief in her eyes. He went on looking at her for a moment in silence, and then said abruptly: "What's your name?"

"Hilo."

He stared. Then he began to laugh. He laughed and laughed, and Hilo knew it was because he would rather cry, so she said nothing. "Of course," he spluttered, still laughing. "What else could you be called? The heights and the depths. You know them all. Don't you?"

"Yes."

He was quiet for a while. "Is that really it?"

"Yes." She saw him wait, and went on slowly. "I had a swing once."

"A swing?"

"It was – like your piano."

Comprehension came into his face. "Your private Eden. Yes. And – ?"

"They cut it down."

"They?"

"My – my mother."

He heard the reluctance in her voice, and did not pursue it. "So." There was a brief pause while he looked at her with sudden kindness. "But it's still there, Hilo, if you need it. What are you worrying about?"

For a long, astonished moment she gazed at him in silence. Slow tears once more crept into the edges of her eyes, but she would not let them fall. To be understood like this was terrifying – and she didn't know whether to welcome it or to run from it. At last she brushed a hand over those tell-tale eyes in a childish, angry gesture and repeated his earlier complaint, "You know too much, too."

He spread his hands out in protest and grinned. "No invasions, Hilo. I told you. You're as safe behind your flaming gates of Paradise as I am. Quits?" He held out a friendly hand.

After a small hesitation, she took it. "Quits," she said.

*     *     *

41

It wasn't easy. She was cautious about allowing the extraordinary rapport between them to develop too fast. Where would it lead her? In any case, she was a bit awestruck by Max's talent. He couldn't really want her hanging around, with all that music inside him, could he? So she stayed on in the overcrowded West Indian house, and visited Max when she was lonely.

He respected her independence and never asked her to stay longer. She would climb the stairs, hearing his piano as she came up from the three dusty warehouse floors below. Max would not look up from his playing. It was doubtful whether he even knew she was there. She would curl up quietly on one of the big white cushions on the floor and listen without comment until he returned to her.

Sometimes he would be playing his own work, which was difficult and strange but which never failed to move her. Sometimes he would be stopping and starting and scribbling things down on bits of manuscript. And sometimes he would go back to Beethoven or Bach, and she discovered them all over again, too. Her father had liked Beethoven, especially the late quartets, she remembered. He had played them on his old record-player, and the piano sonatas, too, when he got the chance. But her mother always got him to "turn that damn thing off", complaining that all that heavy stuff gave her a headache. He had sighed but never answered back, never resisted. Her domineering voice had shouted him down, shouted Beethoven down, and he had said nothing. He had just looked a little greyer and sadder each time it happened. Hilo remembered that shuttered sadness, and it made her ache. Beethoven made her ache, too. But Max's own music made her ache most of all.

She found out that Max called his violin his "money-grubber" – useful for busking, and, as he put it, to use when he felt "splurgy and concerto-minded". Then he would put on an orchestral tape to accompany or play against. ("A lot of buskers do that these days," he told her. "Sounds richer.") He could have done it with piano concertos too, he explained, but you couldn't cart a piano around the tube stations. And anyway, it felt a bit like cheating. She didn't understand this distinction, but accepted that he had his own peculiar code of musical ethics. He even found out that Hilo could play the flute, and bought her a penny whistle. ("Couldn't manage a flute, sorry, but it's better than nothing, and you can always raise a bit of cash if you can manage a tune or two.")

Hilo soon discovered that Max was not only a good pianist, but a wildly inventive improviser as well. Only, as he told her, he was mostly too lazy to write any of it down. She knew, obscurely, that he could make Beethoven speak with the voice of truth. But he could do that with his own music, too, and she found herself not only shaken by its power, but somehow angry that he did nothing with it.

One day she said, over their usual coffee: "Can I ask you something?"

He raised one quirky eyebrow. "What if I say no?"

"Then I won't ask."

He reached out for the sugar. Hilo watched those sensitive blunt-tipped fingers and suddenly found herself remembering the feel of them on her shoulders. She was shocked. But then she told herself it was because it had been the first purely kind touch she had felt since her father died. And that shocked her, too. No wonder she felt shaken.

Max was watching her, looking at her suddenly as if he really saw her, and she wondered if he knew how much his strange, sparky magnetism shook her. But if he did, he made no comment. "Well?"

"What are you *doing* here? Why aren't you doing something with your music?"

He laughed. "Good question." He lit another cigarette – the same kind of hand-rolled one with the extra-sweet scent – and inhaled deeply. "I was a music student, of course. But my grant got cut. I couldn't afford to go on. And a heavy student loan didn't appeal a lot. When would I ever pay it off? So I quit."

She sighed. "And – ?"

"Oh – period of penury." His grin was wry. "Couldn't find a job. Not even washing up."

She grinned too. "I've done that. It ruins your hands."

"Exactly."

When he didn't go on, she prodded him again. "So?"

He patted the piano, as if it was an old friend that needed placating. "Sam rescued me. I really was about starving when he found me. I'd even hocked my fiddle." He laughed at her

43

horrified face. "Took me into the club, gave me a meal, found out I could play jazz – and that was it, really. It's a jazz club, you see. Not pop – the real old smoky-dive stuff." He looked round the big room with cool appraisal. "He thinks I've got 'promise', so he lets me use this place. It's his piano – his equipment. Sometimes other jazz players crash out here, too, if they're stuck for a bed. There's a lot of floor."

She followed his gaze round the airy white space and nodded. But she was not to be deflected. "Yes. But your *own* work?"

He shrugged. "No money in it. Pure self-indulgence."

She was angry with him then. "I don't believe that."

His mouth suddenly curved upwards in a surprisingly sweet smile. "Champion Hilo? Far too optimistic." He paused, and then added with careful nonchalance:

"But I have done a few bits here and there. Sam puts things in my way if he can."

"What things?"

"Oh . . . arrangements. Incidental stuff. Radio. Telly now and then. But it's difficult to get. Lots of competition." He sounded absurdly casual.

"But you can't stay buried here for ever," she told him fiercely.

He laughed. "Buried? Yes, I suppose jazz sessions are a bit like a wake."

He paused again and then added rather too carelessly: "I'd like to go to the States and do electronics. Widen my scope. But I couldn't afford the fare, let alone the fees."

Hilo looked at him severely. "Doesn't Sam pay you?"

"Not a lot. But I live free – and I eat free. Believe me, that's a lot today."

"I do believe you," said Hilo fervently.

There was a moment of silence and then Max shrugged his expressive shoulders and murmured: "Something'll turn up sometime, I daresay. "

"You've got to *make it happen*," said Hilo, glaring at him.

But Max did not answer. He just shrugged again and turned away.

That evening, when Hilo got back to the house in Hammersmith, she found the whole place boarded up, windows and all, and wild-haired Rufty sitting on the steps, waiting for her in the rain.

"What happened?" she asked.

"Re-possessed," said Rufty. "No warning. They just came and threw us all out." He looked up at Hilo and held out her precious folder and her shabby blanket and duffel bag. "I saved your things."

"Thanks. Not that they amount to much," said Hilo, too shocked to make any protest. What was she going to do now? "What happened to the others?"

"Relations," grinned Rufty. "Uncles at every turn. Useful things, uncles."

"You fixed up all right?"

"Sure. More uncles. Crowded but cosy." His grin was full of cheerful mischief. Then his expression sobered as he looked at Hilo. "What'll you do?"

"Oh – I'll find something."

"You could pile in with me."

"No thanks, Rufty," said Hilo, and then smiled at him to soften it. "It's OK. I'll be fine."

"Well, if you're sure – " He still sounded doubtful but, looking into her face, he knew it was no use. So he swayed gracefully to his feet, squeezed Hilo's shoulder, and sloped off into the rain.

Hilo walked the wet streets for hours, wondering what to do. It was too late in the evening to begin looking for another room, or even part of a room to share. It was too wet to sleep out in the park. Even a shop doorway would be a soggy resting place tonight. She might get into a hostel for the night – if she could find one. Or maybe sit in one of those soup-kitchen places, like the crypt of that redbrick church on the corner. They sometimes let you stay all night, even though they didn't run to any beds or mattresses. Even a floor would do – anything to get out of the rain.

She wandered on, getting steadily wetter and colder, and finally drifted into a shabby church hall where a lot of hunched figures were warming their hands round bowls of hot soup and mugs of tea. It was warm and steamy after the wet street and she sank gratefully on to the nearest bench.

"Soup?" said a brisk, kindly voice. "You look pretty wet," and a brown bowl was dumped down in front of her, accompanied by a thick hunk of bread.

Hilo's teeth were chattering, but she managed a shaky "Thank you."

"We don't have a drier here," went on the brisk voice, "but I can hang your coat near the stove."

Hilo hesitated. A coat was a coat, however wet. She might never see it again – and she certainly couldn't afford another.

"It's all right," said the voice, sounding amused. "No-one'll pinch it here."

Reluctantly, Hilo struggled out of her wet duffel coat and handed it over, but she clung fiercely to her folder of papers.

The woman who took her coat was oldish and squarish, with short grey hair and an unexpectedly encouraging smile. "Eat up," she said. "No-one will bother you."

There was an overall smell of steaming wet clothes, soup and tea, mixed with the unmistakable aroma of tired and unwashed human bodies in the shadowy hall, and Hilo found it oddly comforting. We are all in the same boat here, she thought. Stuck. Nowhere to go. No need to keep my end up any longer. I don't have to pretend anything to anyone here . . . she found herself almost nodding over her soup as the warmth of the room and its human flotsam enfolded her.

I've still got that part-time job at the newsagent's, she said to herself. I can go there tomorrow wherever I've slept the night . . . But while she was half dozing in exhausted relief, another woman came in through the door and stood looking around her. She was carrying a small clipboard in her hand and seemed to be looking from one to the other of the shadowy figures with searching interest.

There was another girl sitting not far from Hilo on the same bench, and she suddenly leant forward and spoke to Hilo in a low voice. "You want to avoid her."

"Why?" Hilo was watching the newcomer pick her way across the hall towards a group of young people near the back.

"If you don't want to get picked up – "

"What for?" Hilo sounded quite truculent.

"How old are you?" countered the other girl, still keeping her voice down. "No. Don't tell me. And don't tell *her*, either. Or you'll get taken into care."

*"Care?"*

"Well, you could call it that." The girl's voice was dry. "They try to catch the youngest ones. It makes sense, I suppose. Safer that way." She looked at Hilo out of a pale, dark-eyed face that seemed neither old nor young, but only tired. "Or they send you home."

Hilo looked startled. "Can they?"

"Oh yes. If you're under age." She nodded at Hilo with tired emphasis. "The street's a dangerous place to be, after all."

"Not so dangerous as home," muttered Hilo, and got rather wearily to her feet.

The other girl smiled. "Like that is it? Well . . . good luck then," she said.

Hilo fetched her wet coat from the corner by the stove, and slipped out of the door unnoticed. It was still raining.

By now it was very late, and Hilo was very tired. She scarcely noticed the other people in the street hurrying home against the rain. Hurrying home . . . Well, there was still the newsagent's job tomorrow – that was something. But if she was going to keep it, she'd have to find somewhere to live, or she would soon be too scruffy and exhausted to be presentable. Just a bolt-hole, she told herself. *Anywhere.* Just a small bit of roof over my head to keep out the rain . . . But there was nowhere to go, and the night was getting older and colder.

Then she thought of Max. Did she dare? Would it bother him, or annoy his mysterious boss, Sam, if she turned up and asked for shelter? Would he think she was invading his privacy? (No invasions!) Or just trying it on . . .? She shuddered when she thought of the contempt she might see in his eyes. She didn't know where Sam's jazz club was – Max had never told her. But it was nearly two in the morning now, so he would be going home soon anyway . . . Maybe it would be all right if she waited for him downstairs in the warehouse yard . . . It would be better than being picked up by the police for loitering. Already, one man had tried to detain her, mistaking her profession . . . she felt vulnerable and cold – unable to cope for much longer . . . Better get under shelter somewhere fast.

After arguing with herself along several more shiny wet streets that were mercifully empty, she found herself outside Max's warehouse. The building was dark and shuttered on the first three floors. There was no light in Max's window. Either he wasn't home yet, or he was asleep.

She went into the dark, empty yard, and leant wearily against the door. It was locked, of course. No-one would dare leave a building open to squatters these days. But it had a sort of drunken porch of rotting wood which kept off the rain a bit. Sighing, she curled herself up in as small a knot as she could, and went to sleep.

Max found her there when he came home, an hour later. He did not show any particular surprise or dismay. He simply hauled her to her feet, dragged her up the stairs, and made her strip off all her wet clothes and wrap herself in all the blankets he could find. Then he unceremoniously pushed her down on to the soft futon on the floor and left her alone, while he went upstairs and arranged himself on a spare mattress near his piano.

"Sorry –" began Hilo, her tongue slurring with weariness, "to do this to you –"

"Shut up," growled Max. "You're all right here. Relax."

"I have to – have to go to work – " she protested, drowning in sleep already.

"Not this morning, you don't," snapped Max. "Go to sleep." Hilo did.

When she woke it was late morning – she could tell that by the light from Max's windows. And she was alone. She looked round the big, empty room and wondered where Max had got to. Had she driven him away, afraid to get entangled with a clinging, helpless female? She shivered, and looked round for her clothes. They were draped over a small electric radiator which seemed to be the only means of heat in the place. Her jeans were still damp at the edges, but her T-shirt was dry enough, and Max had put out an ancient sweater of his own for her (so he couldn't be very angry), since hers seemed to be incurably sodden and caked in mud. Had she fallen down? She couldn't remember. Max's was much too big and made her laugh, but it was warm and dry.

Then she began to explore. She discovered a small washroom and lavatory on the floor below. It was primitive, but the water ran and the flush worked. There was also a cracked white porcelain sink on the same landing, with one dripping tap. Upstairs, she found no cooking arrangements except an electric kettle and a small, old-fashioned electric grill, both of which were plugged into one socket on the wall. Basic, she thought. But possible. Especially as he eats at the club every evening.

At this point in her thoughts she heard footsteps on the stairs, and Max appeared, carrying a stick of French bread, a packet of butter and a pint of milk.

"Breakfast coming up," he said. "Have you switched on the kettle?"

He would not let her talk until they had finished eating, sitting cross-legged together on the floor, and then he turned to her and said gently: "How old are you, Hilo?"

"Fifteen." She did not elaborate.

He nodded. "No-one waiting for news at home?"

"No." She shook her head decisively. "They couldn't care less."

Once again he nodded. "And you've had more than enough from someone, haven't you?" He did not wait for her to answer, but continued steadily: "Well, you can stay here as long as you like – and you won't need a sword with me." His smile was almost tender for a moment. "But I've got to tell you – I'm death to be with. I'll forget you half the time. I'm a more than average liar – and a cheat. I let people down all the time, and I don't even notice much when they get hurt. And in the end I always leave when the pace gets too hot. Always."

"Yes," said Hilo.

He looked incredulous. "Just like that?"

"Just like that."

"Hilo, I'm twenty-five. I know someone's wrecked things for you – and it'll probably take you a long time to trust anyone again. Well, don't trust me, that's all. I can't be the one to put things right. I'm much too old, and you're much too young. But – " he hesitated then, and Hilo prompted him softly.

"But – ?"

"We've got something going for us, Hilo – and I think it's

49

too good to waste." He looked at her straight. "And I don't mean sex!"

Hilo breathed a long sigh of relief. "Oh, thank God you said it!"

They looked at each other and laughed. Then Max leant forward and hugged her briefly. "That's better. We'll be all right. We might even have fun. You look as if you could do with some."

She grinned. "So do you, come to that."

"Leave our weapons at the door?"

"Sure," she said. "Pass, friend."

They giggled feebly together and had another mug of coffee, into which Max poured a generous dollop of rum.

At first, Max managed to keep his three lives separate. There was the jazz-club, to which he never took Hilo. There was his own music at home, where he worked oblivious of anyone. And there was Hilo.

It was funny about Hilo. He couldn't understand himself, really. Usually he wasn't very conscientious about people. He was used to being pretty successful with girls. He was reasonable to look at, and they rather liked his burning fiery furnace air, they told him. He didn't take their admiration seriously and went his own way regardless. And – as he told Hilo – he didn't notice much if they got hurt.

But with Hilo it was different. To begin with, she was much too young to play about with. She was so vulnerable, so easily scared by unexpected pressures. He remembered that first time when he put his arm round those stiff shoulders, she seemed to go rigid with shock. Her eyes dilated in terror and begged him silently to let her go. But there was a strange conflict of loneliness, grief and pride in her face – even then. And it was worse now, because she was getting fond of him, in spite of all his warnings, and he was getting fond of her, too, and he knew it was no good – no good at all. There were many deep scars to heal, many deep fears to dispel before anyone dared breach the high walls of Hilo's bitter defences. And it mustn't be him. He'd be going away soon, and he wasn't going to let her get hurt. He *mustn't*.

But however hard he tried to keep things separate, they began to merge. He was suddenly aware, one night at the club, of a lonely Hilo curled up and solitary in the empty warehouse room, waiting for him to come home. Though she would never have said so. She paid him rent now, – not much, but what he could afford out of that crummy job at the newsagent's, and she insisted on cooking him funny little meals on the old electric grill. That way, she told him, she could still feel independent. It was the only way she would agree to stay. And he wanted her to stay, – oh yes, he wanted her there. He had to admit it. While little Hilo remained safe and warm and fed, he felt safe, too. He didn't know quite why, but he did.

Loneliness, though, was something that hadn't bothered him much up to now. He was pretty self-sufficient, always wrapped up in one project or another to do with his music. He didn't have much time to be lonely. But Hilo did – too much time – and she had no-one but him to turn to. Sometimes there was Freddie, the blues singer from the club, who spent an occasional night on his floor when the club sessions went on too late for her to get home. But she was mostly asleep all the time Hilo was there, and did not wake in the morning till after Hilo had gone to work. She was a kind enough girl, was Freddie – warm-hearted and easy – but she was never there on the long, dark evenings when Hilo was most alone.

So the next night he suggested casually that Hilo might like to come down to the club with him. She was doubtful – worried about encroaching on his other life. But he persuaded her to try it. "You may hate the noise and the fug, Hilo. But it is high jazz, not pop. And we don't use amplifiers. Your ears are safe."

She went, distrustfully, and found that she rather enjoyed the insistent rhythms and the free, unrestricted improvisations of the players. There were three of them besides Max – a saxophone, a double-bass and a drummer – and they wove extraordinary patterns on the listening air. Sitting alone at a shadowy table, hazed by cigarette smoke, she let the insidious beat of the music take her, and watched the play of light on Max's face as his fingers moved in an endless, bitter-sweet interweaving tangle of wit and golden nostalgia. She was too young even to recognize most of the old, re-worked tunes but they got to her just the same.

Max's dreaming mouth was set in a straight line of flippant concentration, his wicked black eyes sparked fire, and his face was pale, both with the effort of swift creation and with his own special brand of sardonic self-contempt. Hilo began to ache inside.

At this point, as if he had been called, Max lifted his head and one expressive eyebrow twitched in her direction. He smiled, and went on playing.

But Hilo suddenly began to panic. The beat was too insistent, the sweetness too beguiling, the "blue" edge to the chording spoke too clearly to her of twisted ideals and unfulfilled promise. It was all too clever, too slick and too sad. Even its satire swung back against itself. Life is a joke, it said. It smashes you to pieces until there is nothing left to believe in. You can only laugh . . . The walls of the smoky club began to close in on her. It was a hot, dark, shuttered world of airless isolation, fierce ritual noise and desperate exclusion. She began to hear a more terrible cry of grief behind it than its performers knew. Terrible and incurable . . . She pushed the table away in a sudden movement of revulsion and fled, pursued by Furies.

Max saw her go. He did not try to follow. In any case, he couldn't leave the piano in the middle of a number, but his brilliant fingers played on without his mind.

How to reassure this frightened, freedom-loving creature? Every shadow was a threat. Every moment of careless enjoyment a snare. *A snare.* He had a sudden image behind his eyes of the small, frantic birds threshing about in the nets that the Italian hunters put out during the time of migration. Wildly, despairingly beating their wings against the imprisoning, tangling webs until they died of exhaustion.

*The time of migration?*

He almost ran through the four-o'clock streets, still seeing the appalling tumult of those dying wings. He flung himself up the stairs, put his key in the lock, and all but fell into the quiet room.

But she was gone.

The folder of poems was gone from under the neat futon on the floor. Her duffel coat and bag were gone from behind the door. The room was empty. Colossally empty.

"Oh dear God," said Max, and sat down at his piano and tried to think what to do. He might have wept, but he knew that Hilo would despise him for that, too. Too? Was it because she couldn't stand him wasting his talents in the pursuit of high jazz? No, she wasn't that kind of a snob, he thought. She was too young to make such judgements, thank God. But what, then? What had driven her to run from him with such swift and final terror? He did not know. He only knew he had got to find her somehow, and persuade her to come back – to face the hazards of the day.

It took him a week to find her. And in the end he didn't find her at all. She came back. After seven long days of fruitless search in all the parks and along the embankments, in the hostels and squatters' hide-outs, and among the groups of dossers and campers-out in the various cardboard cities, he came back late and tired to his empty room and found her crouched on the stairs.

She looked very small and thin, huddled in her old grey duffel coat, and her face was pinched with cold and almost as grey as her coat.

He was suddenly stupendously angry. "You tramp!" he shouted. "You coward! You feckless brat! Where the hell have you been?"

She sat there, still in a tight, small knot of despair, looking up at him in white silence, while the tears slid down her face and made grimy rivulets on her cheeks. She looked about six years old. "I lost my job," she whispered. "I'm sorry – " And went on sitting there, helpless and defeated.

Max forgot his colossal anger and sat down beside her on the stairs, rocking her in his arms. "It's all right," he said. "It's all right. You made it. Don't you see? You came back – of your own accord."

She seemed unable to hear him at first, but went on saying: "I'm sorry . . . I'm sorry . . ." in a shamed, whispering little voice full of tears, and shook with strange rigours of grief in his arms. But Max went on repeating: "It's all right," until she stopped shaking. Then he pulled her to her feet and half-carried her up the rest of the stairs to his room. Once there, he sat her down on the floor and brought her coffee.

"Now, you listen to me," he said, wrapping her chilled fingers round the coffee mug, and keeping his own over hers for extra comfort. "You've got to stop running, Hilo. Nothing is as bad as it seems . . . Next time, just take a deep breath and say: "Max said I was a coward, but I'm NOT. Because I came back." He looked to see if there was a glimmer of a smile in her eyes, and there was, tired though they were.

"That's better. Say it."

"What?"

"I'm not a coward."

She shut her eyes as the tears threatened to spill out of the corners. "But I am."

"No." His hand lay on her hair, stroking it absently. "If you beat against the bars, you'll die," he said obscurely. "But if you keep still and wait, you'll survive – like the other brave migrants."

*Brave migrant*? she thought. Me? Not true. He doesn't know the half of it. But Max was pouring out more coffee, and the world was warm again.

Max thought that with each small victory, she got stronger. But there were still times when she retreated in swift panic and became the pale, silent ghost she was when he first met her.

There was the time he introduced her to his boss at the club. Sam was a stringy, shrewd man who was a jazz-player himself and sometimes took over at the piano when Max's fingers got too tired. He also understood the other side of Max's music as no-one else seemed to do. When the club finally closed in the early hours of the morning, they would often sit on discussing Max's work and what they ought to do about it.

Hilo was frightened of the technicalities at first, and sat in bewildered silence while the talk flowed round her. She nearly ran away again then, telling herself that she was only a drag and a hindrance in Max's high-powered world. But Sam gradually drew her in to the conversation, discovering that she had an instinctive understanding of Max's purpose without knowing how or why

"It's the *width*, you see," she said earnestly, looking at Sam's

54

seamed, unsurprisable face with entreaty. "It has to have room to breathe – "

"Yes?" Sam was looking at her with sharp attention. "So?"

"I just . . . I'm not sure it belongs in an ordinary concert hall at all . . . I mean, with tapes you can have the sea – or the wind – or whale songs – or a curlew . . . Space, I mean – and echoes . . . Maybe it ought to be played *out of doors*? Maybe it ought to take *all day*?"

"The Hollywood Bowl?" murmured Sam. *"All day?"*

They all laughed. But Hilo went on, intent on her picture of what Max's music was about.

"I mean, the pace ought not to be hurried. Music is always in a hurry to get to the end. But this – " She broke off, confused, and then added: "And the – the pauses? . . . the rests?"

"Yes. Rests."

"They ought to take as long as they like . . . only people haven't the time or the patience to listen – to wait for it . . . It all has to be so – so potted and frenetic."

"Like jazz?" Sam's smile was wry and dry.

"Like jazz," she agreed, and shivered.

Max smiled. "You're talking about the impossible."

"Am I?"

"A willing captive audience in an outside auditorium, prepared to spend all day listening? *In England?"*

"They listened to Pavarotti in the rain!"

This time even Hilo laughed at her own joke, and Sam gave them all another coffee on the house.

"Clouds are slow," said Hilo. Her voice was strange and distant. "Sometimes they take all day to pass . . ."

The two men were silent, looking at her. But she did not see them. Max got up, breaking the spell. "Come on. Stop asking for the moon. I'm taking you home."

Hilo's eyes came back into focus and she smiled at them. Sudden radiance touched her, and they both blinked. "It might happen," she said.

Max laid a careless arm round her shoulders (he could do that now without her flinching) and took her away, still laughing.

But Sam looked after them thoughtfully, and with a kind of exasperated sadness.

One day not long after this conversation, Max looked up from his score, laid down his pen and said: "It's Sunday."

"So?" Hilo was curled up on a cushion on the floor reading, and looked up in mild surprise.

"Would you like to go out into the country?"

"The country?" She was mystified. "Why?"

He wrinkled his nose at her and a smile began behind his observant gaze. "All this talk about clouds . . . I thought you might like some space?"

She frowned. "What about your work?"

"Finished."

"*Finished?* I didn't know you *ever* finished!"

He laughed, and leapt to his feet, full of the bubbling release of achievement – a height scaled, a wild dream accomplished. "I didn't tell you, Hilo. I finished most of it before . . ."

"Before what?"

"Before now." He was still laughing at her serious face, seeming irrepressibly cheerful today. "This is just the – last bit. I promised Sam I'd give it him today – and he's given me a holiday in return."

"What for?"

"Oh because – " He saw her doubtful look and held back his laughter. Hilo was almost belligerent about his music. She would not let him neglect it. But he went on, still half-laughing: "Because I was working under pressure to meet a deadline – because I needed a break – because even jazz pianists get stale – and because . . ." he paused and grew suddenly serious, "all your talk about width and space and the Great Outdoors impressed him."

"Really?"

"Don't look so astounded. Sam does listen to other people sometimes. He sees a lot more than he lets on, you know. And he rather likes you."

She still sat there looking up at him, not quite sure how to take all this. "What's that got to do with anything?"

"Quite a lot," said Max, and put all his manuscript together, shoved it in an envelope and tied it up with a piece of pink nylon string that was lying about on his table. "We're going to drop this off on the way. And then we're going to catch a train to the wild west. Are you with me?" He reached out and pulled her to her feet.

"Is it good?"

"Is what good?"

"Your music, you clot. Are you pleased with it?"

He paused, and then brushed a careless hand over her hair. "Funny Hilo. I believe you care more about it than I do."

"I daresay. *Is it?*"

He shrugged. "Yes. Probably. We'll see." He seemed to hesitate for a moment, and then went on, still sounding deliberately offhand. "At any rate, it's going to be *played*, Hilo. Think of that!" He whizzed her round the room, out through the door and down the stairs.

They went to a place of wide hills and tall beech woods. It was beautiful and immensely quiet. Out on the short turf of the hills, the sky looked enormous.

But at first Hilo was strangely tense and stiff. Max looked at her oddly once or twice, but he said nothing until they were lying back on the scented grass looking at clouds. Then he gave her a small shake and said: "What is it? I thought you'd be pleased. Don't you like the country?"

"Like it?" She was silent for a moment. When she turned her head to look at him there were angry tears in her eyes. "You don't understand a thing, do you?" She drew a shaky breath of control and went on. "The country was . . . my childhood – my father – and my escape. I left it all behind when I ran away. I've never been back. I didn't dare."

Max was silent for a little while, then he said patiently: "Hilo, I keep telling you – there's no need to run away. Everything is still there – unspoilt." His piercing gaze raked her, willing her to see it. "What are you afraid of?"

She looked at him with dilated eyes. "I'm – "

"Say it. Go on."

"Say what?"

*"I'm not a coward. There's no need to run away."*

After a slow, painful silence, Hilo repeated it. But in the

middle of a word she suddenly began to weep. The tears poured down her face and she sat there on the warm grass, helpless and ashamed. She could not tell him – and Max could not know – that it was the first time she had really wept since her father died – since the awful days of Steve when her world of innocence was destroyed.

But Max could at least recognize real grief and real release when he saw it. He took one look at her face and simply folded her in his arms. It was time, he knew, for comfort, whatever the risks. And love, of whatever kind, was important to little Hilo – especially now.

They had a wonderful day. But somewhere along the way, Hilo began to realize that Max had brought her there for a purpose. He was shatteringly kind to her, and she didn't like it. He kept looking at her, as if to reassure himself that she was happy, and as if he was on the verge of questions which he did not ask, or statements he was afraid to make?

At last Hilo could stand it no longer. She sat cross-legged on the grass like a child and looked into his face with bewildered candour. "Max – what is it?"

He began to say: "It's nothing – " but changed his mind and took a deep, shaken breath. "Hilo – I'm going to America."

Her eyes widened. Then suddenly her whole expression changed and she was all generous excitement. "Max! That's wonderful. What for? I mean – how?"

"I've – Sam has got me some sort of award. It's a bit like a – like a Harkness Fellowship, only less grand." He paused, looking at her with doubt in his eyes. "There's a super electronic workshop there – plenty of scope for experiment . . . and – " again he paused.

"And?"

"Guess what, Hilo? There's an out-of-doors auditorium! You – you said it might happen, and it has!"

She hugged him fiercely. "It's absolutely fabulous!"

"Sam fixed it all. He has friends everywhere. But I think you were the one who pushed him into it.

"I was?"

He grinned. "That space pep-talk you gave him!"

"But that was only a week ago."

"Yes, well – they were already looking at some of my stuff. I didn't tell you because – "

"Because it might've fallen through. I know."

But he was still hesitating, not rejoicing much, and it troubled her. "What else, Max?"

He looked down at his hands, almost as if he hated them and their facile brilliance, and he looked up into her face, clearly under stress about something. "Hilo – I can't take you with me."

She stared back at him in astonishment. "Of course you can't take me with you."

"If – if you were older," he said, sounding miserable and truculent both at once, "I could – we could – "

"No, we couldn't," snapped Hilo. "Don't be idiotic." She glared at him ferociously. "I never heard anything so silly."

He shook his head, still miserable. "It's not silly, Hilo . . . I – at least it would give you some sort of – of security or something . . . I mean, protection?"

Her face softened. "You have the daftest ideas, Max Torelli. I don't need protection. Not any more. I've grown up." She was looking at him now with open affection. "But it's lovely of you even to think of it – in the midst of everything else. Only, let's face it, Max, even if I was old enough, the last thing you want now is any encumbrance."

"You're not – not an encumbrance." Unaccountably, Max was suddenly near tears.

"Oh yes, I am. And you've been wonderful about it. And – and I shall miss you very much. But – it's time to go."

Above her head, somewhere in the blue air, a late lark was soaring and singing. She felt the short turf beneath her fingers, warm and spiky, and the curve of the earth under her hand. It seemed to her that the world had been still for a moment, but now it had moved on, and life began to teem and surge all over again. "Time to move on," she said softly.

Max did not argue. He could not. In the face of that black courage he could not say anything. But he took her hand, and wandered silently on over the quiet hills with her beside him, while something within him wept for the bright days of careless companionship that were lost to them now for ever.

\*       \*       \*

59

They were together for another week. During that time, Hilo gravely helped Max to tidy up his music and his life. They got his tickets and his passport fixed, and filled in a lot of unintelligible forms and applied for his precious Green Card. They bought him some new jeans and a white pullover because he refused even to consider a suit (which he couldn't afford, anyway). They bought him a hairbrush and a sponge-bag which he hated on sight, and several notebooks for lectures, and a new pair of trainers because his old ones were a disaster. Then Hilo went out quietly by herself and bought him a smart briefcase with the whole of her last week's wages (she had a new job by now) and Max tried to be angry and couldn't.

The last night arrived, and they went down together to the club for the last time, and Sam stood them a free meal on the house. They got fairly lit on cheap wine, and Max played like a frenetic fiend for the last time, with lots of encores and requests thrown in, and Hilo surreptitiously thanked Sam for all he had done in case Max forgot. Then Max thanked him all over again, and Sam gave everyone another drink. At this point, Freddie, the blues singer, came up to Hilo and murmured in her ear: "Anything you want, kid – any time you get stuck, just ask for me. Understood?"

Hilo looked at her in astonishment. She had not even realized that Freddie noticed her existence. She smiled, and saw the other girl's strong, friendly face break into an answering grin.

"Understood," she murmured back. "Thanks!"

Freddie gave her arm a sudden squeeze of reassurance. "Tough old world, kid. I know." And she moved away before Max or Sam could overhear. But Hilo knew she understood better than the two men how much this parting was going to mean to her and her future.

But she mustn't show it – of course she mustn't. So she laughed and joked with the rest of the staff, and then Max tucked her arm in his and walked home in the half-dark of the late-night city. They both of them felt limp and tired and strangely hollow inside, but neither of them said so.

"You will be all right?" he said.

"Of course."

"You can stay on in the room as long as you like."

"Who says?"

"Sam." He was grinning a little. "It was part of the deal."

Hilo laughed. "You needn't have done that."

"No," he agreed, kicking viciously at an empty tin in the gutter with one angry foot. "But I'd feel better if – "

"I told you. I am perfectly capable of looking after myself."

"That's what you think!" He pulled her close against his arm as they walked. "You're as crazy as a coot, and twice as feckless!"

"I like coots."

"Why?"

"They make lovely patterns when they swim. And their nests are a total mess."

Max laughed.

They climbed the stairs and stood looking at one another almost shyly in the big white room. Max did not know quite how to handle this parting, and he was surprised and rather confused to find how much he minded leaving Hilo behind. He was used to cutting loose when the time came to move on – he had done it often before. But this time it bothered him. He didn't want Hilo to feel bereft, but he didn't want to make their closeness seem too important to her. After all, she would have to go on with her own life without him. But he felt bad about it somehow. It was probably the first time he had ever thought purely of someone else's welfare rather than his own. He wasn't very proud of himself for allowing them to get so close. But at least now he must end it with kindness.

But he didn't get a chance. Hilo took matters into her own hands. She untucked her arm from his, looked up into his face and said, smiling: "It's all right. Everything's fine. Better get some sleep. You've got an early flight."

"You won't – ?"

"Be too lonely? No, Max, I won't. And I won't sink like a stone, or get lost, or fall by the wayside, or *run away*. Not any more. I'm a survivor. Like you."

"Will you write?"

She hesitated. "I'll write. But whether I'll write to you – I don't know."

"Why not?"

She could not say: You'll have a new life. You won't want

reminders of the old one. They'll only make you feel guilty . . .
But aloud, she said: "Maybe this will tell you."

It was the first time she had ever shown Max anything she had
written. And even now she was shy about it. A sort of fan-poem,
she told herself, and simple enough and childish enough to make
him smile perhaps. But it was his release and she had to give it
to him.

> "You only have to lift a finger
> And worlds flower.
> Auroras bloom,
> Clouds tower,
> Seas rise, and comets fall.
> A fragile universe,
> Precious and rare,
> Grows in each sounding echo,
> Lives in each shape you build.
> Never deny it. Never let it die."

Max looked down at it while slow tears blurred his eyes. He
could not say a word. Hilo did not speak either. She simply
reached up a shy hand and touched his face with a curiously
adult and consoling gesture, and smiled at him gently.

"Goodnight, Max," she said firmly, and turned away to her
own corner of the room, lay down on her mattress and did not
look round.

Max stood there, looking at her doubtfully, but then he
understood her determined firmness and turned away himself
to his own sleeping quarters near his piano. Hilo had chosen how
to handle it, and he knew she was right. Any emotional gesture
might lead them into God knows what entanglement, and it was
both too early and too late for anything like that . . . He was tired
after the long day and his final performance at the jazz club, so
he sank very swiftly into oblivion, telling himself that he would
say a proper goodbye to Hilo in the morning . . .

But in the morning, she was gone.

There was no note, but the alarm had been set and had gone
off at the right time for him to catch his plane. Max looked round
the empty room with tears in his eyes. It was so like her. No fuss.

No recriminations. No tender farewells. A brief, swift severing and a silent departure. He had a sudden very clear picture of Hilo walking away from him, her thin figure very erect and black against the sky, growing smaller and smaller . . . and farther and farther away.

He got up, packed his overnight flight bag, and left the big white room for the last time. The sound of the door slamming behind him was sharp and final. It was over, then. The high, airy refuge, the laughter, and the love they had known but never acknowledged. Over.

He drew a swift breath, went down the stairs and out into the street without looking back. A taxi cruised by. He hailed it and got in. God speed, little Hilo, wherever you are . . . wherever you go . . .

The taxi gathered speed, and he sat looking forward, watching the morning sky.

Hilo, walking swiftly away down the road, also watched the morning sky and wondered why it looked so empty and cold.

# IV

# THE MARKET

Ben was the kind of boy who usually fell on his feet, one way or another, and even this time he did at first. The lorry driver dropped him off by a roundabout at the end of the motorway, and said with a friendly jerk of his thumb: "If you're stuck for somewhere to stay tonight, the Travellers down there might help." Ben followed the direction of his thumb and saw a line of not-very-new trailers parked on the grassy wasteland behind the slip-road.

He wandered down the road towards them, wondering if he dared approach. It was getting towards evening and dusk was falling swiftly on the tired grey streets. It was time to find somewhere to stay, before it got too late.

One of the trailers had an open door, and music and lamp-light spilled out of it. Also two lurcher dogs and a couple of boisterous children came tumbling out, almost at Ben's feet, and a woman's voice called out: "Sharpish! It's getting dark."

The children scampered off down the road to the corner, where a mobile fish and chip van was standing, lit up and waiting for custom, on the edge of the pavement. Fish and chips! thought Ben, his stomach churning with longing. He hadn't eaten all day, except for the hunk of bread and cheese he took from the kitchen when he left. But that was yesterday . . . He had spent the first night in a lorry-drivers' café somewhere on the road, waiting for another lift going south. And in the morning he had been in too much of a hurry to catch an out-going truck to wait for breakfast, even if he could have afforded it. But that truck had taken him a long way round to a trading estate somewhere, and he had to

64

get back on to the main road and wait for another hitch before he got safely on his way south again. So he was both hungry and tired, and the thought of those fish and chips was uncomfortably tantalizing.

The next thing that fell out of the trailer was a paraffin stove, smoking profusely, and a very angry woman coughing her heart out. "Bloody useless!" she shouted, at no-one in particular. "First it won't light, and then it goes up in flamin' flames!" She turned to Ben as if he was just another member of her sprawling family, and not a total stranger passing by. "Know anything about stoves, do you?"

"I might," said Ben hopefully. "We had one once . . ."

"Explode all the time, did it?" she snorted, and gave the smoking ruin a kick with her foot.

Ben stooped over it and gingerly reached out a hand to turn the wick down. The little brass knob was hot to the touch and almost burnt his fingers. "Wants the wick trimming," he muttered. "Got any scissors?"

There was another snort of rage from beside him, but in a few moments a hand appeared, holding a pair of kitchen scissors with red plastic handles.

By this time Ben had the top off the stove, the smoke had died down, and he had turned the wick up again to have a look at it. The edges were furry and blackened, burnt off in uneven spikes and far too dry. "Paraffin's not getting through properly," he said to himself, and started poking about round the edges of the wick. A whole lot of charred debris came away in his hand and the wick shot up with a sudden spurt of movement. "That's better," he said. "Got a match?"

The hand reappeared with a box of Swan Vestas, and the furious voice (a little mollified) rasped in his ear: "Tamed the ruddy thing, have you? Mind it doesn't go up in your face. Spiteful it is."

But the stove seemed definitely tamed. It sat there, hissing faintly, and the circular flames glowed blue in the encroaching dark. Carefully he picked it up and turned to carry it inside. "Where d'you want it?"

"I don't want it at all, the blurry thing, but the kids'll want their tea, won't they? Put it down over there."

When it was safely set down in the trailer's small galley, and showed no signs of smoking or exploding, Ben turned to leave.

"Gotta pad for tonight, have you?" pursued the rasping voice, sounding a lot more alert than its incipient anger allowed for. She knew a boy on the loose when she saw one.

"Er – no. I've only just arrived," said Ben, and stepped down into the darkening night.

"Notta lotta room in here," pointed out the voice, reaching out to him in the gloom. "But you're welcome to the floor."

Ben's curly smile lit up his face in the pale glow from the door. "Well, thanks," he said. "If you're sure – "

"Not sure about anything," said the voice. "Not in this flaming world. But you can have the floor. Come in."

Ben climbed back in and stood looking at the owner of the voice for the first time. She was big, plump and angry, with strong arms and a pinkish face beneath a fuzz of stringy yellow hair, but though her mouth was still set in lines of furious irritation, her eyes were unexpectedly kind and full of half-suppressed merriment. She looked about to burst into laughter at her own absurd rage over a mere stove, and the vagaries of the ridiculous world she lived in. But she didn't laugh. Instead, she filled a blackened kettle from a bucket on the floor, and set it over the blue flames of the little paraffin stove.

"Daresay there'll be enough for four," she said, hearing the voices of the children returning with their wrapped paper parcels of fish and chips. "If the blurry dogs don't get there first!"

So, without any painful searchings or slammed doors, Ben's first evening in the city was safely arranged. Dora Lee, she said she was called, ("We're mostly Lees round here") and the kids were Lonnie and Lindy, twins, and a handful if ever there was one. Their father was off on a scrap-dealing trip (as usual); he'd come home sometime, maybe, but he was a shyster, that one, you never knew where he'd be or what he'd be at. "You gotta job to go to?"

"No," said Ben, happily munching chips.

"Difficult," nodded Dora. "Could try the market. They aren't so fussy as some."

Ben agreed. He knew markets and the cheerful haphazard folk who ran the stalls, from his home town. Maybe it

66

wasn't such a bad idea at that – for a start. Any job would do.

So the next morning he set off for the local street market, having said goodbye to Dora and the twins, and offered to pay for his board and lodging and been furiously shouted down.

"What d'you take us for?" yelled Dora. "Blurry council officials?" (They were the meanest people she could think of at the moment.) But when she saw Ben looking a bit confused, she stopped yelling and added kindly: "You can come back if you're stuck, mind." She seemed to have taken quite a shine to Ben, really, though she wasn't going to admit it. "Rotten old world out there."

"I know," grinned Ben. He stood looking up at her as she stood on the step of the trailer, big and belligerent, but somehow not angry at all underneath. "Are you – do you stay here all the time?"

She laughed. "Fat chance. We get moved on, often as not. Though in winter they usually lets us stay. Sometimes they even plug us into the mains." She looked over his head at the sullen grey-black skies above him. "But, come spring, we'll be on the move again, I shouldn't wonder."

Ben nodded. "I'll – I'll probably see you before then."

She folded her fat arms and squinted down at him severely. "I hope not!" Then she added, quite softly, as he turned to go. "But if you do – you're welcome."

Honestly, thought Ben, his curly mouth lifting in a smile of farewell, aren't people just marvellous? I don't know what I've done to deserve it.

"See ya, Ben!" chorused the twins as he walked away.

He didn't find the market people very marvellous, however. Not at first. They all seemed totally uninterested in anyone wanting work. Either they were too busy selling to listen, or too laid back, drinking cups of tea with their feet up on the end of a stall, to bother to reply when he spoke to them. One woman running a cheap china stall did go so far as to let him wrap up the purchases in old newspaper while she kept a beady eye on him and a firm hand on the cash. But when he had finished wrapping the last cup and saucer for the last customer before the market closed, all she could offer him was £2 and half a cheese sandwich.

"Can I come back tomorrow?" asked Ben, wolfing the sandwich.

The woman shrugged. "Can't guarantee." She looked at him out of tired, not unsympathetic brown eyes. "Trouble is," she volunteered suddenly, "there's too many of you."

Ben looked uncomprehending.

"Too many out of work – and too many villains on the look-out for a quick make. People get nervous."

Ben nodded. "But I'm not a villain," he protested mildly.

A faint smile touched the woman's weary mouth. "Should I believe you?"

Ben laughed. "Probably not." He got up from the orange box he had been sitting on, and prepared to move on. "Well, thanks anyway – "

She watched him go, and then called after him: "Try again tomorrow. Ask for Al."

*Ask for Al*. At least he'd got some kind of introduction to someone. But that left this evening to get through, and nowhere to stay.

He had been doing some serious thinking about his predicament, and he realized the prospects weren't very good. To begin with, he couldn't go down to the job centre to register unless he had an address. And he couldn't have an address unless he had a job to pay for a room. On top of that, his past experience wasn't very encouraging. One part-time job demonstrating computer software, from which he was sacked for being supposedly involved with a gang of ram-raiders. No reference there. One job in a factory design office on a government training scheme, which he left of his own accord without any notice. No references there, either, and not much hope of being taken on for another training scheme unless he explained the whole sorry story about his father. And he couldn't do that. He supposed he could ask social security to help with housing, but there were sure to be long waiting lists, and they wouldn't consider one seventeen-year-old boy's needs compared with the claims of a couple with children. He supposed they might give him some emergency money, but they were more likely to tell him to go home. And he couldn't do that.

Well then, he told himself, I'll have to get casual work until I can get something better, and I'll have to live where I can until I can afford a room. Even part of a room would do.

He was not unduly depressed by all this at first. He was naturally cheerful and optimistic. He would manage somehow – and things would get better soon.

That night he bought a hot dog and a mug of soup at an all-night stall, and slept curled up in the corner of an abandoned building site, sheltered from the wind by a broken hoarding. It was cold, but at least it didn't rain. Towards morning a couple of cats began yowling nearby and a lonely dog came snuffling round the building site: and later on, an old man shuffled across and began poking about in a pile of rubbish across the street. Ben lay and watched him, and wondered what he hoped to find in that heap of unwanted garbage.

In the morning, he went back to the market. There was a wonderful smell of bacon frying from the market cafe on the corner, but Ben resisted the temptation to go in. His money would never last if he squandered it on unnecessary food.

He wandered among the empty trestle tables, looking for Al. People were already arriving to set up their stalls, unloading vans and humping suitcases and spreading out bits of material and lining paper on the trestles to protect their goods from the prevailing London grime.

He stopped one man who was setting up a doughnut stall and said: "Where can I find Al?"

The doughnut vendor grinned and jerked a thumb over his shoulder. "By the shop-fronts," he directed. "Posh end – over there."

Posh end? thought Ben, peering through a forest of bare wooden tables, iron grilles and support pillars, rusty rails and torn canvas awnings over a row of lock-up shops and dingy display counters. At the far end of this decaying row, someone was crashing about with metal loading trays. Al?

He went forward hesitantly and found himself looking into the face of a powerful young black man, wearing tight jeans, a bright red sweat-shirt with the words: "*I have lift-off*" emblazoned

69

across the chest, and a yellow baseball cap on his curly black head. He was hurling the piles of loading trays on to a metal stacking frame against the wall with extraordinary ferocity, and seemed to be enjoying the exercise.

"Are you Al?" asked Ben, between crashes.

"Could be." The polished arms gleamed with bunching muscle, the dark face lit with what was almost a smile. "What can I do you for?"

"Can I do that for *you*?" countered Ben, and stooped to pick up a tray. He hadn't expected it to be so heavy, but he managed to lift it and hurl it on to the pile.

Al looked him up and down and laughed. "Not your scene is it, humping trays?"

"No." Ben managed to heave another one on to the rack. "But I can have a bash."

"Have a bash is right!" grinned Al, and hurled another one on to the pile himself. Then he stood looking at Ben for a moment longer before he shrugged fluid shoulders. "OK. But there's not a lot going, workwise."

"Anything will do," begged Ben, trying not to sound too desperate.

"Like that is it?" The smile flashed out again briefly. "Well, finish that lot – and we'll see." He strolled off, leaving Ben to fend for himself, and began bawling out someone else (unseen) for failing to put out all the waste cardboard for collection.

Ben finished the job without much difficulty (though it made his shoulders ache) and stood looking round, wondering what to do next. Since no-one was around to tell him, he picked up a broom and began sweeping up the piles of paper still left over from yesterday's trading. While he was doing this, Al came back, carrying two mugs of tea in one hand, and – oh bliss! – two bacon rolls in the other.

"Here," he said. "Your lucky day. But as for work – it's dodgy."

Ben took an ecstatic bite of bacon. "Thanks. What's dodgy about it?"

"The Team," said Al succinctly. "The other guys."

"Oh." Ben sighed. "Too late, am I?"

Al leant against a flaking wooden lintel supporting a rather drunken-looking shop-front with a closed sliding shutter in front of it. He regarded Ben lazily over the rim of his mug of tea. "Man, you were too late before you began." He grinned at Ben's disconsolate face and went on to explain. "I got a Team, see? Mostly, the stall-holders set up and take down and clear their own patch. But there's always some cleaning up to do – and we do structural maintenance, what there is left of it!"

Ben nodded, glancing round at the ramshackle little shops and the clutter of metal supports, trestles and pallets strewn around them.

"It looks a mess," agreed Al, rightly interpreting Ben's expression. "But the guys are used to it." Then he added, as if offering some consolation. "Still, there's usually someone off sick . . ."

"And –?" Ben looked up hopefully.

"Daresay there'd be something, if you don't mind fitting in."

"I don't mind anything."

"Couldn't pay a weekly wage," Al told him, still summing him up out of clever, hooded eyes. "Best if I settle up each day. And there may be some days with nothing – understand?"

"Yes," accepted Ben, struggling to keep the disappointment out of his voice. After all, it was better than nothing.

"Best I can do," drawled Al, but there was a lively, knowing kind of sympathy in his observant dark eyes. "At least you'll eat – most days!"

Ben grinned. "That'll be a big help." He wasn't being sarcastic, but Al shot him a sharp glance.

"Don't leave it too long, kid," he said suddenly.

"Leave what too long?"

"Getting a real job."

"Just tell me how!"

Al's wry smile flickered. "Tough, isn't it?"

Ben agreed. "Trouble is – " He hesitated, uncertain how much to say.

"Yeah?"

"No address – no job. No job – no address."

Al nodded. "No address, no social benefit. I know. Catch twenty-two." He looked at Ben hard. "Snag is, kiddo, you go on knocking about and sleeping rough – soon look like something the cat brought in. Then no-one wants you. Plays hell with your clothes – English weather!"

Ben looked tired. "You don't have to tell me."

Al laughed. Then he asked casually: "What *do* you want to do?"

"Graphics," said Ben. Then he added, in case it sounded too cocky: "I mean – I was training, but – "

"But things fell apart," nodded Al. "Yeah. They always do." He was looking at Ben now with a curious expression of mingled exasperation and understanding. He seemed to be making up his mind to say something more, and Ben felt a fleeting sense of surprise – even gratitude – that this powerful and confident man who was clearly the boss around here should waste his time talking to him at all.

"D'you know what I was doing before I came down here?" Al said, a grim flick of humour in his lazy voice. "Studying law."

Ben stared. "*Law?* Where?

"Hull University."

Ben whistled. "That's a five-year course, isn't it?"

"Yeah. That was the trouble."

"Why?"

"Funds ran out. Usual story. Thought I'd do better down here." He glanced round him, still touched by grim laughter. "Look at it!"

Ben looked. "Well, – at least you're the boss."

"Not exactly the well-heeled company creep though, am I?"

It was Ben's turn to laugh. "Is that what you wanted?"

Al looked thoughtful. "I don't know . . . suppose I had ideas about the law and justice, and so on . . ." He shrugged again, somewhat sadly. "The black community needs more lawyers . . . But I guess high-flown plans are a waste of time . . ." He finished his tea and stopped leaning against the sagging lintel. "And this won't win the war, either."

"I wish I knew what would," said Ben.

He stayed with the market for about three weeks – too long, Al said, in between putting plenty of work in his way and nagging him regularly about getting a "real" job.

The Team, when he met them, were less formidable and less

72

prickly than he had feared. There were four of them, though – as Al had admitted – one or other was usually missing. Mike, the tallest and most responsible, was long and thin, with a pony-tail at the back of his narrow head and one gold earring in one protruding ear. He looked frail and rather vague, but he was, in fact, enormously strong and very much on the spot, though he tried to disguise this by being very laid back and slow to get moving. Vic, the shortest, was wide as well as small, with the build of a wrestler, and his powerful shoulders seemed unafraid of any weight they had to tackle. He simply lifted things up from one place and put them down in another, when asked, and rarely bothered to talk. But he had a slow, rather heart-warming smile when anything pleased him. Jacko – so called because he had long, gorilla-like arms that were exceptionally hairy – was also very strong, but more talkative than Vic and always willing to stop work and chat up the girls, particularly Kathy at the Indian stall. Rigs, the fourth one, was wiry and quick on his feet and had won his nickname being extremely daring and swift as a scaffolding rigger. But he had been dashing once too often and had damaged a foot. He was no longer considered safe up aloft, so he stayed on the ground and took what work he could get, including any framework construction at which he excelled.

They all liked Al and respected him as a fairly tough boss, and they were mostly a reliable bunch, though Jacko sometimes got drunk and stayed away with a hangover, and Rigs sometimes went off on another job he fancied and came back when it was done. They all looked Ben up and down and decided he was harmless, and handed on what bits of work they thought he could tackle, without resentment. After a while, they even began to treat him like a kid brother.

During this time Ben spent two more nights on the street and one in a hostel where he managed to get the luxury of a hot bath and an even hotter meal. The day after this, Al took him aside and gave him the key to a small store room at the back of the market. "This is unofficial, mind, and only temporary," he said, glaring at Ben ferociously. "But it's better than the street."

"Will you get into trouble over it?"

"No. Unless you burn the place down."

Ben grinned. "I don't smoke."

"Well, that's something!" Al pointed a precise brown finger at the archway at the end of the market with its open metal gates. "Those gates are locked when the market closes, and so are the ones at the other end. But you can get into the store-room from the street side – only you've got to keep it locked, or you'll have all the drunks from here to Hammersmith coming in."

"Not only drunks," said Ben sadly.

Al nodded. "I know. Well, keep 'em out, OK?"

"Yes," said Ben. "Thanks."

"It's not much," shrugged Al. "No heat. Plenty of corrugated and boxes, though. You could set up your own cardboard city right here!" His sardonic grin was somehow sadder than it was meant to be. "Maybe I should rent them out," he added bitterly.

Ben sighed. "There do seem to be . . . rather a lot of us out there." He waved a vague hand at the dark wet street beyond the glow from the market lights.

"Too many by half," growled Al. But he had made sure that Ben was at least safe and dry at night.

Most of the market people knew Ben by now, and he made himself as useful as he could. It wasn't exactly a calculated policy – he wasn't that kind of boy – but he reckoned that so long as he did what was asked with a minimum of fuss, they would probably ask him again.

Melly, the woman with the china stall who had first befriended him, even let him mind the stall (and the takings) while she went off for a cup of tea. She was a thin, birdlike creature with brown wispy hair dyed a fiery red, sharp brown eyes and a fierce manner which failed to disguise the fact that she was soft as butter underneath her tough exterior of frayed blue jeans and ancient black leather jacket, with a seamed, leathery face to match.

"No price-cutting while I'm away – and no breakages either, or I'll dock you. Wanna doughnut?"

"No, Melly. I'm OK."

"On the house?"

"Oh well – "

She nearly always came back with something to eat – a bag of left-over chips, a bruised pear, a squashed cake or a tired

74

sandwich, and Ben was not nearly proud enough (and much too hungry) to refuse.

George, the doughnut man, usually found a few "damaged" doughnuts at the end of the day and made absurd grumbling noises about the lack of jam in the middle, plastering the last few with an extra dollop of the extraordinary pink strawberry concoction that passed for jam in the doughnut world.

But it was Tony, the fruit and veg seller, who discovered what Ben was really good at – and what, it turned out, was most use to them all. Tony was a good market salesman, full of lively patter and shouts of encouragement. "Give away prices! Where else but Tony's? Cox's, 40p a pound – never get 'em cheaper . . . Lovely ripe peaches, smooth as a baby's bottom, two for the price of one – Come on, where's your initiative?" . . . and so on . . . But the customers did not flock to his stall these days, and he was worried. "What we want is somethink eye-catching," he said, seizing a bit of cardboard and writing ORANGES 2 for 10p on it in scratchy red chalk. "Somethink visual."

"Visual?" asked Ben, who was helping him unload some crates of bananas.

"Show-stopping," nodded Tony, viewing his attempt at poster-writing with a jaundiced eye.

"Here, let me try," said Ben and he looked round for some better chalks and a whiter bit of card.

"Janey's got some stuff over on Toys," suggested Tony. "she might have somethink bright."

Ben went to find out and soon had a packet of fairly vivid blackboard chalks and some clean white card. "Wax crayons last longer," Janey explained, "especially if it's wet – but these are *brighter*."

"Thanks," said Ben and set to work. "I'll do you one, too, if you like," he added, which was the best payment he could offer.

"You do that, Benny-boy," she told him, "and make it *showy*."

For Tony, Ben found himself drawing a green-and-golden orange tree beside an incredibly blue sea bordered by an unbelievably yellow strip of sand, and across a blazing tropical sun he stretched the flaming red legend: "BUY YOUR SUNSHINE

AT TONY'S." It was crude, and so bright it made you blink, but Tony was delighted.

Before long, Ben was busy making posters for everyone. The two girls who ran the Indian sari stall also asked for one. Shona, the beautiful dark-haired Bengali with sloe eyes wanted a Bird of Paradise, but Kathy, spiky-haired and cheeky and thoroughly English rose, wanted a Peacock. "Showing off," she explained. "Lots of flash!" Ben laughed and drew both under a banner headline: "EXOTIC BIRDS – GET YOUR FINE FEATHERS HERE!" Shona was a bit shocked, but Kathy had a fit of the giggles and said it was smashing. Then there was Ranjit who ran another Indian stall specializing in spices and teas and unusual vegetables. He wanted an elephant, but Ben couldn't for the life of him think how to link an elephant to curry powder in the grey old market. Finally, he wrote "EASTERN PROMISE – GET CARRIED AWAY!" across a highly ornamental elephant with a jewelled howdah. Ranjit glowed with pleasure.

"Nice and bright!" approved Janey, looking from Ranjit's elephant to her own poster of teddy bears and fire engines for the toystall. "That'll rock 'em on their heels. Why don't you do a pavement?"

"A pavement?" Ben was mystified.

"We had a 'pavement' here once. He did dogs so's you could see every hair. And puppies – all gooey-eyed. And fluffy kittens. Fair made people drool."

"Brought 'em in, too," agreed George. "Folks like something to look at."

"Something *bright*," repeated Janey, who seemed to have only one important word in her vocabulary. "Come on, Benny-boy, have a go."

So Ben had a go. It was his first attempt at being a pavement artist – and he had no idea how important it was going to be to him later on. But even that first day, when he drew a chocolate-box cottage garden full of flowers and a kitten chasing a ball, he found the admiring public dropping coins into his cap.

"You see?" crowed Tony. "Told you they'd lap it up."

"Cheers the place up," approved George.

"Keep it *bright*," said Janey.

So Ben kept it bright. In between working for Al and the Team and anyone else who asked he spent a lot of time with coloured chalks and grey pavement stones, or bits of white cardboard. He got quite skilled at presenting the obvious in an oblique or vaguely cocky way, and quite skilled at making primary colours turn subtle under a rubbing finger. He reflected, as he worked on an untrodden corner under the leaden winter sky, that it was teaching him quite a lot about layout and what caught the public eye – about graphics, in fact, in a practical way that he would never have experienced at his tidy classes at Tech.

It was while he was working on a more ambitious drawing of purple mountains under a garish sunset that he felt the ground shake a little under his hand. The underground ran close to the market at this end, and the trains often made the floor shake and the old shop-fronts rattle. But this minor earthquake felt slightly worse than usual, and he looked up in surprise. He was just in time to see the end shop with the crooked lintel begin to bulge outwards in a disintegrating arc of falling bricks and timber. It was right next to the huge pile of metal trays that had been stacked up for the day, and Al was standing in front of them, with his back to the collapsing wall.

"Look out!" yelled Ben. He sprang to his feet and across to Al in one swift bound of terror. He only had time to shove Al violently sideways out of the direct line of fire before the cascade of bricks, broken timbers and metal trays began to descend on them. The mass of metal seemed to slide with appalling slowness, and then coalesce into a sort of tangled arch hanging over them. Two trays slipped off sideways and fell on to Al's legs, trapping him where he lay, and one turned upside down and landed on Ben's arm. He felt something give and a brief flash of pain, but as he stood there, half-crouched forward, he realized that he was in some way acting as a buffer to the falling metal trays, not exactly supporting their weight but preventing them from crashing down any further. If only he could keep still like this until help arrived.

Help wasn't long in coming. The Team had heard Ben's shout, as well as the sudden roar of falling débris, and so had some of the stallholders. Everyone came running.

"Be careful," said Ben, very distinctly. "It's holding by a thread. Get Al out *quick!*"

They got Al out, and then someone grabbed Ben just as the vibrations of their combined efforts set the cascade of metal crashing to the ground.

"Phew!" said Melly, who had pulled with the rest. "That was close. You all right, son?"

"Yes," said Ben. "But I don't think my arm is." And he passed out cold.

At the hospital, they set his arm and painted over the gash on his head made by a flying brick. That was what made him pass out, they said. But Ben thought it was probably sheer fright and was rather ashamed of himself. They made a bit of a fuss about Address and Next-of-Kin, but when he pointed out that it was a minor injury and his family were over 200 miles away, they relented. But they insisted on keeping him in overnight. Head injuries, they said, wanted watching, and it was one of their rules.

He didn't mind being kept in, it was rather a relief. He asked about Al, and was told he was having the lacerations sewn up on his legs, but he wasn't too bad at all.

Finally, they landed up in adjoining beds in Men's Surgical, and it all seemed rather cosy.

"What's the damage?" asked Ben, leaning over to have a look at Al.

Al grinned. "One cracked tibia – the rest OK. I was damned lucky."

"Could have been worse," agreed Ben.

"Worse?" Al's grin got wider. "Could've been dead, you mean." He looked at Ben and winked. "I owe you, Benny-boy."

"'S mutual," slurred Ben, thinking of all that Al had done for him over the past weeks. But what with all the excitement and the anaesthetic to set his arm, and the bump on his head, he felt extraordinarily sleepy. The bed felt wonderful, and so did the warmth and comfort of the clean white ward. Before he could think of anything else bright and cheerful to say, (keep it *bright*, Benny-boy) sleep overcame him and he sank into happy oblivion.

Al decided to go to sleep too. It was simpler than worrying about the future.

In the morning they told Ben he could go home after lunch when he had seen the doctor, but Al would have to stay two or three days to let those lacerations start to heal. This upset Al, who couldn't imagine the market getting on without him, but while he was fretting and fuming, Mike came in from The Team and told him that everything was under control, everyone was doing their bit, and the whole bloody shoot was working like a greased diesel, and here were some offerings from his mates. There was another pile for Ben, too, and Mike screwed up his face in a ferocious smile and pulled at his one earring fiercely. "You did a good job there, mate," he said, which was praise indeed from anyone as tough as Mike. Then he sloped off rather fast, saying that Sister had only let him in for a moment because he'd persuaded her that Al was the worrying kind, and he'd better get going before she got stroppy.

The next lot of visitors for Al came in the early afternoon, while he and Ben were still waiting for the doctors who were late on their rounds that day. The new lot consisted of a whole gaggle of dark-eyed, curly-headed children and one very handsome dark girl with braided hair, silver-gilt earrings and a 100-watt smile. They swarmed all over Al until Sister came along pretending to be severe and said "Two at a time is the *rule*!" and then some of them scampered off again and hung about outside the ward door, jumping up and down and laughing. The girl came across to Ben and held out her hand.

"I'm Jo. Al says you saved his life."

"Oh well," began Ben, awkwardly taking her hand in his left (unplastered) one. "No, it was just – "

"Well, thanks anyway!" said Jo, the smile getting even more dazzling, and the various little dark faces that were still bobbing in and out all beamed too, and all chorused: "Thanks, anyway!"

When they had gone, Ben turned to Al in amazement. "They aren't all yours, are they?"

Al laughed. "In a way – they're my brothers and sisters."

"Oh. Then Jo – ?"

"My girlfriend." He paused, and then thought maybe some

79

explanation was necessary. "I told you, funds ran out on law school."

"Yes?" Ben was still mystified.

"My Dad got killed on a building site. So Mum was left – with all that lot."

Ben nodded. He saw it now. "Tough."

"Yeah. Jo helps out when Mum's at work. We all live in a – in pretty cramped space." He looked at Ben almost as if he was apologizing about something. "No room to swing a cat – if we had a cat."

Ben realized all at once that Al really *was* apologizing – for not taking in a stray seventeen-year-old and offering him shelter. It was absurd, especially when Al had given him the store-room key, – and put all that work in his way.

"Does Jo work, too?"

"Sure. She's a beautician. Good at it, too." His grin flashed out again. "And she can take time off in emergencies. Helps a lot with all those kids."

"I'll bet."

"Benny-boy, I been thinking – " began Al, sounding suddenly hesitant. But before he could say any more the doctors came on their late round, and after a few crisp questions Ben was told he could get dressed and go home.

"Had your lunch, have you?" asked the woman doctor, who seemed to know a lot more about Ben than she should.

He had discovered from the other patients in the ward that she was affectionately known as Little Doc Never-Stop, because she always seemed to be on duty, always rushing from one crisis to another, but never too busy to listen, to smile, and to offer what encouragement she could. It was somehow clear to Ben that in this busy city hospital she was well aware of the plight of the homeless and jobless like Ben himself, and did what she could to help them along when she had a chance.

"Don't hurry," she murmured to him as she passed. "You're not using up a bed." She gave him a cheerful wink, and added over her shoulder: "Take things easy today."

He did as he was told, and took things easy. Dressing was awkward, and though he managed it, he began to worry a bit about how he was going to cope on his own. At least I needn't take my clothes off again, he thought, and wondered vaguely how long his arm would take to mend, and how long anyone could wear the same clothes without them falling off with sheer wear and tear – or London grime.

But while he was thankfully drinking a cup of tea from the passing trolley before going home, Sister came across and told him someone was waiting for him.

"For me?" said Ben. "Can't be."

"Go and see," said Sister, pointing a commanding finger at the door.

Ben went.

Outside, sitting on a bench in the corridor and glaring belligerently at everyone, was Dora from the Travellers' site.

"Come on," she said, as soon as Ben appeared. "Can't wait all day."

"Sorry," said Ben, though in truth he was glad – exceedingly glad – to see that tough, uncompromising figure waiting for him. "How on earth – ?" he began.

"Grapevine, dearie," grinned Dora. "News gets about, you know."

Ben still looked astounded.

"We got connections with the market," Dora went on. "They sells our stuff for us sometimes – " She saw his disbelieving face and laughed. "'S'matter of fact, it was the kids brought the news home last night. It was all over the neighbourhood about the accident and Al nearly getting killed and you saving his bacon." Her grin was mischievous now. "Fair chuffed, the kids were, to know a hero."

Ben scowled. "I didn't do anything except stand there!"

"I dare say." Dora patted his plastered arm kindly. "Hurt, does it?"

"No."

"Good." She got to her feet, as if everything necessary had been said. "Let's get going, then."

Ben stared at her uncertainly. "Where to?"

"Home, of course. Where else?"

Home, thought Ben . . . The market by day and the store-room at night? . . . He hadn't often thought about home – real home – since he left. Better not to, really. But something about the hospital and all the anxious relations hovering round the beds, (not to mention the awkward questions they had asked him about Next-of-Kin) had made him think about his mother. Was she all right? Had she and his Dad managed to make a go of it? And would she worry at all about what was happening to her wandering son? Maybe he ought to have sent that Message Home when the lorry driver suggested it. Well, it was too late now. He couldn't exactly tell her he was living rough in a store-room, could he? . . . And here was someone else being kind to him, like Al, and offering him shelter when he didn't deserve it one bit.

He sighed. "Dora, I can't – "

"Oh yes, you can. It's all arranged." She was glaring at him now, the old mock rage lighting her face and putting sparks in her eyes. "The kids are expecting you. Can't disappoint them, can we?"

"But – "

"Listen to me, young man," snarled Dora, sounding more exasperated than ever. "You can't hump crates and live in a packing shed with that arm, can you?"

"I could manage."

"Oh sure – you could manage." She snorted. "But you don't have to – the market people fixed it."

"The *market people*? What do you mean?"

Dora looked as if she would like to shake him for being so dense. "What I say. The market folk got together and had a whip round, see? Saved their boss, didn't you? And you was useful to them, too, so I heard, what with your posters and such." Her voice was still fierce but somehow bordering on laughter underneath. "So I said I'd see after you, and they give me the money, and a few bits and bobs instead, those as couldn't raise any ready. Understand?"

"No," said Ben, sounding even more astonished.

Dora swore gently. "Gorramighty – the boy's an idiot." But suddenly the rasping voice softened and the angry eyes grew unaccountably wistful. "We're going away, Ben. Moving on. Thought you might like to come with us."

"Where to?"

She looked quite eager, and suddenly much younger – almost like a girl looking forward to a holiday. "A permanent site, down Sheerness way. Electrics and water laid on and all." She peered at him, almost anxiously. "Better for the kids, with winter coming on – and for you, too."

He began to protest again, but she interrupted him. "Just for a while, Benny – till that arm mends. How long will it take?"

"Six weeks."

"Well, then – " she looked at him with challenge. "Six weeks won't kill you."

"Won't it kill you?"

She began to laugh then, but suddenly changed her mind and seemed all at once to be almost embarrassed about something. "There is one thing, Ben – "

"Yes?" He wondered what was coming – what kind of restrictions she was going to impose that could cause that uncomfortable glance.

"The kids'll be able to go to school down there – just for the winter. I was wondering if – ?"

"If what?"

"If you could learn 'em to read?"

There was a strange, tingling silence, and then Ben said cautiously: "I could try."

"You see," Dora explained, not looking at Ben now, and not sounding fierce or belligerent at all any more, only shy. "I never learnt, Benny. Nobody never taught me nothing. I picked up what I could. I can figure out money – especially with one of them calculator things. But I never learnt reading – and I want the kids to have a chance."

Ben nodded.

"They'll find school hard, Ben – running wild like they do all summer. I thought – maybe you could . . . kinda help them along? Make it easier, like?" She took a deep, shaky breath, and Ben understood from that quivering sound that this mattered to Dora a lot. "I'd be ever so grateful, Benny-boy. More than pay for sleeping on my floor!" she added, slyly.

She dared to look at him then, and the two pairs of eyes met in sudden sympathy and understanding.

"It's a deal," he said, and held out his good hand. "But I must just tell Al what's happening."

"You do that, son," agreed Dora, grasping his thin left hand with enthusiasm. "But don't be long. The kids'll want their tea."

When Ben told him what was happening, Al thoroughly approved of the idea and told him severely to start looking for a proper job as soon as his arm was fit to use. He looked at Ben speculatively for a moment and then added:

"You could push knobs anyway, couldn't you – one-handed?"

"What?"

"Get a bit more training? Use the cash for a course, or something?" He looked at Ben urgently. "Get out of the vicious circle, Benny-boy. It's important."

Ben nodded. "I know, Al. I'll try."

"That reminds me," said Al, "there might be a bit of compensation for you, as well as me."

"For a casual worker?"

"I don't know," said Al slowly. "That end of the market buildings was a disgrace. Broke all the laws, I'm sure. Maybe the landlord'll be only too glad to pay up to avoid a row." He winked at Ben from his hospital bed, and allowed his smile to grow wide and affectionate. "Anyway, leave it with me. Come back and see me when your arm's OK." He hesitated, and then shook his head at Ben in half-rueful dismissal. "You know you can always get a spot of casual with me – but I hope to God you don't have to!"

Ben laughed, grasped his arm for a brief moment of unspoken gratitude, and hurried away to Dora who was making faces at him from the door.

"That's it," she said, grabbing his good arm and steering him towards the lift. "Make it snappy. What we need's a nice cuppa!"

The new site wasn't exactly beautiful. It consisted of a squared-off clearing between some long-since derelict sheds at the edge of an old, disused factory on one side, and a walled-in housing estate on the other. The ground was mostly cinders, black and crunchy underfoot, and hell for the kids who constantly fell down

84

on it. What grass there was grew in wispy tufts round the edge, or sprouted up through the ancient cracked concrete. One or two stunted buddleia trees had seeded themselves among the ruined buildings. But, as Dora stoutly pointed out, there was water laid on, and electricity, and there was even a public toilet, though no-one looked after it much. There were about a dozen caravans and trailers as well as some campers and lorries parked on the site, and a few stringy dogs ranged about with the dark-eyed children who played in and out of the decaying sheds at the back of the clearing.

"It'll do," said Dora, and set about getting the trailer plugged into the mains. Then she joyously hurled the old paraffin stove out of the door, shouting: "Good riddance!" and began to cook some supper.

There had not been time for Ben to go round and see the market people before he left, and he felt rather bad about this. But after supper, Dora produced a bundle from under the bunk beds and spread it out on the table in front of him.

"These are yours, Benny – along with the cash," she said. "I'll count it out for you in a minute," and she reached for the old biscuit tin that stood on a shelf in the corner.

Ben stared at the collection on the table with misted eyes. "I never thanked them," he muttered.

"Didn't want it, love, wouldn't have known where to put theirselves. Best left as it is," she told him, and fingered the clothes with an appreciative hand. "It's good stuff, Benny. They done you proud."

They had indeed. They had provided a new pair of jeans, a couple of T-shirts in cheerful stripes – two pairs of underpants and two pairs of socks from the factory "reject" stall – and a really thick seaman's sweater from the "Leisure Wear" stall that used to sell everything from cagoules to cut-price trainers. But best of all was something which Dora reached down for on the floor and unrolled with a flourish, as if she was a magician doing his most impressive trick. "This come from The Team, they said. They reckoned it'd come in useful wherever you got to."

Ben could only gape. For it was a sleeping-bag – a thick, waterproof, well-padded, brand new sleeping-bag that would keep him warm and dry wherever he slept. Something he could

85

never have afforded to buy, and something he had often longed for and wished he'd had the sense to acquire when he had a job and was living comfortably at home.

He shook his head in disbelief. "I don't know what to say!"

Dora grinned, and then solemnly counted out the small roll of notes in her hand. "There's sixty quid here, Benny-boy. Not bad, considering." Her glance was shrewd. "Mind, it's gotta last you six weeks at least – till you're fit to get a job."

"But you ought to have it."

She looked as if she was about to hit him. "Benny! They collected it for *you*!" Her eyes sparked fire. "Anyway – you're going to be a teacher, remember?" She turned round to the twins who were staring round-eyed at all those riches spread out on the table. "And you can start right now!"

"OK," said Ben meekly.

"OK," said the twins, not sounding meek at all.


Teaching the twins was far from easy. They were as bright as buttons – as Dora admitted – but they had minds like quicksilver. They darted from thought to thought as fast as they ran from one wild escapade to another. They climbed all over the derelict sheds at the edge of the site, shinned up the grimy brick wall that separated it from the old factory buildings, and skittered down the other side among the the rusting ramps and pulleys, dodging in and out of the empty warehouses and disused machine sheds like liquid shadows. And their minds dodged about like liquid shadows, too – mystified by the tedium of school reading books, impatient of any imposed discipline that kept them from the swift and lively activities they loved.

Dora was quite firm, though. Stay in they would, until they learnt to read. Anyway, the evenings were much too dark now for all that larking about. Dangerous, it was. So they might as well stay in and get used to it.

"Oh, Ma!" protested Lonnie.

"Oh, Ma!" echoed Lindy.

"Don't you Oh-Ma me!" growled Dora. "Sit down there and listen to Benny – and don't you get up till I come back!"

Two disappointed faces glowered at Ben, while Dora stumped off to one of the other trailers. But in fact they liked Ben well enough, he was all right and didn't get at them much. So they did what they were told, and tried gamely to hurry the tiresome process of learning so that freedom could return.

Ben understood their impatience. He also discovered that they could already read quite a lot of words, especially street signs and bus directions and price labels on food. They were mad on food – always hungry – and Ben used a simple form of bribery to get them to work.

"Get through a page, Lonnie, and I'll buy you a Mars."

"Me too," cajoled Lindy, who was very pretty in her dark, curly-headed way, and knew it.

"You too," sighed Ben, reckoning his dwindling money in his mind.

He had put down some of it on a course – as Al had counselled. But he couldn't find a real Graphics course, so he had settled for something called "Lay-out and Office Skills" which he could just about manage one-handed so long as they let him use one of the college desk-top computers. There was usually a queue as there weren't enough to go round and he had to hang about a lot, which annoyed him, but still, it was something, and he was learning a bit about what he wanted to know.

"I'm learning something, too," he told the twins, smiling at their disconsolate expressions. "I know it seems too slow."

"Too slow!" they chanted. "Too blurry slow!"

But they were learning, too.

"How d'you spell *slow*?" asked Ben. "And what about '*blurry*'?"

And the twins fell about laughing.

He went down to the job centre pretty regularly. But he was under eighteen, and they hadn't got much to offer. Time seemed to hang heavy while he was one-handed and unemployable, so he was thankful to get a part-time job sorting newspapers for delivery at a newsagent's down the road. It meant getting up very early, but he didn't mind that, and the shopkeeper usually gave him a cup of tea when he arrived. But that still left a lot of the day free and he wandered about the streets and waterfronts of Sheerness, and found himself admiring the strange, starkly functional silhouettes of the old dockside buildings, black against the sullen skies. There was not much work in the town, they told him, except on the ferries, and they were mostly run by a continental workforce.

Things were very quiet at the moment, what with the recession and such. Very dead.

But Ben felt alive. And the twins felt alive. Live wires, they were, God help 'em, said Dora, and born to trouble as the sparks fly upward. They were like sparks, Ben agreed, and just about as able to keep still. But he got quite fond of them. One day he brought them home a new book about Batman and got them to read it to Dora.

"See?" grinned Lonnie. "I can do it!"

"I can do it, too," boasted Lindy, and snatched the book from her brother.

Dora was impressed.

"You done 'em proud, Benny-boy," she said. "We'll have fried chicken tonight. Here, kids, go and get it."

They went, delirious with delight. Freedom had come back.

Dora looked after them fondly – much more fondly than she would admit if they were there. "Done 'em good, it has, settlin' down here for a bit," she said to Ben. "Difficult for 'em – always on the move."

Ben nodded. "How long will you stay here?"

She shrugged. "As long as Jack stays away. He's the traveller – not me."

Ben looked at her in surprise. "Not you? Aren't you –?"

"No. I just married one." She sighed. "Tell you the truth, I'd kinda like to stay put nowadays. Gettin' tired of it all." She looked sideways at Ben and laughed. "Must be middle-age creepin' on. But Jack, he's the one with itchy feet. Come the spring, we'll be away again – you'll see. That's why I came down here – near the ferry. Jack'll most likely want to go across to the big meeting in France, come the summer."

"Is Jack a real Romany, then?" Ben was interested.

Dora's plump shoulders lifted again. "Are there any left, nowadays? . . . Thing is, Benny, it's all got kinda diluted. Mixed. People marry – like me. Was a time, no-one dared marry outside the clan."

"Clan?"

"Well, that's what I call it. There's one trailer here where they keep it up. The girl, Rosa, was going out with a Gorgio. They beat her up something cruel, – and chucked him in the river."

Ben was shocked. "Not – drowned?"

"No. But pretty near. Someone fished him out – " she laughed, but not too happily.

"And – ?"

"No and. Daresn't show his face around here. And Rosa – they never lets her go out."

Ben whistled disapproval. "It's barbaric."

"It's that all right . . . Romanies go a long way back."

A thought struck Ben that horrified him. "Your Jack wouldn't do that to Lindy?"

"Oh no." Her smile was more comfortable now. "I told you – we're *mixed*. He's not that fussy. But the travelling bug's still in him, – and I guess it always will be." She sighed. "So – the kids and me – we make hay while the sun shines, so to speak!"

"Chicken coming up," shouted Lonnie from the dark.

"We got Tandoorie," added Lindy.

"And chips – "

"With curry sauce – "

"Good!" chuckled Dora. "Let's have a party."


Ben had noticed Rosa before, but then she had just been a pale, sullen face at the caravan window. He had wondered vaguely why she always sat there, staring out at the black cinder square where the other trailers stood, and never seemed to want to go out or talk to anyone. He had tried smiling at her once or twice, but got no response. He was surprised when one day the twins waved at her on their way to school and she waved back.

Now, knowing her history, he understood why she never smiled and never dared to come out of the trailer, and he was sorry. She seemed terribly alone, shut in there, and he felt an irrational longing to see that shuttered face light into warmth and happiness.

Some hope, he thought, with that fiery-looking man, Nikko, watching her every move.

As it was, the other trailer families kept very much to

themselves and did not mix a lot. This was partly because there were three distinct factions there – each of them convinced that their way of life was best. There were the few Traditional Travellers, with Romany blood and strict Romany laws to go with it, proud and prickly and fierce, like Nikko and his brood of silent children with their smouldering eyes and white, unsmiling faces. Then there were the Ordinary Travellers (mixed, like Dora) who were more easy-going, moved on when they felt like it, and indulged in a good many dicey deals (some of them legal) involving trips away and lorry-loads of mysterious scrap metal and left-over goods. They were matier, more open in their dealings with other people, and Dora did sometimes go across to talk to one or other of them in their none-too-tidy trailers. She also went out selling various small items by day. Ben never did discover where they came from, the sprigs of white heather, lucky silver pigs, bits of lace and bright-coloured rag rugs, but the old biscuit tin in the corner seemed to keep full enough of ready cash, and he knew it was best not to ask where it came from.

Besides these two disparate groups there were The Others – what Ben privately called the Latter-day Hippies. They didn't have neat trailers, but old buses, ex-rental vans, broken-down lorries and even an old London taxi (most of them painted in vivid old-fashioned psychedelic colours). The girls (for they were mostly young people and children bursting out of these shabby vehicles) wore long skirts which trailed in the mud, and long hair to match. The boys wore long hair, too, and earrings that flashed in the winter sun when there was any, and their clothes might be anything from tattered sheepskin to caftans or Hari Krishna saffron robes or purple satin shirts, or mud-spattered jeans, or several of these at once. They were for the most part gentle and friendly, played guitars a lot, and let their grubby children and dogs wander about all over the site, getting in everyone's way – and never seemed to get worked up about anything. (Ben knew they smoked pot round their smoky camp fires – the scent was unmistakable – but it seemed to keep them happy and they caused no trouble.) They called everyone "Man," and talked a lot about following ley-lines and the Natural Way of the Earth.

90

In the summer they all moved off in a straggling, unsteady line towards the southwest and the summer solstice celebrations as near to Stonehenge as they could get. A lot of them never got there (so Dora told him), their vans broke down or got bogged in muddy fields – but they all tried very hard to follow their chosen Natural Way, and believed with soft but obstinate persistence in the Magic of Mother Earth.

Ben talked to some of them and was almost sorry he couldn't believe in it too. They seemed so convinced and so committed.

"Got to believe in something, man," one long, thin boy told him, waving an expressive arm in its pink silk open shirt and nodding the skimpy ponytail at the end of his bare, shaven head.

"The Earth calls," murmured a gold-haired girl close by. "You can feel it even in winter." She looked round at the bleak cindery wasteland and sighed. "Even here . . ."

Ben sighed too, and wished he believed her. It would be nice to believe in something.

Dora was a bit contemptuous of their untidy, casual ways, and warned Ben to steer clear of trouble.

"But they don't seem to be trouble-makers," protested Ben, watching them rather wistfully as they strummed old sixties tunes round their packing-case bonfires.

"Not a-purpose," agreed Dora. "But it comes, trouble does, to that lot. You mark my words. Seem to attract it, somehow. Best keep away, I say."

Ben didn't entirely agree, but out of loyalty to Dora, and also from a certain reluctance to join that haphazard bunch, he mostly kept away.

So it was with a sense of shock that he heard shouts and roars of rage, blows and crashes from across the site one afternoon. He had only just come back, having fetched the twins from school for Dora since she was going to be late, she said. He promptly pushed the two of them down on to the bench by the caravan table and said "Stay there – that sounds like trouble!" before he went to the door to have a look.

A scene of carnage met his eyes. Nikko from the Romany corner seemed to have gone berserk. He was standing by the Young Travellers bonfire, swinging an enormous iron bar in his hand and laying about him at anyone and anything within range.

Children ran about screaming, dogs barked, men shouted, and the girls ran in their long skirts to protect their children. Lorry windows smashed, the glorious psychedelic paintwork got irretrievably scratched, wings got bashed in, doors and fragile body-work crunched and sagged under the onslaught. And all the time, a stream of furious abuse came from the angry mouth of Nikko, the dark-eyed gypsy.

"What's happening?" asked Ben, running across to the nearest girl and helping her to pick up a sprawling, bawling child.

"His daughter, Rosa – " panted the girl, holding the child in her arms and keeping a wary eye on the flailing iron bar.

"What about her?"

"Scarpered. Ran away."

"When?"

"Today. While Nikko was out. He thinks we helped her."

"Did you?"

"No." She smiled at Ben's anxious face. "Wish we had. But none of us knew anything about it."

"Have you told him that?"

She waved an expressive hand towards the demented figure ahead, who was now attacking a bus. "How can we? No-one will go near him!"

"I will," said Ben. "He can't have anything against me – I wasn't even here."

The girl held him back. "Be careful. He's dangerous, man."

"Not really," said Ben, suddenly remembering his father wielding the heavy lump hammer and swinging it towards Ben's defenceless head. "Just scared."

"*Scared?*" The girl's incredulous glance went from Ben to the rampaging figure of Nikko and back again.

"Of change," said Ben softly, and went across the stretch of black cinders to speak to Nikko.

"They don't know anything," he called out, above the sound of splintering metal and glass. "You're wasting your time."

Nikko paused in his mad orgy of destruction and swung round to glare at Ben. "And what do you know about it?"

"Nothing," said Ben. "No-one does. I'm sorry."

"*SORRY!*" yelled Nikko. "My girl's gone off God knows where with a Gorgio, and you're sorry!"

"The police are coming," called one of the boys, seeing Nikko's hand starting to swing again, and dangerously near to Ben at that. "Better calm down."

Nikko let off another stream of abuse directed at the f – police who were always on his back, but he dropped his arm and turned back to Ben.

"NOTES were passed," he said darkly. "I found one." His hot black eyes raked Ben. "Someone must've helped her."

"Why?"

"She can't read or write."

"Christ!" said Ben, suddenly angry. "And I suppose *that's* your fault, too."

He thought for one tingling moment that Nikko was going to hit him, but for some reason Ben's words seemed to shake him, and he put a bewildered hand up to his eyes as if he were blind. "I wanted – I wanted . . ." he stammered.

"To keep her safe?" asked Ben gently. He understood Nikko very well. He was just like Ben's father. Upright. Strict. Frightened of change. Afraid of the new modern world and all its glittering temptations – all its traps and disappointments. Wanting to keep it at bay for ever, and keep his lovely daughter in the safe, restricted, unsullied world he thought he knew.

Nikko did not answer, and behind them they heard the approaching siren of the police car cut off, and the crunch of purposeful feet on the cinders. Nikko sighed.

"Wilful damage again, Nikko?" said the first policeman, quite kindly. "Better come quietly." He took Nikko by the arm, and gently took the iron bar out of his hand.

But Nikko swung back to Ben, a kind of fierce appeal in his angry eyes. "Find out . . ." he muttered. ". . . must know she's safe . . ." He did not say any more, and allowed the two policemen to lead him away without further protest.

Behind him the trailer site came back to life – the children ran about, the Young Ones brewed some more herb tea and strummed their guitars, and Nikko's scared wife and his own even more scared children crept out of the trailer and stood looking in horror at the trail of damage.

Ben went back to the twins, who had unaccountably stayed where they were, safely in the trailer out of harm's way. This was unlike them, and a curious thought had occurred to Ben and he stood looking at them severely.

"Did you – ?"

"Only twice," said Lonnie.

"It wasn't much," said Lindy. And then, seeing Ben's grim expression, she added: "She was so sad, shut up in there."

"What exactly did you do?" asked Ben. "The truth, mind!"

"She said to leave a bit of paper in the launderette, by the soap powder. Bob worked there."

"Bob?"

"Her boyfriend."

"What did the bit of paper say?"

"'CAN YOU TAKE ME AWAY'" recited Lindy promptly, folding her hands like a child at school reciting a poem. "I wrote it for her. I write better nor Lonnie."

"You don't!" contradicted Lonnie. "Anyway, I can read better. I read her what Bob said."

"What was that?"

"'TELL ME WHEN,'" quoted Lonnie proudly.

"That was easy!" jeered Lindy. "I did the next one."

"And what did *that* one say?" Ben was remorseless.

"'TOMORROW MORNING. TEN O'CLOCK,'" grinned Lindy. "That's when everyone else was out, see?"

"How did she get out? Didn't Nikko lock her in?"

"Bob broke it," said Lonnie. "I lent him our screwdriver." He sounded very pleased with himself.

"When was this, then?"

"This morning," they chorused, blithely convinced they had done the right thing.

"And why weren't you at school?"

Lindy looked at Ben with big, beguiling eyes. "We only skived off one lesson."

"Went back after," corroborated Lonnie. "Nobody noticed much."

*Didn't notice*? thought Ben. He supposed a busy school might not bother much about two obstreperous gypsy children. He sighed.

There was a silence, while Ben wondered what to say to these two young terrors. Secretly he was rather proud of them, but he

94

wondered what Dora would say. Or whether he ought to tell them to keep quiet and not say anything about it at all. But that seemed like a betrayal of trust somehow – and he didn't like the idea much. You couldn't lie to someone like Dora.

However, while he was still standing there debating what to do, Dora's sharp voice came from the doorway. "Finished, have you? Told Ben the lot, then?"

The twins gasped a little and looked distinctly wary. But Ben knew that fierce, accusing voice – there was laughter underneath it; as usual Dora rather approved of the twins, too.

"Now, listen to me, kids," she said, coming in through the door. "And I mean *listen*. I don't want to hear you tell *anyone* else about this – not *anyone* – not *ever* – understand?"

"Yes, Ma," they chorused, all humble and dutiful.

"That Nikko's a dangerous man, kids. He'd beat the living daylights out of you if he knew, see? Not sure I oughtn't to, an' all – but I'm kinda peaceable meself." She glared at them. "And anyway, I don't like young things caged, no more than you do. But *you never heard me say so. And you never did nothing, neither*. Got it?"

"Yes, Ma," they said.

"Right then." Dora turned briskly to the kettle. "Praps a cuppa will keep your mouths shut!"

And she winked at Ben over the twins' chastened heads.

It was soon after this that word came to Dora that Jack was coming back. Ben had already begun to think about going back to his former haunts. He had an appointment at the hospital to have his plaster off the following week, and he knew it was time to start looking for a real job and somewhere to live.

It had been October when he first left home – crisp and autumnal on those high hills above the town, but now it was nearly Christmas. He had to get on with his own life now. The halcyon time of respite with Dora and the twins was over.

For it had been halcyon, he thought. Whatever that meant. He had been extraordinarily happy with her and the twins. Happy and warm and safe, and never too hungry. He owed fierce, kind Dora more than he could say, more than he could possibly repay. But Jack was coming home, and it was time to move on.

Even so, Dora didn't like it, and made a half-hearted protest. "But Benny, it's nearly Christmas."

"Can't be helped," he said, smiling. "Jack's coming, isn't he? And anyway, I've got to get my arm done. It's time I got myself organized."

Dora looked at him doubtfully. He still seemed awfully young to her to be roaming the streets, homeless and workless.

"I can always go back to the market," he told her, by way of comfort.

She snorted. "Huh! Some job that is!"

"Kept me going, though."

Dora wagged a furious finger at him. "Only temporary-like, Benny. *Temporary*. You gotta getta move on, see?"

He nodded. "I know."

She thought for a moment. "Wouldn't it make more sense to go up and look for a job *now*, while you're still with me?"

Ben shook his head. "With my right arm still in plaster? They'd laugh." Then, seeing her expression, he tapped the plaster with his good hand. "It comes off next week. Then I'll start."

She still didn't like it, but she saw the logic of it. And since her philosophy was always to get on with what had to be done here and now without complaining, she had to let it go. Let *him* go. For, not allowing herself to go too deeply into the matter, she had to admit she'd got rather fond of Ben, liked having him around. He was a support, somehow, with Jack away so much, and simply wonderful with the kids. She sighed.

"Well, have it your own way. But I tell you what, let's have our Christmas now."

"Now?"

"Why not? We can buy the kids a coupla little things – balloons and such – and I know where I can lay hands on a chicken . . ."

"Dora!" protested Ben, having visions of her raiding someone's backyard and wringing some poor unsuspecting bird's neck.

She laughed. "Not that way, you dope. That's more like Jack than me!" Her infectious chuckle grew, and Ben fancied there was a joke there that he could not share. "No," she spluttered. "You leave it to me, Benny-boy. We'll have it termorrer. Afore you go."

*Afore you go*. Ben knew, too, that he would miss Dora and her belligerent kindness more than he cared to admit. And the awful twins, who had somehow wound their mischievous brown fingers round his heart. Oh hell, he thought, it's no good clinging. *Gotta getta move on*, she said. So he went out and spent some of his careful savings on toys for the twins and a brilliant headscarf with roses all over it for Dora. This reminded him of his mother, and the scarf he had given her. *"Do you remember twirling?"* and how he and she had danced crazily up and down the cramped little living-room till his Dad came home and found them. No, he said. No good clinging. There are new things to do. New things to see. New people to meet. *Gotta getta move on, Benny-boy*.

They had their Christmas – even though it was a fortnight too early. Dora cooked the chicken, and also produced some mince pies, two bottles of beer, and an orange each for the twins. Lonnie got a toy Mercedes car and a squeaker that blew feathers into people's faces from Ben, and Lindy got a skipping rope and a blue hairslide. The twins gave Ben a pair of purple socks – one sock each, they said, and fell over laughing. And Dora gave him a khaki-coloured towel (it won't show the dirt!) and a thick balaclava and a pair of woollen mitts. (Cold weather's coming, Benny. Gotta keep warm somehow.) Dora put her scarf on, and for one moment Ben thought she was going to twirl like his mother. But there wasn't room in the trailer for much twirling, so she preened in front of the tiny mirror instead and said in a pleased, warm voice: "Don't I look posh, then?"

And presently the gold-haired girl from the Young Ones knocked shyly on the door and said: "We heard you were going away, Benny. Would you all like to come and sing with us round our fire – a few carols and things?"

Ben looked at Dora for permission and at her quick nod he accepted, smiling. Somehow, relations had been much more friendly all round since the rumpus with Nikko, who, they told him, was now in the right place – Nikko in the nick – and not for the first time, either. And with him away even his scared wife and younger children dared to creep out of their caravan and join in the singing. Ben, remembering the anguish in Nikko's hot, angry eyes, leant forward under cover of the darkness and murmured to the shy gypsy woman beside him: "Have you heard from Rosa?"

For a moment she seemed to freeze into frightened stillness, then she looked at him sideways and nodded.

"Is she all right?"

Again she nodded, briefly and silently.

"Does Nikko know?"

This time she looked beyond Ben into the smoky fire and slowly shook her head.

"He'd want to know she's safe," said Ben, suddenly feeling brave. "Will you tell him?"

The woman's bleak gaze swung back to him, almost in astonishment. Then she murmured, almost under her breath: "Not yet . . ." and looked away again, as if embarrassed at having said anything at all. Ben supposed he must be content with that. He had stuck his neck out quite far enough already, all things considered. And he was a bit ashamed when he considered that he could worry about Nikko's concern for his run-away daughter, but he couldn't even send a message home to his own mother. Was she worrying, he wondered? Or had she and his father just written him off as a dead loss? Somehow, he didn't think his mother would. Though his Dad certainly might. In any case, he told himself, I can't really send a message until I've got a job and some sort of future lined up. Then will be time enough. It's only all this Christmas lark that is making me sentimental.

He took a deep breath and turned to smile at Dora and the twins as the first guitar began to strum a tune he knew.

So they all sat round in the windy dark and sang carols to the night sky which was too murky to produce any stars – but the sparks flew up from the bonfire instead, and some of the Young Ones lit thin joss-sticks and handed them round, so there were plenty of bright gleams rising to match the young voices in the listening air.

Ben thought suddenly – feeling somehow wise and sad and much older than his years – *I shall always remember this night.* Always. Dora's face, tough and fierce, beaky-nosed and kind in the firelight, and the twins singing like angels while no doubt plotting some devilment at the same time. And the Young Ones, with their long hair and their beaded headbands, and their smoky eyes filled with dreams . . .

"*Silent night, holy night . . .*" they sang, sweet and true, and then, in case everyone got too sad: "*God rest you merry, gentlemen. Let nothing you dismay.*"

He sang with the rest of them and drank their herb tea, and listened to their softly thrumming guitars, and watched all their dreaming faces in the firelight. And later, when the twins were nodding with sleep, he and Dora tiptoed away with them back to the quiet trailer and left the singing behind. Yes, God rest you merry, gentlemen, he thought. Let nothing you dismay. And let nothing me dismay, either!

So they had their Christmas. And in the morning, Ben saw the twins off to school, hugged Dora so hard she could scarcely breathe, and set off himself down the road back to London, alone.

He went first to the hospital where a nurse took off his plaster. His arm looked thin and white and rather feeble, but it seemed to work all right. The doctor who came to look at it was the same friendly Little Doc Never-Stop who had first seen him on the ward, and had been so insistent about his having had his lunch and not hurrying home. But here, the notice board called her Dr Emma Forrester, and her name was opposite the words "Orthopaedic Clinic". Now she looked at him rather hard and said: "You'll need to come back for some physiotherapy. Give them your address downstairs."

"I – er – can't," said Ben.

"Why not?"

"Haven't got one."

She sighed. "Well then, make an appointment downstairs *now*. And make another when you come next. All right?"

"Yes," said Ben, sounding doubtful.

"It's important, Ben," she told him severely. "If you want to use that arm!" Then she nodded a cool dismissal, and turned away to her next patient. At least we can keep some sort of tabs on the kid, she thought despairingly. All these homeless, rootless youngsters. What are we to do with them? But duty called, work overwhelmed her, and she forgot Ben and his plight while considering someone else's

Ben dutifully made his appointment, and went straight on down to the job centre. There wasn't much going, and they told him (again) he was too young for most of the vacancies. But they did agree to put him down on the list for a government training scheme. But there weren't many places, they told him, and there was a queue for them, too.

Ben sighed, and went on to the social services department. They also said he was too young (again) and why didn't he go home? They had a huge waiting list for housing, even bed-and-breakfast, and married couples with children came way ahead of him. But they did have the power to give him a small emergency grant if he was really desperate. Ben said he was. Address? they asked. And when he couldn't produce one, they looked even more doubtful.

However, they did relent a little at his beseeching face. After they had produced a small sum and made him sign for it, he set off to look in the various newsagents and shops for advertisements of local jobs. It was no good looking for a room – he couldn't afford one, anyway.

He followed up several job addresses. They were all already filled. One café said it might have some washing-up next week, if he liked to come back. But that didn't solve the immediate present.

At last Ben looked at the fading afternoon light and thought he'd better go back to his old friends at the market. At least they would give him something to do, and Al might let him have the store-room key again. He walked down a couple of side-streets and came out into the main thoroughfare that skirted the market buildings at the far end where the little shops stood.

And then he stopped in appalled disbelief. For it wasn't there. It simply wasn't there. The whole thing had been flattened – demolished – razed to the ground. There was nothing left but a thin, scraped triangle of derelict land, a few piles of rubble, and a yellow bulldozer like a dead dinosaur abandoned on the sooty gound in a sea of mud.

"My God!" said Ben. "What have they done? Where's everyone gone?"

But there was no-one there to answer. Only a few bits of paper blowing in the wind, and the muffled roar of traffic echoing across the grey, empty space.

For a long time Ben just stood there, staring – the absurd tears rising behind his eyes. He had loved the market and its people. They had been wonderfully kind to him. It was the only place he had ever been able to call "Home" since he came to London. And now it was gone. And its people were gone. Where to, he did not know. And he might never find out. There was nothing left now, for him or for anyone else.

He gave the lonely site one last, despairing glance. Then he turned and walked away. Nowhere now to go. No friends to turn to. He was completely alone.

"Down to bedrock now, Benny-boy," he said. "Where do we go from here?"

Night came down on the cold London streets.

# V

# THE STREET

Hilo did not know how long she had been walking, but when she looked up she was down by the river among the old warehouses and muddy reaches beyond the smart restaurants and elegant houses of the river walk. And it was still early morning.

She stood for a while watching the oily water slide past. Even down here the old river was beautiful, full of eddies and reflections, drifting smoothly down towards dockland and the sea.

The sea . . . Max was over the Atlantic now. She thought about Max and his music calmly and without rancour. It would be all right now. It would grow. She wouldn't be holding him back. And maybe she would see the world more clearly, too. She had to confess to herself that she hadn't been seeing things very clearly – the world had been all Max and music, Max and laughter, Max and warm, undemanding safety . . . Max.

She shook herself a little and began to walk on along the embankment. She knew she had allowed Max and his wicked black eyes to come between her and reality. Reality was finding somewhere to live and holding down a reasonably well-paid job. Not depending on anyone else for comfort. Or for affection. Or did she mean love? Whatever it was, she had got to do without it now.

Presently she came to a steamy café and went inside for some coffee. She sat warming her hands on the cup and thinking . . . Yes, she must find somewhere else to live. She couldn't go back to Max's room, not now it was empty and quiet, in spite of what he had arranged with Sam. Besides, she was still fiercely independent (wasn't she?) and she didn't like the idea that she had been living off someone else – however remotely. She had already got a part-time job in yet another cafe. She would have to ask if they would take her on full-time. Or if not, she'd have to look for another part-time one. Somehow, now, she had got to be Hilo again – alone and self-sufficient. Not Max's girl. Not anyone's girl. Just Hilo.

But even so, the long slow ache for Max's company had begun deep down, and it would be a long time before she was entirely free of it. People encroached. You got too enmeshed in living. Feelings got in the way. You thought you were safe and no-one could touch you – no-one could reach you. But you weren't safe at all. You were much too vulnerable. And someone like Max, with his fiery eyes and his crooked smile, somehow found his way in behind the wall, and you were lost.

Not now, though, she told herself. I'm on my own again now. And one day I'll be myself. One day I'll be completely me.

But, she discovered, it was extraordinarily lonely being herself again. Lonely and self-centred. Max – his music and his future – had been part of her living and her thinking for several absorbing months, and she had forgotten what it was like to be totally cut off from human company. Together they had shared much, not least the careless warmth and protection he had bestowed on her with so much nonchalance – and so much hidden kindness.

Now it was over. Life seemed very cold without him. Very empty. All the same, she told herself, she had come very near to allowing the tall tower of pride and self-defence to be toppled in the dust. She had said "Never again" after the nightmare of Steve, and meant it. But Max had gone past all her bright armour – and now it was painfully hard to rebuild those perilous defences.

She took another room (shared, of course, with two others) and another job. She dropped out of Sam's circle of jazz musicians and friends who still talked about Max, and left no word behind her. Better make the break clean while she had the strength.

But even so, she did not quite manage to escape without a fight because Freddie, the blues singer, came after her as she was

103

taking a last, nostalgic look at the old warehouse room before she left it for ever.

"Where are you going?" she asked, coming straight to the point.

"Somewhere else," said Hilo, mouth set in a firm, straight line.

Freddie had the kind of sad, strongly-sculptured face that went with blues songs, her dark eyes ringed by deep shadows of permanent tiredness, reflecting the white, exasperated patience of someone always holding back strong emotions in a world that had no time for them. She looked at Hilo now with sympathy and understanding, and offered what help she could in her own, oblique way.

"You could crash out with me?"

"No thanks, Freddie."

The other girl paused, looking at Hilo sadly. "It's lonely out there, kid."

"I know." Hilo's mouth was still set.

"You don't need to be so flaming independent."

"Yes, I do," said Hilo.

Then Freddie understood, and smiled. "OK. Have it your own way. But keep in touch."

Hilo sighed. "Freddie, what's the use? I don't want to – to – "

"Be reminded? Maybe not." She hesitated, and then added cautiously: "But I promised Max."

"What?"

"I'd keep an eye . . ."

Hilo smiled then. "Well, keep it, Freddie. You may need it!"

They laughed, but Freddie noted that Hilo's laugh was a little shaky at the edges. She made no comment, though. It was clear that Hilo would allow no interference. Instead, she simply handed over a small package, with the words: "He left you this."

Hilo looked at it doubtfully. She knew that it would be money. Max was always worrying about whether she was getting paid enough or eating enough.

"I can't take it, Freddie."

"I think you must. He said he couldn't go without leaving something for emergencies . . ." She looked wearily at

Hilo's mutinous face. "You owe him that much peace of mind, at least."

Hilo was on the point of saying: "Do I?" when she suddenly saw the logic of Freddie's argument. Maybe it had reassured Max to think he had left that safeguard behind him.

"All right," she said reluctantly, and took the package in her hand. "But I don't need it."

"Not now, kid," agreed Freddie. "But you never know . . ." She patted Hilo's arm with a long, cool hand. "He means well, our Max . . . Heart of gold underneath all that pyrotechnic stuff."

"Yes," agreed Hilo. "I know."

There didn't seem to be anything left to say after that, and the older girl suddenly leant foward and hugged Hilo very hard for a moment. "We all loved him, kid. You're not the only one," she said, and went away without looking back.

So Hilo was really on her own at last. And she put Max's money away to use when an emergency should come up – which it surely would some time.

She managed quite well until she got ill. She did an exhausting job by day, and went out with the two other girls sometimes at night, though for the most part she stayed in and read. She devoured books voraciously, and also tried to improve her typing on an old, battered machine that one of the girls owned. But the trouble was, she wasn't eating enough anyway, and the winter flu bug took hold. She was away from work for too long, and lost her job again. Then, of course, she couldn't afford the rent, and had to dip into Max's savings to eke out her feverish days. Bit by bit the money went down, and she finally decided she must go out and get another job somehow, however ill she felt. She left the other two girls, not without protest from both of them, and decided to look for a smaller, cheaper place to stay. Maybe a squat somewhere – anything with a roof over it would do. And a job – any job, however tough. She was sure she could manage somehow.

She wandered out on shaky legs and found it enormously difficult to decide where to go and what to do next. The flu seemed to have left her mind in a state of woolly inertia, and the streets of London seemed like a faintly heaving mirage as she walked along. It was getting near to Christmas now, she told herself, and the nights were cold. It would not do to hang about too long. She *must* find somewhere soon.

She was walking along one of the wider residential streets when she passed the doors of a church. It stood alone on an island of grass, and as she walked by a sudden thin shaft of winter sunshine struck the old, weathered stone, lighting it with pale, fugitive gold. Hilo stopped, arrested by the unexpected radiance. It seemed, somehow, curiously comforting. Not knowing quite why, except that the warmth of that brief sunlit gleam seemed to draw her, she went up the steps and pushed open the door.

Ben spent that first shocked night huddled by himself in a shop doorway. But when daylight came, he made up his mind to find out exactly what had happened to the market folk. Surely there must be someone locally who would know?

He went to several of the shops nearby. All they could tell him was: the bulldozers moved in and the people moved out. But then he tried the newsagent's on the corner, and Reg, the proprietor, knew a good deal more.

"Are you Ben?" he asked, looking at him hard over the top of his glasses. "I got a message for you."

"Yes?" Ben sounded absurdly eager.

"Your friend Al – he said to keep calling in. There might be news for you sometime."

Ben nodded. "What happened? D'you know?"

Reg shrugged broad shoulders. "What do you think? After the accident, the buildings were condemned. It was cheaper for the landlord to sell out than to repair. And Al was asking for compensation, too. So he just wiped out the lot. Cut and run – the rat!"

"And Al got nothing?"

"Not yet!" Reg smiled somewhat grimly. "But you know Al. He's got some law training, hasn't he? Told me to tell you – he won't give up. I reckon he'll get it, too. In the end." He slapped a few heavy piles of dailies down on the counter with a decisive bang. "Creep like that – deserves to have the whole book thrown at him!"

Ben agreed. But something more than compensation was troubling him. "What happened to the others?"

The expansive shrug came again. "Some went down to Shepherd's Bush Market, I heard. Some just gave up, I guess."

"And Al –?"

"Got another job – some way off. Meant moving the whole lot of 'em, he said." He shot Ben another shrewd glance. "That's why he told me to keep an eye out for you – so keep on coming in, son. He'll do his best for you, will Al."

"I know that," agreed Ben. "Well, thanks – " He turned to go, not liking to ask any more.

"You fixed up, then?" asked Reg suddenly, to his retreating back.

"Er – no," Ben admitted. "Job-hunting."

"I'll keep my ears open then," Reg promised. "Call back, mind."

"I will," said Ben, and went off to another day of fruitless search.

Reg was kind enough, he told himself. He couldn't conjure up a job out of thin air. Not like Al.

After the first night, Ben found himself down by an old railway bridge where there were several other people sleeping rough. There was a brazier with hot coals glowing in the dark at one end, and a small, smoky fire at the other end which sent up sudden little licks of flame into the dark night.

He wondered if he ought to ask permission to doss down among the other shadowy figures – they seemed like a little community somehow, and he felt shy of intruding. But one of them spoke to him across the darting spurts of the little fire. "Come on, then. Room for one more." It was a woman who spoke, an oldish voice and an oldish face to go with it, as far as he could see. He went a bit nearer to the fire, and stood looking down at her.

His first impression was one of layers. Layers of coats, layers of scarves, mitts, woolly hats, layers of blankets, rags and bits of old carpet, and finally, layers of cardboard boxes. Inside all this insulation was a seamy, smoke-grimed face, but it was smiling.

"Annie-Mog, that's me," she grinned. "And if Annie-Mog says there's room, there is." She made a wide gesture with her hand, and Ben hesitantly lowered his duffel-bag and his rolled-up sleeping bag on to the ground.

"What about Uncle Allsorts?" said a younger voice, close by.

Annie-Mog snorted cheerfully. "Never turned anyone off but the once," she said. "And he was a junkie – and fighting mad and all."

The owner of the younger voice leaned over the fire and held out a tin mug of tea to Ben. "You look perished," she said. "Drink up."

Ben looked into the new face and saw that it was smiling too, though guardedly. He smiled back and murmured: "Thanks."

"That's better," said the girl. "Get your hands round that. Does wonders for chilblains."

Obediently, Ben wrapped his chilled hands round the warm metal mug and sighed with pleasure at the rising steamy scent of hot sweet tea.

"I'm Evie," went on the young voice behind the veil of steam and long fair hair that shrouded her face. "Homeless and jobless and usually hungry." But she seemed to be laughing, not complaining, thought Ben in wonder. "But on the other hand," she continued, still smiling at him through wisps of smoke and hair, "I'm young, healthy and free. How about you?"

"The same," said Ben, feeling all at once a curious sense of comradeship alive and growing in the shadowy little encampment. "I'm Ben," he volunteered at last. "And I did have a job – once."

The girl laughed, and he caught a glimpse of white teeth, a generously curving mouth, and two merry eyes that were either brown or black, he couldn't tell which in the murky light.

"That's Pete over there," Evie pointed. "But he's asleep right now. He sometimes gets night-loading at the lorry depot. That's why he's always asleep!"

"He does chip in," interrupted Annie-Mog in sturdy defence. "He's no dead loss." She turned to Ben and held out a grimy cellophane packet of biscuits." There had been three in it, he thought, like the kind you bought on station buffets. Now there were only two. He hesitated.

"Go on, it won't bite," said Annie-Mog. "Share and share alike's the rule here."

"The only rule," added Evie.

"Except – we don't pinch each other's gear," warned Annie, and wrapped her blankets more tightly round her shoulders.

Ben understood that the ground rules of this small community were being laid down before him.

At this point there was a curious yowling behind them, and several lean and hungry cats came sidling into the firelight. They went straight up to Annie-Mog and began rubbing themselves hopefully against her shoulders, the carboard boxes, and any other parts they could reach. Ben began to understand her nickname, for she reached inside her box and brought out a medley of none-too-savoury scraps of food which she tossed to the cats. She watched benignly as they scrambled and fought among themselves for titbits.

Evie looked at Ben and grinned. "She's hopeless," she laughed. "Starving, she'd give 'em her last crust."

"No, I wouldn't," snapped Annie. "I'd *share* it." She also grinned at Ben, gap-toothed and sardonic. "Charity begins at 'ome."

Ben grinned back, and gratefully munched his biscuit. Like a starving cat, he thought. That's me. How have I come to this?

Evie was now regarding him thoughtfully. "There's pickings in cafés," she told him. "Specially stations." When he looked mystified, she went on explaining patiently. "People in a hurry, see? They leave things – a biscuit here – a packet of sugar – a roll or something . . . Annie and me, we do the rounds. Some for the cats, some for us. There's usually something worth having."

Ben nodded.

"Then there's the soupers."

"Soupers?"

"Do-gooders. Specially at Christmas. They come round with soup – or open an all-night shelter, or – "

"Bless 'em," said Annie-Mog firmly. "Do-gooders or not, they sure help. Can't look a gift mug in the mouth!" A cackle of laughter escaped from behind the barrage of wraps.

Beyond her, the bundle that was Pete shifted in his sleep under his pile of wrappings and muttered: "Wha's a marrer?" and turned over and went to sleep again.

Evie was looking down into her lap and slowly counting out a

109

few coins with her stiff, cold fingers. "I got enough here for three hot dogs," she said at last.

"*Four*," corrected Annie-Mog, nodding vaguely in the direction of the sleeping Pete.

Ben reached into his pocket. "I've got some too," he volunteered. The two women looked at him in amazement.

"Rockefeller, are you?" cackled Annie.

"For God's sake," warned Evie. "Don't show it all at once!" She was about to get to her feet and go in search of the hot dogs, when another voice spoke from the dark, and a shambling figure came into the firelight.

"No need for that, Evie. I got provvy."

Ben knew it must be Uncle Allsorts – who else could it be? For the bulky, stooping shape was garlanded all over with "allsorts" – tied on to the piece of rope that held his trousers together, festooned round his shoulders on strings and dangling from the pockets of the enormous, ancient overcoat that covered him from his muffler-ridden neck to his broken-booted feet. Tin mugs, frying pans, knives and forks and tin plates, boxes and bags, old plastic carriers full of rattling junk, rolled-up greyish blankets, bits of cloth, clashing bottles and beer cans – everything that kept a roving man alive seemed to be strewn about his person.

"And he does love licorice allsorts, too," murmured Evie, laughing again in Ben's ear.

"Who's this, then?" said Uncle Allsorts, surveying Ben out of two very shrewd beady eyes.

"This is Ben," volunteered Evie, smiling up at the extraordinary, untidy figure.

"An' 'e's 'armless," added Annie-Mog.

"Armless and legless, too, I shouldn't wonder," Uncle Allsorts retorted, still looking Ben up and down.

"'E's orl right." Annie insisted.

"Geroff," growled Uncle Allsorts, "How d'you know?"

"I can tell," Annie said, with supreme confidence. "Same as cats. I can always tell. Some is all right, and some isn't. And some are right wrong-uns. Like that one!" and she pointed to a flat-eared, vicious-looking tom who was fighting tooth and nail for the last scrap of left-overs. "Bite the hand wot feeds it, that one would." She glared up at Uncle Allsorts. "But Ben wouldn't. See?"

The old, hunched figure seemed to shrug, and all his accoutrements rattled around him. "Have it your own way," he grumbled, and then shot out another question, this time at Ben himself.

"What can you do?"

"Anything," said Ben promptly.

"Humping crates?"

Ben hesitated, looking down at his right arm with some misgiving. "I – I think so."

The old man's lip curled. "You *think*? Hard work scare you, does it?"

Ben shook his head. "I broke this arm humping crates," he explained. "It's only just mended."

"Where?"

Ben misunderstood him and began to lay a finger across his right fore-arm. Then he looked up and realized what was meant. "Oh – over in Pin Street Market."

The old man's face seemed to change. "Are you *that* Ben?" He peered at him more closely in the gloom, and there was something almost apologetic in his glance. "Metal trays, wasn't it?"

Ben stared. "How did you know about that?"

"Word gets around," said Uncle Allsorts, sounding suddenly very casual. He lowered his heavy bulk to the ground, amid a renewed clatter of tins and bottles. Then he began to unpack one of his bags and carefully handed round a hot spring roll to each of them and a big bag of chips to share.

"Where d'you get all this, then?" asked Annie-Mog suspiciously.

"I done someone a favour," said Uncle Allsorts, and closed one eye in a ferocious wink. Then he turned to Ben with a spare spring roll held out in his calloused hand.

Ben looked at Evie doubtfully. "What about Pete?"

"Still some left," grunted the old man. "Thought the other two were still here." He glanced round the dark space between the brazier and the smoky little fire. "Where they got to then?" he asked Annie.

It was her turn to shrug, but she didn't clatter so much.

111

"Gone off, 'aven't they? Maybe they found somewhere better."

"Maybe," agreed Uncle Allsorts, in the sort of voice that didn't believe it. But he was still holding out the paper-wrapped food to Ben, and now he added in a slightly less abrasive voice: "I was told to look out for you."

Ben looked even more astounded. "Who by?"

"Your friend Al."

Bemused, Ben took the proffered food, and said in a dazed voice: "Al seems to have had a lot of friends."

"He did," agreed the old man, biting into his own spring roll. "Good bloke, Al was." His eyes glinted in the firelight as he looked at Ben. "You're not the first beginner he found work for."

Ben was silent. This curious cameraderie of the streets was new to him, – and it seemed to stretch even further across the backways and alleys of the city than he had realized.

"Shame about the market," went on Uncle Allsorts dreamily. "Have to find somewhere else now, won't we?"

This time Ben did dare to question him. "What do you mean?"

The shrewd old eyes looked into his, wrinkling at the corners against the smoke of the fire. "I seen 'em all," he murmured obscurely. "They comes and they goes."

"Who?"

"The ones as wants work – and the ones as doesn't. The ones as helps theirselves along – and ones as doesn't." He spat into the fire. "The ones as is worth a leg-up – and the ones as isn't." The straight, grim old mouth curled sardonically again at the edges. "The ones as is grateful for favours received – and the ones as says: 'Oh, not potato soup agen!'"

Annie-Mog snorted explosively. "They *never*!"

The old head in its woolly bobble-hat nodded vigorously. "Oh yes they did. I heard 'em." He allowed a deep, eruptive laugh to come to the surface. Then he turned back to Ben, suddenly serious. "See, Ben, I was the one that got away."

Ben looked confused. "What?"

"No good," spelt out Uncle Allsorts, shaking his head. "Never was no good at nothing. Never got a real job. Look at me now." The tins rattled round him and he sighed.

Ben looked, but he didn't sigh. He rather liked what he saw.

"So now," the old man went on, with painful clarity, "they uses me, see?"

"Who do?" Ben was still mystified.

"To find out," explained the weary voice. "I hear things, see? A job going here – a bit of casual there – and the ones who'll make a go of it." The clever, tired eyes looked out at Ben from worlds of experience and disillusion. "Not all of 'em will make it – but some will, I dessay." He leant forward and gave the smoky fire a vicious prod with his foot. A few bright flicks of flame shot up into the cold damp air. "It's the best I can do," he added, as if he was arguing with himself over many lost lives – not least his own.

Ben understood now. But he was much too wise to say anything. And, for some reason, the old man's frail, self-accusing voice moved him almost to tears. Tears, he thought? It would never do in this company. Hastily, he swallowed a mouthful of spring roll and tried not to choke.

"What *did* you do?" asked Uncle Allsorts suddenly.

Ben swallowed some more. "Graphics. I was – er – I was training." He paused. "I can do posters – the market taught me – and a bit of pavement stuff . . ."

"Ah, a *screever*?" The old man nodded approval. "The underground station's a good place," he murmured as if to himself. Then he looked hard at Ben again. "There's this bloke, see? Gotta fruit and veg stall nearby." He waved one hand in a curious, outflung gesture, setting off a renewed spate of rattling. "Wants someone to sweep out and set up, mornings – sweep out and close up, evenings."

Ben nodded.

"You could do a pavement in between-like?"

"Sounds ideal," agreed Ben.

"And 'e might like a poster, too," put in Annie-Mog, not to be outdone.

"I'll go there tomorrow," said Ben.

"That's the boy," rumbled Allsorts, with surprising warmth in his old voice.

Evie, beside him, broke into laughter. "Whoops, Benny-boy, you're on your way!"

Suddenly, the warmth and friendliness was all round him like a cloak. He had found a place among friends – against all the odds in this huge, alien city, and he felt absurdly safe and secure, absurdly happy.

"Have another cuppa," said Evie, quite aware of his shamefully choked-up state.

"Thanks," said Ben, and beamed hazily at everyone in sight. "Don't mind if I do."

A kind of pattern began to emerge in Ben's street life – precarious though it was.

In the morning he had to get to the fruit and vegetable stall before people started going to work, so that the pavement was empty enough to sweep and to set up the display stands. The stallholder was a thin, wispy man known to all his regulars as Corky (Ben never did discover his real name). His voice was high and strident, and full of sharp mischief as he exchanged cocky repartee with his customers. Mostly he ignored Ben except to say: "Yeah, that'll do," or "No. Put the apples higher." But at the end of the day he usually handed over some leftovers or bruised fruit, with the dry instruction: "Take 'em away before they rot!"

Once the stands were set up and Corky was satisfied, Ben moved on to the bit of pavement near the underground entrance. He had to be careful not to choose a place where he was too obviously in the way, or he got shouted at or moved on. But he got to know the right places, and he usually managed to produce some garish landscape or other, and quite a few coins rolled into his upturned woolly hat on the cold grey stone. It wasn't quite as bad as openly begging, he supposed, though his strict northern upbringing made him very uneasy about accepting charity. He would much rather work for his money.

He did do a poster for Corky however, and the stringy voice paused in its stream of patter and said: "What's this then? Whizz-kid con tricks?" But Ben could tell he was pleased.

The worst days were when it rained and the pavements were too wet to draw on, or the painstaking work of a morning was washed out in instant diluted mud. And Ben got so wet that he thought he would never be dry again.

But after he had shut up shop for Corky, he would pull his anorak collar up round his ears, collect his carrier bag of chalks and bits of leftover fruit, and slope off to the comparative comfort of the old railway arch and Annie-Mog's fire. She was usually there before him, brewing up tea in her old black kettle, and she always handed him a mug of scalding liquid as soon as he appeared.

He had learnt some of the rules of communal living by now. If he had had a good day, he bought everyone some food. If someone else had done well, they paid out that night. One or other of them always brought Annie-Mog some tea-bags and some milk. Evie was good at scrounging sugar (she didn't say how, but Ben thought it was largely in the cafés and station buffets). And she often brought scraps for Annie-Mog's cats. Pete never seemed to be there when Ben was, but from time to time he brought back half-empty cartons of tinned goods from the lorry depot – corned beef sometimes, or baked beans, or soup. Uncle Allsorts kept an eye on stores (when there were any) and stashed them in odd places hidden from casual predators (animal or human). From somewhere he had acquired a large, long-handled cooking pot, and Annie-Mog was very good at throwing a lot of unlikely ingredients together and making a passable stew. They none of them went hungry for too long, but they did get very cold and wet, and all of them – even the sleeping Pete – had permanent colds and coughs.

But Ben was learning how to survive. Uncle Allsorts saw to that. He taught him where to set out his pavement drawings to the best advantage – nearest to the largest numbers of passers-by, but in the place least likely to annoy the authorities or the police. He told him where the hostels were, and advised him to get into one at least once a week if he could – preferably one where he could have a bath and wash his clothes and get them dried. "Leave it too long, and you gets too scruffy," he said. "You gotta go down to the job centre, remember, and look *likely*. It's no good unless you looks *likely*."

Ben understood this. (Keep it *bright*, Benny-boy!)

"And another thing, Ben, never cheek the police – never

argue. Mostly they're decent enough – turn a blind eye – but if they moves you on, just go, see?"

Ben saw.

And Evie taught him where to pick up unwanted food in crowded cafés – and introduced him to some who actually gave away leftovers free of charge. "Marks & Sparks do sandwich handouts, if you're lucky," she told him. "But you has to know when and where – and there's usually a queue."

It was a constant struggle, but it was possible to live, and the more experienced ones did their best to look after him.

But the cold got ever more intense, and Ben found it impossible to stay in one place for too long, so he walked the streets in a desperate attempt to keep warm.

One afternoon late sunlight pierced the pall of cloud and touched the freezing city just as he came to the doors of an old stone church, and the sudden flush of warm gold seemed to invite him in. He went up the steps, and pushed open the door.

Inside, the church was dim, but sunlight still streamed down from above and seemed to swim in a dazzle of muted colours from the stained glass windows and the sparkling Christmas tree in the corner. Stars danced and tinsel shimmered, and the sudden warmth made unexpected tears rise up in Ben's eyes so that he could not see properly, but he thought there was someone standing by the starry firefly points of the tree, looking up at the roof, so that a splash of purple and gold from the window above fell on the pale, upturned face.

It was a girl, he saw, when he blinked hard enough, and she looked so young, so frail and sad standing there, that his heart ached for her, and he knew at once that he had to speak.

"They almost sing," he said.

Hilo turned and looked at him. "What?"

"The colours." He knew about colours – about blackboard chalks on wet pavements, and how he struggled to make them sing.

"Oh." She smiled suddenly, amazed to find another person who felt the power of light and colour in a bleak, cold world. She did not know it, but more light flooded into her face with that brief smile of recognition, and Ben blinked again.

She looked at him harder then, and saw a thin, brown boy

116

with a curly mouth and curly hair to match, and a sheen of unexplained tears in his eyes. And it seemed to Hilo that he was someone she already knew.

For a moment she was reminded of her first meeting with Max playing his fiddle in the street, when that perilous bridge of understanding had swung untried between them and she had been too scared to take that first step forward.

But this was different. Somehow, she knew it was different. She wasn't scared, and she wasn't alone any more. It was as simple as that.

"I'm Hilo," she said. It was meant to be some kind of defence – I'm still me, you know – but it came out soft and almost welcoming.

"I'm Ben," he answered, and there was a smile in his voice, and absurd gladness welling up inside him.

They stood side by side in silence for a while, looking up at the stained glass saints in their jewel colours, and the blue-robed Madonna and her Child illumined by the last slanting rays of winter sunlight.

At last Hilo said in a strange, dreaming voice: "The dying of the light."

"No," Ben contradicted gently. "Not dying. *Changing*."

And he was right. For as they watched the gleam of sunlight faded, but as dusk came down and the street lights began to come on, the colours in the glass seemed to glow and deepen, and the church itself became an island of light in the surrounding gloom.

"You don't believe in all this, do you?" asked Hilo, sounding almost wistful.

Ben sighed, remembering the Young Travellers on Dora's site, and he answered in their words: "You've got to believe in something."

Hilo turned her head and smiled at him with sudden mischief. "What, for instance?"

He paused, considering, a little shaken by that fragile smile. "I don't know. Light?. Colour?"

She nodded, the radiance still growing behind that smile.

"People?"

Suddenly the smile was quenched. "No!" People meant Steve.

And her mother. You couldn't believe in them. You mustn't allow them to be real.

But then she remembered her father – and Max. Yes, they were real. Or had been real. You had to believe in them. And this boy beside her who talked of light and colour as if they were friends of his – yes, you could easily believe in him.

Ben was watching the thoughts chase themselves across her expressive face, and when she came to consider him, their eyes met.

"Yes," she agreed, relinquishing a whole world of hurt and fierce rejection, accepting a whole new world of extraordinary comfort. "OK. People."

He laughed, and laid a friendly arm round her shoulders. He felt her stiffen and start to recoil, but then she sighed and relaxed, as if shrugging off heavy armour and letting it fall to the floor. "Welcome back," he said softly, well aware of that small surrender.

"To what?" she asked, without any real bitterness.

"To the human race," he answered, and the curly edges to his smile grew even curlier.

Behind them a new voice spoke, older than Ben's and not nearly so full of irrepressible hope, but still warmhearted and friendly. "Are you staying for the carol service?"

They looked at each other doubtfully, and then at the man beside them. Obviously he was the vicar of this church, they thought, and as kind as his voice, grey-haired and grey-eyed and tired. The kind of tiredness that had seen it all, was surprised by nothing, but still minded not being able to put things right. Reassured, Ben smiled and gave Hilo's shoulder another quiet squeeze of reassurance.

The vicar saw that small gesture and smiled back. He knew the homeless when he saw them – there were quite a few in his parish, and they all had that wary, cautious look, that fear of interference warring with longing for simple comfort. His conscience was always stirred by them, but he was much too wise to let his pity show.

"At least the church is warm," he said cheerfully. "We don't often put the heating on in the week – too expensive. But today you're lucky."

Ben agreed. "Feels wonderful."

Hilo said nothing, but it felt wonderful to her, too.

"Soup afterwards," added the vicar over his shoulder, as he hurried down the aisle. "In the parish room. All welcome." He disappeared into the vestry without looking back.

*All welcome.* Ben's spark-filled eyes (more violet than blue, like his mother's) met Hilo's grey ones. Both pairs danced a little with laughter.

"Shall we stay?" he asked.

"Why not?" said Hilo. But she was a little worried that anything to do with music might make her cry. Not carols, surely? she thought. Not that corny stuff. Max would laugh. Then she turned back to look at Ben, and he was laughing already. The shadows seemed to recede when Ben laughed.

They sat at the back and watched the church fill up with a motley collection of people. There were a lot of children. Hilo saw they were all carrying some kind of toy or other. When the first carol began, all the children joined the small procession of choirboys and solemnly laid their toys down in front of the candle-lit Crib which stood by the Christmas tree in the corner.

"For the kids in hospital," murmured a woman close to Ben, and beamed happily as her own child returned, glowing with goodwill.

Ben nodded, smiling, and wondered fleetingly whether Dora's twins would have another Christmas when Jack got home. He looked across the aisle at the painted plaster figures of Mary and Joseph, the haloed Christ-Child, the cows and donkeys in the straw, and the tinsel star glittering overhead.

"Oh well," he thought, "at least They knew about being homeless. It's a funny sort of myth, but I can relate to that part!"

He turned to look at Hilo, and saw that her face was pale and tearless, but somehow too fragile to bear. It looked as if it might shatter like spun glass if anyone touched it. He badly wanted to take the tension out of it, but he didn't know how. So, instead, he lifted up his cheerful young tenor and sang with the rest of them, and waited to see Hilo begin to smile at his enthusiasm. Soon her straight mouth began to curl upwards like his own, and she began to sing as well.

"No-o-el, No-o-el!" they sang, and "Glor-or-ia!" and "O-O

Star of Wonder, Star of Light," and Ben thought that one really suited Hilo, whose eyes seemed to reflect a dazzle of wonder and starlight, no matter how tired and frail she looked.

Afterwards, while they gratefully drank soup in the bare parish room, Ben dared to ask Hilo where she lived.

She looked at him over the rim of her mug of soup and shrugged.

"Nowhere much."

"That makes two of us," grinned Ben. Then he went on carefully: "But I've found a good spot – and some good mates." He paused, and added shyly: "We – we kinda share."

He waited for Hilo to make the next move. And in a little while she did. "We?"

His curly smile lifted hopefully. "You'd be safe with us."

Hilo sighed – a long slow sigh of relief and recognition. "I know that, Ben," she said.

So they went home together. Home. To the sooty bricks of the old railway arch, and Annie-Mog's smoky fire, and Uncle Allsorts and his rattling armour of Useful Gear.

Ben brought Hilo to him first, knowing that the old man's approval was vital if she was to be accepted into the group.

Uncle Allsorts looked her up and down with his bright, shrewd eyes, and did not seem too dismayed by what he saw. But he did not ask her, as he had Ben: "What can you do?" Instead, he said gruffly: "Been ill, have you?"

Hilo hesitated. "A bit." She saw his black look, and hastened to add: "But I'm better now."

He did not smile. "Pretty rough out here," he warned. "You get sick, it's hospital, see?"

Beside him, Ben felt Hilo stiffen into sudden panic, and he laid a quiet hand on her arm. "I'll look after her," he said, and turned in appeal to Annie-Mog.

"Aw, come on, Allsorts," she wheedled, grinning up at him. "Where's your Christmas spirit?"

"Christmas spirit? Lead me to it!" said Uncle, looking round hopefully at the little group, and everyone laughed.

From then on it was Ben and Hilo. They weren't together all the time, but they managed to do most things either together or near by. Ben still set up and took down the fruit and veg stall every day for Corky, and in between usually made a couple of pavement drawings. Hilo rather nervously tried out her penny-whistle on the rush-hour crowds by the underground, and was surprised to find they actually threw her some coins from time to time. She also went with Ben down to the job centre, and to the social services office, because he insisted that if they were badgered enough, they might do something. They didn't, of course. They kept on saying that both of them were too young to qualify and why didn't they go home? But Ben, being Ben, was always hopeful that they might change their minds.

It was only when it came to Ben's physiotherapy session at the hospital that Hilo refused to go with him. Ben had already noticed her sudden panic when old Uncle Allsorts pronounced the fierce word "hospital", but he had not tried to find out why she got so scared. But now he thought it was time to ask. There were a lot of ghosts that needed laying in Hilo's shadowed world and he was going to get rid of them all, one way or another.

"Why, Hilo?"

"Why what?"

"What's wrong with hospital?"

She looked at him in sudden exasperation. "You don't understand a thing, do you?"

"Not a thing," agreed Ben, smiling his curly smile. "But I'm trying."

"Very."

Ben pretended hurt. "So?"

But Hilo shook her head. How could she explain to Ben – cheerful, curly Ben – about the dark moments of doubt and terror after Steve's assaults, after she left home . . . How she had gone, sick and trembling, to the first city hospital she could find, to ask someone – anyone who would listen – about the possibility of an unwanted pregnancy, or even V. D. or Aids? She didn't know anything about Steve or what he had been up to before, except that he was completely selfish and self-indulgent and might have spread his favours almost anywhere . . . But how could she tell Ben about the laconic voice, the contemptuous eyes of the harassed duty doctor. "One night stand, was it? Or several?" And the brisk, hard hands of the

121

uncomprehending nurse as she lay there, stripped and ashamed, while they prodded and poked and finally dismissed her with a bored negative. "You're probably not eating enough. Makes things irregular."

*Not eating enough?* When she had barely enough money then to buy a hot dog or a bowl of soup at the all-night stand? When she felt faintly sick and light-headed all day anyway, especially when she thought of Steve and his hot hands?

She shuddered. No. There was nothing she could say to Ben.

"Hilo," he said, and grasped her by the shoulders and shook her like a kid sister. "Let it go."

"What?"

"Whatever it is that's bugging you – let it go."

She sighed and relaxed. "All right. I'll wait for you outside. But I won't come in."

He had to be content with that. He could see how the black thoughts kept chasing themselves round her haunted mind. Better leave it for now. They would go in the end. He would make them go. Somehow.

But Hilo was remembering Max and his insistent voice: "Say it. *I'm not a coward. There's no need to run away.*" She knew she was still running away, though it was getting better. And, she realized suddenly, one day I will be able to tell Ben about it, – but I could never have told Max, not in a thousand years.

"Here," said Ben, producing a grubby stub of candle out of his pocket. "Will this do? Genuine original ghost-buster."

"Perfect," smiled Hilo, and silently hurled a lot of dark demons back into the bottomless pit they came from.

When Ben came out of the hospital, he was carrying a small red book under his arm and laughing.

"What have you got there?" asked Hilo, joining him on the pavement.

"A book," grinned Ben. "I mean, The Book. You've got a Candle. All we want now is a Bell."

"Ben!" she glared at him. "Where did you get it from?"

He began to laugh again, irrepressibly. "Got given it, didn't I? Said I had a Friend in Need." He clasped his hands together and raised his eyes to heaven. "Only too pleased to oblige, they were."

He lurched happily against Hilo, laughter still spilling out of him.

"Honestly, Ben, you are awful!"

"No, I'm not." He gave a little skip of mischief. "Perfectly legitimate cause."

Even Hilo began to chuckle then.

Ben regarded her approvingly. "Come on. Let's take it home – before they change their minds."

Still laughing, they went off arm-in-arm towards home – that is, to the blackened railway arch and Annie-Mog's smoky fire.

When they got there, Annie was already getting out the scraps to feed her cats, and as Ben and Hilo approached a sudden uproar ensued. It sounded like a hundred tin cans rattling and a hundred cats yowling in terror all at once, – but when they looked more closely, they saw that the noise was caused by one pitiful, scrawny creature which seemed to have its head encased in a ragged metal frill from which were dangling several even more jagged pieces of metal banging and jangling together in frightful cacophany as the terrified animal tried to shake them off. And one of the dangling objects was a small brass bell on a piece of wire. Ben eyed it thoughtfully.

"How did it get itself like that?" he asked, starting forward to try to disentangle the animal.

But the frightened cat only backed away, yowling louder than ever, and as it moved the metal collar clanged louder than ever too.

"It didn't," snarled Annie, looking from Ben to the cat with a kind of smouldering anger. "Someone put that – that damn thing on it a-purpose."

"Can't we get it off?"

Annie's anger exploded in a fit of coughing. "You'll be lucky," she wheezed. But even as she spoke she was sorting out the tastiest scraps to tempt the thin little cat into coming within reach. Annie had a way with cats, there was no doubt about it, and if anyone could soothe the frantic creature, she could manage it. Sure enough, before long the wild terror subsided in the tawny eyes and it crept forward to eat out of her hand. She waited a moment, then reached out a second hand and grasped it firmly round its scrawny body so that Ben could disentangle it from the encircling strip of jagged metal. For a moment the cat went rigid and struck out with sharp, unsheathed claws, raking Ben's hand. But then it seemed to become aware that they were trying to help it, and a sudden passive stillness came over it so that Ben could work unhampered by those desperately flailing claws.

"I'll need to cut it free," he said, and waited while Annie reached out one hand to find a knife among the cooking pots round the fire.

At last the little cat was freed from its rattling torment, and Annie spoke to it gently as she took her restraining hand away. "There! You'll be a lot better off without it."

Ben took the tiny brass bell off the tangle of wire and solemnly handed it to Hilo, with the quick response: "And you'll be a lot better off *with* it."

Hilo looked at him in silence, but she took the little brass bell in her hand and smiled.

Annie was still talking to the little cat. "The rats won't hear you coming now."

"The rats *will* hear you coming now," grinned Ben, sotto voce, and this time Hilo laughed.

Annie gave the cat one last, highly-odorous titbit and turned to watch it go. "There you are then, Yoki," she said, giving it a final farewell pat. But the striped, scraggy body arched itself into a sinuous loop that unexpectedly rubbed itself against her legs, the flat head looked upwards, amber eyes fixed on her seamy, smoke-darkened face with instant adoration, – and then a sudden movement from beyond the firelight threatened danger and it streaked away into the shadows.

"Givin' my supper away agen, wos we?" grumbled Uncle Allsorts, coming into the fitful firelight, armed with yet more bags and boxes and rattling almost as much as the frightened cat.

"Aw, come orff it, Allsorts" wheezed Annie, through yet another burst of coughing, "when did you ever eat rotten fish-'eads for supper?"

"Never yet," admitted the old man, and added darkly: "But the time will come."

"Not tonight, it won't," said Evie's voice from beyond the fire. "Pete's got bangers – a whole string."

"Fell orff the back of a lorry, did they?" asked Allsorts, setting down his clanking collection of bags, tins and parcels in a heap by the fire.

"No, they didn't," growled another, deeper voice from the darkness. "Unloaded four pigs, six sides of beef and three sheep for those," and Pete appeared, carrying the string of sausages in one hand and a carton of bashed-up tins under his other arm.

It was the first time Ben had seen Pete awake, and Hilo had not seen him at all – only a bump inside a mixture of cardboard boxes and old blankets and bits of plastic sheeting. He was tallish and gangling, with strong, bony hands protruding from thin wrists which stuck out of the sleeves of a coat that was obviously too small. He looked permanently tired and unshaven, but his light-flecked brown eyes were surprisingly warm, and so was his sleepy smile.

"Hi," he drawled, lazily crinkling up the corners of his eyes at Hilo and Ben and handing the string of sausages over to Annie by the fire. " 'Nough for all the gang tonight."

"I've got some spuds," volunteered Ben, fishing them out of his pocket. "Corky gave 'em me, – and three apples."

"And six doughnuts," added Hilo, not meeting Ben's eye. She lowered her duffel-bag to the ground so that she could unload some of its contents. It was difficult wandering about the streets with all your gear – all your possessions – slung round you, like Uncle Allsorts. But all of them had the same problem, and none of them dared leave anything of any value behind. Clothes were precious, however shabby, and as for Ben's sleeping bag, that was beyond price in these bitter days of winter.

"Where did those come from?" asked Ben curiously. He hadn't seen Hilo buy anything and he knew she hated begging.

"Played my pipe," she said carelessly. "Outside the hospital." A brief, dry smile touched her mouth, somehow making it look much sterner and older than it had a few moments before. "Melted their hearts as they went in."

The others laughed, but Ben thought that smile was very perilous.

"Oughta boil that bell," said Annie suddenly. "And the knife.

125

Fleas gets everywhere." She glared at Ben. "And wash that hand. Give it here."

Obediently, Ben held out his hand, and Annie dabbed it with a surprisingly clean cloth dipped in her kettle of water, and then ferreted about in one of her innumerable bags till she found a tube of antiseptic ointment and a plaster.

"You're very well equipped!" approved Ben.

Annie-Mog scowled. "Accidents happen – specially on the street." She coughed raspingly into the smoke. "And with them cats, – you never know."

She took the small bell from Hilo and the knife from Ben and dropped them both into her blackened kettle. In a few moments she leaned forward and fished them out again with a metal spoon. The bell looked decidedly cleaner. The knife did not.

"Here," said Allsorts indignantly to Annie, "you aren't giving us boiled fleas in our tea, are you?"

"Why not?" Annie cackled. "Give some body to it."

In a little while they were all eating Pete's sausages and Ben's potatoes (baked in the ashes of Annie's fire), followed by Hilo's doughnuts and Corky's apples, and drinking Annie-Mog's tea without enquiring too much into its contents.

Pete stayed with them to eat this time, and Ben wondered when he had done his sleeping, or whether he was learning to do without it altogether.

"No unloading tonight, then?" asked Allsorts, with his mouth full of jammy doughnut.

"Did a day shift, din't I?" said Pete. "Extra. Got the night off – unless I do both."

"No, you don't," scolded Evie. "You need your beauty sleep." She looked at him affectionately, and laid a careless arm round his shoulders.

Pete winked at Ben. "Nice to know she cares, in't it?" And Evie aimed a half-hearted blow at his head.

Hilo was watching their easy comradeship with some envy. She would like to feel as free and unafraid as Evie – as ready and willing to bring comfort to Ben as Evie was to Pete . . . Maybe one day soon she would be, for it was daily getting easier, and Ben – clever, observant Ben – never asked anything of her that she could not give. She wondered then, a little guiltily,

126

whether Evie was really as carelessly untroubled as she made out, and what had driven her and Pete out on to the cold streets of London.

But it was Ben who dared to ask. "What put you out in the cold with Annie's cats?"

Pete looked at Evie and laughed. "We got evicted, didn't we?"

Evie sighed. "I lost my job first. Then Pete lost his. Couldn't pay the rent." She made a wide, shrugging lift with her shoulders. "That was it. Out!"

She leant forward and poked Annie's fire viciously with a handy piece of broken crate. It was the only sign she gave of whatever inner stress she might be feeling.

"Where was that? Down here?" Ben looked round at the grey London night with sympathy in his eyes.

"Oh no," said Evie, giving the sullen fire another poke. "That was Dundee."

*"Dundee?"* Hilo came in then, sounding surprised. "But you aren't Scottish, are you?"

"Nope." Pete answered for Evie. "Stockport. Both of us." He gave Evie a sideways, crooked grin. "Went north to where the work was, didn't we? Big laugh, eh?"

"A scream," agreed Evie. Then she smiled at Pete with sudden fierce reassurance and added: "We're all right, though. Aren't we?"

"Yeah." Pete's voice was laconic. "We live."

"Don't I take care of you-all?" Uncle Allsorts demanded, spearing another burnt sausage on his fork.

"You do Uncle, you do," smiled Pete.

"You eat. You're warm. You're safe," persisted Allsorts. "What more d'you want?"

Ben and Hilo looked at each other. What more indeed?

"Those other two – " said Annie suddenly, leaning over her kettle to pour out another mug of tea. "Them as went orff – "

"What about 'em?"

"Thought they'd be better orff down by the river some-wheres."

"And?"

"Picked her up half-dead with the bronichals, they tell me.

127

Stuck him in a hostel for vagrants." She peered at the others through the smoky haze of her fire. "They had a house, you know – a real house of their own. Got repossessed."

Uncle Allsorts nodded. "I know. Bad luck." He took a quick swig from one of his comforting bottles. "But they was soft." He glared round at them balefully, contempt in his rheumy old eyes. "Soft! . . . I told 'em – keep dry – wear all the layers in kingdom come – go in nights when you can, even separately. Wouldn't listen. No sense." He swore mildly and had another swig. Then he rounded on Annie: "And you're no better!"

"Me?" Annie was affronted. "What've I done?"

"Nothing," growled Allsorts. "That's the trouble. You got a cough fit to rattle the winders of the 'Ouse of Lords – and shoes that lets in half the Thames – and a coat that's got more 'oles than a sieve – I arsk you! And then you goes and gives away your last crust to them plaguey cats!"

"I don't!" said Annie, but even her indignation made her cough. "Like I said, I *shares*." She glared back at Allsorts with glittering, feverish eyes. "And anyways, what'm I supposed to do about it?"

"Put these on for a start," rasped Allsorts, and disentangled a pair of stout boots from the string around his waist.

Annie looked at them suspiciously. "Where d'you get *them* from?"

"Never you mind," snapped Allsorts. "Get 'em on. And get down to the hand-out shelter and grab yourself another coat."

"Yes, Allsorts," said Annie, with surprising meekness. Then she reached over and took the boots and flashed him a sudden grin. "You're a wicked old man, Allsorts, you know that?"

Uncle Allsorts merely snorted and had another nip of gin. Beside him, Pete echoed Annie's sideways grin.

"T.L.C. all round," he drawled. "Just what we need."

"You can say that again," murmured Ben, and leaned over and took Hilo's cold hand in his.

On Christmas Day Allsorts decreed that they should all go down to the "Soupers" refuge. Fixed it, he said he had, and do-gooders or not, you couldn't say no to a good hot Christmas dinner, could you?

The refuge was in a shabby church hall with a splintered wooden floor and flaking yellow paint on the walls, but it was warm, and the food was wonderful (to Ben and Hilo, at least), and there was enough for everyone even though the room was crowded with cold and homeless bodies in damp and steaming clothes.

They stayed in their own little group at one of the trestle tables, and the organizers said they could stay all night if they liked, but there weren't any beds, not even mattresses, only floors to lie on. Even so, it was warm and out of the wind and rain. Mostly, people stayed, gratefully subsiding into little tired heaps in corners, or stretching out in weary relief on the bare, scrubbed boards.

A few of the more cheerful ones tried to start up some singing, and one experienced Irish busker produced an accordion and a little dancing puppet on strings who capered and pranced to the tune of an Irish jig as he played.

"That's clever," said Ben, and turned to Hilo, smiling. "I could make one of those for you."

Hilo leaned forward and watched the tiny jigging figure intently. "Could you?"

Ben nodded. "If you could jig it up and down and play the pipe at the same time?"

Hilo thought about it. If she attached the puppet strings to her elbows . . .? No. Jerking them would interfere with her playing fingers. Her knee, then? No, her foot. That was what the Irishman was doing. But he had to keep lifting his foot up high and wagging it up and down to the music. It would be tiring, but she could probably learn to do it all right, and learn an Irish jig, too, if she put her mind to it.

"I could try –" she said doubtfully, and then smiled at Ben's hopeful face. "If you could make one, I'll try."

"Done!" said Ben. "A late Christmas present." Then he looked enquiringly at Hilo and added under his breath: "That reminds me – shall we give 'em now?"

They had already agreed that such things as presents were beyond them. But even so they had clubbed together and got a packet of licorice allsorts for Uncle and a tin of sardines for Annie and her cats. For Evie and Pete all they

129

could manage was a Mars bar to share, but at least it was something.

So now Hilo nodded, and they shyly produced their small offerings and handed them round.

Uncle Allsorts looked at the packet in his hand, snorted and blew his nose loudly on a rather grubby red spotted handkerchief, and managed a lopsided grin.

As well as the tin of sardines, Ben had managed to get hold of a bottle of cough mixture for Annie, though he didn't know if it would do any good. Her cough seemed to get worse with every grey winter morning. But she smiled and wheezed with pleasure and promised to take the medicine every day, though the sardines for the cats seemed to please her more.

Then Ben and Hilo looked at each other, still somewhat shyly, and each held out their own small token. Hilo's was a cheap, shiny penknife, bought with a few of her busking pennies at the tobacconist's shop on the corner of the station.

"You must be psychic," said Ben. "I can carve your puppet now!"

Hilo smiled and looked down at what Ben was holding out for her. It was the small, perfect shell fossil he had found on the hills at home.

"It's very old," he said softly. "Puts things in perspective."

She nodded and took it gravely from him. Her fingers felt the fluting on the smooth stone, and somehow the ancient strength of the hills and the timeless oceans seemed to course through them into her hand. "I'll keep it always," she said. Then, as if driven into more speech by Ben's expression, she added, smiling: "What with this, and my bell, book and candle, I should be impregnable."

"That's what I hoped," said Ben.

Towards morning, Hilo began to feel restless. It wasn't exactly the crowded room, or the smell of drying clothes and unwashed bodies, or even the snoring, but somehow the pressure of all those sleeping people, their hopeless searches, their dreams and dark despairs, seemed to weigh on her. She got up from her corner near Ben, picked up her duffel-bag (not safe to leave it

130

behind) and slipped quietly out of the door into the street to look at the sky.

The night was dark and almost silent, though there was still a faint hum of traffic and the permanent dim glow of a big city behind the black barricade of the rooftops. Just a glimmer of stars if you looked high enough behind the haze, but they too were faint and far.

"Can you hear them?" asked Ben softly, from close beside her.

"Who?"

"The stars? . . . Angels?"

"Music of the Spheres?" Hilo laughed with equal softness. "I used to think I might – if only I listened hard enough!"

"Me too," said Ben. He looked up at the sky in absurd and touching hope.

Across the sleeping city a small wind blew, and on the wind came a snatch of song, a hint of music swinging on the lifted air. A choir? A radio? Some drunken revellers weaving their way home? An open door and a stereo behind it . . .? It didn't matter. The music was there – the magic was there – and the dark night hummed with distant mysteries.

Hilo and Ben turned to each other, enchanted.

"There!" whispered Ben. "Miracles do still happen!" And he turned Hilo towards him and added: "Happy Christmas, Hilo," and smiled at her rapt, upturned face.

They did not feel like going back inside, so they wandered on down to the river to watch the dawn come up with the tide. It was still dark, but a pale promise of light was beginning to grow in the eastern sky, and fingers of silver reached down to stroke the sullen Thames.

A couple of wild duck thrummed by on urgent wings and called to one another in high clear voices as they passed. There were no more snatches of music, but to those two the morning was still enchanted. A primrose bloom washed the grey winter sky, and the river's molten silver was touched with faint gold. The barebone trees on the far embankment swam up out of the shadows, reaching stark arms towards the sunrise, and strange, shivering reflections formed and dissolved beneath them on the unbroken surface of the water. Colours began to glow behind

131

the grey, and a sudden elusive gleam of crimson touched the cloudscape that veiled the sun.

They were watching this marvellous upsurge of light when they heard a sudden shout from the river terrace above the embankment, and Ben got a confused impression of something falling. There was a heavy splash in the river, and the sound of feet running.

"Quick!" shouted a voice. "She's gone in. Lend a hand!"

Hilo and Ben peered over the embankment wall and saw a sodden bundle being carried downstream towards them by the sluggish tide. On the river bank below them a man was flinging off his shoes and coat and trying his weight on the oily mud at the water's edge.

They did not waste time talking, but both climbed over the locked embankment gate on the shallow steps leading down to the water. By this time, the man was already in the river, swimming out to the waterlogged heap of clothes that was still turning and bobbing helplessly in the slow-moving stream. But Ben and Hilo were ahead of them on the long spit of sandy mud at the edge of the bank.

"Don't go in," said Hilo, seeing Ben prepare to jump in after them. "Only make things worse." She looked round wildly, and then added: "That bit of wood – that long bit . . . it might reach."

Together they tugged the long, broken spar out of the mud and manoeuvred it down to the edge of the thin slick of mud reaching out into the river. The spar wavered and swayed as it met the water, but it seemed to right itself and lie across the flow of the current as it came down.

"Just might –" said Ben, reaching out with it as far as his arms would let him. Hilo, without being told, caught hold of him round the waist and hung on grimly while he leant out over the mud.

Then the man reached the bundle in the water, turned it over so that the pale blur of a face was uppermost, and began to tow it towards the bank. The sinking heap of clothes seemed to struggle feebly, two arms flailed out for a moment, and a wet gold head broke the surface before disappearing again beneath the oily surge of the current. But the man had grasped the soggy clothing around the neck with one firm hand, and now reached out his other arm in a desperate attempt to catch hold of Ben's piece of wood.

"A bit further . . ." begged Ben between gritted teeth. He edged cautiously a little further into the clinging mud. "Hold on, Hilo."

Hilo didn't need telling. She was holding on like grim death. Grim death, she thought – and it isn't very far away at this moment, either.

The floating spar swung precariously in the tide, and it almost looked as if the heavily-burdened man was going to miss it altogether. But then the thin piece of wood swung back the other way, and the tired swimmer could grasp it with his outstretched hand.

"Pull!" breathed Ben to Hilo. "Pull me backwards if you can."

"I am pulling," panted Hilo. "Don't slip in the mud. Go slowly."

They went slowly. Inch by slippery inch they moved backwards across the treacherous river mud, and inch by inch the rescuer and his sodden burden came a bit nearer.

"Hold on," called Ben, afraid that the exhausted fingers might suddenly give up and let go.

But they didn't give up. They held on, and soon the man's legs were touching ground and stumbling up through the muddy water on to the slippery edge of the river bank, dragging the limp body of his rescued victim behind him like a drowned rat.

*Drowned?* Hilo rushed forward then, and so did Ben, clasping both rescuer and rescued in their arms.

"Over here," called another voice, and they saw that someone had opened the embankment gate and a small knot of people, including a passing policeman, were waiting for them on the embankment.

From then on it was out of their hands. An ambulance was called. Someone who turned out to belong to the river police and was just going home off duty administered brisk first aid and pumped the water out of the girl's sodden body. Someone else offered blankets and hot tea to Ben and Hilo, who were both soaked and caked in mud, and to the heroic rescuer who agreed to go in the ambulance with the girl to have a check up. He didn't know her, he said. He just saw her jump. He was on his way home after a Christmas party. But he would do what he could to see her looked after, as he was there.

The girl herself lay limp and white and somehow utterly quenched on the uncaring ground. Everyone was very busy bringing her round and wrapping her up, but Hilo thought they did not really understand the problem, or know how to solve it. So she bent over the pale, lost face and waited till the wet eyelashes lifted from the tired brown eyes.

"Why?" said Hilo softly.

"Why not?" sighed the girl. Her eyes seemed to focus on Hilo for a moment, and she tried to make some kind of explanation. "Too much . . ." she murmured. "All too much . . ." The sigh got longer and wearier. "Not any more . . ." Her voice faded and bubbled with water still. "Can't cope any more . . ." she said, and shut her eyes again.

Beside her, Ben reached out a muddy hand and grasped the girl's wet one in his. "Yes, you can," he insisted, smiling straight into her eyes as they opened again in faint and weary protest. "*Life –* " he added, obscurely, "not to be sneezed at . . ." and then he sneezed with enormous ferocity, and everyone laughed. Even the half-drowned girl managed a pale, thin smile.

Then the ambulance took the two of them away, the constable and the river policeman went off on their own pursuits, and the woman who had brought the tea and blankets turned to Ben and Hilo with abrupt kindness. "Would you like a bath?"

Hilo glowed. A bath? A real hot bath? Would she? "Yes, please," she said politely.

"If it's no trouble," added Ben, and promptly sneezed again.

The woman laughed. "Come this way."

They picked up their duffel bags which they had left just inside the embankment gate before they ran down the steps to the river, and followed the woman home.

The next couple of hours were, for Ben and Hilo, like something out of the Arabian nights.

The woman took them into an extraordinarily elegant house on the river terrace, and led them upstairs. They were both very conscious of leaving muddy footprints everywhere, even without their shoes, but she didn't seem to mind.

"Here you are," she said, opening a door. "It's all yours."

They found themselves looking at a veritable suite – bathroom, shower-room and dressing room, all sparkling with white and chrome.

The woman, who said her name was Maude, as in "Come Into the Garden . . ." had thrown up her hands in horror at the state of their clothes. "I'll chuck them all in the washing machine," she said. "But they'll take a while to dry, even in the big dryer. I'll leave you a couple of spare robes. Come down to the kitchen when you're ready."

So Hilo and Ben took it in turns, revelling in the most luxurious bath they had ever had. When they came down, damp and delighted, and cleaner than they had felt for weeks, they found Maude cooking them an enormous breakfast. The kitchen was just as elegant as the bathroom.

Truly, Ben thought, this was a remarkable Christmas!

Maude was a fairly tough, sensible woman, with grown-up children of her own, but somehow the sight of these two, fresh from the bath, tendrils of damp hair still clinging to their heads, and a kind of softened vulnerability about them as they stood there, shyly clutching their borrowed robes around them, made her feel strangely disturbed.

"Sit down," she said. "Breakfast's ready."

They didn't need any telling, but Hilo tried to be polite. "It's very good of you – "

"No, it isn't," said Maude, "after what you two did – "

"We didn't do much," protested Ben. "Except pull. It was the man who saved her."

Maude grunted. "Joint effort, I'd say."

"What will happen to her?" asked Hilo suddenly. The girl's white, defeated face still haunted her. She still wondered uneasily whether they had been right to bring her back.

Maude stopped to look at Hilo, and thought to herself: Yes, this child knows about despair, too. And so does the boy, I shouldn't wonder. Aloud, she said vaguely: "Oh, I expect they'll keep her in overnight."

"Which hospital?"

135

"Hammersmith, they said."

"And then –?" Hilo's voice was bleak. Back to the streets? No job? No home? Like me? She did not say it, but Maude sighed, and put another fried egg on her plate.

"What were *you* doing down there by the river at that hour, anyway?" she asked, by way of counter-attack. "Out all night?"

Hilo hesitated, but Ben had no such qualms about answering. "Christmas in a Refuge," he explained. "We came out for some air."

Maude looked unsurprised. "I thought so."

"Why?" This time it was Hilo who asked.

"The state of your clothes!" said Maude, laughing. She filled up their mugs with more tea and their plates with more toast, and then sat down at the table beside them with a mug of tea for herself. "Tell me about it," she said.

Ben looked at her thoughtfully, with his mouth full of toast, and decided he could trust her.

On consideration, it was a good face he was looking at – a dependable face, squarish and unruffled, with a broad forehead framed by a straight-cut cap of iron-grey hair. The eyes looking into his were brown and uncritical and there was a hint of tolerant amusement about the upturned mouth. And concern. After all, she was the only one in that street of opulent houses who had come out to help. Yes, concern, but not too intrusive an interest. It would be all right to talk to her.

"Why did you come out?" he asked suddenly.

The neutral face smiled a little. "I was letting the cat out. I heard the shout."

Ben nodded. But she needn't have bothered, he thought. The others didn't. Yet she did.

"And anyway, my sister's a doctor," she added, watching the thoughts chase themselves behind Ben's expressive eyes.

"Is she? Where?"

"Here. At the Hammersmith Hospital."

"I suppose she isn't the one they call Doc Never-Stop, is she?"

Maude laughed. "I believe so, yes. Why? Have you met her?"

"She set my arm." He was looking at Maude with less caution

now, even with a glint of mischief. "And she made sure I'd had a hospital dinner!"

"Was that a hardship?"

"No, it was a luxury."

She laughed again. "Well then, what are you worrying about?"

"I'm not," said Ben, sounding quite positive at last.

"So?" Maude was no fool. She knew she had somehow passed the test. "My sister is a caring sort of doctor. And my brother is – " But she didn't go on with that for some reason. Instead, she grinned and added quietly: "I'm just inquisitive."

Ben grinned back. "What do you want to know?"

"Everything." She was still smiling. "From the Refuge backwards."

Ben sighed. Then he began to talk.

He told her about his training in graphics, his leaving home, his friends in Pin Street Market, his stay with Dora and the twins, and the present set-up with old Uncle Allsorts and Annie-Mog, – and how he and Hilo were managing somehow, in spite of the cold and the wet. And here he smiled at Hilo and added softly: "We're a team, see?"

Maude saw. And then she turned to Hilo and prompted her. "And you?"

Hilo still hesitated. But at last she said abruptly: "I left home because I had to. And since then I've had various jobs and various rooms or bits of rooms. But then I got 'flu – " She looked at Ben uncertainly, and then went on: "Once you get thrown out on the street, it's hard to get back." But Ben's encouraging smile was irresistible, and she suddenly smiled back and echoed his words: "Still, as a team we manage pretty well – one way and another."

Maude was looking at them now with a kind of despairing admiration. She thought of her own family, well-launched and out in the world, and probably sleeping off a self-indulgent Christmas somewhere safe and warm and comfortable. And she compared them in her mind with these two uncomplaining children, with their tough, streetwise endurance and their unquenchable optimism about the future. At least, the boy was optimistic – even his mouth curled upwards with hopeful good humour, but with the girl she was not so sure. It was on the tip of her tongue to say: "What else can I do to help". She knew she ought to do so, they so clearly needed a break, but something – maybe her innate caution – made her hold back. She was a bit ashamed of this, and of her next question, which carefully did not commit her to anything.

"What will you do now?" she asked, watching the curious shadows in Hilo's eyes.

"Go back to Uncle Allsorts," said Ben promptly. "And keep looking for a job. Something will turn up." He looked at Hilo, and said with deliberate calm; "Miracles do happen. Don't they, Hilo?"

Light suddenly flowed into Hilo's eyes, banishing the shadows. "Yes," she said, smiling. "They do."

Maude looked from one to the other of them in silence and could not think of a word to say.

They went back to the Refuge to look for Annie and Uncle Allsorts, and were told they'd already gone. Evie and Pete were still there, asleep on the floor, but they didn't disturb them. Let them get what warmth and rest they could.

ˌ "Ben," said Hilo, as they made their way back along the cold winter streets towards Uncle Allsorts and the railway arch, "I think we ought to – "

"I know," agreed Ben, knowing her thoughts before she spoke. "But we'd better ask Allsorts first." He grinned at her astonishment and then added: "Anyway, how will you feel about visiting?"

"Awful," admitted Hilo. "But – I must."

Ben grinned. "You're getting better."

Hilo sighed. "Am I?" She kicked an old coke tin in the gutter. "I'm still an awful coward."

"Aren't we all?" muttered Ben, and kicked the coke tin even harder and even further.

Uncle Allsorts, when approached, grudgingly admitted that there might be room for another girl, if she was desperate.

"She was that all right," said Hilo, and went off with Ben to try to find her. It was the same hospital that had dealt with Ben's arm, so he knew his way around. But at first they were very unhelpful – especially as neither Ben nor Hilo knew the girl's name, nor even the name of her rescuer. But when Ben finally admitted that he and Hilo had helped in the rescue of a girl who nearly drowned (and they couldn't have had more than one of those in a day, could they?), at last they paid him some attention.

And then little Doc Never-Stop came hurrying down the corridor towards the reception desk and overheard the conversation. "Oh, it's you again, is it?" she said, smiling at Ben. "Were you the rescuers?"

"Only the – assistants," said Ben truthfully.

"But she might need a friend," added Hilo, looking appealingly into the little doctor's face.

"So she might," agreed Doc Never-Stop, smiling. "Come with me, then. I'm going that way."

They were led to a long, busy ward, at the end of which they found the quenched white girl they had helped to fish out of the river.

"Some friends to see you," said the doctor, looking down at the girl with smiling concern. Then she hurried off to another patient.

"How're you doing?" asked Ben, looking anxiously into her exhausted face.

"Hi," added Hilo, holding tight to Ben's hand for comfort. "We wondered if – if you needed any help?"

The girl stared at them in tired acceptance. "Was it you?"

Ben nodded. "And the man – what happened to him?"

She sighed. "He went off . . ." Then she seemed to recollect something and added in a small, shamed whisper: "He left me ten pounds . . ." For some reason this simple statement seemed to shake her air of uncaring, flat calm, and she looked about to cry.

"What are you going to do now?" asked Hilo, getting down to essentials.

But this seemed to be the last straw, for the tears began to spill out of the girl's deep-shadowed eyes in childish rivulets. "I'm going home," she said, sounding like a lost child. 'They sent for my mum, you see." The tears had got into her voice, too. "They said – they said she'd been looking for me – looking and looking, they said . . ."

"How long for?" asked Hilo, still intent on essentials.

"N-nine months," the girl stammered, gulping back tears. "I didn't know," she added, her voice a mixture of tears and disbelief. "I didn't realize . . ." She took a shaky breath. "But she's coming, they said – coming, to take me home."

Hilo and Ben looked at one another and smiled. "That's all right then," said Ben. "Isn't it?"

Both he and Hilo watched her then, waiting for her reply. They both knew from their own experience that going home might not be all right – it might be a disaster.

But the girl nodded and tried helplessly to wipe the tears out of her eyes before she spoke again: "I'll – it'll be OK." Then she took a deep, shuddering breath and added, looking at them both with a sudden flash of awareness: "Thanks."

Hilo was remembering the girl's first whispered words when they pulled her out of the river, and now she asked one more probing question. "*Really* thanks?"

"Yes, really," said the girl, and tried to summon up a watery smile. She looked at Ben and a faint spark of mischief touched her tears-tained face. "Not – not to be sneezed at, you said!"

Ben laughed.

Satisfied, Hilo turned to him, signalling urgent things with her eyes.

"Good," Ben said, looking curlier and more cheerful by the second. "We'll go then – since everything's laid on." He looked down at the girl and added softly: "Good luck," before he turned away, with Hilo's hand firmly in his, and made swiftly for the door.

"That wasn't too bad, was it?" he asked, still holding on to Hilo's hand and feeling it still tremble a little in his.

"No," sighed Hilo, and shut her eyes for a moment, taking a long slow breath of resolve. "But I'm glad it's over."

Ben nodded, swinging her hand like a cheerful child as they dodged the puddles in the wet pavement. "She'll be OK now," he added, and gave a little extra skip of hopeful reassurance to underline it. "Happy ending!"

Hilo looked at him and smiled. He's irrepressible, she thought. I wish I could be as absurdly optimistic as he is! Aloud, she said in a sad, quiet voice: "I never asked her name."

"Just as well." Ben skipped over another puddle. "Probably glad to be anonymous – after all that." He tugged at her hand. "Come on. I'll buy you a coffee."

"What with?"

"I do work, you know. And I make something most days with the pavements."

But Hilo was still looking at him oddly. "Ben – what about *your* Mum?"

He stopped dead in the street. "What about her?"

"Mightn't she be – looking for you? Looking and looking, like the girl said?"

Ben shook his head. "No. She knew why I'd gone."

"But she'd have *minded*?"

Ben looked away from Hilo's insistent gaze. "Oh yes," he said carelessly, "she'd have minded."

Hilo was silent for a moment. It was difficult for Hilo, with a mother who had always been an enemy and a source of danger, to imagine someone loving and caring – caring enough to be desolate when her only son left home. After all, she thought, with a sudden shock of awareness, I'd be desolate if Ben went away now.

"I think you should send a message," she said finally.

"How can I? No job and nowhere to live – she'd have a fit."

"You don't have to tell her *anything*," Hilo persisted. "Only that you're alive." She gave his arm a little tug. "Think how she must be feeling."

Ben thought about it. "Well – " he said at last.

"Come on." Hilo tugged harder. "Let's do it now." While you're feeling softened by that girl, she thought. And while I'm feeling braver than usual. I know what to do.

"How?" asked Ben, allowing himself to be towed along the pavement.

"Sally Army," said Hilo. "They run a Message Home thing. No questions asked."

"Are you sure?"

"Sure I'm sure. And I know where to find them."

She did not tell Ben that on one of her worst nights alone they had picked her up and given her soup and a bed in one of their hostels – and asked very carefully if there was anyone likely to be worried at home. "No," she had said then.

141

"Good riddance, I'm afraid." And they had sighed and left her alone.

Now, she pulled Ben purposefully along till they found the little office at the side of the hostel and made him tell the man in charge his name and address at home.

"I'm all right," Ben said, the cheerful mouth still curling hopefully upwards. "Just tell her I'm all right."

The man nodded kindly. "Anything else?"

"No," said Ben. Then, feeling some explanation to be necessary, he added: "Can't go home because of my Dad. She understands."

Once more the grey head nodded, the eyes met his in neutral sympathy. "Suppose – " he said carefully, "any message came back here –? Would you call in again, in case?"

Ben hesitated. But Hilo nudged him and said for him: "Yes. He would."

Ben opened his mouth to protest but, seeing Hilo's face, he closed it again and said nothing.

"All right," said the Salvation Army officer, smiling with less caution. "Call back soon. Remember."

Ben murmured a non-committal "Yes," and dragged Hilo away. "You bulldozed me."

"I know. Sorry." She looked up at him seriously, willing him not to be angry. "Might be important."

Ben conceded that it might. He was a fair-minded boy. And Hilo was only trying to help. It would do no good to scold her. She was still much too sad anyway, without him making things worse. He thought of the strange happenings of the day, and sighed a little, though there was a glimmer of a smile behind it.

"It was a funny old Christmas, wasn't it?"

"Yes," agreed Hilo and gave him a sudden lopsided grin. "It was."

Ben observed that grin with some relief. "I think we've earned that coffee," he said.

They sat in a warm little sandwich bar where the steam from the coffee machine made patterns on the windows, and an overhead speaker blared out a cheerful stream of sound that

142

might have been music. Ben allowed himself to relax and thaw in the comforting warmth, and hoped Hilo would soon begin to look less pinched and cold.

But Hilo had pulled out an old, battered notebook from her duffel-bag and was scribbling something down in it, oblivious to the roar of the coffee machine or the piped music or the general clatter of the customers. She had never yet shown Ben anything she had written – never even admitted what was in her shabby folder. (After all, she had only ever shown Max one piece.) But this time when she had finished writing, she handed it to him without a word. Somehow, that anxious look of his, wanting so much to see her smile, so relieved when she did, had shaken her out of her private darkness. That, and the sudden realization of how much she would miss Ben if he went away – how much she had come to rely on his unfailing cheerfulness and courage. So now she simply gave him her newest bit of writing as a spontaneous gift, – since it was sparked off by him anyway. Maybe it would reassure him more than a mere fleeting grin could do.

Ben took it in his hand and read it slowly and carefully. He could scarcely believe his eyes. But it was there, all of it – the magic and the sadness, the miracle and the darkness – and his own words staring up at him from the page.

"I thought I heard it once, –
The singing of the stars,
Sweet seraphim?
Far voices echoing?
A snatch, a glimpse,
Light-glancing sound,
Ephemeral, enveiled.
A music filled with distance, –
While worlds,
While universes
Still rolled round.

'Miracles still happen,' you said,
Turning your listening head.

143

But then a girl fell, broken,
Like Icarus from the sun,
A falling star
Quenched in the muddied waters, –
No miracle for her.

The singing was gone then, –
A silent, empty sky.
But you said '*Life*,'
And I heard the stars go by."


"*Hilo*," he said, in a voice soft with wonder. And then added, almost under his breath: "I might've known . . ."

"Known what?" She was looking up at him with puzzled shyness.

You are as much of a romantic as I am, and just as hopeful, really, he thought. But he did not say it. Instead, he simply took her hand in his and murmured obscurely: "Safe . . ."

Hilo did not misunderstand him. She gave a long, long sigh of release and extraordinary gladness. So it was all right. He would not laugh. He would never laugh at her work. Their thoughts marched together – dreams and illusions, all safe. That strange, secret innermost core of the heart which she had fought so fiercely to protect was safe. Understood, unspoken, but safe.

Slow tears began to rise and shimmer behind her eyes, and Ben saw them. He smiled and stretched out his other hand to touch the shadows beneath them. "Beautiful," he murmured, and she did not know whether he meant the words she had written or her own face. But it did not matter. There was recognition in his voice, and something more that made it pulse with certainty.

"Beautiful," he said again, "and safe . . ."

And Hilo's wilderness suddenly flowered.


The half-hearted promise to "call back" at the Sally Hostel reminded Ben that he had also promised to call back at the papershop near the old Pin Street Market site. It wouldn't do any harm to ask if there was any news of Al, he supposed, and

144

now that he had a bit of work at the fruit stall, he needn't seem to be begging for a job.

He took Hilo with him this time, in between setting up the morning stall for Corky and getting down to his pavement drawing, before Hilo had time to get cold playing her tin whistle to the passing crowds.

"Ah," said Reg, the newsagent, looking at Ben over the top of a great pile of glossy magazines. "Gotta letter for you."

"For me?" Ben looked astonished.

Reg reached under the counter and brought out a crumpled envelope. "Someone from the old market gang brought it – name of Rigs. Friend of Al's, was he?"

"Yes," said Ben, feeling a surprising wave of longing for the old market days with their cheerful comings and goings. "He was."

He took the envelope from Reg and after a moment's hesitation opened it there and then in the shop. For some reason he could not explain he felt he owed it to Reg, who had kept the letter for him so faithfully and never tried to look inside. He took out the single sheet of paper, and as he did so, three ten pound notes fluttered out on to the floor.

He looked from them to Reg, almost apologetically. "Did you know what was in it?"

Reg grinned cheerfully. "I might've – "

Ben shook his head in disbelief. Hilo, meanwhile, stooped down and picked up the notes and handed them back to Ben. They were much too precious to leave lying about.

"What does Al say?" asked Reg, still sounding cheerful. "Is he in the money, then?"

"Not yet." Ben was rapidly scanning Al's spidery handwriting. "He says he's going to court and he's got a good case, and so have I." He turned the piece of paper over and looked at the other side. "And he's doing all right, so this is just an instalment." He looked from Hilo to Reg with rueful protest. "Honestly! He doesn't need to do this."

"He thinks he does," said Reg seriously. "Worries about you, he does."

Ben almost scowled,– except that his curly mouth refused to do anything so downhearted. "I'm OK, Reg. You can tell him

145

that if he calls in again. And thank him, of course." He moved towards the door, suddenly embarrassed.

"There's a bit of a job, early mornings," said Reg suddenly, "sorting and such – if you want it?"

Ben paused. "I'm working early," he explained, "setting up a stall. But thanks for offering."

"Could I do it?" asked Hilo, and turned an appealing gaze on Reg. She saw him hesitate, and added: "I'm quite strong, and I can come as early as you like."

Ben was looking at her doubtfully. "Hilo – " he began, but she interrupted with swift determination.

"I can do it Ben – when you're setting up for Corky. I've got to start *somewhere*!"

Reg looked her up and down, half-smiling, and turned an enquiring face to Ben. "Mate of yours?"

"Sure."

"And you're a mate of Al's." He was grinning more broadly now. "Can't lose, can I?"

"I hope not," said Ben.

"Of course not," said Hilo.

Then they all looked at each other and laughed.

But even so, Ben was worried at the idea of Hilo working. She was still very thin and fragile after the recent bout of 'flu, and she still had a cough, though it was not so bad as Annie-Mog's which worried him even more.

"Are you sure you want to do this?" he asked, turning her round to face him in the street. "You don't have to."

"I *do* have to," Hilo contradicted, her mouth straight. "I need to earn something, Ben. I can't sponge on you for ever."

"You don't sponge. You earn quite a bit, busking."

"Not enough." Her mouth was still a straight line of defence, and Ben hardly dared to mention what he wanted to do next. He knew it would start another argument. But he had to – oh yes, he *had* to . . . He looked at her warily, wondering how to go about it, and then lost his nerve and began to walk on again, saying nothing.

But Hilo gave him the opening he needed. She stopped looking belligerent and smiled at him with sudden warmth.

146

"You worry too much." And when Ben did not respond but kept on walking, she laid a hand on his arm and said: "Where are we going?"

Ben took a deep breath. "To buy you a sleeping bag."

"*What?*"

He sighed. "Hilo, it makes sense. Don't be angry." He made a curious little appealing gesture with his hand, almost as if warding off a blow. "It's the only way – the only time we're likely to have that much money all at once."

"Ben! Al sent it to *you*"

"So he did," agreed Ben. "And I've decided what I want to do with it." His voice was unexpectedly firm and unyielding. "I got mine free, Hilo. I was lucky. Now it's your turn."

She shook her head. "I can't – "

"Yes. You can pay me back in stages if you like, but you're going to have it – *now*."

"But Ben – "

"It's important," he insisted. "Don't you see? If you get ill again, where will you be? Remember what Uncle Allsorts said – about hospital?" It was unfair of him, he knew, but he wanted to scare her a little. He saw her shiver, and waited a little longer to see if she was near persuasion. Then went on, pressing it home. "This way, at least you'll be warm at night. It may make all the difference."

Hilo just looked at him despairingly. "What am I to do with you?"

"Trust me," said Ben, beginning to smile as he scented victory. "Come on, we'll try the cut price army surplus on the corner," and tucking his arm through hers before she could protest any further he led her away.

They had just reached a narrow alley before the corner when it happened. Hilo heard the footsteps first and just had time to shout a warning before they attacked. There were two of them, both heavier and tougher than Ben, and they fell on him with practised violence. Ben twisted sideways under the assault and pulled free, landing a couple of glancing blows on his assailants as he did so. But they waded in again harder than ever.

Hilo, with swift and instant reaction, blew two loud, shrill notes on her tin whistle – it might sound enough like a police

147

whistle to bring assistance. Then she started hitting out wildly at whichever head she could reach with the hard little metal pipe. The two attackers yelled in surprise at this unexpected assault, and Ben followed up the moment of advantage with a couple of well-timed punches in strategic places. Hilo closed in, still hitting out with her pipe and landed a fierce kick in the groin for the nearest thug. He doubled up and howled in anguish, but Hilo saw the other mugger reach inside his belt and produce something that gleamed wickedly in his hand.

"Look out!" she shouted to Ben. "He's got a knife." And she took time out to blow another shrill blast on her pipe.

At this point, a policeman actually did appear round the corner – and at the same time Ben landed a hard, chopping blow on the flailing arm that wielded the knife. The two attackers saw the approaching uniform and suddenly decided they had had enough. They had seriously underestimated their victims' resistance. Now they fled down the street, leaving their knife behind. The policeman gave half-hearted chase, but he knew he could not catch them once they got into the maze of back yards behind the alleyway. After a few minutes he strolled back to see how the victims were. Clearly they were not too bad, for they were picking themselves up and dusting each other down.

"Are you all right?" asked Ben and Hilo both at once. Then they began to laugh.

"Are you all right?" repeated the policeman, who had seen quite enough to sum up the situation. After all, it was common enough. "Did they get anything?"

"No," grunted Ben, putting a quick, protective hand on his inner pocket where Al's money was still safe.

"They must've followed us," Hilo said suddenly. "They must've seen us in the paper shop."

"Why?" The policeman's eyes were alert and questioning.

"Well, I mean, look at us," Hilo pointed out. "No-one in their right mind would expect *us* to have anything worth stealing, would they?"

"So?" The questioning glance was still on them.

Ben explained about Al's letter and the bank notes fluttering to the floor. "They must've been outside," he said. "Looking for a quick grab. I suppose they just took a chance – " He shrugged helplessly, and discovered that various parts of his shoulders and arms hurt quite a lot when he moved.

"Well, if you're sure you're all right," said the constable, and suddenly smiled at Hilo as he turned to go. "That was a good idea – blowing that pipe of yours."

Hilo grinned. "It has its uses!" But she caught Ben's eye and did not elaborate. After all, busking was probably illegal anyway, though mostly the police didn't bother them about it.

They stood together, watching the constable out of sight before they went on towards the cut price shop on the corner.

"Have you been mugged before?" asked Ben.

"Why?"

"You seemed so – certain what to do!"

Hilo laughed. "Instinct!" She glanced at him sideways. "Yes, I have, though. When I looked more – er – respectable . . . And things got stolen in most of the squats I was in. Jungle law." She sighed. "You learn the hard way."

Ben grinned. "Streetwise, they call it."

Hilo was still smiling at him. "Is that why you took me to Uncle Allsorts?"

"Of course. It's safe there, at least."

She nodded. She did not say: "Safe and warm and protected – and you are absurdly good to me," because she knew it would only embarrass him. Instead, she submitted meekly to being bought the best sleeping bag that Al's money could buy, while secretly resolving to pay back every penny of it with whatever she could earn.

They carried it home in triumph, and that night Hilo slept warm and comfortable for the first time in many weeks. But it did not altogether stop her coughing. Ben woke once or twice at the sound and worried about it in the small hours. He also worried about Annie-Mog, whose cough seemed to be getting worse with every cold winter dawn that came. Even the little stripey cat, Yoki, who had attached herself permanently to Annie, seemed disturbed. She prowled round Annie's restlessly-turning body, cringed at each racking bout of coughing, and then crept close again when it subsided, curling into a warm, comforting ball against Annie's side.

In those bitter mornings it was usually Annie who got up first,

149

Annie who started the fire and boiled the first kettle of tea. And the little cat got up when Annie did and went off on her own day-long forage for food and warmth. But now Annie seemed to find it harder and harder to get up, and Yoki stayed with her, curled up in a tight ball of protective warmth. Now it was Ben who got up first, and Ben who got the fire going, by which time Hilo had got up too, and had filled the kettle from Uncle Allsorts' big plastic water-bottle and set it on the reluctant flames of the damp wood fire.

Uncle Allsorts himself was usually sleeping off the latest attack on the gin bottle, but even he was getting worried about Annie-Mog, watching her anxiously out of bloodshot eyes when she began to stir. The only comfort he could offer was more gin – or sometimes rum if he'd been lucky on the daily scrounge. But Annie accepted either cheerfully enough, and went on coughing and wheezing by the smoky fire.

Ben and Hilo took to coming back at lunchtime from their busking and pavement drawing to see if Annie was all right. She had almost given up her usual daily wanderings. She stayed hunched by the fire, accompanied by the anxious little cat, Yoki, who never left her side, not doing anything very much. This worried them more than anything for Annie had always been a vigorous and active scrounger, with her own private round of likely spots and sympathetic stallholders and small shopkeepers. They all knew Annie; she was a practised "collector" of useful objects – almost as good at it as Uncle Allsorts – and always seemed to know where extra food or extra blankets might be obtainable. But now all that daily routine seemed to have been abandoned, and it fell more and more to Ben and Hilo, or Evie and Pete, to bring in the group's subsistence rations. Uncle Allsorts did what he could, when he remembered and the gin fumes did not befuddle him too much, but the weaker and frailer Annie became, the more Uncle seemed to sink his anxieties in his latest bottle, and his temper became even more unpredictable.

Even so, Ben managed to make Hilo's little puppet to go with her pipe, hoping it would bring in more cash from the intrigued passers-by. He brought home some broken crates from the fruit stall, and saved the best pieces for the puppet while Hilo fed the rest to the fire to keep Annie warm. He carved a rugged little head with a pointed nose and chin and a wide, smiling mouth. Then he looked round for something for her hair.

"Pull orff a bitta fringe," wheezed Annie, waving one of her tattered wool scarves at him. And while Ben carefully unravelled the old brown wool, Hilo filled an empty gin bottle with hot water and wrapped it in a bit of blanket to put by Annie's feet, to compensate for the lost bit of fringe.

"You look so cold," she muttered, wrapping yet another bit of blanket round Annie's shoulders.

"Huh!" snorted Annie staunchly. "Used to it, aren't I?" Then she instructed Ben in great detail how to boil up a few old fish heads to make a strong, usable glue.

The carved head acquired a wealth of stringy brown wool hair. Then Hilo brought back a needle and thread from the corner shop, and Uncle Allsorts sacrificed one of his grubby red spotted handkerchiefs to make the puppet a skirt. And Evie and Pete, getting into the spirit of the thing, brought back some nearly-empty tins of paint from a building site, so that the puppet could have a painted face.

"The colours are a bit weird," said Evie apologetically, "but there's a bit of red for her mouth."

"And some black for her eyebrows," added Pete.

"What shall we do with the green?" wondered Evie.

"Give her long fingers and toes, Ben, and we can paint them green, like a witch," instructed Hilo, smiling.

Finally, Ben bought some eyelet screws from the DIY store, and carefully linked all the tiny puppet's arms and legs and nodding head and clacking feet into a well-strung whole.

"Look!" he said, jigging the strings up and down from their two wooden crossbars, "she dances quite well!"

But the question was, could Hilo make her dance and play the pipe as well? After various attempts and experiments, they discovered it was possible if Hilo attached the wooden crossbar to the end of her pipe and jigged it up and down rather more markedly than necessary as she played. The Irish jig was a great success, once she got good enough at it to forget about her fingers. Even Uncle Allsorts grinned approval.

151

"We'll try it out tomorrow," said Ben, and smiled encouragingly at Hilo. "It'll be a cinch!"

Hilo looked at Annie-Mog and played the jig again, hoping to make her smile. And this time the thin little cat, Yoki, seemed to recall some dim memory of her kitten days and pounced and dabbed with her velvet paws at the little puppet's clattering feet, seeming to dance a jig of her own. Then even Annie's ravaged face broke into a delighted grin.

"There!" she cackled happily. "Even a cat can dance!"

But her laughter sparked off another bout of coughing. The others looked at each other anxiously and tried not to show their concern.

The next day they tried out the puppet by the underground station, and drew quite a crowd of fascinated onlookers. The money in Hilo's upturned cap grew steadily, and she played till her fingers ached.

That evening they took home a special tin of chicken soup for Annie and heated it over the fire. But though Annie tried to drink it, she found it difficult to swallow. Her breathing seemed to have become very fast and shallow.

Ben went to Uncle Allsorts and tackled him head-on. "What are we going to do about Annie?"

The old man shrugged in apparent unconcern and waved a half-empty gin bottle at Ben. "What can we do?"

"A hostel?"

"Won't go. I've tried." He took another angry swig. "Obstinate," he added, stating the obvious.

"Hospital?"

"You'd have to carry her. Kickin' and screamin', most likely."

"What then?"

Allsorts shrugged again. Ben wanted to shake him but he knew, really, that the old man was simply covering his own sense of despair. There was nothing they could do for Annie. She wouldn't let them.

"Been on the street a long time," said Allsorts, by way of excuse. "Can't see her leaving now."

"She might have to." Ben was getting desperate.

"Huh!" grunted Allsorts. "Feet first!"

Ben gave up. He went back to Hilo, who was trying to persuade Annie to drink something hot – anything to keep some warmth in her wasted body. But Annie seemed almost beyond understanding what was happening, – almost gone from them into a land of cold shadows where no voice, no friendly touch could reach her.

Hilo looked at Ben in despair and laid down the cup and spoon on the frozen winter ground. They had built up the fire higher than usual, and brought Annie as close to it as they could, piling blankets, newspapers and cardboard boxes all round her to keep out the chill air. They had filled two more empty bottles with hot water, wrapped them in anything they could find and laid them near Annie's feet, but nothing seemed to make her warm, even though her head felt burning to the touch. Great rigors shook her from time to time, and in between she seemed to drift into even deeper oblivion. The only thing that roused her was Yoki, the little stripey cat, who crept out of the shadows and folded itself into the crook of Annie's outflung arm and tried to warm her with its thin, mangy body.

Ben and Hilo decided to sit up with Annie and keep the fire burning all night, but they were both tired with the day's work and the long hours on the streets, so towards morning they both fell asleep to the sound of Uncle Allsorts' spasmodic snores and Annie's laboured breathing – and the fire burnt low.

They woke with a start, well before it was light, and wondered what had disturbed them. For a few moments they both lay where they were, listening to the familiar night sounds, – a distant train – a taxi in the street – a tug hooting down river – and the usual rhythmic reassurances of close breathing. Only it wasn't usual, that was the trouble. They could hear Uncle Allsorts' mingled snores and grunts, – and Evie and Pete further off behind the archway. But from Annie, who was nearest, they could hear nothing at all.

Hilo started up first and went swiftly across to lean over the crumpled heap of blankets by the fire, and Ben was quick to follow.

They looked down and could see nothing in the darkness,

but Hilo stretched out a hand and touched Annie's face. It was cold. Stone cold. Deathly cold. The only thing that was warm was the tightly curled furry body of the little cat that was still lying close in the crook of Annie's arm, refusing to move.

"I think she's dead," said Hilo in a strange, flat voice.

"I think so too," agreed Ben. He put his arms round Hilo, holding her tight against the terrors of the night.

The usual nightmare of death and swift despatch ensued. An ambulance was called. The police were told. Questions were asked, and very gruffly answered by a shattered Uncle Allsorts, who was either too drunk or too overcome with grief (or both) to give a coherent account of anything.

Ben and Hilo said what they could, and so did Evie and Pete. But the situation seemed clear enough to the police. A homeless old bag lady had died on the street – probably of pneumonia due to the cold. It was a common enough occurrence these days, and did not really excite much comment. No doubt a hospital doctor would confirm what had happened – and that would be that.

But Hilo, white-faced and curiously angry, sat down by Annie's smoky fire, beside the desolate little cat, and wrote her rage and grief down on a clean white page.

### GOD IS DEAD.

"What d'you expect?" they said.
"God's dead."
But I didn't believe them.

I pointed at sunsets and starry heights,
And new beech leaves, and a wild duck's flight,
And a stranger's smile, and all that crap.

They said they hadn't any tears on tap
Right now. It was too cold to cry.
Much simpler to die,
Like God, they said, who was dead.
But I didn't believe them.

154

I said I wasn't that kind of dope,
And I was perfectly sure I could cope.
You've got to believe in something, I told them,
And hang on to dreams, if you can hold them.
After all, no-one can live without hope.

"Just so," they said.
"And God is dead."
But I didn't believe them.

And then someone stole my last pair of socks,
And even my matches and my cardboard box.
"You see?" they said.
"We told you God was dead."
But I didn't believe them.

After all, I said, we have survived
So far, by hook or crook.
There's always something to scrounge if you look.
But then my friend lay down and sighed
"It's cold out here," and quietly died.

"I told you so," they said.
"God's dead."
And I believed them.

When she had finished, she sat there looking at it with tears in
her eyes, until Ben came and found her and read what she had
written, leaning over her shoulder beside the smoky fire. Then
he said in a strange, broken voice: "Oh Hilo – oh no. No, Hilo,
no . . ." and folded her in his arms and rocked her to and fro like
a child until her tears really came and she wept helplessly in his
hard embrace.

It did not last long – Hilo was always ashamed of tears – but
she felt better afterwards, and Ben took her walking by the river
and said nothing else at all, only watched anxiously to see the
colour come back into her face, and then bought her a coffee at
the all-night stall by the embankment.

In the afternoon he persuaded her to go with him and play
her pipe and make the little puppet dance while he did a new
pavement drawing. (Make it *bright*, Benny-boy!) He thought

being busy and reasonably independent was the best thing for Hilo at the moment.

"Play for Annie," he said. "It made her laugh, remember? And the little cat danced."

He looked at Hilo sideways, willing her to understand. And Hilo suddenly lifted her head and smiled. "All right," she said. "I will."

And her fingers began the Irish jig, and the little puppet danced and danced on the pavement, tossing her spotted hand-kerchief skirt and nodding her wooden head with its crown of stringy woollen-fringe hair, and tapping her little green wooden feet on the hard cold stone like a demented thing.

Well, if ever Annie-Mog wanted a lively wake, she's got it now, thought Ben. And Hilo, meeting his eyes, thought the same thing. She went on playing till there was no more rage, only a kind of rueful pity, left in her heart – though she could not be sure whom the pity was for, Annie or herself or Ben, or all the heedless world?

"That's it!" said Ben. "Make it dance!" (Keep it *bright*!) "Play Annie home."

From then on, it seemed to Ben, Hilo began to lose heart. He managed to make her laugh from time to time, but the brief glances of sunlight did not last, too often she returned to a sombre silence.

He took her walking through the parks or along the embank-ment, and tried to divert her by every means he could muster, but nothing really dispelled the look of bleak disillusion behind her stoic gaze. She didn't complain, but her strength was failing and her cough was getting worse. Remembering how Annie-Mog had been before the end, Ben was getting frightened; he knew he had got to do something to change the comfortless pattern of their lives.

He went down to the job centre and badgered them some more, (after waiting about for nearly four hours before he could talk to anyone). But they told him to try another centre some way off – there might be more vacancies in that area. He walked across London to the other regional centre, and found he was too late for that day, the office was closed. The next morning he had

156

another four-hour wait before he saw anyone, and then was told to go back where he came from.

The same thing happened at the social security offices – more waiting – more stone-walling – more indifference. He was too young for the dole – there was no emergency fund for which he qualified.

He went back to the housing department, and they told him yet again that their waiting list was already too long for them to cope with – even for couples with children, let alone stray single youths who should be in a hostel. Even bed and breakfast had to be allocated to really *deserving* cases. Ben wanted to tell them that Hilo *was* a really deserving case – who more so than a sick, homeless girl of fifteen? But he knew their answer would only be: "Well, then, a children's home or a girls' hostel – if they've got room, which they haven't."

He went away in despair and tried to talk to Hilo. But she only smiled at him rather dimly and said: "I'm all right, Ben. Stop worrying," and went on playing her pipe by the underground station entrance as the crowds came home from work.

One day she fainted in the street, and Ben had to half-carry her home. Home? A windy street and a dripping railway arch? Half a plastic sheet and a couple of thin army blankets? And one good, draught-proof sleeping bag?

It wasn't enough. He knew it wasn't enough to save Hilo – and he had got to do something about it. Now. But first he had got to talk to Hilo, – and in order to do that he had got to get her on her feet again, at least for the moment.

With this thought of immediate revival uppermost in his mind, he steered her into the nearest steamy café and led her to a table near the wall where she could lean back and rest until she recovered a little.

"How much did you eat today?" he demanded, putting a mug of hot soup into her cold, stiff hands.

"The same as you."

Ben frowned. That meant a hunk of hard bread and a piece of stale cheese for breakfast, and half a tuna sandwich at lunchtime. "Not enough," he growled, shaking his head. "Not when you're ill." He got up and went over to the counter to see what else he could afford. Steak-and-kidney pie? That would be fairly filling, and reasonably nourishing as well, – if she would eat it.

He carried it back to her and sat down opposite the weary, disconsolate figure at the little table. "Hilo, we've got to talk."

She raised heavy-lidded eyes to him, obedient but strangely disinterested. "What about?"

"You."

She sighed. "Lost cause, Ben. Don't waste your breath."

Ben wanted to shake her. "You are *not* a lost cause. But you will be unless we do something positive."

"Such as?"

He hesitated. He knew the alternatives, but he hardly dared to spell them out to her. "A hostel?"

"No."

"Why not?"

"They wouldn't keep me more than a night."

"How d'you know?"

"Tried it. They said I was too young." She laughed a little wildly, but it made her cough, and this time when she coughed Ben saw her wince.

"Then –" he began, even more hesitantly.

"The alternative?" There were tears of pain in her eyes now, but she shook them out fiercely. "A home for delinquent girls off the streets? No thanks."

"But what are we to do?" Ben sounded quite desperate.

Hilo looked at him and smiled. "Nothing. I'll get by." Then, seeing his distress, she put out one hand and patted his arm kindly. "Stop worrying. It's only a cold – it'll go." And when he still looked unconvinced she added: "And I've got my sleeping bag." She gave his arm a little shake. "Honestly Ben, I'll be OK. You do far too much for me already."

He blinked a little in the light and warmth of the café, telling himself that it was the steam, not tears of frustration, that blurred his eyes with broken images.

"I don't like you being ill," he muttered. "But I've tried everything . . ."

"I know you have."

"Even a squat."

"Which one was that?"

"Over by Mill Street. But they said they were full up – and anyway . . ." he glanced at her warily, "I didn't much like the set-up."

She grinned palely. "What were they on?"

"Not sure. But it looked a bit lethal. Two of them were out to the world, and one was fighting the wallpaper."

She nodded. "Better away from all that."

Ben felt he was getting nowhere fast. "But if you get really ill –?"

"I won't," said Hilo, and set her mouth in a firm line of determination. "Here – have a bit of pie, and dry up."

Ben sighed. "Hilo – I'm serious."

"I know." Her voice was suddenly soft. "I know, Ben. But it's all right." She closed her eyes for a moment, summoning strength, and Ben could see the shimmer of tears beneath her lashes. He did not know that it was his absurd concern and kindness that made her come so close to weeping into her soup.

"You know what Uncle Allsorts said about hospital," he warned. "And – and he's got very edgy since Annie went."

Hilo nodded. She knew about Uncle Allsorts and his uncertain temper, – and his increasingly fuddled dependence on his gin bottles. "It won't come to that," she said, trying to sound convincing.

Ben just looked at her, seeing the tired droop of her shoulders and the lustreless fall of her hair round her pale, shadowed face, and the way she still fought so gallantly not to let that vulnerable mouth look less than straight and determined. It was still a fighting face, but it was transparent and paper-thin, and his heart ached when he saw how hard she had to struggle to keep her frail resolve intact.

"We'd better go," she said. "Can't fall asleep in here." She got groggily to her feet and waited for Ben to follow her.

He put a steadying arm round her shoulders and together they went out again into the cold winter streets. Nothing was resolved, he thought, – and Hilo was clearly almost too ill to stand. Something had got to be done.

"I'll curl up by the fire," she said, hugging Ben's arm close to her side. "Pete brought in some more broken crates last night. We'll be fine."

"Oh yes," sighed Ben. "Fine." But he felt like Canute trying to turn back the tide.

It was a day or two later, while he was walking alone down by the river, that he remembered Maude. He remembered the opulent house on the river terrace – the white and gold bathroom – the wonderful warmth of the kitchen, and the lavish breakfast . . . And he remembered Maude's neutral, compassionate face, and how he had felt instinctively that he could trust it. She had been a good listener – sympathetic but uncritical, and he remembered that she had been the only one who had come out of that row of well-to-do riverside homes to offer help. Would she help now? But it was one thing to rush out when an unknown girl jumped in the river, – and quite another to give shelter to a sick and homeless waif like Hilo. It would be committing yourself to more than just a momentary crisis. He couldn't really imagine that happening . . . But her sister was a doctor – that brisk and caring young woman known as Little Doc Never-Stop. And some of her caring nature had clearly rubbed off on Maude. Maybe she would help . . . Or maybe get Hilo to hospital? The decision would not be his, at least . . . But that seemed like betrayal somehow. Could he do that to Hilo?

Once more in his worried mind he went over the alternatives – the people he knew – the hopeless round of endlessly closing doors – social security offices and their rules and regulations – hostels – care orders and homes for delinquent girls – hospital. Hospital. It would come to that in the end if he didn't do something – and Hilo still trembled all over and her eyes went black with terror at the mere mention of the word.

Then there were the people he knew . . . Al was away somewhere unreachable. Reg at the papershop was friendly enough, especially since Hilo had begun to work for him in the mornings. But she had been too ill even to do that these last few days. Somehow he didn't think Reg would put up with someone who was sick and a liability. Life was hard enough for him already . . . Then there was Corky who ran the fruit stall. But he didn't live there at all, – he only arrived each morning in a van loaded with stock. He never told Ben where he lived or if he lived anywhere but in his van. No, that wouldn't do . . . And of course, there was Dora – tough, warm-hearted Dora and the twins and the cramped space of the cosy little trailer. But her Jack was back now; there would be no room for strangers. No, *no room for strangers*.

He sighed, remembering that he had left Hilo asleep by the fire for too long without checking. Better go back and see how she was. He stopped at the coffee stall and bought two hot dogs and some hot soup in a plastic container, then hurried back to the railway arch and the dubious protection of Uncle Allsorts.

Hilo was awake when he got back. She smiled hazily in his direction, but he got the impression that she did not really see him very clearly. There were two spots of high colour in her white face now, and her eyes glittered with fever.

"Can you drink this?" he said, propping her up against his arm.

She tried gamely to swallow the hot liquid, but it made her choke and cough. The hot-dog she could not manage at all.

Ben's heart sank. He was sure she was worse today. Somehow he had to keep the fact from Uncle Allsorts, who would get very fierce and start muttering about hospital again, which would upset Hilo even more.

As he thought this, the old man himself appeared from round the corner, rattling as much as ever in his armoury of tins and bottles, and wheezing with the effort of struggling along under the weight of all that unnecessary gear.

"Huh!" he growled, glaring at Hilo. "Sitting up and taking notice, are we? Just as well."

Just as well what? thought Ben, and scarcely dared to go further in his mind.

"Hullo, Uncle," whispered Hilo, giving him a dazzling, unseeing smile. "Lovely sky . . ."

"Lovely *wot*?" rasped Allsorts.

"Sky," repeated Hilo sighing a little. "Clouds . . ." She looked up at the lowering storm clouds that were chasing themselves across the faintly sunlaced London haze, and smiled at them as if they were old friends. Then she lay down again and closed her eyes. But she wasn't asleep, for one hot and burning hand came out and grasped Ben's in a silent demand for comfort. Ben gripped it firmly in his and sat on in the twilight, wondering what to do next.

In the morning Ben went to work without rousing Hilo, scurried madly through the setting-up process and got roundly cursed by Corky for being clumsy with the tomatoes, and then decided to rush back to see how Hilo was before getting down to his usual pavement drawing. But while he was turning away from Corky's stall, a shadow fell on him and a figure detached itself from the early morning gloom.

"Hullo, Ben," it said. "I've been looking for you."

Ben stood still, heart thumping. The police? Had he done anything wrong? But it wasn't the police. In the half-light of a winter dawn he had mistaken the uniform. It was the Salvation Army officer he had met at the hostel when he sent his message home.

"Me?" he said, sounding a bit squeaky with surprise. "Why?"

"We had a message back," said the voice, and the figure came nearer so that Ben could see his face. It was a rugged, kindly one and, posed no particular threat. But it looked concerned. "We've spent a bit of time finding you," said the man, smiling a little grimly. "But old Uncle Allsorts usually knows where people are."

"Was it him?" Ben was confused. "He didn't say anything to me."

"Left it to us," the man shrugged. "Usually leaves things be, does Allsorts." The smile was still a bit grim.

Ben looked at it with misgiving. "Well then – what's the message?"

"I'm afraid it's bad news," said the officer, no smile apparent now. "Your father's had a stroke, and is not expected to recover."

"Oh, my God," said Ben, and then gave the Sally Army a fleeting smile of apology. "Sorry! . . . Did – was it my mother who left the message?"

"I don't know. It was just a telephone call. 'If you can find Ben, tell him his father is dying.'" He was blunt now, but at the same time he laid a kindly hand on Ben's arm. "I'm sorry, son. But you had to know."

Ben nodded. He was thinking furiously, wondering how to resolve the various crises which had suddenly descended on him. Hilo was ill. Too ill to leave. His father was dying. His mother would be coping alone. He must go home. He had no money to deal with either situation. What was he to do?

"Got any money?" asked the officer, sounding brisk and practical.

"A bit," admitted Ben cautiously. (But not enough to be any use, really.) "And I can hitch," he added, half to himself. "But – " he wondered if he could tell the friendly man about Hilo, and then decided against it. A hostel would be the answer, they would say, or one of their Homes for Girls. He shuddered, picturing Hilo's face.

"Here," said the officer, "it's all we're allowed to give at one time – but it may help a little," and he handed Ben a ten-pound note.

Ben smiled at him gratefully. "Thanks. It'll help a lot."

The kindly face regarded him seriously and a hand patted his arm. "Go home, Ben. They need you there." He turned away, and called over his shoulder: "Good luck!"

Sighing, Ben put the money away, wondering which of various urgent things he ought to do with it. The price of a room in a hostel for two nights? But two nights would not cure Hilo. The price of a really good, nourishing meal – (or two?), but Hilo wouldn't be able to eat it. The price of another warm blanket – or a waterproof cape to spread over everything at night when it rained? But Hilo needed more than that. She needed a roof over her head, a warm bed, a place of comfort and safety, away from the bitter frosts and drenching rains of winter. Where was he to find it? He knew now, really, but he was afraid to take the risk. Afraid to commit her to someone else's care and go off without her. What if they refused? What if she was left even more stranded – even more destitute and deserted – than before? How could he leave her, not knowing what would happen to her?

He made his way back to the railway arch and Hilo, racked with indecision. On the way, he bought some more take-away soup and a carton of milk. At least he could keep Hilo going for today, if she would only take it.

As he arrived back at the corner, he met Allsorts coming out.

163

He was carrying an old billycan in one hand, and when he saw Ben he looked a bit sheepish and explained: "Gotta getta drop of water – she drank some tea."

Ben smiled at him with a sudden rush of gratitude. This battered, broken old man, riven by his friend Annie's death, still had time to look after Hilo – as best he could.

"Rice puddin'," he said unexpectedly. "That'll do her good. I know a place as does it." He looked hard at Ben, and added in a rough, brittle voice: "You goin', then?"

Ben shook his head. "Not till she's better – or safe somewhere."

"Better getta move on, then," growled Allsorts. "She's bad, Ben. Real bad." He hitched a few more tins at a less rakish angle and prepared to move off. "I tell you" he added, sounding very fierce indeed, "if she's no better termorrer, I'm calling the ambulance." His hot, angry eyes bored into Ben's, willing him to understand. "Annie was bad enough," he muttered, still angry and belligerent. "Can't let it happen *agen*." He gave Ben one last, furious glare, and stumped off down the road.

Ben went quietly across to Hilo and sat down beside her. She seemed to be asleep, but her breathing was getting very fast and shallow – like Annie's – and he was afraid.

"Hilo?" he said.

She did not answer.

He tried again, but she only sighed and turned over in her sleeping bag, breaking into a fit of coughing as she did so.

After that he was afraid to rouse her. It only seemed to make things worse. He debated whether to try to get a spoonful or two of soup down her throat, but he was scared of making her choke. Instead, he simply built up the smoky fire with the rest of Pete's broken crates, and laid his own blankets and his coat round Hilo in an attempt to keep the winter chill at bay. All day he sat beside her, debating in his mind what he should do.

Once she roused herself a little, and he hastened to warm up some milk on the fire in one of Allsorts' old tins. She could not hold the cup, but submitted meekly enough to swallowing it spoonful by spoonful as Ben held her head up. Then she sank down again, murmuring: "Ben? . . . Better . . . soon . . ." and seemed to drift off before he could answer.

164

She woke once more, with a sudden start, seeming frightened and lost for a moment, looking round her with scared, over-bright eyes as if she did not know where she was. "Ben?" she whispered, and when he answered: "Yes, I'm here," she fell back again as if reassured. And even in her exhausted state she managed a faint smile. "Sky?" she said. "*Sky*?" and when Ben leant over her, saying: "Yes, it's still there," she sighed and fell asleep.

He watched over her until the dusk set in. Then he made up his mind. Uncle Allsorts still had not returned – he was probably on some drunken jaunt or other – and Evie and Pete were out somewhere as well. It made what he had to do a little easier. He collected the best of the blankets and wrapped them round Hilo as tightly as he could, hung her duffel bag and small possessions round himself like Uncle Allsorts and his tins, and picked her up in his arms and staggered off down the darkening street.

He went gamely on, feeling her weight pitifully light under the blankets, until he came to the river terrace. There, he paused for a moment, looking up and down the dimly lit street. There was no-one much about at this hour. People were at home having their tea or their early evening meal. Work time was over. The evening's activities had not yet begun. Good. He was glad it was quiet. It made things less difficult.

He drew one long, frightened breath of resolve, and then tightened his grip on Hilo's limp, uncaring body. She had hardly stirred as he carried her, seeming oblivious of the change of position, the uneven lurch of his stride or the night air blowing on her face from the river. Only once she stirred in his arms, sighed and murmured: "Put me down, Ben . . . I can manage." But she had drifted off again before he could answer.

Carefully, he carried her up the steps to the river terrace, along the raised-up flagstone path in front of the houses with their gracious porticos, until he came to the door he knew. It was Maude's house all right. He could not mistake that white, elegant exterior. There was a light in the window, too. At least someone was in. Gently, he laid Hilo down on the top step in front of the blue-painted door, and beside her he put down her duffel bag with her folder of poems (her most precious possession, he now knew), her bell, book and candle, her cheap tin whistle with the little dancing puppet, all wrapped up in old newspaper against the damp, together with the little fossil from the hills of home. Beside these he placed his note – the only thing he could say to Maude – and wedged it safely with the wooden crossbar from the puppet strings, alongside a screw of paper containing the Sally Army £10 and all the other money he had. The note said simply: "*Please take care of Hilo. I can't any more. The street will kill her. Thank you. Ben.*" (He thought desperately: maybe if I thank her, she won't be able to refuse.)

Then he rang the bell once, very loudly, and melted away into the shadows and hid. He watched from his hiding place behind the tree in the corner as yellow lamplight spilled out on to the pavement when the door opened.

There was a soft exclamation of surprise, but it was not Maude's voice he heard. It was a man's, – low and quiet, and oddly gentle. Ben was reassured by that voice – almost satisfied. But still he waited in the dark to see what would happen next – *what would happen to Hilo*.

"Maude," said the gentle voice. "Look at this."

There was another movement by the door, and then the voice Ben had been waiting for answered from the doorway: "What is it?"

"We can't leave her here," said the first, deep voice. "There's ten degrees of frost outside. Give me a hand, will you?"

"Of course," said Maude. "Let me help."

Ben saw them stoop over her, and then, after looking up and down the street for a moment in a searching, puzzled way, together they carried Hilo into the house and shut the door.

The yellow lamplight was gone, the step was in darkness, – but inside that warm, kind house, Hilo was safe.

Absurd tears of relief blurred Ben's eyes – relief, and grief, too. For he knew now that he loved Hilo deeply, and he did not know if he would ever see her again.

Straightening his shoulders against this sudden assault of emotion, he turned away from the beautiful house and its tall, golden-lighted windows, and slipped quietly out of the shadows and down the windy street.

Hilo was safe. If he had done nothing else right with his life so far, at least he had done this. *Hilo was safe.* Oh Hilo, he said as he walked away, stay safe and warm till I come back. For I *will* come back, one day.

Then he went on to Uncle Allsorts' camp, collected his own belongings, and walked to the motorway roundabout where he could pick up a lift to the north.

Before more than half-an-hour had gone by, he was on his way – alone, and penniless – and Hilo was left behind.

# VI

# THE DREAM

"What do you think?" said the voice that was kind – a deep voice, but gentle and slow and somehow filled with quietness.

"Pneumonia, I should think. She'd be better in hospital."

At this, something shrieked in Hilo's mind – a small, mouse-shriek that grew enormous. She remembered Steve, and the heedless cruelty of his hot hands. She remembered that hospital, and how they had looked at her with cold contempt and said: "Keep still!" in tones that reduced her to a piece of unwanted flotsam. Something in her mind had screamed then. It screamed now.

"No!" she screamed. "Not hospital! *Please*!" She thought her voice was loud, echoing hugely in those narrow antiseptic corridors, but it was a mere hoarse whisper, bubbling and scarcely audible.

She struggled wildly, but hands held her down. The more she struggled, the firmer the hands were. "No!" she whispered. "*Please*!" and went on fighting. But the hands were inexorable. She could not escape them. *"Please!"* The high, thin scream reverberated in her head. But the hands still held her and she fell back in despair.

"It's all right." The voice had an even deeper kindness now. "No hospital. Relax."

"No hospital?" She could scarcely articulate the words, her throat was so dry and parched, her tongue so heavy.

"No. You're staying right here."

She gave a small, shaken sigh and fell into the dark.

The two people looked at one another in mutual question, the man's face as full of puzzled compassion as Maude's.

168

"What was all that about?"

Maude was frowning, an unwilling understanding in her clear gaze. "These city hospitals can be pretty soulless, Emma tells me. And she should know."

The man sighed. "Can we get her over to take a look?"

Maude nodded. "She's coming in this evening anyway – off-duty for a few hours." She looked down at the exhausted girl in front of her and made a slight grimace of mingled anger and pity. "Though she won't thank me for an extra case!"

The man smiled a little, lightening the whole cast of his face. "If I know Emma, she won't refuse a patient!"

Maude agreed, somewhat ruefully. "She'll probably say hospital would be best."

The man looked swiftly at Hilo – in case that dread word had penetrated her oblivion. But she did not stir. "Maybe . . . But we'll stave off that kind of panic if we can." He looked down again doubtfully at Hilo's ashen face. "Ought we to tell the police or something?"

Maude hesitated. "I know something of her history. She told me a little. But she clearly didn't want to talk about it."

The man grunted. "Any idea why?"

Maude was no fool, and she had taken in a lot that Hilo had left unsaid behind her brief, unwilling account of her life before she left home.

"I don't know . . . But I had an idea it might be some sort of child abuse . . ."

The man's face changed. "I see. One of those . . ." He looked down at Hilo once more, the lines of compassion even deeper in his face. "Well, – we'll have to see what we can do."

"It'll be a chore, David, I can tell you. And it'll mostly fall on you, since I'm out most of the day, and so is Emma."

"I don't mind," he said mildly. And then to Maude's doubtful look, he added: "In an emergency!" and smiled at her.

Maude still looked uncertain. "Will she be all right in here?"

"Yes. Someone's got to keep an eye on her."

"Won't it disturb your work?"

He shrugged a little wearily. "Doesn't matter."

Maude shook her head. "We'll wait and see what Emma says." She was watching him a little warily, and when he looked up he found her eyes fixed thoughtfully on his face. "You know, David, it's no use – "

He broke in swiftly: "Yes, it is. It is, Maude believe me. Someone else to look after is quite a good idea." There was the same weariness in his voice now as in that tired lift of his shoulders, but it was a weariness born of some deep, inward grief, not just the despairing acceptance of yet another stray casualty of the big city's uncaring heart.

Maude was still looking at him in some exasperation. But something in the strained darkness of David's glance seemed to sober her. "Well, have it your own way," she said, and gave his shoulder an awkward, affectionate pat. Then she turned to look down at Hilo. "I wonder why Ben ran away?" she mused, straightening a blanket over Hilo's unconscious form.

"So that you couldn't refuse," said David, who knew much more about Maude's gruff kindness than Ben did.

Beside them, Hilo sighed unevenly and whispered: "Ben? . . . *Ben, put me down!*"

Several times during the next few restless days and nights she swam up to the surface, but she did not seem to know where she was or what was happening to her. Once or twice she called wildly for Ben, and seemed frightened and defeated when he did not answer. But either Maude or David was there to quiet her, and she sank again into dream without really waking.

But at last one morning she opened her eyes to pale winter sunshine pouring through two long windows opposite her divan bed in the corner. It came in a slanting, transparent shaft, and there were bright motes drifting in it. She watched them for a long time before she began to notice the room behind them.

Then she began to worry as memory nudged at her dreaming mind. "Ben?" she called. "Ben?" But her voice was weak and husky, and no-one seemed to hear.

Once more she tried to focus her failing attention on her surroundings. It was a quiet, airy room, with elegant proportions lit by those long sunlit windows, – and there were books everywhere. On three walls they stood in orderly rows on white-painted shelves, but they also lay in random piles on the chairs and tables, and even on the floor. Along the fourth

170

wall, below the tall windows, stood a long drawing-board spilling over with papers and the accumulated clutter of a busy working draughtsman or artist.

Artist? . . . But there were no canvases or pieces of stone lying about, no paints or palettes. And most of the papers on the drawing-board were small and the images on them, so far as she could see, were clear-cut and neat. An illustrator, then? A comic-strip artist? A cartoonist? Or a designer? . . . But there was no computer for graphics – and that instantly made her think of Ben, and she called out again more urgently: "*Ben? Ben – are you there?*"

But still no-one answered, and her mind flicked away from terror and tried to concentrate on something else.

The furniture. Look at the furniture. Or the pictures. Anything to keep frightened memory at bay . . . There was a photograph on one wall – an enlarged print of a man kneeling by some water and holding what looked like a baby seal in his arms.

Her eyes wandered round the room, restless and bewildered – even puzzled. For there was something wrong with this room. Something missing. She could not tell what it was, or why she was so certain about it. But a memory of another face – not the man in the photograph – came to her, too, a face with strength in it, a longish jawline, a straight nose and thick dark eyebrows, and eyes that were kind (like the voice, yes, she remembered the voice, too), eyes that regarded her without judgement or reproach. But – she remembered this, too – eyes that were darkened by some kind of sorrow and seemed to be waiting for something. Or someone. And they were very close to despair, she thought, Not like Ben's, which were always laughing, always full of hope.

And at this thought, longing rose up in her and she cried out again, more loudly this time: "Ben? *Ben – where are you?*" and tried vainly to lift her heavy head and look for him.

But as she spoke, the owner of those tired, waiting eyes came through the door carrying a glass of milk. "Were you calling?" he asked, and set the milk down on a small table beside her.

"Ben?" she repeated. *"Where's Ben?"*

171

David hesitated, and then sat down on the edge of the divan beside her. "He's not here just now, I'm afraid."

"Where is he, then?" Again she started up, trying to rise, but he put out a hand, restraining her, and she sank back, defeated.

"Give me a chance," said David, smiling at her persistence. "I'll explain what I can."

Hilo looked up at him in puzzled bewilderment. "I suppose," she said, in a voice between tears and laughter, "it's silly to say: *'Where am I?'*"

David laughed. "This is Maude's house. You remember her, don't you?"

"*Maude's* house?" Hilo tried to collect her flying thoughts. "How – ?"

"Your friend Ben brought you here," said David, sounding calm and reasonable about extraordinary happenings. "He asked Maude to take care of you, so we did."

"We?"

"I'm Maude's brother, David."

She gazed up at him and confirmed what memory had told her. It was an arresting face, strong and quiet, with a smile that had compassion and great sadness in it, but a distinct quirk of humour, too.

He picked up the glass of milk then, and when she tried to move, he said quickly: "No. Don't try to sit up yet. You'll feel much too swimmy. Drink it like this." He slid a practised arm under her shoulders and lifted her up. She drank obediently, realizing in a dim way that he must have done this before – he or his sister, Maude.

But the kindly gesture somehow brought Ben back into her mind more urgently than ever. He had held her like this when she was too weak to drink their smoky tea, or the precious bowl of soup he had bought for her.

"Then why isn't Ben here?" she asked. "I don't understand."

David was watching her somewhat anxiously. He could see that this boy, Ben, meant a lot to her, and he wondered what the news that he had just left her on their doorstep and gone off without a word might do to her.

Finally he explained it gravely and carefully, even fetching

172

the note Ben had left for Maude so that Hilo could see it for herself.

"Just *left* me?" said Hilo, disbelief and hurt making her voice even hoarser than before.

"He had to, Hilo," said David patiently. "You were dying out there. He had no choice."

Hilo was silent. She was beginning to understand what Ben had done – the black courage he had shown in taking such a calculated risk on her behalf – and why he had gone away, leaving her in Maude's care, hoping and believing that she would be safe . . .

"Oh Ben," she whispered aloud, in helpless, childish grief. "Oh Ben, how could you?" and she began to weep slow tears of weakness and despair.

"It's all right," said David, putting a kind arm round her. "You have to get well now, you see? That's what Ben wanted, after all."

But it wasn't all right at all. Not without Ben. And she went on weeping helplessly until exhaustion overcame her and she drifted off into merciful oblivion.

The next time she woke, Maude was sitting in a chair beside her, and there was no sign of David.

Hilo moved her head restlessly, she almost began to call for Ben again when memory flooded back and she sighed instead. I will look for him soon, she thought. Soon. When I'm well enough. He's bound to be somewhere within reach, probably still with Uncle Allsorts. I'll find him . . . But she knew she was still too weak to stand. It would have to wait . . . And she sighed again.

Maude noted that the sigh still had a catch in it – the child's breathing was still not right. She made a mental note to tell Emma when she called in next. Aloud, she said briskly: "You're awake. That's better. Would you like a drink?"

"Yes, please," whispered Hilo humbly.

But when Maude returned with a tall glass of lemonade, Hilo looked at her calm, unharassed face and dared to ask a question. "How – how long have I – ?"

"Ten days." And at the rising protest in Hilo's eyes she added, smiling a little grimly: "You were out to the world. What else could we do?"

Hilo tried a washed-out smile in return. "Hospital?"

Maude stared, and then laughed. "After the scene you made?"

"Did I?" Vague recollection came to her and she gave a small, uncontrollable shudder.

"I can see the idea doesn't appeal," said Maude drily.

But Hilo was remembering Ben, and her bell, book and candle – and how he had always managed to dispel the shadows some-how. Where were they now, she wondered, – the ghost-layers he had so carefully acquired for her? (And where was the little stripey cat they had christened 'Yoki' because of that awful yoke of clashing metal?) And where, most of all, was her precious folder of papers that she had carried round with her for so long?

But before she could even ask, Maude sat down again beside her, with a look of determined purpose on her face. "Hilo, my child, there are things we have to talk about."

"I'm not a child," said Hilo automatically, looking so absurdly young and vulnerable that Maude almost laughed, – only it wasn't really funny, it was sad.

"I know. You're Hilo – the cat that walked by itself. But all the same, you've been pretty damned ill, and if you'd died on our hands, who were we supposed to tell?"

Hilo's dark gaze was almost opaque. "No-one." Except Ben.

"My dear girl, there must be someone who needs to know."

She shook her head, and repeated it. "No-one."

Maude sighed. "Well, at least tell me your name."

"Fielding. Rebecca Fielding." She shut her eyes for a moment against the memory of her mother's acid voice: *What sort of a name is Hilo? At least Rebecca makes you sound almost normal.* She sighed. "But it won't help," she said.

"Why not?"

Hilo's face seemed to blanch still further with the effort of explanation. "I left home when – when I was fifteen . . ."

"How old are you now?"

"Sixteen."

"Sixteen – and on your own. Why?" The question was blunt, and Hilo blinked.

174

"My – my father's dead. And my mother – " she hesitated.

"Yes?" Maude was inexorable.

"She couldn't care less."

"Are you sure?"

"*Quite* sure." She sounded oddly clipped and abrupt.

But Maude persisted. "How do you know?" And when Hilo did not answer, she pursued it. "At least let me try."

The pale pain-washed smile flickered. "You can try. The police tried once when they picked me up in the park one night. She just didn't want to know."

"*What?*"

Hilo knew she ought to say more, but she was reluctant to spell it out. The shadows all came back too close if she spelt it out. "She – had a lodger . . ." she began, and then her throat closed up and she could not go on.

But Maude seemed to see the implications at once and her face softened. "I see."

"She said I'd walked out of my own accord and, as far as she was concerned, I could stay out."

There was a disbelieving silence. Then, seeing the bleak truth in Hilo's face, Maude leant forward and with a strangely maternal gesture brushed the hair out of Hilo's dilated eyes. "All right. Leave it. But I'd better have the address – just in case."

Listlessly, Hilo gave it to her, and then turned her head away to hide the useless tears. "When can I get up?"

"Not yet. Not till Emma says."

"Emma?"

"My sister. She's a doctor at the hospital. Ben called her Little Doc Never-Stop, remember?"

Hilo remembered. She remembered Ben's uptilted, curly mouth and how he had come out of the hospital laughing, with the little red Book in his hand. And at the memory her tears began to fall faster than ever. "I'm sorry," she said, ashamed of such weakness. "I'm – I'm all to pieces."

"I know," agreed Maude with tranquil acceptance. "Try to sleep now. Things will look better tomorrow."

When tomorrow came – she supposed it was tomorrow – David was back, working at his drawing-board, and Maude had gone.

She watched him for a moment as he bent over his work, and then his careful absorption and his fingers moving on the paper reminded her about that folder of papers which should be among her belongings. Was it really there? She hadn't checked for herself, – she was still too weak to stand. She had tried secretly, when no-one was looking, and had promptly fallen over in a heap on the floor.

But now, somehow, watching David at work made her want to be sure – to be certain her own work, such as it was, still lay safely hidden in its folder somewhere close by. Her eyes searched the room in terror.

"Did you – did I have – ?" she began.

He understood at once. "Your things are over there." He pointed to a small table in the corner. "Your friend Ben left them for you."

Hilo stared across the room with tear-darkened eyes. Even in this, Ben had not failed her. "A – a folder – ?"

"Of papers?" He nodded, smiling. "That, too." There was a hint of laughter in his voice now. "No need to panic." Then, seeing her face, he grew grave. "Are they that important?"

She lay looking up at him and something flashed in her eyes. "Only to me."

He looked at the tired resignation in her face and was moved to say gently: "I'm not so sure about that."

Hilo stared at him blankly, not quite believing what she heard. He seemed to know about the contents of the folder and her attempts to set down the highs and lows – the ecstasies and despairs – of the world she knew. He was looking at her now with the same compassion and tenderness in his face that she had glimpsed before. But he turned away and looked down at his work table, fiddling with the pencils in absent abstraction. He had withdrawn into some private grief of his own, his head stooped, the whole line of his tense shoulders one of shuttered pain.

She thought he had forgotten her, but presently he said in a voice schooled to quietness: "Writing is hell, isn't it?"

She jerked alert. "What?"

He did not sigh this time – just laid down his pencil rather

176

carefully and turned back to look at her. "I'm sorry, Hilo. I just meant – I should know."

But he is an artist, she thought. A draughtsman of some kind. Not a writer. How can he know? How can he understand what my father understood – the endless search – the ceaseless ache that beauty leaves in the mind – the struggle to set down, set down before it is too late . . . to set down each fragile, spun-glass moment of truth among the nightmares and mirages of despair? How could he comprehend the urgent need of a homeless drop-out with no education and no money to buy it – the need to preserve those shining, jewel-bright images, those vivid words and phrases that were her only riches in a cold grey world gone mad?

"You – *read them*." There was a note of appalled accusation in her voice.

He nodded. "I'm sorry – I had to, you see. You were so ill. I was looking for some kind of clue – to know who you were."

Who I was? Who I am? . . . Do I really know any more? I don't think I do, she thought, in sudden panic. *I don't know who I am.* Not without Ben.

Her eyes were shut now. Tears trembled under the lashes. Her world, her private world invaded once again . . . The swing lay on the scuffed earth in a pool of sunshine. Light gleamed on her father's shears – on her mother's triumphant smile . . .

But a shadow fell across her, and it was not the bitter shadow of her mother.

"Hilo, listen to me. Are you listening? They're good. Do you know that?"

Pain flicked across her face. Her eyes opened and fixed themselves on his in dread and longing. "Are you sure?" She leant up on one arm, searching his face. It was so easy to lie – to offer crumbs of comfort.

"Yes," said David firmly. "Some of them are very good indeed." He waited a moment to see if she believed him. But her eyes seemed to cloud and dim as he watched her.

"Sky?" she said, incomprehensibly. ". . . sky?" and passed out cold in her tumbled bed.

She woke this time to a murmur of voices.

"Only shock," said one – a woman's voice, but not Maude's. Come to think of it, she did recognize it, though. It was the voice of Emma Forrester, otherwise known as Little Doc Never-Stop. She had only heard it once in the hospital when they went to visit that girl who had jumped in the river, but you couldn't mistake that voice, it was so quick and brisk and full of cheerful kindness. (Rather like Ben's.)

The other voice was David's, sounding quite close and warm. She thought Maude was there too, but further away and drifting out of the room, for she heard her say: "Back later" before the other two went on talking.

"She's not ready for it yet," that was Emma's voice, half-laughing about something.

"I'm sorry, Emma. I ought to have had more sense."

"Well, I daresay you'd have passed out if someone had told you your work was that good – at her age!"

He laughed. "Probably." But he seemed to sigh and then go on more slowly. "What does one do about talent, Emma? It's a bit frightening."

"I know. If you foster it and make life easy, the impetus goes. If you don't, it dies anyway, – either from frustration or starvation."

"She's had some of that already by the look of her."

"Oh certainly. This collapse is as much due to malnutrition and neglect as the pneumonia."

There was a pause, as if both speakers were contemplating her. But there seemed to be something heavy on her eyelids and she could not open them. She drifted further.

"What do we do now?"

"Wait. She'll be all right. These things take time."

Time. It swung round her in a wide arc. It was huge. It was vast . . . and she was drowning in it, drowning in wide air. It was taller than sky, taller than stars. It turned and wheeled and grew . . . humming in a spiral of echoing space . . .

"Taller than stars," she murmured, and sank, drowning.

David and Emma looked at one another and sighed.

"She'll sleep now," said Emma. "I've given her another shot." Then, seeing the other's face, she laid a kind hand briefly on his arm. "Honestly, David, stop worrying."

His answering smile was difficult and strange. "I'm a fool. I always think – "

"I know what you think. But you're wrong. Maude and I keep telling you. You're quite wrong, and you must stop blaming yourself."

"If only I'd – "

"Yes. If only we'd all been twenty-four hours in one place and twenty-four in another at the same time. If only we'd all never been tired or distracted. Never made a mistake. Never forgotten anything. If only we were infallible. If only we were God."

She spoke with quiet passion, her tired, observant blue eyes fixed affectionately on her brother's face. David's own eyes – a darker blue made darker still by grief – widened in surprise.

"You?"

"Of course, me. Is there a doctor in the world who hasn't thought these things? It's no good, David. You've got to stop saying "If only . . ." You must stop torturing yourself. Or you're going to end up as ill as that child."

David's glance strayed back to the thin, sleeping face under the fallen wing of hair. "She isn't –?"

"Suffering from remorse? How do you know? Most of us are, one way or another. And there are certainly shadows there of some kind. Maude told me so."

He nodded, and went over to the corner table. "What you need is a drink. And so do I." He ran a hand through his hair, visibly trying to pull himself together, poured out two stiff drinks and carried them across to Emma who was still standing by Hilo's bed. On the way over, he glanced down at his drawing-board and made a face at it.

"Work no good?"

"Not much."

"Does having her in here disturb you?"

"Not really. Gives me something else to think about."

Emma nodded. "And if you put her in a room on her own, you'd only keep running up and down to have a look, I know!"

He laughed somewhat ruefully. "You know too much!" Then he gestured to a chair, and bent down to switch on the electric fire. "Can't you sit down for a minute? You look whacked." And

179

when she laughed too, and sank gratefully into the nearest chair, he added, rather crossly to himself: "I'm a selfish bastard."

Emma grinned and sipped her drink. "Aren't we all?"

They sat in companionable silence for a while, taking their drinks slowly. Hilo's breathing was still a bit shallow and fast, but it was deepening into real sleep at last.

"You know what I think?" said Emma.

"What?"

"You need a holiday."

David gave a sudden snort of laughter. "You say that to me! You work all day long and half the night at a busy city hospital. You're on call nearly every night. And on top of that, as soon as you get home for a spot of rest, I call you out to look at another patient who isn't even yours!"

Emma smiled. "They're all mine, David – in a way. That's my job, and I opted for it. And I do sometimes have a holiday. So does Maude from that unrelenting publisher's office of hers. But you haven't stopped flogging yourself since – "

"I know, I know," he interrupted, his voice rough with sudden anger. But he checked himself and went on in a more level, reasonable tone. "Work is my salvation, Emma, just now."

"Maybe. But a working artist needs a break, David. Your ideas will dry up otherwise.

"They already have."

"Well, then!"

"Emma, I couldn't – "

"Yes, you could." Her voice was firm. "Maude's here, isn't she? In the same house. And so am I, most days. If anyone came looking for you – "

"No. It's impossible."

The young doctor sighed and rubbed a tired hand across her eyes. "All right. You never liked being bullied." She grinned at him cheerfully. "But that child could probably do with some sun as well, you know."

David gave her a shrewd, half-humorous look. "You're a cunning little devil, aren't you, Doc Never-Stop?"

"I try to be," she admitted smugly.

David leant over and gave her a playful push. "Sometimes I hate you, Emma."

"Yes, I know. I do, too."

They laughed, and Emma rose rather groggily to her feet. She moved like someone on whom tiredness was fast catching up. "Better go before I fall asleep. I'm on duty at seven." She yawned and stretched, giving herself an admonitory shake. "I'll look in on the kid tomorrow."

"Bless you."

"And tell Maude I agree with every word she says."

"What about?"

"You!" She gave David one sharp, hard glance and turned to go. At the door, she looked back, smiling, shook her head at him and went out.

Behind her, David moved restlessly about the room, unable to settle. He took another look at the quiet sleeper on the divan in the corner, wandered over to his drawing-board, picked up an unfinished drawing and put it down again, and walked over to his bookshelves and took out a book. As he did so, something fell out of the pages. He stooped to pick it up, and stood suddenly still, rigid with shock. Then he straightened slowly, looking in a blind, helpless way at the thing in his hand. It seemed to be a photograph of two people laughing together – two men in a boat with some kind of big, brown bird between them. One of the men was David himself. The bird had one wing spread out awkwardly so that its white underside showed up clearly, and its tired white head with some kind of fluffy crest on it was resting confidingly on the other man's shoulder in perfect trust. Behind the small white boat was a working fishing port with a miniature quayside and a jumble of other fishing boats alongside and above it, a neat terrace of little colour-washed houses at the edge of the water.

He stared at it for a long time in shuttered stillness. Then he shook his head at it ruefully and, turning back to the bookcase, thrust the small coloured print far back on the shelf, moving several books to stand on top of it. Buried, he thought. Dead and buried. But he didn't throw the photo away.

The sleeper in the corner had stirred suddenly, almost as if the charged atmosphere of the room had disturbed her, or that moment of tension had actually reached her. She lay drowsily half-watching the man as he returned to his drawing-board, put one hand over his eyes for a moment as if to clear them of mirages, then settled down steadily to draw. The solitary, concentrating figure reminded Hilo too acutely of Ben, also with his head bent and solitary, drawing one of his 'pavements' on the cold winter ground. Oh Ben, she cried inside, where have you got to? Why did you leave me? Couldn't you at least come back to see me? But she knew he could not do that – or he would think he could not. He would stay away so as not to cramp her style, to give her a chance. That was what Ben was like. He did not understand that she needed him much more than all this luxury and careful kindness. Yes, she was safe and warm and looked after (and she knew she ought to be enormously grateful for it), but it was Ben she wanted. Only Ben could make her whole again, and he did not know it.

Sighing, she shifted a little in the bed and turned her head away from the light. It was no good. Ben was not there – and he would not come. She had to get well first – well enough to go out into the street and look for him. And then she would find him – and everything would be all right.

"All right . . ." she murmured. "*All right, Ben, I'm coming . . .*" and her eyelids closed over her tear-laden eyes and she fell asleep.

When she next woke, her bed had been moved near one of the tall windows. For a moment she was panic-stricken, not knowing where she was, then she recognized the room from a different angle and sighed with relief. Her eyes turned hopefully to the window. She could see great white clouds sailing with enormous slowness across a nearly-blue sky, and below them a pattern of house-shadows on the ground, a sheen of river water, and one leafless tree.

It was so unexpected and so marvellous – all this new width and space outside – that tears fell out of her eyes on to the sheet. She brushed them hastily away with one rather weak hand. She cried much too easily these days. Normally, she told herself fiercely, Hilo never cried.

"I thought you'd like it." David's deep voice was reproachful and made her jump. "What are you crying for?"

"I do. I mean, that's why." She turned her head and saw that he had shifted the drawing-board and all his work further down the wall to make room for her divan. "But why did you –?"

182

He smiled. "You kept on about stars and sky."

"Did I?" Her eyes grew bleak for a moment as they remembered her father lying on the summer grass and whispering: "Sky." But then another great fleet of clouds sailed over, and new warmth came into her face. "I love clouds," she said in a drowsy voice of content. "The sky looks bigger when it's cloudy."

The silence behind her was suddenly so loud that she turned her head again to look at David. For an instant she caught a look of such naked anguish on his face that she was shocked. But at once it was hidden, and he smiled with quick reassurance at the concern in her eyes.

What had she said? The sky looks bigger when it's cloudy. What was wrong with that?

"I thought it might cheer you up to see that the world was still there."

Even his voice sounded shaken. But he schooled it. Everything about him was disciplined, she thought. Too disciplined. As if he held a torrent in check.

"Or maybe you'd rather it wasn't?" There was a dryness about his voice now.

She looked out at the sky and sighed. "I'm glad *that's* still there."

She lifted a hand towards the white, piling clouds. Better not say it aloud if it troubled him. "But should you – ought you to move all your work? There won't be enough light."

He smiled. "Of course there will. I've still got one window."

"In any case – "

"Well?"

"I ought to get up soon."

"Not till Emma says so."

She looked at him in a troubled way, confused to find her thoughts flying with the clouds. Scarcely to be grasped. She was still frighteningly swimmy – but something must be said.

"David – I can't accept all this."

"Why not?"

She shook her head helplessly, unable to find an answer. There was too much to say, and no way to say it.

"No job . . ." she whispered. "No money . . . No p-prospects

183

of having either . . . I can't even – can't even . . ."

"You don't have to." Deliberately he answered the question she had been afraid to put into words. "It's good for me to have someone around. Therapeutic, Emma would say. And Maude agrees with her. Stop worrying."

She looked at him doubtfully. For a long time she seemed to search his face, seeing the tired kindness, the swift reserve when she came too close, the sorrow so carefully controlled and hidden. It was almost a beautiful face, she thought, with the kind of scraped beauty of winter trees, fined down to the bone. It was a still face – still and distant with pain – but it was compassionate, and it posed no threat.

He nodded, seeming to understand her probing gaze without being told. "Yes. I know you've had to get very wary. But you're all right here."

She flushed under his half-humorous gaze, and then went even paler than before. To her shame, tears of quick relief rose behind her eyes again, and she turned swiftly away to look at the moving clouds beyond the window.

But he had seen. "Hilo, the world's a pretty brutal place. Everyone needs some kind of sanctuary sometime."

"I know."

"Well, then?"

"It's just – " She drew a quick shaken breath. "It reminds me of my – my father." *And Ben.* "And Ben."

"What does?"

"Kindness," she said. "Just plain kindness." With no strings. But she did not need to add that. Not to David.

"No strings," he said, echoing her thoughts. "I don't believe in them."

She heard the sudden grief in his voice, and did not look round. Nor did Ben, she thought. Dear, laughing Ben, who asked for nothing and gave me everything . . . I must go and look for him soon. She repeated it aloud, on a slow sigh of resolve. Perhaps it would make it seem more real and possible. "I must go and find Ben soon."

"Just go on getting well," answered David, smiling at her in swift encouragement. "That's enough to concentrate on for the moment. Ben will wait for you."

*Ben will wait*, she told herself, trying to believe it. But something within her denied it and made her want to get up that instant and go out into the winter streets to find him. Only, she was too weak. Too tired. Suddenly she hated her fragile body – hated herself for lying there waiting for strength to return. It was taking too long.

"Be patient," said David to her mutinous face. "It will come."

But Hilo was not so sure.

It was a couple of days later when Hilo made her first attempt to get up. She had been thinking of her father's reassurance when she had been ill once before. *"Spring's on its way, Hilo. The willows are turning yellow."* The willow branches . . . down by the brook at the bottom of the garden . . . only they weren't exactly yellow, more golden-red, almost garnet-coloured in some lights . . . translucent . . .

"Garnet willows."

She was not aware that she had spoken aloud, but David raised his head from his work and smiled.

"Spring, Hilo? London sickness, we call it." He laid down his pencil and looked at her thoughtfully. "Would you like to get up today?"

A pale hope glimmered in her face. "Can I?"

"Emma said you could try."

*"When?"*

"Now, if you like." But, seeing her begin to move, he got up hastily and came over to the bed. "Take it easy. You'll be very wobbly at first."

She had never stopped before to think about the practical details of this pneumonia of hers. How had David managed? What about the ordinary necessities of life? And where were her clothes?

David stood there, laughing. "What are you worrying about now?"

"David, how – ?"

"Emma's a doctor, remember? She told us what to do. And Maude takes over at night. It's all laid on." He put an arm round her, easing her carefully out of bed. "Maude even put you into that glamorous nightie."

Hilo looked down. Never since she left home had she owned anything so ridiculously frivolous. Sleeping in what she stood up in had been the usual pattern – in as many clothes as possible to keep out the cold. And someone's floor the least rough of the places she had found to sleep on.

"How stupid . . . I can't stand."

"Not surprising. Try sitting on a chair."

The room seemed to heave and tilt, then righted itself. She sat, helpless and ashamed on the nearest chair, and waited for her head to clear.

David thought he had never seen such a pathetic waif in his life. But he knew he must be very wary of helpless waifs. They were his weakness. His, and another's . . . But that was a different story.

"At least – at least I can get to the bathroom."

"All right. Try."

But he had to hold her steady, half-carrying her as they went, and he left her at the door with some misgiving. "If you feel like passing out, call me."

But she managed. And after that she struggled back to the chair in David's room on her own.

"David – can I talk to you?"

"Why not?" He came across to her, this time gravely, and sat down opposite her on the end of the bed. "Well?"

"How – how long have I been here now?"

He considered, counting in his head. "Fifteen days, I think."

Her eyes widened. "*Fifteen days*? How have you coped all that time?"

He grinned. "Maude's very practical. And Emma kept looking in. We managed."

She shook her head, almost angrily. "But it's awful. I can't just *use* you like this. Isn't there somewhere I could go?"

"Like what?"

"Oh . . . a – a hostel?" (She couldn't admit to him how much she hated and dreaded hostel life.) "Or – or a convalescent home or something?"

He put his head on one side and considered her. "Let's get a few things clear. First, in your present state – let alone

186

what you've been like up to now – a hostel would just about kill you."

She stared at him. So he knew how she felt about hostels. She couldn't think how.

"Secondly, since you've not been in hospital, a convalescent home isn't easy to lay on, though I daresay Emma could fix it. But my guess is, you'd curl up and die there, too."

"But – "

"Hilo, I don't think you quite realize how things have been. It isn't only the pneumonia – or the fact that you probably hadn't had a square meal in weeks."

Glancing humour touched her. "I've always wondered what a square meal was."

"Steak-and-kidney pie, I should think. Don't interrupt." He was smiling too, – but there was a serious purpose behind his direct gaze. "It's something else, Hilo, isn't it? You're terrified of hospitals, terrified of enclosed places with no sky. Pretty scared of men – except your young friend Ben, and possibly me." He paused then, allowing his smile to take over for a moment.

No, thought Hilo, I'm not scared of Ben – or you. I wasn't really scared of Max either – though he was much more dangerous. But the others – the ones like Steve – yes, I'm scared of them, and I always will be.

"And wildly defensive about your writing," went on David, watching the denials and acceptances chase themselves across her vulnerable young face. "I'd say you were as near nervous collapse as you could be when you came, Hilo – on top of the chest infection. I don't somehow see you venturing out into the wide wicked world alone again just yet."

But I won't be alone, she thought. I won't be. Ben will be there. I will have found Ben by then. She did not say it, silenced by the amount David seemed to know already. She waited a while, thinking it out, and then said in a hesitant, unsteady voice: "Then – what next?"

"Wait till you've got your legs back."

"And then – ?"

"Emma suggested a holiday."

"I couldn't do that. I must go back and find Ben." She looked at David's doubtful face and added painfully: "David – please – I'm not – not a – "

"A sponger? I know that, Hilo. Ben told Maude you wouldn't beg, and you'd rather walk than thumb a lift."

"Did he?" She seemed bewildered. "I'd forgotten that."

He smiled. "Maude hadn't."

She bent her head, ashamed that the slow tears of weakness were rising again behind her eyes at the mention of Ben's name.

David thought, watching her, that the hair falling over her face looked like a tired brown wing. "Only temporarily grounded," he murmured. He went suddenly over to his work table, picked up the drawing he had been working on and held it out to her.

It was the sketch of a bird – or rather a series of swift pen drawings in sequence – the first a tumbled heap of feathers, limp and forlorn – the second a frenzied, distressed creature trying to fly out of a cage – and the third a beautiful, clean-swept wild thing flying free.

She looked at it in silence, willing the tears not to spill out of her dazzled eyes.

"D'you think I can draw, Hilo?"

Astonishment made her eyes dilate even further. "Draw? Like Michelangelo." But something in the question made her pause. "Why?"

"It's just . . . I've had an idea . . ." He glanced at her, almost shyly she thought. Or was it embarrassment that made him sound so hesitant?

"What kind of idea?"

He wandered restlessly away from her, and then turned back to face her across the room. "Hilo, I've made myself a bit of a name as an illustrator. I – er – used to collaborate with . . . several well-known writers quite successfully . . ." He paused again, and she could feel him trying to steady his voice, to sound rational and calm.

"So?"

"Do you think you could bear . . . would your work stand illustrating?"

She caught her breath. But before she could answer he rushed on, as if afraid she might refuse.

188

"I don't mean – a literal translation into visual terms . . . It would have to be oblique . . . subtle . . . I mean, your words don't need illustrating at all, really. They say it all themselves. But – but maybe it could help to *promote* your work." He rubbed a hand distractedly over his hair, knowing he was being clumsy. "You see, publishers aren't all that keen on poetry anyway – it doesn't sell, even written by established people. But if it had a – an extra name to boost it – even a mild name like mine, I mean, it might be useful?"

"Oh David, stop!"

He turned, looking so anxious and so humble that she laughed. "Don't go on *apologizing* for offering me the earth!"

"What?"

"Of *course* I would like it. I – I'd be honoured. More than that – overwhelmed. You must know that."

He looked enormously relieved, and suddenly much younger. "Oh God. You're such a proud, independent creature, I was afraid I'd upset you."

"Upset me? An offer like that?"

He rubbed his hair up the wrong way again with one nervous hand, sighed, then laughed as shakily as she had done. "Then – you won't mind if Maude reads them?"

*"Maude?"*

"She's an editor, Hilo. A publishing editor. Would you be willing to discuss it with her?"

She looked at him incredulously. "David – what can I say? I'll do whatever you suggest."

"She'll have to see them first."

"Of course."

"You don't mind? You looked as if – "

"As if what?"

"As if I'd committed rape when I told you I'd read them."

She went very pale at that word "rape". But then she smiled. "I didn't know then – "

"Know what?"

"That you wouldn't laugh."

He swore softly. "Is that what they did?"

"Everyone. Always." Except Ben. (And Max, who only saw

189

one.) "I mean, *poetry!*" She laughed herself a little. "That's why I – "

He nodded. "Hid everything that could hurt."

"Was that cowardly?"

His smile was sorrowful. "We all do it, Hilo. We none of us grow enough armour."

This time it was Hilo who looked suddenly stricken.

He was quick to notice. "What have I said?"

"It's nothing . . . My father always told me to grow some armour." (And so did Ben). She turned to him ruefully. "I thought I had, that's all."

His answering look was compassionate but humorous. "No way out, is there? If you were invulnerable, you wouldn't be a poet."

"I'm not a poet," said Hilo, suddenly serious. "I wouldn't dare call myself anything so grand. I just . . . love words, that's all."

"Isn't it the same thing?" asked David, with enormous innocence.

Maude, when she had spent some time on her own leafing through Hilo's folder, was brisk and business-like.

She came into David's room, carrying the sheaf of papers, and sat down in a chair midway between David at his drawing-board and Hilo, still shaky but up and dressed and perched on the end of her divan.

"Well, Hilo, David was right. Some of them are certainly usable." She looked over her glasses at Hilo rather severely and added: "Poetry is a dead loss to a publisher usually, you know. But David's name isn't – you understand?'

Hilo nodded dumbly, too shy to speak.

"We can't do them all, of course. Are you willing to let me choose?"

Hilo, who had been pale and silent so far, spoke suddenly. "No. If David wants to illustrate them, he must choose."

They both looked at her with respect. David said quietly: "Don't you have any say in the matter?"

She shrugged. "There are one or two I think are bad. I don't want those in. Only – " she took a deep breath and looked at David uncertainly, "the thing is, I know I'll be lucky to get *any*

190

of them in print and I can't start making conditions – but – but they are about *us*, you see. People like Ben and me, I mean, – the young ones – the jobless and homeless, and what life is doing to them. They're about – well, I suppose they're about hopes and disillusions and – and what's left to believe in, if anything!" She turned her fierce, appealing gaze on Maude for a moment. "We're not all morons out there," she said, sounding absurdly young and belligerent. "Not all junkies and mindless layabouts . . ." She drew another shaky breath. "We do think sometimes – when we're not too cold. We – we would *like* to get things right, to go on hoping . . . to have something to aim at – even the dim chance of a job or a room of our own one day" She tried valiantly to hold on to her composure. 'So I – if it gets into print at all, I want it to speak for *them*. We've got to include the ones that would matter to *them* – do you see?"

The two others looked at her in shaken amazement.

"It's not really *poetry*," went on Hilo, trying to explain something unsayable. "I told David – it's more . . . the way we think – the things that still turn us on, in spite of everything – or the things that don't. It's too – *plain* for poetry. High-flown words frighten them, you see." (Down to earth, my girl!) "I can't – I don't want to – to phase them by sounding too – pretentious?" But even the word "pretentious" sounded like a betrayal somehow, too clever, too grand for the basic simple facts of street life that she was trying to portray.

But how could she tell them about Uncle Allsorts and his drunken despair about Annie-Mog and her wheezy chest and her heart of gold, the blue faded eyes that still hoped for reprieve, and never found it? About the little stripey cat, Yoki, who went away, thin and alone, to grieve by itself when Annie died . . . Or about Evie and Pete, always hopeful, always waiting for a break, a room in a house, a steady job, – but always sturdily together, stoically enduring the cold, not blaming the world for its heartless toughness but still fighting back . . . Or Ben? But she could not tell them about Ben, and all he meant to her – his unfailing cheerfulness, his enormous kindness, and more than anything his unshakable belief in the future – in the fugitive beauty of the earth around them – in miracles. ("*Miracles do still happen!*")

191

She took one more uneven breath, trying to push down the rising longing for Ben that these thoughts engendered. *Oh Ben, where are you? I need you so*. Then she added in a voice that shook a little with the tears she held at bay: "I want – I want to tell them what Ben said . . . that the miracles are still there – they do still happen . . ."

The tears nearly overwhelmed her then, so she did not see the other two look at each other, also with suspiciously shiny eyes, too overcome to speak.

At last, Maude said in a strange, uneven voice: "Hilo. You put us to shame."

But Hilo had not finished with them yet. She smiled suddenly at them both. "You are one of Ben's miracles, don't you see? And I'm the lucky one. But even so – I – I don't want either of you to be kind about this idea unless you think it will work. I wouldn't want to do anything that might harm David's reputation as a – as an artist or whatever. I know he's collaborated with some pretty famous people – he told me so. It's no good throwing all that away just to – just to help an unknown scribbler along."

There was an extraordinary silence after this speech. David had turned away so that she could not see his face, and Maude seemed too stunned to speak. But at last she said with unexpected crispness: "My dear girl, I am a hard-headed business woman, with David's interests at heart. You need have no fears on that score." But somehow she had contrived to get between Hilo and David, and was making a great show of leafing through the folder again.

After a moment, David went out, muttering something about drinks all round. Hilo felt the tension like a steel web across the room, and found Maude's solid, unruffled presence curiously comforting.

"Maude?"

"Mm?"

"What did I say?"

Maude raised her iron-grey fighting head like a warrior scenting battle and smiled at Hilo a little grimly. "It's nothing, Hilo. A bit of ancient history. If David hasn't told you, he has his reasons. Let be."

"I can't," said Hilo, sounding desperate. "I keep saying things that shake him to the core. I must know what it is, – otherwise I shall keep on hurting him needlessly."

Maude stared at her with a kind of cool appraisal mixed with doubt. Then she seemed to make up her mind. "Can you remember any of the things you said that upset him?"

"He wasn't upset. He's too disciplined for that. He was just – silent."

Maude nodded. "I can imagine." She waited patiently for Hilo to go on.

"I remember one thing. When he moved my bed near the window so that I could see the sky . . . I said: *'The sky looks bigger when it's cloudy.'*"

The silence was almost as absolute as David's when she had first said it. At last Maude sighed and murmured: "No wonder he was shaken."

"Why?"

For answer, Maude reached out to the white bookshelves and pulled out a book. As she did so, the photograph that David had pushed so far back on the shelf among the other books fell out on to the floor. Maude stooped and picked it up and after looking at it for a moment in silence handed it to Hilo, together with the book.

Hilo saw a colourful dust-jacket of mountains and water, and two figures bending over a strange young deer with a stripey body and small straight horns. One of the men was David, the other was a striking, powerful man with a golden beard and a remarkably beautiful profile. The title of the book was "The Wilderness is Wide" by Sylvester St Cloud, illustrated by David Forrester.

Hilo looked down in wonder at a smiling, gentle-faced David looking ten years younger, and his companion who was also smiling, half at the young animal and half at David with unmistakable tenderness.

The same shining compassion seemed to shine out of the single photograph, which showed an even younger and more carefree-looking David, and his companion without the golden beard, also looking young and happy, both of them concentrating protectively on the white-headed bird cradled between them in the small open boat. She turned the photo over, and it said simply: "*Saving the osprey*" in David's neat script. No name, but it was clearly the same startlingly attractive man in both photographs. Hilo felt strangely drawn to him and to the almost palpable happiness that seemed to shine between those two companions. "Who was he?" she asked.

"We called him Cloudy," said Maude.

Hilo's head jerked up. "*Cloudy*? Of course. I see!"

"They were the most famous team in the conservation field. They'd been together for years. Cloudy was a brilliant naturalist and a fine writer – David was his illustrator. They went all over the world together on all kinds of weird and far-flung expeditions. And always when they came back they brought a book with them. A marvellous book – each time. A publisher's dream. Each one a greater success than the last."

She was silent so long that Hilo prompted her. "And – ?"

Maude got up for a moment and went to the door, listening for sounds of coffee-making from the kitchen – but there was no cheerful noise of rattling crockery. As she stood there they both heard the front door click quietly shut and footsteps going away down the river terrace.

"That's all right. He's gone out," said Maude, and came back to her chair, still half-reluctant to go on.

"What happened?" persisted Hilo.

"Someone rather like you."

"What?" She was shocked.

"It was Cloudy's own predilection for waifs and strays that did it." She smiled apologetically at Hilo. "David was just as bad. They never could say no to a creature in trouble – whether four-legged or two."

"So?"

"They picked up this girl. She was a dancer – out of work and alone – and they were both enormously kind to her. She was very pretty in a thin, febrile sort of way, and Cloudy fell for her, hook line and sinker." She laughed a little, but there was a grimness behind it which Hilo knew spoke of trouble. "After a while, Cloudy asked her to marry him. He thought she needed some permanence in her life, he said – though how she would get any with him and David away most of the time, he hadn't really stopped to consider. However, he was absurdly chivalrous and romantic about women – David was always teasing him about being gullible, but this time he didn't listen. So it was all arranged and everyone seemed very pleased." Once again she paused, and once again Hilo had to prompt her.

"And then – ?"

"And then, disaster. The girl – Candice, her name was, and never was a name less suitable, either – wasn't content with just one of them. She made a dead set at David, too. He tried to avoid trouble by going out, – he even went away by himself for a bit, but Candice came after him. And Cloudy walked in on a heavy clinch – engineered by the girl, of course." She glanced rather bitterly at Hilo. "In the normal course of things, neither Cloudy nor David would have made a thing about it – they had both had various girlfriends before. But Cloudy was the most unselfish of men, and he was also fastidious and proud. He would never contemplate *competing* with David about anything, – least of all over a girl. He would simply have bowed out and left the field clear. And so he took certain things for granted that he shouldn't have."

"Like –?"

"Like David being really fond of the girl and afraid to hurt Cloudy. Like thinking life would be simpler for David if he really did bow out. You know the scene." Once more the bitter glance rested on Hilo, not really seeing her. "The classic destruction of a perfect friendship by one stupid, predatory girl." Her voice was almost too edged for Hilo to bear.

"So?"

"So he just went."

"Where?"

"God knows. David nearly went berserk. He searched every place he could think of – he even got Interpol on to it. No trace. Not anywhere. Cloudy simply dropped out of sight."

"And – no-one's found him since?"

"No-one."

"But it's crazy!"

"Oh yes. It's that all right. And David's been driven very nearly crazy, too, in his attempts to find him."

Hilo understood that all right, and something within her ached for David as he searched and searched in vain in a heedless world for the one person who really mattered in all that lonely wilderness outside.

"What happened to the girl?"

Maude's face got even grimmer. "That was worse still. There was an awful row, of course, and David accused her of deliberately breaking things up between them, and went off again on some desperate search or other, leaving her alone in the flat. When she realized what she'd done, and that neither of them really wanted her, she took an overdose."

"Oh God."

"David found her when he got back. She'd been dead a week."

Hilo was silent. It was almost too awful to contemplate. She could understand a lot of things about David now that had puzzled her before.

"But –" she was very hesitant now, "what I don't understand is – "

"Yes?"

"After all that . . . how could he bring himself to take me in – how could *you*, come to that? History repeating itself . . .?"

"Don't you understand? He has never ceased to blame himself for that foolish girl's death, – or for his own idiocy in letting her grab him – or for Cloudy's disappearance – the whole lot. He sees it all as his fault, – and none of it is at all."

Hilo shook her head. "That's what your sister meant – "

"Emma? What did she say?"

"I heard her talking to David once when I was supposed to be asleep. Something about – if only. If only we could all be twenty-four hours in one place and twenty-four hours in another. If only we'd all . . . never been tired, never made a mistake, never forgotten anything, if only we were infallible, if only we were God, I think she said . . . something like that."

"Yes," said Maude sadly. "Emma's a very dedicated doctor – she should know." She smiled at Hilo, aware that the child might be feeling bad about all this. "But you were another chance, you see, Hilo. Another chance *not* to make a mistake, or forget, or be in the wrong place at the wrong time, or let another human being die in despair because he wasn't there to stop them."

"But he didn't owe me *anything*."

"He didn't owe that wretched girl anything, either. But he knew that Cloudy would never turn away any creature in distress, so he had to be the same. He still feels like that. He owes it to Cloudy."

Hilo sighed. "And what does that make me – some kind of conscience-sopper?"

Maude's smile grew kinder. "His salvation, Hilo, I should think. You've given him something to do for someone else – and someone else to think about besides Cloudy. Why else do you think we left you in this room where he works? You've been good for him!" She grinned at Hilo's doubtful face. "And this proposed illustration of your work – it was his suggestion, you know, not mine. It's the first time he's shown any interest in his own work for over a year. He hasn't touched another book till now. He turned all my offers down, and everyone else's as well."

"What has he been doing, then?"

"Just free-lance stuff – and an occasional dust-jacket for a friend. Marking time, you might say."

"Do you think – he's waiting for Cloudy to come home?"

"I'm sure he is."

"Oh God, Maude, it's terrible."

"Yes. It is pretty terrible. And pretty bad for his friends to watch. Especially for Emma and me – our wonderful hero brother." She sighed again. "I honestly do thank God you came along, Hilo. You really have helped."

"Have I? I don't much like pity, you know."

Maude laughed and leant over to pat her shoulder. "Nor do I. But it isn't pity, Hilo. It's something much more subtle than that. It's a kind of – of extended love, really."

Hilo looked at her incredulously. "Love? Isn't that Cloudy's prerogative?"

"Possibly. But David sees you as someone Cloudy would have loved and cared for – like any sick animal – so he feels the same. Is that condescending?"

"No," said Hilo, thinking of Ben and the way he had loved and cared for her without a word but with everything understood between them. "No, it's – *not to be sneezed at!*" and then her eyes filled with tears as she quoted Ben's absurd words.

But Maude remembered them too – and their context. "Ben knew his values."

Hilo nodded. And so do I now, she thought. When it's too late. But aloud she said mildly: "But I am me, you know – not an extension of Cloudy."

Maude laughed again. "I can assure you, he's well aware of that!"

Hilo had the grace to grin, too. "I'm glad to hear it."

"At least you've made him alive again. I got the feeling once or twice that he was going to die of an old-fashioned broken heart."

"I've thought that, too – though I didn't understand why. It was like – like – "

"Mm?"

"Like a deep lake slowly freezing over."

Maude nodded. "Exactly."

"Is there anything I can do?"

"Only what you are doing. Go on getting well. Stay here a bit longer – I know you're itching to get out of here and look for Ben, but you're not up to it yet, Hilo. Just – keep David working on this book, if you can."

A shadow touched Hilo then. "It isn't *only* a vehicle for David, is it?"

There was such humility and such entreaty in her face that Maude was touched. "After all you've said about it? The lecture you gave us! Of course not! I think it may be quite important, in its way." She smiled again, (with sincerity, Hilo believed). "And I told you – I'm running a business, not a charity. Much as I love my brother, I couldn't insult him or you with that sort of deal."

"Good." Hilo was almost satisfied.

Maude looked round David's room with a faintly rueful expression. "This was my husband's room, and his house, you know. My own children are all grown up and gone. It was pretty empty after he died, till David and Emma agreed to share it. And someone young in it seems right, some-how."

Hilo thought Maude was being very kind indeed now, and did not know how to answer.

But then they heard David coming back, and Maude hastily

198

began to talk about Hilo's poems and such things as spacing and pages.

David saw them there with their heads together, and smiled. It almost felt like coming home to a real family welcome. And then they both looked up and smiled back, and it did.

As soon as Hilo's legs were strong enough to carry her, she determined to go out and look for Ben. But it wasn't easy to get away. Maude was decidedly disapproving, Emma flatly forbade her to venture out yet in the cold, and even David looked doubtful.

"Out of the question," snapped Emma.

"You'll get ill again, and undo all the good we've done," said Maude, sounding quite brisk and fierce.

"Can't you wait a little?" asked David.

But Hilo couldn't wait. She slipped out when no-one was looking, and seized her old duffel coat from the hall as she went. That should keep the cold out. She didn't want to get ill again, either – or be more of a burden to them than she was already. In fact it was high time she left altogether, really, and got on with her own life. Only she knew she wasn't ready for that yet. But she had to find Ben. She *had* to.

She went first to the old railway arch to look for Uncle Allsorts. But he wasn't there. No-one was there. The fire was cold, the ashes rained-on and soggy. There were no boxes or bits of cardboard lying about. Everything looked empty and untenanted. There was no sign of Evie and Pete either.

But while she stood there wondering what to do next a strange, shaggy boy with an untidy backpack and a blanket slung over his shoulders stopped by the archway and lowered his gear to the ground with a practised shrug.

"You looking for someone?"

Hilo went up to him warily. "Yes. Uncle Allsorts. Is he around?"

"Not any more," said the shaggy young man, spreading out a layer of newspaper on the ground before he laid down his blanket.

"Where's he gone then?" Hilo hardly dared to ask such a

loaded question. Somehow, the empty space round the cold fire filled her with dread.

The boy gave another laconic shrug. "How should I know?" Then, seeing Hilo's expression, he relented a little and added: "Friend of yours, was he?"

"Yes," said Hilo, suddenly very sure of it. "He was good to me. I wouldn't want anything awful to happen to him."

"Well, it did," drawled the boy, turning back to sort out his gear before settling down for the day.

But Hilo stood her ground and asked again: "What happened?"

"Got so drunk he fell down." The boy turned a tired, stubbly face in her direction and decided to say a bit more. "Got picked up and taken off to some hostel. Haven't seen 'im since."

"Since when?"

Again the careless, indifferent shrug. "Three or four days – a week – I don't remember."

"What about Evie and Pete?"

"What about them?"

"They were here, too." Hilo was getting exasperated by this stone-walling. "They didn't get picked up, too, did they?" If he shrugs again, I'll hit him, she thought.

But he didn't. He laughed – a mirthless, weary little laugh that might almost have had a hint of tears behind it if he had allowed it. "They got a pad," he said. "A bed-sit – after four months on the street." He glanced up at Hilo with sardonic, glittering eyes.

"How?"

The sardonic glitter got brighter, the laugh yet more mirthless. "She got pregnant, see?"

Hilo saw.

"Pity I can't do the same," said the boy, looking at her sideways. "Care to oblige?"

Hilo laughed too. Only then did she dare to ask the most important question of all. "And Ben – was – is Ben here?" *Is Ben here*?

The boy looked at her in puzzled incomprehension. "Who's Ben?"

Hilo's heart sank. A great wave of despair seemed to descend on her as she looked into the blank, unhelpful stare of the youth beside her.

"He – was a boy I knew," she said helplessly. "He was here, too – with the others."

"Not when I came." He twitched his blanket into place, and reached in his pocket for a packet of cigarettes. "Smoke?"

"No thanks," said Hilo, turning away.

But something about her despondent figure seemed to get through to the boy and he called after her: "Sorry – "

Hilo paused, looking back over her shoulder. "If he comes back – tell him I was looking for him," she said.

"Who's asking?"

"Hilo."

He nodded. "Tell Ben Hilo's looking for him? OK." He gave her a crooked, apologetic smile – clearly regretting his earlier indifference. "If I hear anything, where can I get you?"

"You can't," said Hilo. "I'll call back."

"You do that, kid," he told her. "I'll be here. Name of Marc."

Hilo realized that even admitting to a name was a concession from this fiercely defensive young man, and she must not take advantage of it. So she merely answered his smile with a more open one of her own and said: "Thanks," before going off along the street alone.

No Ben there. It was a blow, but there were other places to try. Maybe he had gone into a hostel for a few days – or found a squat or a corner of a room somewhere. He would probably have kept on the job with the fruit stall, so the next person to ask was Corky.

"Ben?" he said, sounding both annoyed and harassed. "Went off, didn't he? Left me stranded."

Hilo looked shocked. "Without a word?"

Corky snorted. "A word you *could* call it. Did the evening stint – said he might get held up next day – and that was it."

Hilo was nonplussed. It wasn't like Ben. Not like Ben at all, to throw up a good job without a word. "I'm sorry," she said, apologizing on Ben's behalf. "Something must've come up." She couldn't think what else to say, and turned away miserably. No Ben – no word of Ben – no clue about Ben's

201

whereabouts. Only one rather disgruntled stall-keeper, and a cold, windy street.

"Hi," shouted Corky, calling after Hilo's retreating back, "Hi, kid – I just remembered something."

"Yes?" Hilo swung round eagerly.

"Sally Army," said Corky. "That's who it was."

"Who what was?"

"Came after him – I was packing up the van, see? Just caught a glimpse." He looked at Hilo uncertainly. "Thought maybe they was offering shelter – but it might've been somethink else."

"Yes, it might," agreed Hilo with a sudden joyful smile. Now she knew where to try next. "Thanks, Corky!" She almost ran down the road.

But when she got to the Salvation Army Centre, they were cautious and uncommunicative until she explained with heartrending honesty: "We were together, you see. But I got ill – and he left me in someone else's care. I've only just got better." She looked at the grey-haired man who had heard it all before, and willed him to understand. "I just – I just want to know where he is, and if he's all right."

The tired face of the kindly officer did not change, but all the same he was touched. "He went home, I believe," he said gently. "His father was ill." And at her look of shocked disbelief, he added sadly: "I'm sorry."

Hilo was silent for a moment, – too shaken by this news to answer at all. Ben gone? All the way back up north to his parents' home? Then had she lost him for ever? Would he ever come back? He would be safe and warm again at home – like she was in Maude's house. So would there be any reason for him to come back? . . . Would he ever feel the need to come looking for a stray girl on the windy streets of the big, heartless city? . . . *He might never come back again.*

"Are you all right?" asked the friendly officer, concerned by her pallor and her continued silence.

"Yes," said Hilo, in a small, quiet voice. "Thank you for telling me." She turned away and wandered off down the street with no clear direction in mind.

It was cold in the street, and a piercing wind still pounced on her round the corners. She knew she ought to go back

202

to Maude and David who would be worrying about her and probably cursing her for being so obstinate. But somehow she couldn't seem to concentrate on where she was going – and her legs were getting more and more shaky with every tired step she took. Ben has gone, *Ben has gone*, *Ben has gone*, said her feet as they lurched along. How was she going to get through, if Ben had gone?

She wandered on, directionless and unseeing, while the world seemed to grow steadily colder and emptier around her as her footsteps kept echoing "*Ben has gone*" with a kind of bitter drumbeat in the recesses of her mind.

At last she was too tired to go on. She sank down into a doorway on the pavement and sat there stupidly while the incessant drumbeat of loss went on and on in her head.

It was there that David found her, having combed the streets round his house and the railway arch neighbourhood with exasperated anxiety until he was almost as tired as the exhausted creature he sought.

He picked her up and shook her, almost angrily because he was so relieved to find her, but when he said: "You stupid child – you'll get ill again!" she looked up at him piteously and whispered:

"I'm sorry . . . Ben has gone, you see," and began to weep there in the street for the bright-eyed, laughing companion she might never see again.

Hilo was ill again for another week and it was during this time of restless nights and high fever that the dreams began.

At first she was searching for Ben, wandering through endless city streets on legs that felt too heavy, too full of aching exhaustion to lift. People kept drifting away from her, their dim forms shifting and weaving, mirage-like, in insubstantial wisps, and she kept trying to catch up with them but she never could, and they were never Ben . . . There was no Ben anywhere.

But then the scene seemed to change to an island – a small, sunlit island in a sea she did not know . . . (Not the flat sea of Weymouth where her family holidays were spent, but a strange, grey, stormy sea beneath a sky of sailing clouds . . .) The clouds were important in her dream, and she seemed to see glimpses of that photograph of the white-headed bird and the two men in the small boat . . . But then the image faded and she was back in the streets of London again, looking for Ben.

"Ben?" she whispered, aloud. *"Where are you, Ben?"* But there was no answer. There was never any answer.

The next day she was barely conscious, the fever had got so high, and she heard voices round her, sounding anxious. She wanted to say: "I'm all right," but her tongue wouldn't let her, and instead a different hoarse whisper came out: *"Put me down, Ben. The sky hurts . . ."*

Above her head David and Maude looked at one another and shook their heads, but Emma's brisk, cheerful voice said: "Only a temporary relapse, the silly girl. She'll be all right." And then the voices went away and the dreams came back.

The search for Ben got more desperate this time, and she kept asking the drifting, insubstantial passers-by if they had seen him. But when they turned their faces towards her, they were strangers, blank and uncaring, – or sometimes they were those two in the photograph again – David and his friend, Cloudy – and the island was back instead of the London streets, with the sea all round it and the clouds racing in the sky.

The next time she heard voices, they seemed closer, and David's sounded oddly urgent and troubled. "Must do something . . . seems to be sinking . . ."

I'm not sinking, Hilo tried to tell him. I'm looking for Ben, and I can't find him. That's why I'm so tired – I'm looking for Ben.

Aloud, she murmured Ben's name again and sighed, and then added in a fading whisper: *"The wrong sky . . . too cloudy . . ."* and sank again into dream.

She was too far out to see how her words affected David as he and Maude stood looking down at her.

When she woke next it was daylight, and her head was clear. But the ache for Ben was still there, and so was the strangeness of the dream – particularly that nameless island . . . She lay there puzzling about it, wondering why it seemed to matter. There was something about it that felt important in some way, but she couldn't think why.

I am better, she thought. I can't lie here idling while Ben is lost, – and this man, Cloudy, is lost and no-one knows where to find him. The thought bothered her. Was that persistent image of the island anything to do with it? . . . She tried to remember what the sunny coloured photograph had shown. The bird, with its white underwing exposed – the two men – the small white boat – and an ordinary little fishing port behind . . . but no island. And in any case, that photo had been taken a long time ago – it had nothing to do with now.

Anyway, lying here worrying about it wouldn't solve anything – wouldn't find Ben, or Cloudy either. Better get up and find some clothes and get herself back on her feet. She wondered vaguely where David had gone, but she was rather glad he wasn't there to scold her for getting up too soon.

She got groggily out of bed and managed to weave over to the corner where her possesions still lay in a tidy heap. Her duffel bag was still there, and she reached inside, feeling for any spare clothes that might be left there – the ones she had been wearing when she went to look for Ben before – seemed to have vanished. Her folder of poems lay on top where David had put it after the discussion with Maude. But someone – probably dear, careful Ben – had wrapped the rest of her belongings in old newspaper. She brought the package out and began to unwrap it. Where on earth had Ben got hold of the *Dundee Courier*, she wondered? Then she remembered Pete and Evie, and how they had told her that they had come south again from Dundee to look for work. As she laid the crumpled sheets aside, a small headline caught her eye, and the word "*osprey*" sprang at her out of the page. The words on the back of that photo "*Saving the osprey*" came instantly to mind, and she bent to look at the small printed paragraph more closely.

"The ospreys have returned to the west coast – to a certain nameless island – after several years absence since one of a breeding pair was shot by unknown vandals. Though rescued and nursed back to health by conservationists at the time, the incident clearly caused the birds distress and they did not return to their usual breeding ground the following year. Now they are back, and their secret whereabouts has been declared a protected nature reserve, closely guarded by one dedicated observer who, for the sake of the birds' safety, must also remain anonymous. This time, perhaps, the ospreys will be able to breed in peace."

*Anonymous observer*, thought Hilo. Could it be . . .? Would he go back there, not telling anyone . . .? Have I had the information that David was searching for here all the time, under his nose?

She looked at the date on the old newspaper and found it was April of the previous year. That figured, she thought. The birds came back in the spring and they will be gone again by now. But would Cloudy have stayed on? An anonymous observer on an anonymous island? . . . But David will know where it was – if I dare ask him – or Maude. Yes, I'll ask Maude first. Can't raise David's hopes yet – it's all so problematic and unlikely. But – she sighed, hoping against hope that her hunch might be right.

I could be wrong, she thought. So wrong. The dream could easily be a kind of auto-suggestion thing in my head, with that photo to trigger it off. But I don't think so, somehow. I think it *could* be possible. But I must ask Maude first.

So when Maude came in with yet another cup of sweet, milky coffee, Hilo decided to go into action.

"Where's David?" First things first.

"Gone to deliver some drawings, I believe."

Hilo sighed with relief. "Maude – can I talk to you?"

"Of course." Maude sat down on a chair and looked at Hilo's pinched white face. "What is it?"

"I think – I think I know where Cloudy might be."

*"What?"* Maude looked totally astounded.

"Please," begged Hilo. "I know it sounds far-fetched – but please will you listen?"

"Go on," said Maude.

So Hilo went on. She described the dream as it came, each time, mixed up with the search for Ben in the streets of London. She described the persistent image of the little island in the sun, and the curious importance in her dreaming mind of the cloud-laced sky overhead, and the repeated glimpses of that sunny photo with the white-headed bird between the two men in the small white boat.

And Maude listened with increasing bewilderment.

"And then there's this," said Hilo, bringing out the crumpled page of newsprint in a sudden burst of courage.

The silence while Maude read it went on so long that Hilo was almost frightened. "Do you – do you think it's possible?" she asked at last, begging Maude with her eyes to take her seriously.

"I don't know," said Maude slowly, brushing a distracted hand over her iron-grey head. "I simply don't know . . ."

"That photo," prompted Hilo, "the osprey one – could I see it again?"

Without speaking, Maude got up and fetched it from its hiding place behind the book '*The Wilderness is Wide*'. As an afterthought, she brought the book too, and handed them both to Hilo.

She looked from the single photo to the book-jacket and back to the photo again with a sense of curious recognition. There had been no little fishing port or row of small terrace houses in her island dream, but the boat had been there. She could even read its name – *Morag II* – painted on the white stern in black letters.

"Was this their boat?"

Maud looked uncertain. "I don't think so. They usually hired one, or borrowed one. Some old fisherman took them across, I think he told me." She looked at the photo again, more closely. "I suppose he must have taken this for them."

Hilo nodded. "Do you know where it was?" she asked at last.

Maude shook her head. "Scotland, with ospreys, obviously. As that press report says: somewhere on the west coast – but where, I don't know."

"But David would?"

Maude looked at her grimly. "Oh yes, indeed."

"Then – could you ask him?"

"I – suppose so." She still sounded doubtful and reluctant. But Hilo understood her hesitation.

"I know we mustn't raise his hopes – not yet. It's such a long shot. And I could be completely wrong." She looked appealingly at Maude. "But if – if I knew the name?" she paused, thinking hard, and then added half to herself: "Of course that was a fishing port in the photo. It might not be on the island at all."

207

"Probably not," agreed Maude, also peering at the photo again. "Most likely they were bringing that bird in to be treated by a vet or something."

"But the island wouldn't be very far away?" persisted Hilo, pursuing her own thoughts. "Surely it's worth a try . . ."

Maude was suddenly gruff and disapproving. "Hilo – you're in no fit state to go off on a – on what may be a wild-goose chase."

"I know," agreed Hilo cheerfully. "But I will be – soon."

Maude shook her head again, and looked even more disapproving.

"At least ask him," Hilo begged. "Or will it upset him too much?"

"No-o." Maude still spoke with reluctance. "Not if I can keep it casual." She took the photo from Hilo for a moment and stared at it even harder. "But he may smell a rat," she added, still sounding troubled. And when Hilo looked at her enquiringly, she broke into abrupt explanation. "The thing is, he's tried it. He's tried *everywhere* – everywhere they'd ever been – and Cloudy wasn't there."

"Not *then*," said Hilo. "But he might be *now*."

Maude sighed. "Oh Hilo, I hope to God you're right." But her voice clearly doubted it.

Hilo sighed a little too. "We can only try – we've got nothing to lose." And when Maude did not respond, she added almost shyly: "I know it sounds daft and improbable, but – " She became serious all at once. "Do you think there's anything in – in dreams and telepathy and such?"

Maude looked at her uncertainly. "I don't know." What could she say to this thin, large-eyed child with a visionary mind that no-one quite understood?

"I suppose . . ." Hilo was arguing with herself, "my mind could have invented the whole island thing, after you showed me the photo and told me about Cloudy?"

"Yes," agreed Maude, her face curiously bleached and stern. "But you didn't invent *that*," and she laid one finger on the crumpled press report.

"Coincidence?"

"I don't believe in coincidences," said Maude flatly.

"Or fate?" murmured Hilo, half to herself. And this time Maude did not answer at all.

But all at once Hilo felt suddenly drained – the effort of trying to convince Maude – and herself – had been absurdly exhausting. There were too many implications in all this for her to take in all at once and trying to piece it together had made her mind tired.

There were so many things she ought to say to Maude – so much care and kindness to thank her for – so much generosity which she could never repay, (and there was no earthly reason why Maude or David should have done any of it). How could she begin to thank them? Or Emma, Little Doc Never-Stop, either, who need not have bothered to help her at all?

And then there were so many plans to make – so many insoluble problems, not only about David and Cloudy, but about herself and her future – a job to make her independent again, and a room of her own to find somewhere. And Ben, dear, brave, unselfish Ben to look for, (far more important to her than this mirage-man, Cloudy). How could she reconcile all these things in her crowded mind and still know what to say to Maude?

"You're tired now," said Maude, seeing her sudden pallor and the heavy shadows under her eyes, – and feeling a pang of guilt at their cause. This child – who really had been at death's door when she came to them – was in no fit state to wrestle with such imponderables. "Better sleep for a bit," she said. "We'll talk some more later, when you're rested."

But Hilo could hear that there was still doubt in her voice, – still a bitter reluctance to let herself believe in the possibility that Hilo might be right.

"I've got to do this by myself," said Hilo to herself, before she obediently lay down to rest.

The man stood looking up at the sky and the swift-moving clouds beating their way from the fading brightness of the west towards the dark, and sighed. But then he remembered the small creature at his feet and how his private grief seemed to disturb it, shadowing its leaping joyousness, so he turned back to talk to it again, kneeling down beside it on the shore.

The young otter had got used to him by now. It went on playing happily in the rock-shaded pool, not bothering much about the tiny silver fish that darted in and out of the shallows. It had caught a couple earlier on, and now hunger was not imperative. Some kind of playful communication with the man seemed to be more important at the moment. After a little more swimming and diving the slender, gleaming body stood up in the water and the otter let out a cheerful bark.

Well, the man reflected, it was *called* a bark, but it was more like a friendly crow. "I quite agree," he said, smiling. "That's just what I was thinking."

The otter crowed again, and dived in a spectacular arc through the fast-moving water of the stream as it flowed down to the sea. This time, when it had finished its curving dive, it splashed out of the water and came up to him, barking another welcome. It was only as it moved on land that the unevenness of one badly squashed paw became apparent. In the water it was as swift and lissom as the stream itself.

The man put out a hand and laid it softly on the wet, smooth head. "You're doing fine," he told it. "Just get well, my friend. That's enough to concentrate on for the moment."

The otter seemed to laugh at him, barked again once, and then slid away into the water. For a while the man and the otter talked to one another and watched each other with unwary eyes as the winter darkness came down.

The man himself sat quietly on the bank of the stream, a notebook beside him in which he occasionally wrote some observation. But for the most part he just sat there, watching the eddies of the stream and the dark, bobbing head of the otter, and answering its cheerful conversation with a smiling gentleness.

That was the noticeable point about this quiet watcher; his smiling gentleness with the young otter, his kind, blunt-tipped fingers on its wet head, and the warmth and simplicity of his recognition. Here was a friendly creature making overtures – well, he would make them back.

But there was a stillness about him that was beyond the otter's necessity; there was a shadow of patient grief that even those sinuous antics could not dispel. His eyes, looking beyond the twilit gleams of glancing water, were dark with memory.

At last he noticed the gathering darkness that threatened to quench the faint afterglow of sunset on the sea. Night was coming and it had grown cold. He shivered a little and began to cough. The otter, startled at the sound, stood up again in the water, head cocked in enquiry. The man coughed again, and the otter decided it was a bark like his own and came out of the water, laughing.

But when it came near, something about the man's quiet figure disturbed it, and it thrust a cold wet nose into his hand like a dog – both seeking and giving comfort.

"It's all right," he said gently. "All right, my friend. Only a way of saying good-night." He rubbed his hand across the intelligent, questioning head. "Go on home now," he told the otter. "It's time we were both in bed."

He stood up and the otter barked again happily and slipped away into the water. It gave him a brief display of private rejoicing, and then headed away upstream into the deepening shadows of rock and tree.

The man stood looking after it, watching the silver darkness settle on the water. Then he sighed again, picked up his note-book and his anorak and turned away from the stream into the darkening hills.

The fisherman was getting old now. It was a long haul out to the islands, and since the engine had packed up, the pull of the oars was heavy against the swell. But the fishing was better out here, and besides, he had some stores to deliver.

He looked up at the sky, assessing the weather with a practised eye. There was a blow coming. It would be best to abandon the fishing and put into the small island before the sea got up. That was the trouble with this coast – a storm could blow up out of nothing. It could come sweeping across like lightning – sometimes *with* lightning, too, and the seas grew so mountainous that a small boat could scarcely live in them. They might subside as quickly as they rose, or they might go on hurtling and pounding against the rocks for days. The islands could be cut off for as long as a week when things got really rough. Best to run for shelter while the going was good.

Only he couldn't run. He could only go on hauling at the oars against the tug of the increasing swell, and glance over his shoulder to see how near the little horse-shoe bay was growing.

It was hard work and it hurt his chest, but he kept on. The grey granite cliffs got nearer; he could hear the crying of the seabirds now. One seabird in particular kept circling round his boat and swooping down over his head, but he had nothing to give it now. He couldn't stop to fish.

He loved this little island. *Eilean Diomhair*, they called it – the secret island – and most of the other fishermen wouldn't go there. They said it was haunted or something, – but what part of this ravenous coast wasn't? The ghosts of old ships haunted every rock and every cresting wave.

But this island was kind. Welcoming. Even before Mr McLeod came back and turned it into some sort of nature reserve. Behind its fierce cliffs, the perfect little horse-shoe bay was a natural harbour – tiny but safe. Once get the boat into the lee of the rocks at the entrance and it would drift into calmer water of its own accord; then he could stop his furious rowing.

He didn't dare to stop yet, though. The wind was increasing and the sea was beginning to turn black and choppy. Waves slopped over the gunwales, but he didn't stop to bale. He went on, driving and pushing the frail craft through the water. Now he had to watch what he was doing, because the rocks were very near. One stroke too close and the boat would fall apart like matchwood. He stroked it gently past the nearest jagged tooth, took a wide circle round where he knew the others were beneath the surface, and pulled hard across the mouth of the little harbour. For a moment he thought he was going to overshoot it. The swell took him further than he meant to go and he had to pull back even harder. But all at once the roar of the surf against the cliffs and the screaming wind were behind him. He shot into quiet water and let the boat take its own course to the shore.

He was very spent now, and leant on his oars, panting. There was a roaring in his ears that was not the sea. But above the roaring he could hear a voice call sharply, and two strong, sinewy arms caught hold of his boat and beached it on the sand.

"Angus, are you crazy? Putting out in this weather!" The arms helped him out and steadied him as he stumbled on to the wet shore. He shook his head, shaking the spray from his eyes, and

212

managed a salt-caked smile. The pain in his chest was subsiding now. He felt better.

"I was being foolish, Mr McLeod," he admitted. "The weather came up on me. And the engine failed."

The arms – or one of them – still held him steady. "Better come up to the house and get warm. We can have a dram."

Angus tried to gather his dignity together. He straightened his back and let his mild blue gaze rest on the arresting face of the man before him. It had a kind of piercing quality, a strange, hawklike beauty of structure, pared to the bone with hard living and self-denial – and there was a darkness about the eyes that spoke of deep-hidden sorrow – or precarious health – or both. Angus was used to it now. He knew that there was a profound gentleness behind that hard-driven exterior. He had seen how those hands dealt with an injured animal or bird, how those eyes watched with a half-smile of compassion in them when one of his wild companions showed off or suddenly got frightened and backed away. He had seen him with seals and otters and, of course, the ospreys when they were here. He was a good man, Angus thought – as men go. A good man and one to be trusted.

"I was bringing the stores in any case," he said, trying to justify his foolhardiness. Then he caught the gleam of amusement in the other's eyes, and smiled. "You are right," he said. "I could be doing with yon dram."

They walked up the beach in comfortable silence, carrying the stores. Behind them the sea grew darker and fiercer beyond the little bay, and the wind hit them as they reached the top of the dunes. The seabirds circled in a wide, flashing arc, their voices calling wildly against the approaching storm. It won't blow itself out tonight, thought the man. I'll keep him with me till tomorrow.

"Tomorrow, Angus," he said aloud. "No venturing out in that sea now."

Angus nodded.

Outside the whitewashed croft both men stopped and looked at the sky. Clouds were flying fast, piling and hurling from the seaward horizon. The sea itself was whipping into crests of white, and the swell of each wave grew ever more mountainous before that tearing wind.

213

Angus shook his head. He did not speak. But the other laughed and opened the door to let him in. A black and white collie bounded out with cries of welcome. Firelight flickered within. The two men left the stormy night behind them and went inside.

"May as well settle down," murmured the man, pushing Angus into a chair. "We're quite safe here."

In spite of Maude's insistence that Hilo should rest and get strong before any decisions were taken about anything important, Hilo knew at the back of her mind that talking would resolve nothing. Actions spoke louder than words. And she was the one who would have to take that action, disregarding Maude's doubts and curious reluctance, whatever the result.

So she waited three days for her strength to return, and until Maude had managed to put that casual, loaded question to David. "By the way, this fell out of the bookcase. Where was it, d'you remember?"

"That?" David had snapped. "Portleish." He had glared at Maude like a wounded lion. "And I've tried that – like everywhere else!" And he had gone back to his work with furious concentration.

Maude said nothing but quietly slid the offending photo into Hilo's hand. She knew Hilo had heard the important word – Portleish. The rest they would have to decide later, when David was out of the way.

But Hilo did not believe in "later". Now was what mattered. Those glimpses of that smiling island in the sun and the two smiling men in the little boat had seemed so charged with happiness in her dream. And here was David still shuttered in this awful sadness. She must do something. Now.

She had to wait a bit longer, till Maude was at work and David had gone out for something or other. Then she collected her belongings from the corner where they had been left and prepared to go on a journey. She found Ben's money – with the Salvation Army's £10 – still intact. That would help. But she would have to hitch. Scotland was a long way. She hesitated about her precious folder of poems, but decided in the end to take them with her. Maude had already made copies of the ones

214

she thought they could use, and David had already begun a few tentative drawings. The rest was up to them, and Hilo knew very well that once she had left, she ought not to come back. Make the break clean. They had done enough for her already. And with every succeeding day it got harder and harder to leave. But she couldn't go on being dependent on their kindness for ever. It was time to go.

Fleetingly, she thought of Max, who had gone when it was time to go. Gone without a backward glance (as far as she knew), and accepted thankfully Hilo's own decision that it was right.

Well, it was right now. She must go and find Cloudy – if he could really be found. It was something she had to do for these two who had been so good to her. Maybe, if she succeeded, it would be some recompense for all their care and kindness.

And then she must put her own life in order. Find Ben, who had gone when it was *not* the right time to go – who had gone, rather like Cloudy, out of unselfishness and the need to spare the one he cared for from unnecessary suffering. Only it wasn't unnecessary, Ben, she said. I'd rather have been ill on the street with you beside me than be cut off from you for ever in this lonely world.

But I will find you, she said. I will find you somehow. I know you had to go home for some family trouble, but you will come back, I'm sure. Just let me get this strange Cloudy business sorted out, *and then I will find you*!

She shrugged herself into her old duffel coat, hoisted her bag over her shoulder, and crept down the stairs and out into the street. It was cold outside but it wasn't raining. She looked up and down the river terrace, and then walked away towards Shepherd's Bush and the motorway roundabout. It would do for a start, till she could get on to the M1 for Scotland. She just hoped her legs would hold out till she got a lift.

Hilo arrived by the small quayside of Portleish harbour towards dusk on the third day, just as the fishing fleet was setting out for the night catch. Too late for the island tonight, she thought. No boat would take her there after dark. Better wait for the morning.

There didn't seem much point in looking for somewhere to

stay – she couldn't afford it anyway – so she simply curled up by a heap of lobster pots and a tangle of nets and tried to ignore the cold. But one of the fishermen found her there and took her home to his wife, saying gruffly: "Too cold for sleeping rough." He handed her over to a thin, quiet-eyed woman called Mora, who didn't seem at all surprised.

Hilo protested that she had no money, but the woman took not the slightest notice and sat her down by the kitchen fire with a bowl of lentil soup. "It should by rights be porridge," she said drily, "but that'll have to wait till the morn." Hilo protested that anything hot was wonderful, and did not dare confess that she much preferred soup to porridge anyway.

Then she thought of asking some relevant questions. "Does – does anyone round here own a boat called Morag II?"

Mora handed her another piece of warm, home-baked bread and smiled. "Old Angus? He'll not be out with the fleet tonight. Getting too much for him these days." She saw Hilo's expression and added comfortably: "You'll likely find him down by the quay tomorrow, mending the nets."

Hilo nodded. She was suddenly so tired that she could scarcely hold her head up, and the warmth of the fire and the hot soup made her even more drowsy.

"Best take the spare cot," said Mora practically. She led Hilo over to an alcove behind the chimney breast where a raised wooden shelf was built into the wall. A thick woollen blanket served as a mattress, and Hilo allowed herself to be steered on to it without protest. It was a lot warmer, and a lot less hard, than the street.

"No bad weather tonight," explained Mora kindly. Hilo looked uncomprehending, trying vainly to keep her flying wits together.

Mora laughed a little at her blank stare. "Sometimes, in bad weather, we get the islanders stranded here – and other stormbound boats put in for shelter. Then the spare cots are all full."

"I see," murmured Hilo. "I'm lucky, then." But her eyelids were already drooping, – exhaustion was catching up on her.

"We have a saying here," said Mora, laying another knitted blanket over Hilo without fuss, "that folks bring their luck with them." She stood looking down at Hilo for a moment in silence, an unexpected softness in her face, and added in an odd, quiet voice: "And I think you have."

But Hilo was already far out, and did not hear her.

In the morning she went down to the quay, as instructed, to look for Angus. She found him, as Mora had said, sitting in his boat, Morag II, mending his nets. She was not in the least sure how to approach him, or how to set about the whole strange busines of Cloudy and the island, but in the end she simply began with first things first.

"Are you Angus?"

The old man looked up at her doubtfully from under shaggy eyebrows, but his fingers did not stop their intricate weaving of the fine yellow thread of his nets. "I might be."

"If you are," Hilo went on, crouching down beside him, "and if you're the owner of this boat, maybe you'd know these two people?" and she handed him the sunny photograph of Cloudy and David with the osprey in the boat, Morag II.

Angus screwed up his eyes and pretended to peer at the photo as if he had never seen it before. But in truth he knew it perfectly well. Hadn't he taken it himself on that fiddly great camera of theirs, with those two sitting in his boat and smiling at him with the injured bird between them? But that was in the days when those two were working together, and nearly always smiling when he came to bring the stores. And now it was only the one of them looking after the birds and the otters, and he scarcely smiling at all and looking like a man with the heart gone out of him. But he liked his independence did Mr McLeod, and even the merest hint of concern about his welfare could make him freeze into icy stillness, so Angus was very wary of anything that could seem like an intrusion. Careful he had to be, and this young woman (girl, rather) coming here asking questions would have to be careful too.

But then he caught the girl's anxious expression. And something about it troubled him, so he gave her a cautious answer. "I might . . ."

Hilo sighed. This is going to be difficult, she thought. I've got to get through to him somehow. Then, on impulse, she said her thoughts aloud: "I know this is difficult, Angus. Could I tell you the whole story?"

He stared at her for a long moment in silence, seeming to assess the honesty of her intentions, even her deepest hidden motives, with his canny seaman's eyes. "Maybe you could," he allowed at last.

So Hilo did. She did not say much about the reason for David's and Cloudy's estrangement, or about the girl, Candice. She felt that was probably too private, and Cloudy would not like it discussed. But all the rest, including the little press report in the *Dundee Courier*, she told Angus as clearly and sensibly as she could. Even the dream, because somehow she knew that Angus, with his strange, Highland heritage, would not be surprised.

When she had finished there was a long silence, and then Angus murmured half to himself: "So that was the way of it."

"You see how it is, Angus," Hilo explained. "They ought to be working together again – and if David is to come up here and find him, I have to be sure it is the right one." She brought out the book '*The Wilderness is Wide*' which Maude had given her and pointed to the bearded Cloudy on the cover.

"Is – is he there . . . on the island? Are you sure he is the one?"

Angus nodded. He scarcely needed to look. But he was puzzled by the name 'Sylvester St Cloud'. He had always called himself McLeod on the island. Maybe it was the same thing with a different spelling. "He calls himself McLeod up here," he said.

Hilo was not surprised at this. "This is probably his pen name." She looked earnestly into the seamed face before her. "He didn't want to be found, remember"

"Aye," agreed Angus. "He hass made that clear."

Hilo smiled at him a little ruefully. "So what are we to do?"

Angus pondered, not knowing how to answer her. But in truth he was strangely stirred by the girl's story. Her dream of the silver island in the sun seemed to him all part of his own boyhood background: the same myth and magic he had been brought up with and known all his long life. There was nothing surprising about it to him, except that the girl was a lowlander, and a lowlander's mind was usually locked against such things. But

218

that clearly did not prevent her from having what he called The Sight, and he recognized the signs of that ancient, inexplicable gift in those visionary young eyes.

"I suppose," said Hilo slowly, "the birds have long gone . . ."

Angus looked dreamily out to sea. "It iss the otters now," he said.

Hilo was pursuing her own thoughts, searching her mind for a clear recollection of that elusive dream. The island had been there, sure enough, shining in the sun, with the skyful of racing clouds above it. And had there been a small boat beating its way towards it across that grey, stormy sea? She couldn't quite remember. But Angus's words about the otters had triggered off a faint image in her mind's eye, an image of something small and dark leaping in and out of a stream near the shore . . . Or had there been? Maybe she was just imagining it.

"The thing is," she said, still speaking slowly, in a voice full of doubt, "we don't want to scare him."

Angus wasn't quite sure if she was speaking about the otter or Mr McLeod, so he decided to stay silent.

"If I go over to see him," went on Hilo, trying to make things clear to herself as well as Angus, "and he doesn't want to know, mightn't he take off again and disappear?"

"He won't leave the otters yet," said Angus, with sudden certainty. "Especially the one who wass injured."

Hilo's eyes came back into sharp focus. "Won't he? Then – will you take me over?"

Angus pondered again. But somehow he knew it was important. He was fond of Mr McLeod, for all his fierce, independent ways. He would like to see him happy. And the other one, too. David Forrester. He had liked him as well.

They were both good men – caring about the creatures they worked among more than for the usual rewards of money and power that people seemed to strive for. As for him, old Angus Murray, he liked a quiet life himself, and quiet men like those two deserved what help he could give.

"I will take you over with the stores," he said simply.

"I won't want to stay," explained Hilo. "Just give me time to talk to him, – and if he is angry you can take me away again very fast!"

219

Angus permitted himself a seamed and salty smile. "I will do that," he said.

The sea was calm that day, flat and silver, like her dream. Hilo marvelled at its beauty – its subtle colours and changing reflections – as the small boat ploughed its sturdy way through the quiet swell. It had been so long since she had seen anything except the grey London streets or the enclosed space of her sick room that she was overwhelmed by the sense of space and light. Overhead, the same wild cloud patterns chased themselves across the sky, but they were moving more slowly than in her dream, massing and piling in great drifts of grey and snowy white over the silver sea. It was almost too beautiful to bear, and Hilo found that there were tears in her eyes long before she got to talk to the man she was looking for. (Be careful, Hilo, she told herself severely. You cry much too easily these days. Keep it all calm and sensible, if you can.)

He came down to the shore to meet the boat as usual, but stopped short when he saw Hilo in the bows beside Angus.

"I wass bringing you a visitor," said Angus, paving the way for Hilo as best he could. "She hass promised not to disturb the otters – and she says it iss important."

The man looked hard at Hilo and for some reason that he could not explain to himself rather liked what he saw. She was a thin child, with the marks of recent illness in her face, but her eyes were brave and clear. They were watching him now with a curiously adult compassion.

"Are you Cloudy?" she said, without preamble. "If so, perhaps I'd better show you this." and she held out the sunny photo for him to see.

But he did not need to see it – one glance was enough. That, and the name she had given him. He went slowly ashen-pale and, after a long, echoing silence, said in a taut, shaken voice: *"Where did you get this?"*

"It's a long story," said Hilo, looking into his face with entreaty. "Shall we – could we walk along the shore?"

He continued to gaze at her in silence for a moment. Then he seemed to make up his mind and gave a quick nod of consent. "I'll be back to help with the stores, Angus," he said, and strode off down the beach rather too fast, with Hilo close behind him.

Angus looked after them with a mixture of affection and exasperation in his perceptive gaze, then he shook his head gently and set about unloading the stores.

Cloudy went on till he reached a convenient rock sheltered from the sea wind, and there he sat down and waited for Hilo to join him. "Now," he said, still in that taut, driven voice: "What's all this about?"

But Hilo did not immediately sit down beside him. Instead, she stood before him very straight and said: "Before I begin – will you please hear me out, and not blow your top, or tell me to mind my own business? Because it really is important."

A faint smile twitched at the corners of Cloudy's gentle mouth as he looked up at this fierce, compelling child who was confronting him with so much reckless courage. He knew she was nervous, and he could never bear to hurt a nervous creature. "I'm not much given to top blowing," he said mildly.

"Not now," said Hilo, and looked at him very hard. Then she sat down and began to talk.

When she had finished she added quietly the words she had said to Maude about David long ago (at least it seemed long ago in the story she had been telling). "He – he is like a deep lake slowly freezing over . . ."

Cloudy did not reply. At some stage in the story he had put up one hand to shield his face and now he kept it there and did not look round.

Hilo waited a while and then asked the only important question. "Will you still be here – if he comes?"

There was a long, long silence. And then Cloudy answered in a muffled voice: "I will be here."

"Is that a promise?"

"Yes."

"I'm looking for someone too, you see," she said gently. "For Ben. And I know how awful it is – especially when you go somewhere, feeling all hopeful, and he's not there after all."

Cloudy did not answer. And on an impulse Hilo felt in her pocket and brought out Ben's ancient fossil and held it out to him.

"He gave me this," she said. "He says it puts things in perspective . . ."

Still Cloudy did not answer. But Hilo knew she had said enough. After all, she reflected, they had got to work it out for themselves – the pride and the hurt, and the long, long exile – and Cloudy had got to know that David came of his own free will, and not under pressure. There was nothing more she could do for them now.

She waited a little longer in case he said anything more. But when he did not speak again, she got up quietly from the rock and stood looking down at him for a moment. "It is up to him now," she said softly. "But I know he will come."

Then she walked swiftly away back to Angus and went with him in the little boat, leaving Cloudy alone on the shore.

Once back on the quay at Portleish, Hilo went into action. She had been trying to decide what to do next all the way across the silvery sea between the island and the mainland. Now she turned to Angus for one last bit of help and advice.

"I am going to send a postcard, Angus, from Portleish. Has the island got a name that David Forrester would know – but wouldn't give things away to the tourists?"

Angus smiled. "It is called *Eilean Diomhair* – the secret island," he said softly. "And Mr Forrester will know it. "He looked at her out of shrewd, assessing eyes and added, half to himself: "But not many others would know it."

Hilo nodded, well satisfied. "Then – if David Forrester comes, will you take him out there?"

"I will do so," promised Angus, "if you are sure Mr McLeod will like it?" He spoke with his own special brand of cautious Highland dignity, and Hilo was somehow touched by his unceasing loyalty to that solitary man on the little island.

"I am sure," she told him firmly. She waited to see that he believed her, then made her final request. "I would like to stay on here for just a couple more nights – until I know David has come." She looked at the old, weatherworn face beside her, wondering how to explain her lingering doubts and fears. "I don't want him to see me – that might embarrass him. I just want to know he's arrived." She hesitated, and then added, almost to herself: "If he doesn't come, I may have to go back . . ."

Angus understood her quandary. "I am sure Mistress Fairlie will be glad to have you stay."

Hilo sighed, feeling ashamed, not for the first time, of her penniless state and her inability to repay the hospitality of these generous people. "I can't offer her anything in return . . ."

"As to that," Angus spoke with the same quiet dignity, "Mr McLeod hass always been a good friend to us here in Portleish. And if anything should be a help to him, we would be verry pleased."

Hilo nodded and touched him gratefully on the shoulder with one diffident finger. "I am glad the dream was true," she said obscurely.

The wise, faded eyes looked into hers with perfect understanding. "Up here," he said softly, "we do not take dreams lightly."

So Hilo went down to the post office and bought a sunny postcard of Portleish and a stamp with her last remaining change from Ben's Salvation Army £10. On it she wrote the name of the island – "*Eilean Diomhair*" – and added just nine noncommittal words. "*Wish you were here. Weather very cloudy. Love, Hilo.*"

That should do it, she thought. He will ask Maude what it is all about, and she will tell him. And it doesn't sound too interfering, I hope. It is still up to him."

She addressed it to both Maude and David, stuck the stamp on and thrust it in the box on the post office wall. There was nothing to do now but wait. *Oh David, do come*, she prayed silently. *Do believe it*. Then at least I will have done something positive to repay you and Maude for all your kindnes. And Cloudy's eyes will no longer reflect such loneliness and pain – and nor will yours . . . *Do come!*"

She waited patiently for three days, knowing he could not get there sooner, and then she began to fret. In the meantime she had tried to help Mora with the work of the house and had been initiated into the mysteries of making girdle scones on top of the kitchen range. She had also attempted to help Angus with his nets and had even gone out with him once to the nearest fishing grounds. She knew, humbly, that she was not much use to either of them, but they both humoured her and allowed her to feel faintly helpful.

223

It was on the fourth day that she looked up from helping Mora hang out a billowing line of washing and saw the local bus arrive and a familiar figure descend from it.

She watched him look round for a moment at his surroundings like a man returning home, and then make his way rather swiftly down to the quayside. She did not dare to follow him too closely – she knew this was something he must do alone – but she saw him greet Angus and hold a quiet conversation with him, and then the two of them climbed down into Morag II and set off from the little fishing port into open water.

The sea was still calm and silver, the sky above was still full of scudding clouds, but there was blue between with a hint of sunshine behind the winter grey . . . And the small white boat went out into the silver sea and moved steadily away into the distance.

There he goes, thought Hilo. It is all right now. At least one search is over. It seemed to her that even the little boat, Morag II, was performing her own joyous dance on the glittering surface of the winter sea . . .

Well, I've done what I could, she thought. Now it is time to find Ben. *Time to find Ben!* So she collected her old duffel bag, said goodbye to Mora Fairlie, turned her back on the sea, and set out for the road to the south.

Angus ran the boat gently ashore and David stepped out on to the smooth wet sand. There was no-one waiting for him, but if he was disappointed he did not show it. He simply turned back to Angus with a lift of one enquiring eyebrow.

"He will be up at the otter pool," said Angus. "He iss there most days."

David nodded and turned to walk along the little curving beach. "Thanks, Angus."

"Will I need to be waiting?" the lilting highland voice called after him.

For a moment David hesitated and then – with sudden resolve – gave a decisive shake of the head. "No," he said, and smiled back over his shoulder. "You go on home."

*Go on home*, said his feet, crunching on white shell and golden shingle. *Go on home*. And the cloud shadows raced ahead of him over the pale, tide-washed sand.

Cloudy heard his feet coming. He stood up slowly to meet him and the little other leapt and crowed for attention at the edge of the stream as he moved away.

For a moment the two men stood still, dark glances meeting and locking in mutual enquiry, and then flooding with a kind of joyous relief which neither of them could hide.

At last David said in a faintly uneven voice: "Well, I hope I'm welcome, after all the trouble that child has taken."

Cloudy just looked at him and laughed. "It would be a pity to disappoint her," he said. "Come and meet another hopeful optimist."

And together they sat down by the stream and watched the young otter play.

Back in the little boat, Morag II, Angus was heading for home and thinking to himself, in the same words as Hilo's before: I am glad the dream was true.

# VII

# THE REAL WORLD

Ben had a difficult journey home. Lifts were scarce and too short and a cold sleet fell on him as he waited by the roadside. But at last he arrived, cold and tired, only to find the house locked up and no light on anywhere inside.

He was just turning away in despair, when a neighbour came out of her house and looked him up and down.

"Come home, have you, Ben? About time, too."

Ben sighed. He knew he would have to face a lot of this from his mother's friends, so he did not try to make excuses.

"Is – is my Dad – ?"

"On the way out," said the woman bluntly. "Your Mam's at the hospital now."

"Oh – " He did not know how to respond to this. So he simply picked up his backpack again, pulled up his anorak collar round his ears and prepared to go on to the hospital on foot. It was a long way across town but he hadn't any money left for a bus fare.

Behind him the woman's voice seemed to soften a little as she called after him. "Bring her back here when she's done. I'll see to a meal."

"Thanks," said Ben, flashing her a grateful grin over his shoulder. He knew that in this bleak town her offer was a real concession.

He did not see her shake her head after him, with genuine concern looking out of her sharp black eyes.

At the hospital he was directed to a ward called Spenser, which looked bright and cheerful enough, but which he knew from past visiting mostly dealt with the terminally ill. His heart sank still further when he saw its patients, but the blunt warning of his neighbour had prepared him for the worst.

He found his mother sitting, dry-eyed and calm, by the high hospital bed, with his father's hand in hers. But nothing had prepared him for the shocking change in his father, and he stood there awkwardly, unable to say a word.

But his mother looked up and saw him, and a great smile of relief and welcome lit her face as she realized who was standing beside her. Gently, she placed her husband's shrunken hand back on the sheet and simply held out her arms to her son.

"Oh Ben – you came!"

"Of course," he said, encompassing her in a fierce, comforting embrace. "Of course I came – as soon as I could."

For a moment neither of them could say any more, but then his mother withdrew a little from his consoling arms and patted the chair beside her. "Sit down, then, and tell me how you've been."

Ben obeyed her, but he looked down at his father's grey, twisted face with a wrench of awful pity. What could he do – what could anyone do – to help this broken wreck of a man?

"Is – is he – ?"

"Conscious? No, Ben. Hasn't been since it happened." She clutched at his arm with one hand and gave him a small tug of reassurance. "Better this way. Understand?"

Ben nodded. He did indeed understand. But at the same time he felt a great sadness that he could no longer reach his father – could not be reconciled with him after the awful scene over the computer and his precipitate flight from home. It was too late now. He would never be able to explain to him why he had fled, or tell him that there was a bond between them still that could never be broken, despite their differences.

"Don't fret, son," said his mother. "Things went wrong for him that could never be put right." She looked down at her husband with a curious expression of mingled tenderness and resignation. "Never came to terms with it," she murmured, reaching out a hand to smooth the thin wisps of hair on the top of his head.

Under her hand Stan moved his head very slightly and sighed

227

a long, deep sigh. Then his eyes opened slowly and fixed themselves on her face with a look of unexpected awareness in their faded depths. At first they seemed to focus on Edie's anxious gaze, then they moved on and settled on Ben's young face beside her. Something seemed to stir and change in their expression then, and for a brief, heart-stopping moment clear intelligence and recognition shone in them. He knew his son, Ben, and a faint stricture that was almost an attempt at a smile touched the corner of his mouth. The two pairs of eyes met and locked, and to Ben it seemed that a whole lifetime of experience, misunderstanding and forgiveness passed between them in unspoken accord. Then the light of understanding faded within Stan's eyes, and the heavy eyelids closed over them again in silent surrender.

Edie did not speak and nor did Ben. They went on sitting there quietly until a nurse came by. She took one look at Stan and led them gently away.

"I'm sorry, Mrs Roberts, dear," she said in a kind voice that struggled to say the right thing. "But at least it was peaceful at the end."

"Oh yes," said Edie carefully. "Yes. It was that all right."

Ben said nothing, but he put his arm round her and took her home.

It wasn't until after the funeral that Ben and his mother sat down to talk. Until then, it was all arrangements and relations, neighbours and Stan's old workmates, cheap sherry and ham sandwiches. Ben did his best to be a tower of strength and took on everything that his mother would allow – which wasn't as much as he would have liked. But when he thought about it, he realized that Edie Roberts was not the sort of person to lie down under adversity. She was a fighter and a survivor – just as he was – and she needed to be furiously busy just now, so he would be doing her no favours by taking everything off her shoulders, even if she would let him, which she wouldn't.

But at last everything was over. The relations and the neighbours had departed, the house was tidy again and there was time to breathe. So Ben made a cup of tea and carried it in to his mother and Edie said with brisk decision: "Now then. You've stalled long enough, Benny-boy. Tell me all."

Ben grinned at her determined face and obeyed like a dutiful son. He told her about Dora and the caravan trailer and the twins he had taught to read. He told her about Al and the market and all the market folk and how good they all were to him one way and another, especially when he and Al got injured in the accident. He told her about Al's further kindness, too, and his efforts to get compensation for them both which still might come to something.

Then he told her about Uncle Allsorts and Annie-Mog and the cats, about Evie and Pete, and the unexpected warmth and friendship he had found on a windy clearing beside a broken railway arch in the heart of the city.

And then he told her about Hilo. He didn't leave anything out – not even Hilo's secret folder of poems – because he knew his mother would understand all too well how someone could still have dreams and visions in spite of hardship. (Hadn't she danced and twirled with his silk scarf, with unquenched, youthful joy still in her eyes?) But when he came to that Christmas night when they heard music in the starlit air, he found that he could not speak of it at all, it was too precious. So he went on to the girl in the river, and their meeting with Maude in the beautiful house in the riverside terrace.

At last Ben came to Hilo's illness and the awful choice he had had to face. His voice almost faltered then, and he hurried on to the moment when he left her on Maude's doorstep and waited in the shadows to see whether she was taken in. And as he came to the end there were tears in his eyes, and tears in his stumbling voice, too.

"I had to, Mum," he said, turning towards her in desperate appeal. "Do you understand? She was so ill . . . I didn't dare leave her out on the street another night – and I knew they'd do something for her, one way or another. Maude had been kind to us before – and then there was her sister, Little Doc Never-Stop, we called her. I thought she'd help; either they'd put Hilo in hospital or they'd look after her somehow. And that was more than I could do." His voice broke a little then and he took a deep breath before

229

he went on: "But I – I felt like a traitor, leaving her, and I still do."

His mother nodded again and said gently: "I can understand that – but you did the right thing."

"Did I?" Ben was asking himself more than his sympathetic mother. "I hope to God I did." Then his natural ebullience seemed to return and cancel his doubts for the moment, and he smiled at Edie and added: "Anyway, I reckoned you needed me here, so I came."

If Edie was surprised at all this long saga, or the fact that Ben was no better off and no nearer a job and good prospects than he was when he left home, she did not say so. But now there was the future to think of, and she knew she had to get a few things clear between them.

"What will you do now?" she asked.

Ben's expression changed and his eyes fixed themselves on her face in concern. "That depends on you."

"Does it?" She faced him levelly. "Why?"

He looked confused for a moment, and then said awkwardly: "I don't know how you're fixed for money – or whether I could get my old job back up here?"

"You couldn't," said Edie flatly. "The factory closed down completely soon after you left."

Ben blinked. "So all that row with Dad – "

"A waste of breath. Yes." Her smile was bleak.

Ben noted that smile with misgiving. "Then – another job?"

She shook her head doubtfully. "I don't know . . . unemployment's very bad up here – worse than London, they say."

"It couldn't be much worse," growled Ben. Then he went on, anxiously prompting his mother. "But you'll need some money coming in, won't you?"

"I've got my own job still," she said. "Stan didn't bring in anything lately."

"What about the redundancy money?"

She shrugged. "Ask the Crown and Thistle."

Ben sighed. "The house – ?"

"The Council will let me stay on, if I can pay the rent . . . even though Stan let it mount up a bit."

"Did he?"

Edie sighed. "Owed money all round, in the end. So I'll probably move, if I can."

He looked surprised. "Do you want to leave here?"

"*Yes*," said Edie, with sudden passionate conviction.

Ben was astonished, seeing a side of his mother that he had not known about. "Where would you go?"

"Almost anywhere," said Edie, "where no-one knew about Stan and no-one was sorry for me."

Ben nodded. He understood that. "Would you – if I could get fixed up somewhere in London – would you come?"

Edie looked at him consideringly. Ben had grown up a lot since he left home. He was somehow stronger and more reliable than he had been – even if he hadn't yet landed a steady job. But he was also more independent and already making his own private commitments and relationships. This thing with the girl called Hilo was a lot more serious than she had expected, perhaps even more serious than Ben himself realized. So how would he feel about having a widowed mother on his hands? Wouldn't it cramp his style? And did she really want to depend on Ben for company – for support?

"I could always go and live with Auntie Flo," she said suddenly.

Ben grinned. "Do you want to?"

"No." She was honest about that, at least.

He laughed. "So I thought." Then he grew serious again. "You haven't said if you'd come?"

She hesitated. "I do the accounts at the bakery now. I'm quite good at it. I suppose I could always get another job, with that behind me." She paused again, still hesitating. "But – would you want me to?"

"Yes." Ben was quite definite about that. He had to be. But he also had to be honest. "Only, there's the question of Hilo." He also paused, trying to think what to say. "I'll have to go back and find out what happened to her – d'you see that? I mean, they may have got her life sorted out for her, or they may not. She's very independent, you see. And if she's out on the street again she'll need help." Once again he stalled, unable to put into words what he felt about Hilo. "And anyway, I think – I think we probably need each other, somehow."

231

His mother was both wise and far-seeing, in a way that Ben did not fully realize. Now she said gently: "I can see it's important to you. Of course you must go and find her. And help her, if she needs it."

He looked at her gratefully. "Are you sure? I mean, I'll stay on here if you need me."

"No," said Edie. "You go and find Hilo. I'll get things settled up here. Then – if you get yourself fixed up, we'll talk about all getting together – if you think it would work?"

Ben's curly mouth could not help curling upwards in relief and gladness. "I'm sure it would work," he said. Then he added obscurely: "Hilo likes twirling, too."

Edie did not answer that. But she understood Ben completely.


Ben waited another week before he left, and even then he was not a bit sure that he ought to leave his mother on her own. Her steady, sensible calm seemed genuine enough, but there was something about her eyes that bothered him – they still seemed to be a bit too bright and clear, too dilated in shock, to be natural. He tried once to ask her if she was all right, but he could not get past that steadfastly cheerful face, and he came to the conclusion that she needed to keep up appearances at the moment, and shattering that fragile serenity might do more harm than good. He rather wished she would cry, but he knew, somehow, that if she did it would be in secret, and not for his father's death, but for the slow, tragic decline that had overcome the strong, handsome man she had once loved so much. When he reached this point in his thoughts he looked up and saw her watching him, a half-smile of tender amusement lifting the corners of her mouth.

"It's all right, you know," she said. "I won't break in two."

Ben's answering smile was still anxious. "All the same – "

Edie interrupted him firmly. "Ben, I think you should know – I'm glad it's over. It's no joke watching someone you love go to pieces – especially when you know they could snap out of it if only they'd try." She drew a steadying breath and went on quietly. "Stan was his own worst enemy. I knew that long ago – and I always hoped he'd change." She shut her eyes for a moment, as if remembering too many things, then seemed to summon up more strength. "But a man like Stan can't change, Ben. It's not in his nature. All I could do was – sort of *cushion* him against his own mistakes." She sighed. "It got so that I couldn't even do that towards the end."

She shook her head in sorrow at the memory of those many scenes and rages. But Ben could see that she was not upset by the recollection of them, just filled with a kind of resigned and gentle pity for their perpetrator. He realized then that there was a hidden, steely strength about his mother that he had not recognized before, and he understood too that Stan's death was much more merciful and much less devastating than an even more prolonged and dreadful period of decay would have been.

Edie leant foward and patted him affectionately. "That's it, Ben. See it clear. He's all right now, my Stan. Let him rest in peace."

She got up then, brisk and cheerful as ever, and went to put the kettle on, saying over her shoulder as she went: "So just you get on and find that poor child, Hilo, before she gets into any more trouble. We might as well salvage something from the wreck!"

Ben was so filled with admiration for his mother's unfailing courage then that he felt like crying himself. But instead he followed her into the kitchen, laid an arm round her shoulders, hugging her close, and said a little gruffly: "You're smashing, Mum, d'you know that?"

But Edie just lit the gas under the kettle, and laughed.

When he got back to London, Ben went straight to the house on the river terrace to look for Hilo. Feeling anything but brave, he rang the bell, and hoped that Maude would come to the door, not the strange man who had been with her when Hilo was left on their doorstep. At least he knew Maude, and he thought she would probably not be too cross with him for having taken her generosity so much for granted.

His mind was full of explanations and pleas for understanding and protestations about Hilo's worth and her desperate need for shelter, and he found himself rehearsing passionate speeches as he waited there on the doorstep. But nothing happened. No-one came to the door. He tried ringing the bell again, but still nothing happened. There was no-one at home – the house was clearly empty. But then, where was Hilo? What had happened to her? Had she been so ill that they had been obliged to send her to hospital? Or – or had it been even worse than that? Could Hilo have succumbed – like poor Annie-Mog – to the rigours of life on the street in a London winter? No, he thought. No! I'd know if anything bad had happened to her. I'd know if Hilo was dead. And he shivered when he thought how terrible that would be. How cold and empty the world would be. For if Hilo was ever to die, something inside him would die too. He knew that now.

But she *wasn't* dead – he gave himself a mental shake. Of course she wasn't! She had just gone away somewhere. The question was, where? And since neither Maude nor the strange man seemed to be in he would have to go and search for Hilo on his own – and maybe come back later to see whether anyone had returned and he could ask where she had got to. Yes, that was it. Go back to all the places Hilo and he had known together and ask for news of her. If she had gone off on her own again, she must be somewhere.

He gave one last look at the silent house, and then turned away sadly and went off down the road towards Uncle Allsorts and the old site by the broken railway arch. But when he got there he found – like Hilo – that the whole set-up had changed. There was no Uncle Allsorts, no Evie and Pete, only a group of strangers and one very laid-back young man with smouldering eyes and a casual tongue who spoke in lazy monosyllables and volunteered nothing.

"So where did Uncle Allsorts go?" asked Ben urgently. "Where did they take him?" He didn't like to think of the old man shut away in some kind of restricted space when he had been used to the freedom of the cold streets and the night sky. "It'll about kill him, shutting him up," he muttered.

The boy looked at him curiously. "What is it with you guys? All this fuss about an old drunk who got paralytic and fell down?"

Ben shook his head. "You don't understand – " and then something about what the boy had said made his mind snap to attention. "What d'you mean 'all this fuss'? Did – did someone else come asking about him?"

234

"Sure," agreed the young man wearily. He seemed disinclined to say any more, and Ben wanted to shake him. (Just like Hilo.)

"Who, for instance?"

Marc shrugged fluid shoulders. "Guys."

"Was – was a girl called Hilo one of them?"

There was a pause, and the smouldering, angry eyes fixed themselves on Ben's face with surprising alertness. "Would you be Ben?"

"I would."

He nodded. "Gotta message. Hilo's looking for you."

Ben could not hide his eagerness. "She *was* here, then?"

"Yeah."

*"When?"*

Once more the vague, dismissive shrug. "Sometime – " and when Ben glared at him in furious frustration, he enlarged upon it a little. "Coupla weeks ago? Maybe longer . . ."

Ben sighed. "But she didn't stay?"

Marc looked round him and made a willowy gesture with one languid hand. "Not here, is she?"

Ben was getting very near to throttling him, when he added suddenly, without prompting: "She said she'd be back . . ."

"Oh." There was nothing else to be got out of him now, Ben realized. Even volunteering that much was obviously an effort. So he gave the boy a fleeting smile and said: "Thanks. I'll be back, too."

"Ask for Marc," said the boy, conceding much at the last moment, as he had to Hilo.

Ben nodded and went off down the street, not knowing where to look next. At least she's alive, he thought. And asking for me. And she must be fairly all right if she can get down here to have a look. He walked on, feeling a lot more hopeful. But he hadn't found her yet, and there were other pressing arrangements to make as well.

He went next to see Corky – expecting a furious ticking off for leaving him in the lurch.

"Oh," said Corky, slapping a bunch of green bananas down on the stall with much too much force to do them any good. "Condescended to come back, did you?"

235

"I'm sorry," explained Ben humbly. "My Dad died."

Corky's indiarubber cockney face changed. "That's different," he admitted in an unexpectedly gentle voice most unlike his usual screech. "I'm sorry, too, kid." He looked him up and down, noting the neat, newly-washed jeans and new thick sweater. Clearly, going home had done the kid good. So why was he back on the street again? "You want your job back?" he asked.

"Didn't you get anyone else?"

Corky shook his head and shrugged, all in one swift movement. "Got by on my own, didn't I? But you can come back if you like."

Ben hesitated. "I would like – but I'm looking for someone . . ."

"Your girl, was it? The one that played the pipe? She was asking for you."

"*When*?" asked Ben, new hope rising.

"Oh – it would be . . . a week – ten days ago?" He paused, considering, and while doing so slapped down a few more unprotesting bits of fruit on to his overcrowded stall. "I told her the Sally Army got to you."

Ben stared. "You saw that? Did she – What did Hilo say?"

"Nothing." He looked at Ben's disappointed face with sudden sympathy. "But she went off like a bat in hell."

She probably went to ask them, thought Ben. I wonder if they'd have told her? And if they did, what would she do next?

He turned back to Corky and said: "Thanks. I'll try and turn up tomorrow morning – but I'd better be off now."

Corky nodded and forbore to ask where Ben was going next, or where he would be staying the night.

But Ben had suddenly thought of something else. "Old Uncle Allsorts," he said. "You knew him, didn't you?"

"Sure. Everyone round here knew old Uncle."

"D'you know where they took him? I'd like to go and see him."

Corky sighed. "You might be too late, son."

"Why? Was he that ill?"

"No-o. But once they took him in the heart seemed to go out of him, they said."

"Who said?"

236

"One of the hostel workers. She buys her veg from me, see?" He shook his head again sadly over the plight of Uncle Allsorts. "Poor old sod," he muttered, then added to Ben: "It's Pen Street – down Chiswick way, she said."

Ben nodded. "Thanks. I'll try and get there."

"Maybe it'll cheer him up to see a friendly face," agreed Corky, balancing some oranges on top of a pile of cabbages. "Here, take 'im a coupla these." He waved Ben off with the oranges just as a customer arrived demanding instant attention.

Ben put the oranges in his pockets and went across the road and up several side streets to his next port of call, which was Reg's paper shop on the corner where the old market used to be.

Reg's face lit up when Ben arrived, and he began to scold him cheerfully as soon as he set foot inside the door.

"Where've you been? You promised to call in, remember? Al's been looking for you."

"*Al* has? When?

"Oh – coupla weeks back. Left a letter for you." Reg was trying to look severe, but somehow he couldn't help smiling, and Ben began to wonder what had come over him. "I think it's good news, mate," added Reg, diving under the counter and bringing out a neat white envelope.

Ben looked from Reg's smile to the envelope, and then opened it with not very steady fingers. Inside was a single sheet of paper, and two five pound notes.

*Good news at last*, said Al's careful handwriting. *The small claims court awarded damages to us both. I get £1500 for injury plus loss of earnings. You get £500 ditto. Not large, but best I could do. If you go to the solicitor, George Brown in the Goldhawk Road – Reg knows where he is – (and take something to identify you) he will pay up. In case you're stuck meanwhile, this will at least get you a bed in a hostel and a meal. Then, Benny-boy, you can get a room and a job. Mind you do! All the best, Al.*

Ben looked down at Al's letter and then up at Reg with tears in his eyes. The impossible had happened – the awful sequence was

237

broken. At last he could get his life in order and have something to offer Hilo in the way of safety and shelter when he found her. *When he found her*. And all because of the persistence and generosity of one tough black ex-student with half a lawyer's training.

"Honestly," he said to Reg, not knowing whether to laugh or cry. "He didn't have to, you know. It's unbelievable."

"He thought he had to," grinned Reg. "'A life's worth something, Reg,' he said. So you make the most of it, son!"

"Oh, I will!" laughed Ben, and suddenly whirled Reg with him round the shop in a crazy dance. "I will! You see if I don't!"

But then he remembered that he hadn't found Hilo yet, and he hadn't found a job or a room yet either, however good things looked on paper. So he grew sober again, got the solicitor's address out of Reg and went off to deal with everything at once on a tide of optimism he simply could not quench.

He would find Hilo soon. He must. There was a future for them now. He must find her and tell her all about it. She couldn't be far away.

In the next few days after Al's money came Ben got a lot of things sorted out. He found a pleasant room in a tall thin house full of students, and put down a deposit for one month's rent in advance. (Amazing, he thought, that he could actually do that at last!) It wasn't all that big as rooms go, but it seemed like a palace to him, and it had a good bed and a sofa. It would be all right for Hilo too – when he found her. If he found her. But he wasn't going to let himself think like that. Of course he would find her.

Then he went down to the Job Centre, with an address and some semblance of respectability in his life at last. He demanded to be put on the list for the government training scheme in computer graphics and also begged to be sent for an interview to any kind of job they thought he could handle. To his surprise, this time they took him seriously – the possession of that small, shabby room near Shepherd's Bush seemed to make all the difference. After two fruitless interviews (he was only allowed to try for three) he found himself being accepted at the third, as a filing clerk who might possibly have the skill to transfer information from old-fashioned files on to a data-base on the office computer. It was something he knew he could do, and he managed to sound so confident and so convincing that they took him on trial. Then it was up to him.

So now he had a room and a job (not very well paid, but it would cover the rent), and he went back to Corky and agreed to help him on the early morning and late evening shifts as well, for old times' sake. What with this and the day-time job there was even a little money to spare. He could scarcely believe in his luck.

There was something to offer Hilo now. He could take care of her – and maybe if his mother decided to come down later on, they could all afford to take a flat together. With this hopeful future in mind, he decided to go back to see if Maude was there in the beautiful house by the river.

He arrived there late one evening to see a glow of lamplight in the house. So someone was there at least. Feeling suddenly shy and nervous, he rang the bell and was relieved to see Maude standing there by the open door.

"Ben! I'm so glad you've turned up at last."

"Is – is Hilo?" He could not get it out clearly.

"She's not here, Ben. I'm sorry. She's in Scotland."

"*Scotland?*" He sounded appalled. Scotland was such a long way away. "Why?" he asked, seeming absurdly shaken and bewildered.

"You'd better come in," said Maude. "It's a long story."

So Ben went into the warm white house and sat down in the kitchen while Maude told him all she knew.

"And two days ago this came – " she said, handing Ben the sunny postcard of Portleish with the cryptic message on it. *Wish you were here. Weather very cloudy.*

"Clever," he muttered.

"Very. It told David all he needed to know. But it took nothing for granted." She smiled at Ben with sudden warmth, looking all at once much younger and happier. "You've no idea what this means to us, Ben. The whole family has been living under this shadow. If David is happy again it will be a different world!"

Ben nodded, swallowing an alarming tendency towards tears

when he translated that thought to Hilo. If he found Hilo again it would indeed be a different world. "I – I'm glad," he said inadequately, and then went on with awkward shyness: "You've been so good to her – I don't know how to – "

"My dear boy," said Maude brusquely, "if this works out, it more than repays anything any of us have done, believe me." She looked at Ben kindly. "She's rather a special person, Hilo, isn't she?"

"Yes," said Ben, swallowing again. "She is."

Maude passed him another cup of tea. "Now tell me what you've been doing."

So Ben told her about his father, and about the possibility of his mother moving down to London – and about the wonderful windfall of Al's compensation money. And about his new job, and his room, and his extra work for Corky. And finally, looking into Maude's face with anxious entreaty, he said: "So you see, I must find Hilo. I can look after her now. I couldn't before, when she was so ill. But I can now. She'd be safe with me."

"I know that, Ben," said Maude. "And when she was ill here she never stopped asking for you. That's how she got ill the second time – looking for you."

Again Ben nodded sadly. "Then – do you think she'll come back?"

"I'm sure she will. My guess is, once she knows David's arrived in Portleish, she'll disappear."

"And come back home?" *Home?* He winced a little. "I mean – come back here?"

Maude hesitated. "I think so. There's this business with her poems. David will insist on going ahead with them, I'm sure. There'll be some money in it, too. Not a great deal, but some. And she'll be needed for vetting the illustrations and proofs and so on, later."

"Will she – will she realize that?"

Again Maude hesitated. "Yes. She's not a fool. She'll know work will be needed on them." She gave a sudden almost mischievous grin. "She subjected us to quite a lecture, you know, – about the plight of her homeless friends, and how she wanted to put their case. She really shook us!"

Ben grinned back. "I can imagine. Hilo can be quite high-powered." He paused, remembering. "That one – 'God is dead, they said' . . ."

"Yes," Maude agreed. "That one, particularly . . ." She looked at Ben again, and laid a hand on his arm. "So I think she'll come back here, Ben – probably not to stay, because she's frantically independent, but she'll come. And I'll either keep her here and send for you, or give her your address, now you've got one! Either way, you'll get together in the end."

In the end? How long would that take, Ben wondered? And what if she didn't come back at all?

"I think you'd better keep calling round," said Maude, worried about his anxious face. "We're bound to have news of her soon."

Ben sighed and got up to go. "I hope so – " He paused and gave Maude a shy, pain-washed smile. "Thank you for everything you've done for her. I – I'll come again soon."

"You do that, Ben," said Maude firmly. "And don't leave it too long."

Ben did not reply to that. How long was too long, he wondered? How long before Hilo came back and life could be good again?

He went away down the street, back to his own small room. *His own small room!* It was warm and cosy when he lit the gas fire, but it still seemed colossally empty. *Oh Hilo, where are you? Please come home! Come soon!*

The gas fire popped and hissed. The students upstairs strummed guitars, and someone's stereo belted out fractured music. Outside, the London traffic went on with its usual muted roar. The night was full of cheerful noise and bustle – but Ben was alone, and to him the silence was deafening.

Hilo's second lift put her down in Edinburgh in the late evening on a mild and rainy night. The street lights shone into pools of rain on the pavements and the neon signs painted cheerful colours on to the oily streets. Hilo walked along, shoulders hunched against the rain, and wished she'd got some money left for a cup of coffee. But that postcard and that stamp had taken the last of it. Then she suddenly remembered that she had still got the tin whistle and the little dancing puppet, and began to look round for a likely spot to do a little busking. There was a theatre near by, with people already going in through the open doors, and a concert hall next to it, with a billboard outside advertising coming events. That had its doors open too, though there weren't many people going in there yet.

She decided on the pavement outside the theatre, and got out her whistle and disentangled the puppet's strings from Ben's careful wrapping. (*Oh Ben, how much your care and kindness come home to me at every turn.*) The rain was not heavy – a mere hazy drizzle – and it was still mild enough to play without her fingers getting too cold.

She began the Irish jig, and then changed it to a Scottish reel (which she could just about manage) in honour of her surroundings and the little puppet danced on the end of her strings and people stopped to smile at her and drop a coin or two into Hilo's woolly hat. (It would get wet, she reflected, and probably muddy. But who cares, if the coins roll in?)

She had been playing for a while when something on the concert hall billboard caught her eye. A name – a performer, perhaps, or an orchestra? Or a new work by a new composer? Something jogged at her memory, and she took a step nearer as she went on playing, and leant forward to have a closer look. The little puppet bowed and bobbed a curtsey on the pavement as she did so.

Then she stopped playing abruptly and stared in disbelief. But it was there, as clear as city lamplight could make it – and there was no mistake.

*Max Torelli and the Aurora Quartet.*
*A programme of American music, including*
*'Cloud Towers' by Max Torelli.*

He's even used my poem, she thought, – "*Auroras bloom, clouds tower . . .*" He must have thought of me, then – at least once or twice. For a moment she was tempted to go in and ask for the Green Room – to find him and welcome him back. But then she thought again, and remembered that he had gone away to start a new life, a new career, in a new country. '*No encumbrances*' she had said, – and meant it. She couldn't spoil it now.

But she could hear his music. That is, if the busking had raised enough for a ticket. She bent down and counted the money in the little woolly cap, then rather timidly went into the foyer and asked at the box office for the cheapest ticket they had. She wondered if they would object to her scruffy jeans and damp duffel coat, but they seemed entirely unperturbed. They were used to students and any audience was better than nothing for a programme of new music. She could just about afford it. But it would leave no money for a meal or a bed. Never mind, she thought, I've done without before. At least it will be warm and dry inside. So she slipped into her seat at the back of the hall and settled down to wait.

When the players came in she was surprised at how her own stomach clenched and churned with nervousness on their behalf. There were five of them, including Max at the piano, and they came on into subdued lighting, looking young and thin and strung-up in their black jeans and sweaters. There was a cellist, a violinist, a flautist and a percussionist with a variety of drums, gongs, glockenspiels, xylophones, tubular bells and nuts, and there also seemed to be some sound equipment with taped background effects, which Max seemed to be in charge of when he wasn't at the piano. Not the usual kind of quartet, Hilo reflected, but they looked interesting.

Max looked the same as ever, the burning fiery furnace air even more marked than before, if anything, and his bow to the thinly scattered audience was brief and business-like. Hilo hoped fervently that when they began they would seem less fragile and vulnerable. It was awful to be new and young in the music world, to be unrecognized, and to have to fight to impress an indifferent, sceptical audience.

But she needn't have worried. As soon as they played the first notes, the magic began. She didn't understand all the music – some of it, she knew, was beyond her, even with Max's training behind her. But all five players reflected the same burning intensity of feeling that Max engendered, – and their electric fervour sang in the air.

When Max's own piece came, she found that she did understand it. There were sounds in it that she had not known could exist – shimmers of starlight, great climbing cloud shapes, breath-taking mirages, and sudden, harsh rages that tried to cancel out beauty and couldn't . . . And always, always, behind it all, the certain promise of light – till it blazed out at the end in a blinding dazzle of radiant sound.

Hilo was riven by it – shaken more than she had known music could stir her – and she found that tears were running down her face when it was over. (*Hilo, you cry too much these days. You ought to be ashamed of yourself.*) But she wasn't ashamed. She was glad. Oh Max, she thought, you've made it! How could anyone fail to be moved by music like that?

The audience seemed to think so too, and went on clapping a long time for him, so that he and the others had to come on several times before the lights finally went up. Then Hilo quietly brushed the tears off her face and slipped out of the door into the street before the rest of the audience came out. Better to get right away. She knew now that Max was on his way up – the move to America had paid off and his music had grown, grown out of all recognition. She couldn't disturb him now. He was all right, and the use of her words – her images – in his music was enough compensation for letting him go.

Good luck, Max, and God speed, she said, and went on down the rainy street alone. Maybe I can pick up another lift soon, she thought. Then I needn't bother about somewhere to sleep. I've got enough left for a Mars bar – that will have to do. And the sooner I get a lift, the sooner I'll get back to London – the sooner I'll find Ben. *The sooner I'll find Ben.*

For she had realized, when the sudden presence of Max in the next building had dawned on her, that she did not really need to see *him*, did not feel the ache of *his* absence any longer. It was Ben she needed – Ben whose absence ached through her every limb and made her world seem so empty and grey.

I've got to find him, she thought. I understand that now. And I'm glad I had the chance to hear Max's music – to find out where my true feelings lie. Max is all right, and his music is all right, but he has nothing to do with me any more. It is Ben who matters. Ben who counts.

She had reached a main road by now, and before long a lorry pulled up beside her, answering her beseeching thumb. She climbed on board and the wheels began to turn. The lights flashed past and the long wet road gleamed before them in the headlamps. She was on her way. London was ahead. She would find Ben soon.

One evening the waiting for news got intolerable, and Ben set off to find the hostel which had taken in old Uncle Allsorts. Feeling rather guilty about Corky's oranges, which he had never delivered, he bought some more, together with a packet of the old man's favourite licorice allsorts, and took a bus down to Chiswick High Street. There he wandered through a maze of unfamiliar streets and finally ran the hostel to earth at the end of a small cul-de-sac near a jumble of warehouses.

But when he went in and asked for Uncle Allsorts they told him the old man had gone.

"Gone?" he said, his heart giving a small flip of dismay. "You don't mean –?"

"No." The woman helper smiled at his anxious face. "I don't mean that. He just went off – the obstinate old so-and-so."

Ben sighed with relief. "Was he all right?"

The woman shook her head ruefully. "Not entirely. I don't suppose his health will ever be 'all right' again. But he would go. And, knowing him, I expect he'll survive. Till the next time."

Ben nodded, knowing that the pattern was already set for old Uncle Allsorts, and nothing would change it now.

"Where did he go, do you know?"

The woman shrugged eloquent shoulders. "Back to his old haunts, I expect."

"Yes," agreed Ben. "That figures. I'd better go and look."

She smiled at him again, this time with more warmth. "If he needs help again, let us know."

"I will," Ben promised, and went off to catch another bus back to the old haunts of Uncle Allsorts.

He approached the old site by the railway arch a little cautiously this time, not knowing what he would find. But the fire was lit and smoking, and there were several shadowy figures hunched round it. He thought he could make out the laid-back figure of the boy, Marc, and a couple of strangers – but standing over them, and weaving on his feet as usual, was the unmistakable bulky shape of Uncle Allsorts.

245

"So there you are," growled Allsorts. "Might've known you'd turn up. Bad penny, is it?"

"I was looking for you," protested Ben.

"Lookin' for me?" rasped Allsorts, glaring at Ben with a red, baleful eye. "Why? I lives here, don't I?"

Ben did not contradict him. He simply handed over the oranges and the packet of allsorts and said mildly: "Glad to see you on your feet." But he privately thought the old man looked as frail as a piece of bitter grass blowing in the wind, and if he got hold of any more gin that night, he wouldn't be on his feet much longer.

"Where you bin, anyways?" demanded Allsorts, taking in Ben's tidier, more prosperous appearance. "Gone all posh on us, have you?"

"Does it look like it?" countered Ben, and was a bit taken aback when the old man said crossly: "Yes!"

But he sat down then, rather suddenly, and allowed Ben to make him some tea in the old blackened kettle.

"I suppose – you haven't seen Hilo?" Ben asked at last, not hoping for much and looking round at Marc as well for a reply.

But Marc merely lifted fluid shoulders in yet another shrug and said in a tired drawl: "Not since . . ."

"Not since what?" demanded Allsorts, aware that he was missing something.

"That was while you were away," explained Ben. "She came once, Marc said . . ."

"Lookin' for you, was she?" The old eyes bored into his with surprising sagacity.

"I – yes, she was," Ben told him. "And now I'm looking for her." He paused and then added slowly: "Where d'you think she'd go, Uncle? Any idea?"

"Back here," said Allsorts promptly. "She'd know you'd look for her here." He took a noisy swig of hot tea and added confidently: "Stands to reason."

Ben sighed. That was what he had hoped, too. But there was no sign of Hilo yet – not in any of the haunts they had known. He had tried them all.

He spent another half-hour talking to the old man, and then sadly got up to go. No luck this time. But there was always

246

another day. He wandered on down to the river, and stood looking out at its shadowy, ink-and-silver reaches beyond the reflections of the streetlights. Hilo had loved the river – maybe even looking at it would comfort him. She would come soon.

Hilo was set down once again at the Shepherd's Bush round-about. Her mind was full of determined resolutions about jobs and rooms and independence. She made her way down to the first set of shops she came to and looked in all the windows for notices of vacancies. But there weren't any that she could handle. At last she came to a newsagent's with a whole display of notices on the door and stopped to read them one by one in case she found something promising. There was one that caught her eye and she read it again with growing interest. "*Small stationers – travel books, maps & magazines – requires someone intelligent who can read.*"

It sounded sardonic enough to be genuine, she thought, so she went in and asked for the address.

"Only twelve doors along," the newsagent told her. "You might just catch him before he closes."

Hilo ran along the street and reached the small shop just as someone was pulling the blind down over the door. She rapped on it wildly, not really having much hope that the owner would take any notice. But he did. The blind remained down, but the door opened an inch and a voice said warily: "Yes?"

"The job," panted Hilo "I've come about the job. And I *can* read!"

There was a moment's pause, then the man inside laughed and opened the door a bit wider. "In that case," he said, "you'd better come in."

Hilo could scarcely believe her luck. She went inside, surrep-titiously trying to smooth her hair down with a nervous hand, and stood blinking around her in the dim light from the passage beyond.

But the owner moved then to a light switch by the door, and the little shop swam into focus before her. There were the usual stands for stationery, pens and pencils on one, and sellotape and glue on another, envelopes and cheap writing pads on a third. And beyond these, two other display racks full of magazines.

247

But on the other side of the room there was a series of shelves containing a bewildering variety of travel books, guides and maps, and there was a curious square, free-standing counter in the middle with a panel of lighted glass on its smooth flat top.

"That's for enlarging maps," explained the man, watching Hilo's gaze as it settled there in puzzled enquiry.

"I see," said Hilo, and went across to look.

"We're famous for our maps," he went on cheerfully. "In fact, we're known as The Map Shop."

"I can see why," said Hilo, a little awestruck by the number of maps stacked in neat piles all along one wall of the room.

"What's your name?" asked the shopkeeper. "I'm Michael Wood, the map man. But most people call me Woody."

"Rebecca Fielding," she answered shyly. "But most people call me Hilo."

He laughed and held out a friendly hand, as if she were an expected guest in his house.

Hilo took it in a state of dazed disbelief. She found herself looking into a pair of very observant hazel eyes – more green than brown – beneath a fairly broad, intelligent brow topped by a lot of rather wispy greyish hair. The handshake was firm and kind, and somehow seemed to engender a certain warmth and confidence in her as she shyly returned its grip.

"So you can read," said Woody, grinning. "What else can you do?"

"Write," said Hilo, greatly daring.

"Do you mean write or write?" asked Woody, and the clever eyes seemed to probe very deep as he watched her.

"Both," said Hilo. And then, as an afterthought: "And I am used to books. My – my father was a librarian."

"That helps," acknowledged Woody. "Can you type?"

She hesitated. "A bit. I taught myself, so I'm not very accurate. But I'm not too bad."

He nodded. "Accounts?"

She looked doubtful. "I never have. Never had anything to account *with*!" A brief grin touched her. Then she added: "But I can learn, if you'll show me."

"That's the spirit," said Woody. "When can you start?"

Hilo blinked. "You mean – ? Just like that?" (Max had said

248

"Just like that?" in just the same tone of disbelief – and it had been simple then. Could it really be that simple now?)

"Why not?" said Woody. "You've told me what I want to know."

"But – you don't even know if I'm honest – "

"Don't I?" he said, and cocked his head on one side like a perky bird. "Well, I'll soon find out, won't I?"

Hilo just gazed at him, while slow tears of thankfulness rose in her eyes. "I – don't know what to say . . ."

"Say yes," he prompted. "Jobs are hard to come by."

"Why – yes, of course!" agreed Hilo, not knowing whether to laugh or cry. "And I could start tomorrow."

"Good," said Woody. "I think we'll suit each other very well. Be here at eight."

He looked at Hilo's pale, incredulous face and added gently: "I daresay you could do with an advance?"

Hilo began to protest. "No, I – "

But he took a five pound note out of the till and handed it to her. "Six days a week – sixty-five pounds. I'll deduct it from that." He hesitated. "It's not a lot, I know. But you're young. And it's all the shop can afford. OK?"

"OK," whispered Hilo, and restrained an impulse to fling her arms round his neck and kiss him.

"I shouldn't, if I were you," he said, laughing – rightly interpreting Hilo's glowing look of jubilation. "I'm quite a slave-driver when the need arises. See you tomorrow. Good night."

Hilo went out of the door in a haze of bewildered goodwill and relief. I've got a job, she said. *I've got a job!* I'm independent! I'm free of the street-life trap! I can get a room of my own! I can have something to offer Ben when I find him, instead of being a drag. (An encumbrance, like I was to Max – and to Maude and David too.) I can be myself at last! And I can go and look for Ben now without any fear of harming him. Because I *was* afraid of that – all the time. But now it's different! *I can go and look for Ben now.*

She almost danced down the street. She was too elated even to think of buying a meal with Woody's five pounds. She simply wandered on, smiling idiotically to herself and not noticing much where she was going, until she found herself in familiar ways down by the river.

Ahead of her was the enbankment walk, and beyond it the night-dark, slow-moving river, full of silver gleams and golden streetlight reflections. It was the place she loved most in the whole grey, winter landscape of London, and its shadowy beauty always drew her close to look down at the glancing whirls and eddies of the tide.

She moved a little closer to admire the whole dully-glittering sweep of the ancient river as it wound its way down to the sea – but instead of seeing the glint of water beyond the wall she found herself looking instead at the shape of someone's head outlined against the sky – someone who leaned on the parapet and gazed down at the water just as she was doing, with the same air of incurable sadness . . . someone whose head she had seen silhouetted against the night sky many times before – with the London haze behind it – with starlight and moonshine behind it – with the smoky light of Annie-Mog's fire behind it . . . She would know that head anywhere.

"Ben?" she whispered. "Ben – is it you?"

And at her soft whisper the head turned towards her, the leaning body grew taut with instant recognition, and the voice, coming to her over the faint lapping of the tide on the shore, was as soft and broken with joy as hers.

"Hilo? *Hilo?*"

And then they were running, arms outstretched, and the stars sang in the sky, and the river sparked with rejoicing. Their world was whole at last.